Dead Horse, Dirty Vengeance

And then, quite suddenly, Slocum felt something wrong. Something wrong with his horse. It lurched down, then up, like a broken carousel, then forward just a stride before he heard the slug—it was a Sharps carbine, if he was any judge—saw the gunsmoke rising from a crag facing his, and knew he'd been had. He leapt clear of the saddle and hit the ground at the same time as his horse. By the time he crawled to his head, the horse was dead, shot through the neck. The shooter was gone. Slocum could hear the distant hoofbeats thundering away.

Earlier, he'd thought of Rafe as a murderer. Masterson had killed a man that Slocum never knew, but now he was a horse killer. That was just as bad, to Slocum's frame of mind. Worse, it was *his* horse. Slocum sniffed, his brow furrowing with anger and intent while he thought, *If and when I catch up with that sonofabitch, I'm gonna by God ram that Sharps down his ugly throat!*

He likely would, too. If he didn't come up with a better place to ram it.

And, knowing Slocum, he just might.

DON'T MISS THESE
ALL-ACTION WESTERN SERIES
FROM THE BERKLEY PUBLISHING GROUP

THE GUNSMITH by J. R. Roberts

Clint Adams was a legend among lawmen, outlaws, and ladies. They called him . . . the Gunsmith.

LONGARM by Tabor Evans

The popular long-running series about Deputy U.S. Marshal Custis Long—his life, his loves, his fight for justice.

SLOCUM by Jake Logan

Today's longest-running action Western. John Slocum rides a deadly trail of hot blood and cold steel.

BUSHWHACKERS by B. J. Lanagan

An action-packed series by the creators of Longarm! The rousing adventures of the most brutal gang of cutthroats ever assembled—Quantrill's Raiders.

DIAMONDBACK by Guy Brewer

Dex Yancey is Diamondback, a Southern gentleman turned con man when his brother cheats him out of the family fortune. Ladies love him. Gamblers hate him. But nobody pulls one over on Dex . . .

WILDGUN by Jack Hanson

The blazing adventures of mountain man Will Barlow—from the creators of Longarm!

TEXAS TRACKER by Tom Calhoun

J.T. Law: the most relentless—and dangerous—manhunter in all Texas. Where sheriffs and posses fail, he's the best man to bring in the most vicious outlaws—for a price.

JAKE LOGAN

SLOCUM
AND THE
SECOND HORSE

J

JOVE BOOKS, NEW YORK

THE BERKLEY PUBLISHING GROUP
Published by the Penguin Group
Penguin Group (USA) Inc.
375 Hudson Street, New York, New York 10014, USA
Penguin Group (Canada), 90 Eglinton Avenue East, Suite 700, Toronto, Ontario M4P 2Y3, Canada
(a division of Pearson Penguin Canada Inc.)
Penguin Books Ltd., 80 Strand, London WC2R 0RL, England
Penguin Group Ireland, 25 St. Stephen's Green, Dublin 2, Ireland (a division of Penguin Books Ltd.)
Penguin Group (Australia), 250 Camberwell Road, Camberwell, Victoria 3124, Australia
(a division of Pearson Australia Group Pty. Ltd.)
Penguin Books India Pvt. Ltd., 11 Community Centre, Panchsheel Park, New Delhi—110 017, India
Penguin Group (NZ), 67 Apollo Drive, Rosedale, North Shore 0632, New Zealand
(a division of Pearson New Zealand Ltd.)
Penguin Books (South Africa) (Pty.) Ltd., 24 Sturdee Avenue, Rosebank, Johannesburg 2196,
South Africa

Penguin Books Ltd., Registered Offices: 80 Strand, London WC2R 0RL, England

This is a work of fiction. Names, characters, places, and incidents either are the product of the author's imagination or are used fictitiously, and any resemblance to actual persons, living or dead, business establishments, events, or locales is entirely coincidental.

SLOCUM AND THE SECOND HORSE

A Jove Book / published by arrangement with the author

PRINTING HISTORY
Jove edition / June 2010
Copyright © 2010 by Penguin Group (USA) Inc.
Cover illustration by Sergio Giovine.

ISBN: 978-0-515-14808-4

JOVE®
Jove Books are published by The Berkley Publishing Group,
a division of Penguin Group (USA) Inc.
375 Hudson Street, New York, New York 10014.
JOVE® is a registered trademark of Penguin Group (USA) Inc.
The "J" design is a trademark of Penguin Group (USA) Inc.

PRINTED IN THE UNITED STATES OF AMERICA

10 9 8 7 6 5 4 3 2 1

1

Slocum checked the poster again. Same hair, same eyes, same everything as the man at the table across the bar from him. Rafe Masterson, wanted for murder and robbery, among other things.

He tucked the poster back in his pocket and took a last drink of his beer. Masterson hadn't done a thing to him. Slocum was just looking for some sport that paid money. And Masterson paid $3,500 in Arizona, according to the poster.

Slocum just wished it wasn't winter, that Flagstaff wasn't in the mountains, and that he hadn't caught up with Masterson in Flagstaff.

But then, at least it wasn't snowing. Or sleeting.

Masterson, who was thankfully no relation to Bat over in Kansas, stood up from the table along with his men. Four of them. Slocum figured to make a dollar or two off them, as well. According to the poster, one was

Max Furling at $700, one was Toby Keith (the glory hog, at $1,000), one was Pete Snodgrass at $600, and the last was Andy Cowl at $400. They brought the total up quite a bit. If Slocum could catch them, that was.

He followed them out of town and into the mountains to the southwest, damning the sheriff, who was out of town visiting his sister. Slocum hadn't asked where. He didn't much care at this point.

But now he was out here, alone, trailing the gang. He rode about a mile, up through the snow-shrouded, piney mountains, before the gang split up. Well, splintered off was more like it. One man rode off to the right, down the mountain. It would lead him either down through the valley that separated this crag from the next or up again, to climb the facing crag.

Slocum followed the trail he was on and chased after the four other riders.

He went about another half mile before they broke into a lope, then an outright gallop. He'd been spotted. Or, more likely, heard.

Shit.

He took off at a gallop, his Appaloosa running full-out as he trailed the men higher up the mountain, then out into the open over a worn path along the edge of the mountainside.

And then, quite suddenly, he felt something wrong. Something wrong with his horse. It lurched down, then up, like a broken carousel, then forward just a stride before he heard the slug—it was a Sharps carbine, if he was any judge—saw the gunsmoke rising from a crag facing his, and knew he'd been had. He hit the ground at the same time as his horse.

By the time he crawled to the Appaloosa's head, the

horse was dead, shot through the neck. The shooter was gone. Slocum could hear his distant hoofbeats thundering away.

He threw his arms around his horse's neck, and a silent tear slid down his cheek.

That spring, Slocum rode down from the San Francisco Peaks with a purpose. Sure, he was angry that he'd been locked up in an old, rattletrap cabin, snowed in for the past two months. Alone. He'd just about run clear out of grub. He wanted a woman, and bad. But he also wanted to get Rafe Masterson, the murdering rat who'd shot his horse out from under him in the San Franciscos in the first place.

After the snow—which had buried the cabin from the ground to halfway up the roof—had melted away enough that he could crawl out through a window, he'd slowly made his way—on foot—to the nearest town. That in itself had taken him five days of cold-to-the-bone hiking. Not exactly prime transportation for a man who'd spent most of his life in the saddle. But he'd made it.

And as luck would have it, there wasn't a woman in town. Not one.

It was really nothing more than a mining camp, and not even a glorified one. But he'd gotten supplies and—miracle of miracles—found himself a fairly nice Appaloosa gelding that had belonged to the deceased mine manager. As soon as he'd closed the deal on the Appy—whose name, he was informed, was of all things "Spots"—he set off to the south, toward Phoenix. Where he was pretty certain that Rafe Masterson had headed.

And where, by God, they had some women!

And by this time he was most of the way down, out of the high mountains. He wasn't on the flat yet, not by a long shot. That'd take him two more nights of sleeping on the ground. But he was looking forward to getting back down to more familiar turf. And he was looking forward to finding Rafe Masterson.

More like, he was looking forward to pummeling Rafe's face into pulp with his bare hands.

Earlier, he'd thought of Rafe as a murderer, but now it was worse. Masterson had killed a man that Slocum never knew, but he was also a horse killer. That was just as bad, to Slocum's frame of mind. And worse if it was his horse.

He sneered unconsciously then began to tear up, picturing that final moment, when the gelding had gone down—gone down galloping, full-out—and he'd realized the horse was dead before he hit the ground with Slocum crouched on his back, still demanding more speed.

Rafe had been up in the rocks to his left, on the opposing mountainside, up there with a Sharps carbine. With Slocum's horse in the sites.

Slocum sniffed, his brow furrowing with anger and intent while he thought, *If and when I catch up with that sonofabitch, I'm gonna by God ram that Sharps down his ugly throat!*

He likely would, too. If he didn't come up with a better place to ram it.

And, knowing Slocum, he just might.

The big man rode into Phoenix three days later.

This, he thought, was the West. No snow, no ice. It was in fact, in the eighties. Birds were chirping out in the desert, which was already greening up, and folks went about in their shirtsleeves, untroubled by inclement weather.

He rode straight to Miss Katie's, where he tied his gelding to the rail and walked on in the front door.

Normally, he would have stabled the gelding right off. But, to tell the truth, he was halfway hoping somebody would steal him.

Oh, he reined well enough, Slocum supposed, but that was about it. Apparently he'd been owned by a lazy rider, and even the few little polishes that Slocum had put on him on the ride down hadn't helped much. All the polishing in the world wouldn't disguise that choppy trot that by now had Slocum's backside feeling like laundry that had been pounded to death at the riverside.

Slocum figured to try and trade him for something a little more promising before he left town. Hopefully on the trail of Rafe Masterson.

He was barely through Katie's front door when he heard, "Slocum! Bless your buttons! Why'd you stay away so long, you big, beautiful hunka beefcake?"

And Katie herself fairly jumped into his arms, kissing him all over his face and neck between giggles and gales of her infectious laughter.

Slocum let her carry on for a while—after all, it had been a long time since he'd been greeted with so much avid female enthusiasm—and then he broke it off, picking her up and setting her down on the floor about a foot from him. "Hey, give a feller a chance to look, Katie!" he said with a broad grin.

She winked at him, then put one hand at the side of her pert face, surrounded by red ringlets, and the other on one hip, striking a pose for him. He broke out laugh-

ing, and she did, too. She wasn't dressed for business—
she had on her street clothes—but then, he figured that
three in the afternoon wasn't her prime time for making
money. He thought maybe he'd change that.

He said, "Katie-Cat, how'd you like to go upstairs
with a poor old saddle tramp that's just spent the worst
two months of his life?"

"Don't tell me," she said. "You were trapped in a place
with no women."

"Correct," he said. "And way too much snow. Take
pity," he added, looking as much like a freshly whipped
hound pup as he could muster.

She slipped her freckled arm through his bronzed,
muscled one and said, "Don't go so heavy on the melo-
drama, sweetie. You'll have me cryin' all over the front
hall." She began to lead him up the stairs, pausing only
to holler down toward the kitchen, "Molly! Watch the
place for a while, will ya?"

Slocum heard a faint "Yes'm!" and then he forgot everything except Katie.

Lord, she was wonderful! She knew his moves better
than he did, and responded in ways that made them even
better. She was full-figured to the point of being volup-
tuous, and red-haired everywhere. Her full breasts were
still high, her hips round and full, and her legs long and
lean.

The bed was neatly made up when they entered the
room, but by the time she'd come three times and he'd
come two, there were bed linens and clothes scattered all
over the place, and a couple of the pictures on the walls
were hanging crookedly.

And Slocum was damned proud of himself.

Katie threw on a pretty pink housecoat and grabbed his hand. "Bet you're starving. You always are."

Sheepishly, Slocum grinned. "Guilty as charged."

"Good. Throw some britches on that handsome ass of yours and meet me in the kitchen, sweetie."

Slocum went all out and put on not only a pair of pants, but a shirt and his boots, too, and went downstairs to the kitchen. He knew where it was. He'd been here before.

He found Miss Katie there, in the company of three other women.

"Slocum!" said Miss Katie. "Meet Julie, Fan, and Blossom." The girls nodded. "Ladies, Mr. Slocum is a good friend of mine, and a good friend to this house."

The girls nodded again and Slocum nodded back. "Pleased to meetcha," he said, and when Katie showed him a chair, he sat down at the table.

The girls joined him.

"Sorry, Slocum," said Katie as she banged the pots and pans about, explaining, "cook's day off."

"You ain't gonna hear no complaints from me," said Slocum. He knew that Katie was a fine cook in her own right, and he looked forward to anything that came from her skillet or oven. His stomach rumbled loudly, and he said, "'Scuse me!"

The girl at his elbow—he couldn't remember if she was Julie, Fan, or Blossom—tittered. He gave her a grin, and she flushed right up to her hairline. Now he remembered. Fan. She was pretty, but Christ she was young! He guessed her to be about thirteen. She shouldn't be here. She ought to be at home finishing her homework, or maybe helping her mother cook dinner.

He asked her, "Where are your folks, Fan?"

When Fan didn't answer him, just looked down and stared at the floor, Katie, from the stove, said, "Her ma died in childbirth, so Fannie never knew her." She paused to stir a pot. "Her pa was a drunkard. Drank himself to death after her ma died."

Sighing, Slocum asked, "Nobody else?"

Katie answered, "She's got an aunt and uncle, but they're over to Californy. And she ain't got a red cent for traveling."

They likely wouldn't pay him one red cent, either, but he had half a mind to ferry their niece home to them. This wasn't the place for her, even with Katie around to watch over her.

"How long you been here, Fan?" he asked gently.

She still didn't look up. But she shook her head and muttered, "Not long."

"Katie?" Slocum asked.

Katie turned from the stove again. "Less than a week."

"Workin'?"

"Not yet."

That answered a heap of questions.

"Fan?" he said. "Fan, look at me."

Slowly, the girl's head lifted to reveal an embarrassed face. "Yes, sir," she muttered.

Christ! Do I look that *old?* Slocum thought. But he said, "Fan, do you want to get to your aunt and uncle in California?"

She nodded. "Yes, sir."

"First of all, knock off the 'sir' bit. Call me Slocum."

"Yes, Slocum."

"Better. Second of all, can you ride a horse?"

"Yes . . . Slocum."

He nodded. "Better yet. And third, would you do me the honor, Miss Fan, of allowing me to escort you west to California?"

Her jaw dropped, and she looked toward Katie.

Katie laughed, then said, "I'd take him up on it if I was you, Fannie-girl. Don't worry. He won't bite. Well, not you, anyways." Chuckling, she turned back to her work.

Fan looked over at Slocum, her eyes still wide with the shock of it. "I . . . I . . . Thank you, Slocum. Thank you very much!"

And quite suddenly, Slocum found himself engulfed in a child's arms. As he tried to loosen her grip, he realized that she was crying, too. *Poor kid*, he thought. At about the same time that he remembered what had put him in Phoenix in the first place. The thing that jumping into the sheets with Katie had temporarily pushed from his mind.

After he disentangled Fan from himself and got her sitting back in her own chair, he said, "Now, I'm gonna need alla you gals to help me with somethin', all right?"

They all sat forward expectantly.

"About two months ago—well, anytime in between now and then—did any of you run into a feller name'a Rafe—" His stomach chose that moment to growl again— loudly—and when it was done, he said, "'Scuse me. Rafe Masterson. It's important to me that I find him."

One of the girls stiffened. Julie or Blossom? He couldn't recall. But he turned toward her. She was, in fact, sitting up so straight that he was afraid she'd snap her spine.

"What?" he demanded.

Slowly, she said, "It was you, wasn't it? He shot your horse."

Katie dropped a pot on the counter and everybody turned. Except Slocum.

Still staring toward the girl, he said, "When was he here?" When he got no response, he said, "Julie or Blossom or whatever your name is! When was he here?"

The girl snapped back toward him. "It's Blossom," she said, adding, "and about a month and a half back, he was through here. He wasn't nice. At all."

The final girl, Julie, asked softly, "He was the one what cut you, wasn't he, Blossom?"

Blossom nodded dully, then looked down, staring into her lap. "He sliced me up, Slocum. Sliced me all acrost my chest and belly. And he said he shot your horse out from under you at a dead run. He told me that to let me know I wasn't safe, now or ever." Tears began to roll down her cheeks and spatter in her lap. "He's a terrible, awful man."

Slocum said, "I'm sorry, Blossom. Right sorry. You got any idea where he went when he left here?"

Blossom shook her head. "West is all I know."

Slocum nodded and said, "Don't worry, Blossom. Once I catch up to him, you won't have to worry about Rafe Masterson anymore."

2

Slocum didn't leave Phoenix right away. He figured that Rafe had a good six or eight weeks' head start on him already, so what did a few more days mean? Of course, Miss Katie's company had a lot to do with it.

And he had to shop around for a new horse, too. He'd decided to just give Spots to Fan—she had fallen in love with him, anyway—and finally found himself a nice five-year-old gelding. He was named Fleet, and unlike Spots, who was a leopard with sorrel spots, Fleet was a black bay with a blanket of dark bay spots scattered over his rump, and a star and a stripe on his face.

The horse trader—with whom Slocum had dealt before—told him that Fleet had belonged to a drummer who got himself into trouble in an argument with a gunman over who was quicker on the draw—men born in Missouri or men born in the Dakotas.

The gunman, born in the Dakotas, won the argument.

But the late drummer had been a fair hand with horses, and Fleet was in good shape and trained up nice. Slocum was pleased with the deal.

He was running low on money, but he managed to put together enough in the way of supplies to get him and Fan over to California and then some.

And so, on the morning of his third day in Phoenix, he made ready to leave. He kissed Katie good-bye and set out toward the western horizon, with Fan trailing behind him on Spots.

They made excellent time until they stopped for lunch. Little Fan didn't say much—or hadn't so far—but she was a trooper and kept up. The moment he stopped, though, she ran behind a big rock. Slocum, loosening both their saddle girths, could hear her making water. He grinned. He had forgotten what tiny bladders children—particularly girl children—had.

She came out from behind the rock about the time he was pulling out the possibles bag, in which he'd stashed his market plunder. He pushed aside the potatoes, carrots, and peas—he figured to make a stew for their supper later—and pulled out the hardtack and the cheese Katie had pressed on them. The boiled chicken she'd given them would go into their stew.

He handed about half the hardtack and cheese to Katie, saying, "Here's lunch. We'll eat light on the trail, okay?"

She nodded in the affirmative and slid down to the ground, where she sat cross-legged, opened her canteen, and broke off a piece of her cheese.

Chewing, she asked, "Are you keeping this cheese in anything?" When Slocum looked at her blankly, she added, "You know, like in butcher paper or cheesecloth or something? Because it'll keep longer without dryin' out."

Slocum grunted, and she gave up. It was just as well. He didn't feel the need to explain that they didn't have all the comforts of a kitchen out here. Cheese just went into the bag, like everything else.

He bit off a piece of cheese, then a hunk of hardtack.

He washed the bite down with water, then asked her, "You got a last name, Fan? Sorry I ain't asked you before."

"It's Forebush. I'm Fan Forebush. My pa was Frank, and my ma was Alice," she said, then sucked down more water.

"What's the name of this town again? The one where we're goin'."

She said, "It's called Palos Verdes. It's south of Los Angeles."

Slocum nodded. He'd heard of it, although he'd never been there. He'd certainly been to Los Angeles, but couldn't think of much to recommend it. Just another cluster of falling-down adobe huts. The only thing that made it stand out from the other little mud villages up and down the coast was that goddamned tar pit outside of town.

"We'll find it," he said. "You're practically sitting right next to your aunt and uncle right now, Miss Fannie Forebush."

She smiled shyly. "Slocum, I wanna thank you again for—"

He waved a hand. "Don't mention it."

"Aunt Mary's bound to press a cake or a pie on you," she said, grinning.

He smiled. "Wouldn't turn it down, that's for sure."

* * *

They rode on, past Monkey Springs, before they stopped for the night. Slocum found them a decent place to camp. There was no aboveground water, but there were some large boulders for cover and some spring grasses sprouting up. He figured the horses would be glad, anyway.

After he tucked in the horses and cooked the stew (which was pretty damn good, even if he said so himself) they were eating—and Fan was telling him some story or other—when he heard, "Hello, the camp!"

He stiffened immediately, dropping his plate in the dirt beside him, and reached for his gun. Travelers looking for a fire and some conversation were one thing, but bandits seeking to rob and kill wayfarers were another.

The call had come from out to the east, so he whispered, "Fan! Get back behind that boulder!" before he called back, "Who's out there?"

He heard the voice again. A voice with a decidedly Southern twang. "A weary traveler lookin' for to share some coffee and a fire. And some food, if you've got any. Smells like chicken stew!"

"You got the coffee?" Slocum called. In truth, they were fixed fine for coffee, but he wanted to see if the stranger actually had something to offer in return for the stew.

"I do! Got peach turnovers, too, made just this morning!"

Slocum smiled. Those would taste awful good, and he knew that Fan had a sweet tooth, too.

"Come on in," he shouted.

"Thankee kindly!" said the voice, and a moment later there emerged from the gloom a figure on horseback. As he grew closer, Slocum made out a tan hat and a brocade vest over a white shirt. The figure rode a light-colored horse—probably gray, Slocum figured—and was coming toward them at a head-bobbing, ground-eating walk. *A Tennessee walker? Out here?* Slocum thought, scratching his head. Well, he supposed that stranger things had happened. Still . . .

The rider came almost into the camp before he dismounted, then led his horse forward. "Howdy!" he said, looking like the fanciest fellow one would dream of meeting on the trail. A riverboat, maybe, or a New Orleans fancy house. "Name's Forsythe, Bill Forsythe." He stuck out his hand.

Slocum took it and gave it a shake. "Slocum here. What brings a fine feller on a Tennessee walker out this way?"

"Aha!" Forsythe cackled. "A man who knows his horseflesh!" He pointed out toward Spots and Fleet, hobbled on the other side of the fire. "And who has two of those exotic Appaloosa horses."

Slocum grinned. "Only one." He turned his head and said, "Fan, you can come out now."

Shyly, the girl poked her pigtailed head around the edge of the boulder. "Is it safe?" she whispered.

Slocum motioned her out, saying, "Fan, I'd like you to meet Mr. Bill Forsythe. Forsythe, Fannie Forebush." And then he laughed. "Seems like we got us a passel too many 'F' names!"

Fan laughed and Forsythe joined in.

"Settle your horse, Forsythe," Slocum said, grinning. "I'll get you a plate'a stew."

Later that evening, after they'd finished the last of the stew and Fan had fallen asleep beside the fire, Slocum and Forsythe sat up smoking cigarettes and gabbing. Forsythe was from Louisiana, he said, and had come west about a year ago. He'd fought in the War Against Northern Aggression, too, and he and Slocum traded war stories for a while until suddenly Forsythe sat up straight and exclaimed, "Don't tell me you're *that* John Slocum! The sniper who—"

Slocum nodded. "That's me, all right. Spent half the war up in a tree, waitin' for a shot. Got quite a few of 'em, too, as I recall." He was pleased that he had a reputation as a good soldier besides the one he had as a tough bastard. Well, at least with one feller he did.

"My goodness, my goodness," said Forsythe, shaking his head. He stuck out his hand. "Even prouder to meet you than I was before."

Both men chuckled softly as Slocum shook Forsythe's hand for the second time.

"So what takes you to California, Forsythe?" Slocum asked. They had already established that Slocum was ferrying Fan out to her family.

"A man," said Forsythe, confidentially. "If you could call him that. A murdering son of a bitch would be more like it."

Slocum's eyebrows lifted. "What's his name?"

"Rafe Masterson. He killed my brother. Shot him in the back. I intend to do the same to him, only I want to shoot his damn face off."

Slocum stared at the ground, feeling the pent-up anger boil his blood. Finally, he looked up and said, "You and me got more in common than the war, Forsythe."

"What's that?"

"I'm out after Rafe Masterson, too."

Forsythe's eyes widened. "I'll be damned. What'd he do to you, or does he just hate Southern boys?"

"I think he just hates everybody and everything, period. The bastard shot my best horse right out from under me. Up north in the mountains. I only wish there was a bigger bounty on the son of a bitch peckerwood. I'm runnin' low on cash."

"Hell's bells!" Forsythe slapped his forehead. "There is a bounty, Slocum. Five grand, dead or alive, in Arizona Territory. Tell you what. Partner with me. Two gunhands are better than one, right? We'll split the bounty right down the middle, no matter who has the honor of takin' him down."

"Deal," said Slocum and stuck out his hand to shake a third time with Forsythe. "Hell, the last paper I saw on him was only thirty-five hundred!"

"Good," cried Forsythe. "Then things are looking up! We have a pact, then."

Across the fire, Fan stirred in her sleep. Forsythe covered his own mouth, then brought his hand back down and whispered, "Didn't mean to wake her. Sorry."

"It's all right," Slocum whispered back. "Think she's dozed off again already."

Forsythe shook his head. "Ah, the sleep of the young and innocent. I envy her."

"Don't be envyin' her too much," Slocum said. "Her folks died, and the only place she had to go was a whorehouse."

Forsythe said, "No!"

"She came out of it untouched, though," Slocum added quickly. "I came along, told her I'd take her to her only livin' relatives. They're out west. Woulda put her

on the stage, but like I said, I'm runnin' low on funds."
A bug tickled his arm and he slapped at it.

"You have my great admiration, Slocum," Forsythe
said, bobbing his head. "You are, indeed, a gentleman."

3

The next morning, the three of them set out with new vigor.

Well, Slocum, at least, was invigorated. He figured he'd just doubled his chances of putting down Rafe Masterson, and doing it legally. He didn't need another murder charge that he'd have to either talk or gun his way out of.

But then he got to thinking. Finally, he turned to Forsythe and asked, "That reward on Rafe Masterson. Is that just for Arizona, or is California in on the deal?"

Forsythe's face screwed up. Finally, he said, "Sorry, Slocum. I was thinking. Once we cross the Colorado, we'll need to check posters, but he may be worth more in California. I mean, isn't everything?" he added with an odd little laugh.

"Just wanted to make sure he was wanted there, too. Hate to get tagged for murderin' the slime."

Forsythe nodded. "I understand completely."

Spots nudged his way between the other two horses and riders, with a puzzled Fan aboard. "What's goin' on?" she asked. "You two been whisperin' like a pair of bank thieves up here!"

Forsythe slapped his forehead and announced, "Curses! Caught in the act!"

Slocum broke out in a laugh, followed by a giggling Fan, who was joined by Forsythe.

They traveled on with few difficulties for the next two days and, in the afternoon of the third, arrived at the banks of the Colorado River. They had come upon it a good five miles down from the ferry, Slocum thought, and so they decided to make camp where they were for the night and ride up to the ferry first thing in the morning.

Slocum had grown to like Forsythe a great deal over the past days, but not so much as Fan had. The poor little thing was besotted by him, constantly making eyes at him. Unfortunately, she was a good bit better at it than other girls of her age, due to having been a very observant bystander at Miss Katie's.

Forsythe couldn't help but catch her at it, and now he was acting as jumpy as a frog on a stove lid, terrified that if he turned his back too long, she'd jump him. Slocum didn't blame him for being nervous. He rode between them as much as possible, creating a comfort zone for Forsythe, who was grateful.

But when they stopped to make camp, Slocum lost what little control he had over the situation. While he saw to the horses and Forsythe made a fire, Fan was right by Forsythe's side.

Forsythe tried to distract her. He had her carry wood, then stack it, then actually build the fire, but nothing dampened her devotion.

When Slocum had finished with the horses, he went to the fire and crouched down beside Forsythe. "Need rescuin'?" he whispered.

"For the love of God, Slocum!" Forsythe pleaded, in visual distress.

Slocum hid the grin he couldn't hold back, then got down to business as best he could. He moved Fan to the other side of the fire on the pretext that he wanted someone trustworthy to keep an eye on the darkened eastern horizon, and Forsythe breathed a sigh of relief.

For the moment, anyway.

It was close to eight before Slocum had their dinner ready. Tonight it was fried jackrabbits and the last of the potatoes, chopped up and fried as well, along with an onion.

Fan finally had something to focus on besides Forsythe, and Slocum saw him relax—really relax—for the first time in a couple of days. It wouldn't last long, but he enjoyed his fried rabbit and potatoes all the more because of it.

After they'd finished and Slocum and Fan had washed the dishes—in water, this time, instead of scrubbing them with sand or gravel—Slocum said, "Well, I suppose we'd best turn in about now."

He knew Fan wanted to kill him for messing up what she must have considered both her and Forsythe's wish to spoon, but he admired the way she hid it. Poor thing.

No, poor Forsythe.

While Slocum packed away the frying pan and supper

things, Fan made her pallet on one side of the fire, then snuggled down into her blanket. Forsythe, on the other side, let his shoulders heave with relief before he dug into his pocket for his tobacco pouch.

Slocum finished his packing and slowly made his way back to the fire. He sat down next to Forsythe and said, "Mind if I join you?"

Forsythe, looking relieved, said, "My pleasure, I assure you." He held out his tobacco pouch. "My distinct pleasure."

Slocum waved off the tobacco. "Still got my own, thanks. River sounds nice tonight, don't it?"

Forsythe lifted his head for a moment, listening to the gurgle of the spring-swollen water as it traveled from the north to the south.

Forsythe said, "I reckon it does. Been a while since I had a chance to camp along a watercourse. This one go dry in the summer, too?"

"You mean like the stream down to Tucson?"

Forsythe smiled. "Yeah, that and every other so-called stream in southern Arizona."

Slocum snorted as he pulled out his tobacco pouch. "Nope. This one carries water all year. Well, not this much usually, but the snow's meltin' off up in the high country right now."

Forsythe nodded as if he needed no further explanation. He said, "When you reckon we'll get her home?" He nodded toward Fan, who might or might not have been sleeping, but she had her eyes closed, anyway.

"Two, maybe three days," Slocum replied, lighting his quirlie. Forsythe's pipe was burned down to almost nothing.

Forsythe had the coffeepot in hand. He refilled his own cup then paused. "More?" he asked.

"Wouldn't mind it."

Forsythe poured Slocum a cup, then set the pot on a hot rock, halfway into the fire. He tamped his pipe on the ground, then hoisted his own coffee and leaned back. He asked, "As soon as we find her folks, we're out after Rafe Masterson, right?"

"Yup."

"Good."

Slocum chuckled softly.

"What?"

"Don't worry, Forsythe. You can't be half as eager as I am to catch up with Rafe."

Forsythe took a long drink of his coffee, then said, "Wouldn't take no bets on that if I were you, Slocum."

The next morning, they had risen, breakfasted, and gotten on their way without incident. They were only about two miles from the ferry landing and riding along the riverbank when Slocum heard a sudden *thump* from directly behind him. While he was turning in the saddle, he said, "What the hell are you—"

But he never got to finish his sentence. He leapt off his horse and scooped Fan up in his arms while Forsythe grabbed the horses and made for the rocks. There was a bullet wound in young Fan's shoulder, and she was unconscious.

He slid down behind a boulder, bringing her with him, and asked Forsythe, "Who the hell's shootin' at us?"

Forsythe had already drawn his gun and was peeking over the rock, toward the rushing river. "Funny, I was about to ask you that same question." Quickly, he glanced back at Fan. "She gonna be all right?"

Slocum said, "Think so. Slug went right through her and out the other side."

"I didn't even hear the shot! Did you?"

Slocum had turned Fan. The wound looked clean, but it was bleeding. He pulled out his bandanna and held it against the back of her shoulder. "If he was far enough out, we wouldn't have. River's making enough noise to cover it. Gimme your kerchief."

Forsythe handed it over. "But why the devil would somebody from clear over *there* be shootin' at us clear over *here*? How the hell could he even *see* us?"

Slocum furrowed his brow. "Maybe . . . maybe 'cause he's not shootin' at us in the first place." Without any warning, he suddenly stood up.

"Are you outta your mind?" hissed Forsythe, who tried to drag him down under cover again.

Slocum snatched his arm out of Forsythe's grasp. "Let go a'me," he said. "Come on. Stand up. It ain't nothin' but somebody on the California side tryin' to shoot a rabbit or a quail or somethin'."

There was a cloud of dust on the distant horizon.

"Or maybe pronghorn," he added. "That's a pretty big dust cloud for a couple'a bunnies."

Forsythe sighed, got to his feet, and gingerly stood erect. After a few moments of scanning the horizon, he shoved his gun back in his holster.

Shaking his head, he muttered, "This place is crazier than a N'Orleans cathouse on a Saturday night."

Slocum barely heard him. He had knelt again to hover over Fan, who was just regaining consciousness.

"Ooh, ooh," she wept. "Daddy, Daddy, I'm hurt! Wake up, Daddy . . ."

"You're all right, honey," Slocum said. "You just got hit by a stray slug, that's all. You're gonna be fine, just fine . . ."

He let her cry a little longer before he helped her up into a sit and gently took the kerchiefs away and handed them to Forsythe. "Rinse those out, will ya?" He turned back to Fan. "Go ahead and cry it out, Fannie. This is the worst it'll be. Bullet went all the way through, no need for me to dig."

She didn't look very impressed.

He said, "Hang on a minute, and I'll get you wrapped up, all right?"

Once again, she responded only with a look that wasn't exactly chipper, but Slocum got on with it, as best he could. He pulled clean rags from his saddle-bag, packed the wound, then bound it up as tightly as possible. This wasn't any too tight, seeing as how he had no intention of asking her to strip to the waist. He did the best he could, though, circumstances—and her modesty—considered.

When Forsythe came back with the washed-out bandannas and saw what Slocum was up to, he quickly lit a small fire and brewed Fan some willow bark tea, which he insisted she drink before he put her up in her saddle again.

Slocum, soggy bandanna tied round his neck, backed him on this. He said, "I don't care what it tastes like, Fannie. Drink it."

"You're so mean!" she whined. "My shoulder hurts because somebody shot me. Shot me! What did *I* do?!"

"You didn't do a thing. And nobody's tryin' to harm you on purpose, you silly girl," Slocum growled. "You're damn lucky that Forsythe had that willow bark in his possibles bag."

Forsythe shrugged, as if it had been nothing.

Steeling himself, lest he haul off and smack somebody, Slocum said, "I know it ain't pretty, but if you drink that down, it'll take away the worst of the pain. Don't you want it to quit hurtin'?"

She didn't say anything, just glared at her hands grasping the mug.

Slocum stood up. He winked at Forsythe, then said, "Well, no skin off my nose. C'mon, Forsythe. I want to get up to the ferry by noon." Forsythe rose, too, and the two men started toward the horses.

"Wait!"

Slocum glanced around to see Fan quickly gulping the contents of her mug, and he pursed his lips to hide a smile. Forsythe didn't hide his, though, and said, "That's a good girl, now, Fannie. Drink it all."

She did, and Forsythe helped her up on Spots.

"How soon will it work, Mr. Forsythe?" she asked from behind lowered lashes.

"Give it about a half hour," Slocum answered.

She tossed him a glare.

Forsythe said, "That's right, Fan. About half an hour."

She smiled at Forsythe.

Slocum would have smacked her if she'd been close enough. This was the last time he'd do a favor for a stupid child, he vowed. But then he thought, *Aw, hell. Stupid's how some folks describe* all *kids, and I've known some awful sharp ones.* And then he thought, *Just forget it. You ain't never gonna win.*

He swung up on Fleet and said, "We're burnin' daylight, folks."

Forsythe was right behind him, leading Fan's horse. After Slocum glanced back, he asked, "She can't rein her own horse?"

Forsythe shrugged. "I'm just leading her till the willow bark kicks in."

Slocum nodded, but muttered under his breath, "Your funeral."

Slocum didn't know how lucky he was.

Forsythe had his hands full with Fan, true, but that also helped keep him from thinking about making advances toward Slocum.

Forsythe was a homosexual, a way of life then frowned on by most of the fledgling United States, tolerated only by the more sophisticated parts of the country—San Francisco and New Orleans, for example.

When he first ran across Slocum, Forsythe had logged him as straight, almost militantly so. Slocum was also too massive and too scarred by bullets and arrows to be Forsythe's type. Or so he told himself at the time.

But when he learned that this was the legendary John Slocum, a famed sniper in the War Against Northern Aggression, and when he had a chance to sit and talk with him around that campfire in the middle of nowhere, his interest had been piqued.

He found Slocum ruggedly fascinating. Well, he found him fascinating, period. But he took great care not to give himself away, by word or by gesture. He had the feeling that if Slocum learned of Forsythe's proclivities, he would murder him where he stood. He looked like he could do it, too.

And through the stories that Slocum told him at night while they waited for Fan to go to sleep, Forsythe had the feeling that Slocum might do it just on principle.

So he kept his feelings to himself. For the time being, anyway. Once they got this silly little girl off their hands and were traveling alone, he'd have a better chance to verbally feel Slocum out. Well, a better chance to *think* about a verbal approach.

Or not.

4

Forsythe went down to the landing and rang the bell while Slocum made a quick trip to the makeshift general store at the ferry crossing. He got them some canned peaches, three oranges, some bacon, and picked up a small tin of heroin pills for Fan. They'd cut her pain better than the willow bark, but he'd have to remember to tell her to watch how much she took.

By the time he got down to the landing, the ferry was just pulling into the dock. Once it got stopped between the tethered, floating logs that made its "stall," first Forsythe, then Fan, got on board, leading their mounts behind them.

Slocum dismounted and led Fleet aboard, too. He tied Fleet to the rail, then opened his parcel from the store and took out the heroin, which he handed to Fan.

She looked at it curiously. "What's this?"

"Medicine," Slocum said. "For the pain. I'd go easy

on that stuff if I were you, though. I hear it's pretty powerful."

Forsythe said, "What's that?" and held out his hand. Fan obliged by surrendering the tin. He squinted at it and said, "Heroin, Slocum? Isn't this stuff addictive?"

"Told her to be careful how much she takes," Slocum replied as the ferry's captain stopped in front of him.

"Fifty cents per person, plus a quarter for each horse," he said expressionlessly.

Slocum dug into his pocket and pulled out his fare, plus enough to cover Fan and her horse, as well. He was glad he hadn't bought a fourth orange.

"Here's me and the little girl," he said, handing the change to the ferryman.

"And mine," Forsythe said, and handed his share over.

"Thankee, folks," the ferryman said as he took the money. "Anybody else comin'?"

"Not that I know of," said Forsythe.

"All right. No reason to tarry, then," said the boatman, and he moved to the ferry's prow.

Actually, there was no prow—the ferry was square, and it traveled on horsepower, provided by two horses turning a wheel on the opposite bank. The wheel was rigged to a chain that traveled from either end of the ferry, up a pole rising more than twenty feet above the river, then across it and down to the wheel.

Slocum wondered how the hell they got back across! It looked to him like a good rig for a one-way trip, but that was all. There were no horses and no wheel on this end.

But when the ferryman clanged the bell, Slocum realized how the dang thing worked: the horses across the river started circling, and slowly, a chain attached to the front of the ferry rose up out of the water.

Eventually, the ferry began to move, and Slocum shook his head. "Well, I'll be damned!" he breathed.

"Probably," said Forsythe at his elbow, wearing a large grin.

Slocum grinned back. He took a quick look around. "Where's Fan?"

"Sleepin'." Forsythe pointed to the benches at the rear of the ferry. She was stretched out on one, sound asleep.

Slocum's brow furrowed. "She take a pill?"

"It would appear so."

Slocum grumbled, "Funny guy," but kept his eyes on the far bank. It wasn't so far anymore.

He'd be plenty happy to make the California bank and get Fan settled with her relatives. Then he and Forsythe could get down to business. He was really looking forward to that. He dreamt about it every night, dreamt of getting Rafe Masterson in his sites, dreamt of pulling the trigger, dreamt of seeing Masterson fall.

He was getting to be a little worried about how good it felt. But not *that* worried. Not yet, anyhow.

They were across the river and pulling into the opposite docking stall before he knew it. Forsythe couldn't wake up Fan, so they lifted her up across Spots's saddle and went on their way.

After an hour or so, they stopped for lunch. Fan still wasn't awake, so they settled for an orange apiece and spent most of their noon rest smoking and dozing and talking and watching the horses graze.

After an hour had passed, Forsythe asked, "You want me to wake her up now?"

Slocum shook his head. "Let's let her sleep as long as we can. Keep her from takin' any more heroin, anyhow."

"I don't like hauling her across the horse. It's like she's our prisoner!"

Slocum tipped his head. "Fine. We'll make her a travois."

"Capital!" cried Forsythe. He pulled a small axe from his saddlebags and set off for a little stand of trees nearby.

"Aw, crud," muttered Slocum, glancing at the sleeping girl, and he slowly gained his feet to follow Forsythe on down.

By evening, they had traveled another five miles. They weren't making good time so far as Slocum was concerned, but dragging the travois slowed down the entire process.

Spots handled it well, though. Slocum had been afraid that he'd have to give up Fleet for the rest of the trip since Spots was the greener of the two Appaloosas, but Spots must have been used to haul something or other at one time. He took to it like a duck to water.

When they stopped for the night, Fan was still sleeping, and Slocum took it upon himself to shake her awake. She was breathing, all right, but she was like a rag doll in his arms.

"Just how many a'those things did she take, anyhow?" he asked Forsythe.

"I got no idea," Forsythe answered with a shrug. "Did you look in the tin?"

"Don't know where she put the damned thing," he grumbled. "Been through her pockets twice and it ain't turned up yet."

"You go through her saddlebags?" Forsythe didn't wait for an answer. He simply went over to Spots and began to rummage around.

Forsythe had luck. He suddenly turned about, holding up a tin. "Found it!" he announced happily.

"How many are gone?"

Forsythe studied the tin, shifting the contents with his finger. He looked up. "Only one. Box says there were ten, and there's nine left."

Slocum scratched the back of his neck. "Well, I'll be damned." He gave up on rousing Fan, and laid her back on the travois. "Well, long as she's out cold, I might as well change her bandages . . ."

This time, Slocum did strip her to the waist. He pulled the packing from both sides of her wound, decided it was no longer needed, and bandaged her up properly before he dressed her again and laid her back down on the travois.

Forsythe, like the Southern gentleman he was, turned his back for the entire procedure, and by the time Slocum had finished, he had a nice little fire going and the coffee brewing.

Slocum slumped down beside the fire. "You think we oughta force some water down her?" he asked.

Forsythe thought a moment. "Perhaps a drop or two."

Slocum nodded. "Okay. You get to be her hero this time. The coffee ready yet?"

Forsythe hauled himself to his feet and grabbed a canteen. "Probably about five or ten minutes more," he said, and walked over to the girl on the travois.

Slocum watched him dribble the water, little by little, on her lips, then stroke her throat to make her swallow. He was mentally kicking himself for buying her that heroin in the first place. He should have settled for the laudanum, he thought. He'd never heard of anybody knocking themselves out with that, unless they drank a whole damn bottle of it.

About the time that the coffee was ready and Slocum and Forsythe were just settling back with a cup, Fan woke up.

"Where am I?" she said, almost drunkenly.

"California, Little Miss Sunshine," said Slocum. "Can you sit up?"

Slowly, she worked herself into a sort of a sit. Slocum could tell that it hurt her, though, particularly when she had to put any sort of pressure on her bad arm and shoulder.

While Slocum watched her slowly ease herself up into that sit, Forsythe dug through Slocum's possibles bag and brought out the last orange. "Here you go, Miss Fan," he said, presenting it to her. "Slocum found it at the store back on the Arizona side."

Her eyes widened and she took it. "An orange? For me?" Gingerly, she cupped it in her hands. "Thank you!"

Had this kid ever had anything? Slocum wondered. He knew they had oranges in Phoenix. He'd seen the trees. And he knew they hauled them in with other California produce, too. But Fan looked as if the fruit in her hand was from Mars. Maybe the heroin had something to do with it.

He got the peel started for her and showed her how to eat the fruit, then sat back with his coffee again and watched her. It took him a moment more to realize that Forsythe was watching him.

"Somethin' the matter?" he asked.

There was a silence before Forsythe said softly, "You look like a father, that's all. I think you're softer than you let on."

One corner of Slocum's mouth quirked into a smile, and he snorted. "Maybe. Maybe not."

Forsythe's grin widened. "Uh-huh."

Slocum grimaced. "Ah, drink your damned coffee."

When morning came around, Slocum allowed Fan some of Forsythe's bark tea but held onto the heroin himself. He wanted to make time today. And besides, he knew the girl was better. He and Forsythe got her up on her horse and cut loose the travois, and they set out for the western shore beyond.

Slocum figured to go to Los Angeles first and ask a few questions, then cut south and take the girl home.

That's what he figured, anyhow.

Two days of hard travel later, the Los Angeles they rode into wasn't much more than Slocum remembered: just a small collection of adobe huts, a couple of wells, and a handful of Mexicans surrounded by farms and orchards. Paradise, it sure wasn't. But he had to give them credit for bringing fresh water in to irrigate the crops. It was pretty amazing what such hopeless-looking land could bring forth if it was watered and treated right. Actually, it sort of made him believe in magic again, like a kid.

In town, Forsythe went to the dry goods while Slocum went into the cantina, both asking after Rafe Masterson.

Neither one came up with anything—except Forsythe, who bought a bag of penny candy and some fresh bandages for Fan's shoulder.

"Well, nobody knows nothin'," Slocum said once they'd ridden clear of town and stopped to change Fan's dressing again.

Forsythe was doing the honors this time. "Well, my dear, things look to be mending fine," he said. He was changing only the part of the wrap that went over her shoulder, which he could do when she had her blouse on: Slocum had torn the sleeve away first thing. "I believe you'll live. And Slocum? Not entirely."

Slocum frowned. "Not entirely what?"

"Can you read Mexican?"

"Better than I can say it."

Forsythe reached into a shirt pocket and pulled out a small, folded piece of paper, which he handed to Slocum. Curiously, Slocum took it and unfolded it, spreading it out on the top of his thigh.

He squinted at it, then said, "He rides south one week gone." He raised his eyes to meet Forsythe's. "What's that supposed to mean?"

"Bingo!" yipped Forsythe. "There's your answer."

"What?"

"Read it again, man. Rafe Masterson rode south, out of Los Angeles, a week ago. And carrying little Miss Fan here all the way to her home has put us dead on his trail."

5

There was what the overly enthusiastic might have called a road leading south from Los Angeles, and the three of them took it. Fan was the least enthusiastic of the group, for obvious reasons.

Slocum figured she had deluded herself into thinking she had Forsythe wrapped up in her "womanly charms" and any second now he'd break down and be forced by nature to kiss her.

Or something.

Slocum couldn't begin to understand the machinations of the female mind, but he knew enough to know that when the wheels started turning, a wise man got the hell out of the county.

And this was looking like one of those times.

She rode between him and Forsythe as they traveled southward. Her left arm was cradled in her lap, yet she rose straight and proud, her budding chest out and her back straight—a position Slocum knew had to hurt, but which Forsythe seemed to be finding . . . attractive?

Surely not. Forsythe had seemed like such a sensible fellow!

Slocum shook his head. Well, they'd be rid of Fan sometime tomorrow, and then they could get on with tracking Rafe Masterson. He smiled, although the grin had no humor in it. There was nothing funny whatsoever about that horse killer. The smile, instead, was one of potential satisfaction, of a wrong about to be righted.

Not that killing Masterson would bring back Dash, he thought, allowing himself to think the horse's name for the first time. Even then, he winced a bit at it. Damn, he missed that horse. Fleet was all well and good, but Dash had been like a partner, a friend.

A man didn't come across a horse like that very often, and the man that pulled him apart from that horse should burn in eternal torment!

"What you all growly faced about?" asked Forsythe.

"Me?" said Slocum, surprised that anyone had noticed. He shrugged his shoulders. "Just thinkin' 'bout Rafe shootin' my horse."

Forsythe set his mouth and sighed. "Still hurts, doesn't it?"

Slocum nodded.

"Don't worry, Slocum. Killin' the bastard'll ease that up a good bit."

"Hope you're right."

"I hope so, too. For my brother."

Slocum nodded and urged Fleet into a jog trot. The others did the same—even Fan, who winced at the change in pace.

Slocum figured it was time to change the subject. He

said, "Once we get a little farther south, we're gonna have to keep our eyes peeled for *bandidos*."

"Here, too?" Forsythe asked. "I thought I'd left that behind in Texas."

"Long border," Slocum replied.

"What time is it?" Fan's sleepy voice piped up from between them.

"It's around four in the afternoon," Slocum said. "We'll be stoppin' in about an hour. That okay with you?"

The girl nodded. Her posture and expression had changed from that of the seductress to one of the exhausted child.

Although Slocum felt sorry for her, the latter look fit her much better than the first one.

The next afternoon, the travelers rode into the dusty hometown of Fan's aunt and uncle, Palos Verdes. Slocum checked at the sheriff's office and got directions out to the orchard—and also inquired about Rafe Masterson. In answer to the first inquiry, the sheriff drew him a map on the back of an old Wanted poster. In answer to the second, Slocum got himself an earful.

Rafe had been there, all right. He'd ridden in, started a dustup at the local saloon, and promptly ridden out again. The sheriff was delighted to hear that Slocum and Forsythe were looking for him—and looking for the reward, as well.

"I ain't foolin' myself," he said from behind his desk. "Masterson would take one look at this badge, and that'd be the last of me, period. Hope you boys get him. I wish you luck."

And that was that.

Slocum did find out that the price on Masterson's

head was $10,000 in California, though, information that thrilled Forsythe no end.

Well, Slocum was glad about it, too.

They made their way out through the countryside until they came upon the orchard. Slocum had thought the sheriff was just being lyrical in calling it that, but irrigation ditches surrounded the fields and ran between the rows of fruit trees. It went on for acres and acres.

"Nice place for you to live in," he said to Fan, who was wide-eyed with it all. "That's quite the irrigation system they got, ain't it?"

"Sure is," replied Forsythe, tipping his hat back with his thumb. "Jeez! Where'd they find that much freshwater out here?"

Slocum shrugged. "In the ground, most likely. Or mayhap they got a secret river close by that I ain't seen yet."

Soon enough, they rode up to the house, which was flanked by a barn and several outbuildings. A woman was taking down laundry from a line and stopped when she saw them.

"Aunt Mary, Aunt Mary!" Fan cried, and was off Spots and hugging the woman before Slocum knew it. He and Forsythe stepped down off their mounts, and Forsythe held the reins while Slocum, hat in his hands, walked tentatively forward.

He had to wait to speak, though, because Fan was babbling on and on about the death of her father and her luck in finding Slocum—and then Forsythe—and her ride west with them. She'd just finished telling how she'd been shot by mistake when Slocum took advantage of a pause in the conversation.

"Ma'am?" he said to the woman.

"Slocum or Forsythe?" she answered, a grin spread wide across her face. She hadn't let go of Fan yet.

"I'm Slocum, ma'am, John Slocum," he said, and nodded his head in a quick little bow. He poked his thumb backward. "That's Forsythe." Forsythe nodded. "That shoulder a'hers is pretty well healed up already, but you'd best keep an eye on it for a while."

"I'm Mary Forebush," she said, hugging Fan with one arm while holding out the other hand for Slocum to shake. "My husband's out in the orchard, but he'll be up soon. You'll stay for dinner? I warn you, I won't take no for an answer . . ."

Slocum figured she looked like a gal who wouldn't. He smiled and nodded curtly. "Be mighty pleased to, Mrs. Forebush. Be pleased to eat somebody's cookin' besides my own."

"Good, Mr. Slocum," she said, smiling wide. "And you'll accept our invitation to spend the night, then, too. You and Mr. Forsythe can put your horses up," she added, without waiting for an answer. Then she was just gone, whisking Fan off into the house and hugging her every step of the way.

"I guess we're stayin', whether we like it or not," Slocum remarked with a shake of his head.

"I reckon you're right," replied Forsythe, equally as stunned.

He stood there a moment, staring after Mary Forebush. And then he blinked. He started toward the barn directly, leading all three horses, with Slocum bringing up the rear.

Fan's Uncle Fred turned up just as they had finished settling the horses and were walking up to the house.

Fan came barreling out the front door and leapt into his arms before he knew what had hit him—at least, that's how Slocum read his expression.

Mary emerged on Fan's heels, saying, "It's your niece, Fred. Frank's girl, Fannie. These two gentlemen have brought her all the way from Phoenix!"

A look of recognition spread quickly over Fred Forebush's face. "Fannie, Fannie! I haven't seen you since you were a month old and only as long as my forearm! What are you now? Thirteen? Fourteen?"

"Thirteen, Uncle Fred!" Fan replied, embracing him anew. "Oh, I'm so glad to be here. I miss Daddy so much!"

"We're all missin' him, Fannie. Frankie was the finest brother a man could ask for."

If Slocum ever had a family, he vowed he was going to name all the kids at least two letters away from each other.

"Fred, put Floss away. I've almost got dinner on the table," Mary said. When he didn't show signs of budging, she added, "Take Fan to the barn with you, Fred."

Slowly, Fan and her uncle Fred made their way to the barn, Fred's sorrel plodding at their backs.

Mary waved at Slocum and Forsythe. "Come in, you two, come in this house!"

Mary laughed into her napkin. "When you get to our aunts and uncles—your great aunts and uncles, Fannie—that's where it really starts to get awkward!"

Fred was grinning wide. "Flotilla and Fortescue, Flax and Ferdinand—"

"And Fester and Franklin and Florida and Farley," added Mary, still giggling.

Fred held up his forefinger. "And Forgetful, Fiery, Festus, Farfel, and Flannel?"

Fannie, who was doubled over with laughter, asked, "Are those even real names?"

"Yes, ma'am, and they're in your pedigree, same's mine," chuckled Fred.

"Come on, Miss Fan," said Mary as she rose from the table. "Help me with the dishes."

Fan obliged, and before Slocum knew it, the table had been cleared and the women were out in the kitchen, washing dishes and laughing.

"Mind if I smoke?" Forsythe asked.

Fred shook his head while he pulled out his pipe. "Not if I can join you."

Slocum didn't bother asking. He pulled out his fixings pouch and rolled a quirlie.

As he scratched a lucifer into flame, Fred said, "Again, I'd like to really thank you men for ferrying Fan out here." He puffed on his pipe, lighting it. "We'd heard about her papa dying, of course, but nothing about Fan." He shook his head, then shook out his match. "I just figured that Frank had already married her off."

Slocum opened his mouth to say something about her daddy's death having almost sold her into a most public sort of marriage, but Forsythe beat him to the punch.

Forsythe didn't have whorehouses on his mind, though. He asked, "Don't suppose you were in town the day that Rafe Masterson came through, were you?"

Fred's jovial expression vanished. "I was," he said, leaning forward and abruptly spitting on the floor.

"I take it you two don't get along?" asked Forsythe.

"He shot a friend a'mine," Fred growled. "Goddamn saddle-burnin' no-account." As he said it, he threw

Slocum a sidelong glance, but Slocum didn't react. He could think of a lot worse names for himself, and a thousand more for Rafe Masterson.

"Well, he killed my brother," said Forsythe. "And Slocum's horse," he added, almost as an afterthought.

"I'm sure sorry, Forsythe," Fred said. "And you, too, Mr. Slocum."

"It's just Slocum," he said out of habit, then, "A feller gets real close to his horse when they've been on the trail together a long time." He didn't add, *when that horse has got you out of a jam or three*, or *when that horse is whistle-trained, or can spin on a bottle stopper, or reins so handy you can ride him with no bridle . . .*

He could have gone on and on, but didn't. Folks didn't understand. If they did, you knew it right off, and he wasn't getting any such ear balm out of Fred.

Only he really knew Dash, only he missed his Dash that much.

And only he could avenge him.

6

Slocum went to bed before the other two had finished gabbing. Forsythe seemed to be the star so far as all the Forebush clan were concerned, but Slocum didn't mind. He was content to let him take the limelight, and went to sleep the minute his head hit the pillow.

When he rose the next morning, he was certain that Forsythe hadn't come to bed at all. The other cot in the room was made up and unmussed, and he'd heard no sounds of rustling around. But when he got downstairs, there was Forsythe, looking rested and bright, enjoying breakfast with the family.

"There you are, sleepyhead!" cried Fan. "We thought you were goin' to snooze away the whole day!"

"Run and fix Mr. Slocum a plate, Fan," said Mary, indicating a vacant chair. "Sorry. We get up at the crack of dawn out here."

"Fruit farmin' takes a feller the whole day," Fred added.

Slocum sat down. "Bet it does," he said. "I been meaning to ask where you get your irrigation water, Fred. I was right impressed with your system."

"Oh, thank you, thank you," Fan's uncle Fred replied as if Slocum had just complimented him on his skill with a forty-five. "We've got a nice creek to the south, and I just diverted part of it to the ditches. There was a Mexican that had this place afore me, so I can't take the credit for layin' out most of the trenches. I take it he grew tomatoes and peppers, though. He had one orange tree. That's what gave me the idea."

Mary piped up, "He was Spanish, Fred."

"Same thing," Fred replied, offhand. He waved at Slocum. "Shove that marmalade over here, would you?"

Slocum complied just as Fannie brought his breakfast. It was a beaut, too. Scrambled eggs, hash browns, bacon and ham, toast and butter, and a big pot of hot coffee.

"Thanks, honey," he said. This must have seemed like heaven to Fan. He supposed they even kept their cheese wrapped up in cheesecloth, he thought, and tamped down a chuckle.

He dug into his breakfast right away, pausing only to say to Mary, "This is sure a good breakfast to have to eat so fast!"

She laughed but said, "Why do you have to eat so fast?"

He was chewing fast to get the ham out of his mouth when Forsythe, bless his heart, said, "We have to get out on the trail. We're hunting Rafe Masterson."

Slocum wouldn't have put it so dramatically, but he

was still chewing, and he nodded at what Forsythe had said.

"Oh," Mary said softly.

Her husband said, "You tear 'em up, boys!"

Little Fan made calf eyes at Forsythe.

And Slocum just kept chewing as fast as he could. He wanted to get out of there and get on the road. Or the trail, or the path, or whatever. He just wanted to get out of there, away from all the "F" names—well, most all of 'em anyway—and get Rafe Masterson in his sites.

At his elbow, Forsythe said, "I believe I'll go get the horses tacked up. All right with you, Slocum?"

Slocum nodded, and Forsythe went on his way, with Fan tagging at his heels.

After weighing them down with baked goods, the Forebushes finally bade them good-bye. Slocum wasn't sure, but he thought he saw Mary physically restrain Fan, who nearly darted after them.

He turned his attention to the trail out of the orchard. *Oh well*, he thought. *She'll get over it. And over him.* A glance over at Forsythe told him that Forsythe hadn't been watching. He had, however, been busy in the time before Slocum got up. Slocum learned that the Forebushes had pressed not only baked goods but a knotted bandanna upon them. Forsythe opened it and found they'd put two ten-dollar gold pieces inside. For that, Slocum was truly grateful.

They swung back through town on their way south, and Slocum indulged himself by buying two packs of ready-mades, along with canned and dry goods for the trek. Again, he went to the sheriff's office, and learned that nobody else had come through town asking about Rafe.

Good, he thought, nodding his head. *That winnows down the competition.*

He and Forsythe, saddlebags—and possibles bags—full, set off. About three miles south of town, the trail split, just as the sheriff had told him it would. They took the fork that would lead them farther inland, away to the southeast.

"Too bad somebody hasn't belled him," remarked Forsythe. "It'd sure make things easier."

It took Slocum a second to figure out what he was speaking of, and then he chuckled. "You mean like when you bell a sheep?" he asked.

"Or a goat," Forsythe said, a grin spreading over his face. "Yup. That's it, exactly."

They made excellent time that day and camped for the night in the center of a loose circle of worn-smooth boulders. Slocum saw to the horses while Forsythe built a fire. They hadn't passed a single bush all day, and Slocum was trying to figure out just what the devil Forsythe had used for fuel when Forsythe said, "When you figure we'll catch up with him?"

"What? Oh. Good question. Depends on how much ground we can make up over the next few days." He took a look at what Forsythe was putting in the skillet for tonight's dinner. "Beefsteak," he said with a smile. "Good."

Forsythe just nodded. Now, Slocum knew he was as anxious as the next man to catch up to Rafe Masterson and give him what for. But he was accustomed to trailing men, waiting them out, trying to think one step ahead. He knew that Forsythe wasn't.

He said, "You gotta start thinkin' like Masterson. Remember, the bad guys don't think like you or me.

Now, thinking like Masterson, I might just figure to go on south, then double back when I find a place that doesn't take any track. Try to find me a good roost, where I could see for miles in any direction. Take my shots from far off. Or mayhap somethin' else."

"Far off, like whoever it was that shot Miss Fan?"

"There you go. I like the way you're thinkin'. Except that wasn't Rafe Masterson. If it had been, there's no way he could have beat us to Los Angeles by a week."

Forsythe nodded. "I get you."

"Don't get anxious," Slocum said. "It'll come round when it comes round." He sat forward and gestured toward the frying pan, which Forsythe had just settled atop the fire. "Can I help with anything?"

"Nope," said Forsythe. He had the coffeepot ready to perk, too, and set it over the fire. "Just with eatin' it. And that'll be a little while."

Slocum leaned back against his saddle then and pulled his hat down over his eyes. "If you don't mind, I believe I'll grab me a little shut-eye afore dinner," he said from beneath it, and crossed his arms over his chest.

"Go right ahead," he heard Forsythe say.

And that was the last peep he heard out of Forsythe.

Something woke Slocum at about seven-thirty. The fire had burned down to embers, and the skillet had been taken off it and set to one side. And Forsythe wasn't in sight.

Slocum pushed himself up to his feet, quickly giving the dying fire a stir as he rose.

He shouted, "Forsythe!" out into the darkness.

No reply.

He froze.

Still no sounds.

What the hell was going on?

He looked toward the horses, but it was too dark to see them. He could hear them, though. At least, he could hear one of them. That was the one good thing, so far. Slowly, he circled the campfire. The grub bags had been put away—at least, he hoped that was the case—and Forsythe's bedding had been picked up.

Aside from the extra footprints, there was no sign that anybody had ever been camped here but Slocum.

What the hell had happened? Had Forsythe just decamped in the night? Did he plan on picking up that reward money for himself?

Well, good luck, you sack a'shit, Slocum thought with a scowl that was anything but kind. *Rafe'll pick you off before you even know that he's there.*

He growled, "Shit!" and made his way through the darkness to the place he'd left the horses, but he found only Fleet still tethered. This elicited a much longer stream of invective and ended with Slocum trying to punch out a boulder.

Forsythe was solid gone, all right, and now Slocum had a hand full of bruised knuckles to boot. He'd left food, though. At least, some of it. Oh, he'd ridden out with the sack of baked goods given them by Mary Forebush and he'd taken the rest of the bacon and ham, but he'd left Slocum with the canned and dry goods he'd bought. He'd also left half the water and all the horse feed. Probably thought that fancy-steppin' Tennessee walker of his could live off the land.

Fat chance.

Slocum walked back to the dying fire and knelt down to stir it back into flame. He'd just given it a fast tickle before. And when he was done, he checked to see if there was any food in the skillet.

There was. He had steak and eggs for dinner—somewhat burnt, and cold as the grave. But he set the pot back on the little fire and had, at least, some hot coffee.

And the whole time it took him to have dinner, he berated himself for having misjudged Forsythe.

Had the shitheel planned this all along? Slocum couldn't convince himself otherwise. Forsythe was probably out there right now, heading merrily south and figuring out all the goodies he could buy with the reward.

Damn it.

Slocum didn't mind so much about the reward. And he certainly didn't mind riding the trail alone. But he did mind being abandoned by somebody he'd thought was a friend, somebody in whom he'd put his faith. Somebody who was most likely going to get himself killed.

If there was one sure thing, it was that Forsythe wasn't trail-wise. Slocum had learned that much over the past few days. He was bound to run out of water and get himself lost out there in the desert, if not ambushed by *bandidos* or taken down by a grizzly or a cougar or a rattlesnake. Hell, a damn black widow!

Or shot by Rafe Masterson. Or somebody very much like him.

The California desert wasn't very forgiving. It was much like Arizona's southern half in the roughness and toughness of its men and women, its climate, and its wildness.

He didn't believe that Forsythe was up to it. Not for a minute.

And to tell the honest truth, at this point he didn't much care.

* * *

At roughly the same time that Slocum finished his coffee and his grumbling and turned in for the night, Forsythe was two miles down the trail in total darkness.

It had been all right for a while, but then the trail had entered this canyon. Once the moonlight was blocked out, he found himself in a peck of trouble.

He got down off his horse and clumsily led it forward, feeling with his booted toe for the path through the scrubby undergrowth.

The dark wasn't the only thing to feel bad about.

He felt bad about having left Slocum back there. Not so bad that he was about to turn around and sneak back into camp, but he did feel bad for him.

He hadn't left because of any dislike or grudge having to do with Slocum, or even because the maddeningly straight Slocum was driving him crazy with desire—which, as a matter of fact, he was.

Very simply, he'd left because all of $10,000 was a lot more than half of $5,000.

Enough to set a man up, practically for life. Certainly enough to cover a nice house in Louisiana, and maybe buy his way into a thriving business.

He stumbled and almost went down to his knees, but stopped himself by hanging onto the horse's reins.

This was not a practice favored by his Tennessee walker, who flung his head up and back, jerking Forsythe roughly back to his feet.

Once he got his balance again, he soothed the gelding with both hand and voice, calming him before he started forward again.

"There, boy. Easy, boy . . ."

The horse moved slowly, and Forsythe kept pace with

him. As long as he was moving, that was enough. But every feather rustle, every soft slide of a snake's belly scales, every sound, mysterious or known, set the walking horse into a panic. Forsythe talked to him more to fill the air with his familiar voice and cancel out sounds the horse might take to be the equine version of the boogeyman.

It was going to be a long, bleak night.

7

Slocum was on the trail early in the morning, following Forsythe's path. He'd decided that Forsythe was going to get himself killed—that was all there was to it—and it was up to him to stop that from happening.

If he could.

He didn't need to feel happy about it, but it was something he felt he had to do.

He had a clear trail to follow, too. Forsythe might as well have posted signs along the way. For instance, at one point going down a small canyon, Slocum could tell that Forsythe had been leading his horse when he'd fallen, been jerked back up, stepped to the side, then gone on his way again, leading his mount.

The skid of his boot heels and the rapid backward skitter of his horse's shoes told Slocum volumes.

Slocum didn't recall the talk between them ever turning to tracking. Now it was obvious why it hadn't.

Forsythe didn't have the sense to hide his track or even disguise it.

And Slocum didn't take Forsythe for a fool.

The only assumption left was that Forsythe didn't know how to track. Now, this puzzled Slocum. Any Louisiana farm boy should have been able to snatch up a rifle and pick off a couple of rabbits for lunch by the time he was ten.

And to snatch up game in a hurry, you had to be able to track it.

Slocum shook his head to rattle some sense into it, but it didn't take. Forsythe was making less and less sense as time went on.

Later that morning, at the other end of the canyon he found the place where Forsythe had camped and probably cooked some of that ham. He found the fresh remains of a campfire and a place that looked to have been used for a lie-down. There were signs of a horse having been tethered nearby.

Slocum rode on.

At noon, he stopped to have a light lunch and rest his horse. He didn't rest himself, though. He was too busy trying to figure what to do next.

After he'd given Fleet an hour's break, he set out again. Forsythe's tracks were so easy to follow in the dusty topsoil that he let Fleet canter for a bit, stretching himself out, before reining him back down to a slow but solid jog trot.

He rode on for a couple of hours, until the trail brought him down a pass in the low foothills, a pass that widened itself out into a broad plain.

He didn't see Forsythe right away, although he was

looking. The plain went on forever, and from his view-point, that meant a good two or three days toward the horizon. He heard the shots first.

He dropped off Fleet as quick as an eel down a chute, then drew his gun and crouched behind some rocks. It soon became apparent that the shots weren't intended for him—they were being fired from across the plain and were focused on a target about a half mile distant.

A quick look with the spyglass told Slocum the tale: their target was Forsythe.

Forsythe was fit to be tied. After a very rough night of stumbling and tripping in the dark, he had emerged on the open plain—only to be driven to cover by some idiot out there with a gun! At first, he'd thought these fellows were just out hunting. Until he'd waved his arms. The next shot sang just past his ear, and he took cover im-mediately, fanning his horse away.

He was completely staggered by this. No one could be tracking him. No one knew he was coming. Cripes! He hadn't even known anybody in California until yes-terday. Still kneeling, he dusted his hands on his lower pant legs and started, very slowly, to rise.

Another shot parted the bushes on his right, and he dropped back down again. Damn it! The shooter was too far off for him to see, but judging by the sound of the shots coming toward him, he was a long way out, and he was shooting with a rifle.

This posed a problem on several levels. First of all, Forsythe didn't own a rifle, and had forgotten to lift Slocum's when he left. Secondly, there was no fixed place for him to aim at. And last of all, the shooter would have to shift very little—perhaps only a fraction of an inch—to nail him if he ran for his horse and tried to hotfoot it out of there.

He would likely never have thought of another alternative, but just then, somebody fired from behind him.

Crouched, he whirled about on one foot. The marksman fired again, and this time he caught a glimpse of a blue and black plaid shirtsleeve. It was enough to make him laugh with recognition, but then he started to worry.

Maybe Slocum was madder than he thought about being left alone out there.

Maybe he'd finally figured out Forsythe's sexual leanings.

Belatedly, Forsythe realized that if their positions had been reversed, he would have been right angry with himself. No, he thought. He would have been downright mad. *Murderously* mad.

And he swallowed hard at the thought.

The slugs weren't coming near Slocum. Those that hit close enough for him to see them thumped dully off the rocks or skidded to the ground like stones skipping on pond water. He wasn't going to waste any more ammunition firing back at them. He stepped out into the open and put his rifle down. Then he cupped his hand around his mouth and, at the top of his lungs, hollered, "Hello the shooters! Who the hell are you?"

He waited. He had no idea if the sound of his voice, booming though it was, would carry that far. He could hear the shots, but a bullet's boom was a whole lot different than a man's shout. He waited with the spyglass to his eye and hoped.

At last, a figure moved in the far-off sage.

A voice, barely heard, shouted back, "Damn! Is that you, Slocum?"

He couldn't tell much about the voice, but he knew the shouter was Mexican. He called back, "Yes, it's me. Who are you?"

A few minutes crawled by before he heard the thin reply echo up to him. "Juan Alba, amigo!"

Slocum laughed, although he was pretty sure the sound hadn't gone out across the canyon. He cupped his hands again and shouted, "*Juan! Mi amigo!*"

He'd been afraid Forsythe would run across Mexican *bandidos*—he just hadn't thought that he'd bump into this one!

Forsythe didn't gain his feet until he could actually see Slocum's approach. And even then, he got up very slowly, with his hand on his gun. He didn't know how happy Slocum was going to be to see him.

As it turned out, he didn't get to find out for a while, because just before he almost rode over Forsythe, Slocum turned out toward the shooters. Forsythe's brow wrinkled. What the hell was going on?

Rising the rest of the way to his feet, he watched Slocum ride away, heading out to meet the men who had just tried to kill him.

It took another half hour, but Slocum finally met the riders coming toward him across the plain. He had ridden the last half mile with his Colt out but pointed down, just in case somebody had had the nerve (and the smarts) to use Alba's name for cover.

But when he was close enough to see Juan's grinning face, he shoved the gun back in its holster and raised his hand overhead.

"Juan!" he shouted. "How goes it?"

The tall, thin man at the center of the serape-clad line of riders laughed. "Good! Very good! And you, my friend?"

"Much better now!" Slocum didn't have to shout it now. He and the line of riders converged. He slid down off Fleet at the same moment that Alba—the most feared bandit in Arizona—stepped down to the ground. They met in the middle and embraced. "Jesus Christ, Juan! I sure didn't expect to run into you out here. What the heck you doin' in California?"

"I should ask you the same question, Slocum," the bandit said, slapping Slocum's back.

"Well, I'm lookin' for a polecat name'a Rafe Masterson," Slocum said. "You seen him?"

Alba nodded. *"Sí,"* he said. "And suffered his passing." Slocum quirked one brow.

"Folks keep thinking we are him. They give us no chance to explain that we are not." Alba shrugged. "Already I have lost two men. Well, one and a half. Pancho, over there, he cannot shoot anymore." He indicated the mounted *bandido* to his left, whose arm was bound to his side. "We go home now. California is too much bother, what with crazy gringo gunmen going before us."

Slocum laughed. He said, "And you mistook my friend back there to be Masterson?" He poked a thumb back toward Forsythe's hiding place.

Alba nodded and Slocum went on, "That's a hoot and a half. He ain't Rafe Masterson, but Masterson killed his brother over a card game back in Louisiana."

"Ah! My apologies, Slocum!"

"I'll let you tell him yourself." Slocum remounted. "C'mon with me."

The rest of the *bandidos* trailing behind them, Slocum and Alba traveled back toward Forsythe's stand.

Alba had been a longtime, if seldom seen, friend of Slocum's for over twenty years. When Slocum first came out to the Territory, Alba, then just starting out on his life of banditry, had jumped into the same cave as Slocum when Slocum was being pursued by a band of pissed-off Apaches.

The two men had finally stopped trying to kill each other when they recognized that they were far more alike than they were different.

And far more likely to be slaughtered by the Indians than by each other.

They had ended that Apache incident by simply hiding themselves and their horses long enough that the Apaches gave up and went away, and they emerged from the cave as strong buddies, pumped up on luck.

Through the years their friendship had grown, even considering how seldom their paths crossed. They were of an age, and they respected each other.

Out here, in this hard country, men had been known to build a lifelong bond out of nothing more than respect.

Sometimes, it was enough.

They camped for the night back at the spot where Forsythe had hunkered down.

He looked skittish when they rode up on him, Slocum thought. *He oughta*, he mused. *Damn deserter.*

But Forsythe apologized to him later. He said he'd

been wrong to just take off like that. He said he wouldn't blame Slocum if he wanted to kill him. And in true gentlemanly fashion, he took a step back, closed his eyes, and held his vest open, fearlessly waiting for the bullet to come.

Slocum could have slapped him just for being so silly.

But he didn't. Slowly shaking his head and grumbling under his breath, he'd walked away.

Juan Alba's apology to Forsythe was much more sincere and far less theatrical.

"Amigo," he said, "my men and I make you the apology. We thought you were another. Rafe Masterson, his name is. Slocum tells us that he has done you harm, also?"

"You thought *I* was Masterson?" Forsythe asked, his face incredulous, yet curiously desirous to hear more.

"*Sí,*" replied Alba. Several men, behind him, echoed his answer softly or bobbed their heads.

Forsythe said, "He killed my brother."

"So Slocum has told us. I am—we all are—very sorry, señor."

"Juan?" asked one of the men. It was Pancho, Slocum saw. "The tortillas, they are done."

"Thought I smelled somethin' interestin'," Slocum said, and smiled. "I still got some cheese for meltin'."

"I got some ham we could chop up." Forsythe joined in. At least he was sharing again. The food, anyway. And Slocum reminded himself that he still had the ten-dollar gold piece that Fan's uncle had given him . . . At least Forsythe hadn't made off with that in the night, too.

One of Alba's men said, "I have two rabbits, and the spices to cook them."

And Alba himself said, "And we already have the beans cooking, do we not, Raul?"

Unseen, another man grunted, "Yes."

Smiling, Juan said, "*Muy bueno*. We will have a very good meal, then."

8

Juan hadn't added that another of his men had a good supply of tequila, and Slocum spent a relaxed and companionable evening. Forsythe, on the other hand, was still concerned. Although he'd sampled it on occasion on his way west, he wasn't really accustomed to the spicy Mexican food.

He nibbled at his dinner, but each tiny bite was hot and spicy. Too spicy. He nearly drank his canteen dry, had four cups of coffee, and it still wasn't enough.

The Mexican bandits made him uncomfortable, too. They looked, to him, like men who'd kill you in your sleep, and he wondered how he was going to make it through the night in one piece.

He saw that Slocum wasn't worried. He laughed and joked with Alba and his men like they were his long-lost brothers! But then, Slocum wasn't exactly feeling brotherly toward him. Forsythe had tried to talk to him several times, tried to make a more detailed apology, but on each occasion he'd found the opportunity, Slocum was called away on some pretext or other.

His throat and chest burning from whatever it was he'd had for supper—ground tarantula and scorpion was his guess—and fear pounding his heart, he found a small amount of soda in his provisions bag. He dumped it in his mouth, then took a big gulp of canteen water and swallowed the soda down to help soothe his stomach.

Slocum was across the camp, deep in conversation with Alba and his right-hand man. Forsythe didn't want to intrude. Well, actually, he was too nervous to intrude on their conversation: too impressed with Slocum and too frightened of what Slocum still might do to the idiot who had snuck out on him.

Bad decision, you old son of the South, bad decision, Forsythe thought, mentally whipping himself. Had anyone ever made such a careless determination? He thought not. Not considering all of the circumstances. Not considering any of them!

He finally gave up trying to figure it out and spread out his blankets. He was so tired he was practically sleepwalking anyway. After surrounding his pallet with a ring of rope—something he'd seen Slocum do, and which he'd always copied—he sank down, then stretched out on the blanket, resting his head on his saddle.

His innards still burning from the supper he'd eaten, he closed his eyes and fell into a fitful sleep, his only companion the murmur of conversation carrying over from the area around the campfire.

*   *   *

"Here's the deal, Juan," Slocum said. The two men had finished their dinner and were sitting apart from the others. Slocum kept his voice low.

"There's a reward on Masterson," he continued. "Forsythe and I have already agreed to split it, no matter which of us takes him down. But I'm willin' to cut you in for a quarter of it. That's half of my half. If you agree to go along on the hunt. What you think, compadre?"

Alba pursed his lips, then took a long drag on his cigarette. Finally, he said, "My men, they can go home and rest?"

"Yup."

Again, there was a long pause while Alba considered this. "For a third," he said at last.

Slocum nodded. "Done. I think Forsythe'll go for it. Well, lemme put it this way—either he goes for it, or he don't go for nothin' at all ever again."

"Yes, yes," replied Alba with a smile and a quick nod of his handsome head. He stroked his mustache. "By the way, amigo, just how much is this prize on Rafe Masterson?"

"Ten thousand. Which means we each get three thousand three hundred and thirty-three dollars. And thirty-three cents."

"And the extra penny?"

Slocum chuckled. "You can take it. Buy yourself some more color for your horse."

Alba laughed out loud. He rode a pinto, dark chestnut and white, with white making up most of the color pattern. He said, "I could say the same about you, my friend."

"Reckon you could. But I like him that way."

Alba, still smiling, shook his head and said, "You always did, compadre. You always did."

Slocum heaved himself to his feet. "Well, I'd best turn in. Been a long day, what with gettin' shot at and all."

Alba stood, too, and dusted the seat of his britches off with one hand. "*Sí*, it has been a long day for us, too, what with shooting at crazy gringos who refuse to die."

Slocum grinned. "But for good reason."

"*Sí,*" Alba grudgingly admitted. "We think so now."

Slocum wasn't sure what he meant, but he smiled and nodded anyway. Now wasn't the time to nitpick. He was honestly too tired. He said, "Night, buddy," and gave Alba a quick wave.

"*Buenas noches,*" came the reply, and Alba disappeared into the darkness.

Slocum crept over to where Forsythe had made his pallet. There, a few feet away, he spread out his blanket, hauled his saddle into place, and pulled out his lariat to ring the saddle with rope. He saw that Forsythe had done the same, and despite everything that had gone on that day, he nodded in approval.

Given enough time, Forsythe just might make a Westerner after all.

Juan Alba waved the notion away. "No one has ever accused the Scourge of Arizona of being a stupid man," he said.

Crouched beside him, Vargas snorted out a laugh. "If they had, they would not have named you the Scourge!" he said.

Pablo smiled, and Alba grinned in agreement.

"There you have it," he said. "I will stay and you will go."

"But, Juan," began Pancho.

"No buts," Juan said, cutting him off along with the argument he knew Vargas was building. "I want you to lead the men southeast. Down into Mexico, to our old hideout in the mountains. I will meet you there, and when I do, we will go into town and drink much cerveza."

His expression told Pancho and Vargas not to argue, and together they said a final "*Sí*, Juan."

Alba nodded his approval, an expression that also told Pancho and Vargas that the conversation was over and that they should leave him. They did, going off to bed down with the rest of the gang and leaving Juan alone.

He laid out and readied his blankets without interruption. A glance to the side told him that Slocum and his friend were already asleep.

That Slocum! If he thought he could tell an untruth to Juan Alba, he was sadly mistaken. Alba knew that he and Forsythe had not been traveling together. The look on Forsythe's face when they rode up on him told a different tale. Forsythe had been afraid—scared of him and his band, and rightly so; but he feared Slocum more. This much was apparent.

But it was also apparent that this fear was not so terrible that it couldn't be overcome by a desire for sleep. Forsythe had been asleep long before Slocum retired.

It was a curious thing. Alba didn't wish to stir the simmering waters up into a boil by poking too much, but the question intrigued him: just who was this Forsythe to Slocum, and what had he done to make Slocum so angry with him?

Alba already had his doubts about Forsythe. He looked and acted like one of those fancy boys to him.

But why would Slocum be traveling with one in the first place?

Or perhaps it was the reason Slocum was so angry with him.

But it was none of his business. They would work it out, whatever it was, in their own way.

As he settled down onto his blankets, wriggling until he found a position where no rock was digging into his flesh, he decided that the Slocum-Forsythe feud was a moot point. Let them glare at each other. Let them disagree. If he was very lucky, Slocum might even end Forsythe's life. That would make Alba's take half of the whole instead of one-third.

He and his men could use the money.

Come morning, Forsythe arose to find he was the last to wake. Alba's men were making breakfast or feeding the horses or cleaning their rifles. Alba himself was sitting on a rock, mending tack. And Slocum was nowhere to be seen.

For a moment, Forsythe felt fear stab through him. Had he been deserted by Slocum? Had he been left with these murderous men so that they could kill him for sport?

Terror filled his heart, and he broke out in a wave of shivers.

And then, from behind him, a voice boomed, "Mornin', sleepyhead."

He whirled in his blanket, reaching for his pistol. He nearly had it clear of his holster, too, when he saw Slocum's face smiling down at him.

"You always take aim at the feller who wakes you in the mornin'?"

"N-no," stuttered Forsythe, in a voice that was far too high and squeaky to be his own. He cleared his throat and put his gun away. "You just startled me, sir, that's all." He got to his feet. "Slocum, I just wanted to say that I didn't mean anything when I—"

"'Nough said," replied the tall man with a wave of his hand. "Came over to ask you a question. I been thinkin' that two's not enough to take out Rafe Masterson. Juan over there," he tipped his head toward Alba, "tells me that Masterson's been stirrin' up a heap of trouble down around these parts. Could be the reward's even bigger than we been told."

Forsythe perked up. "Even bigger?"

"Could be," Slocum said with a nod. "Therefore, I went ahead and asked Juan Alba to come in with us. Thirds. That strike you as all right?"

Thirds? No, it didn't strike him right, but he didn't say so. He was thinking that maybe Slocum had a good idea. Masterson could likely shoot any of them out of the saddle from far off, with no more care than a dog scratched a flea.

Forsythe took the high road. "It's fine," he said, nodding. But then he asked, "What about his men?"

"He's sendin' them back to Mexico. We're better off if there's just the three of us."

Forsythe took a moment to let that sink in. Slocum was right. Three was probably best. He said, "All right. When do we start out?"

"Today. After Juan gets his boys straightened out."

"I see," Forsythe said, even though he didn't. "Fine, then."

Slocum pulled his hat brim down low on his forehead. "I'll let you get yourself ready. There's beans on the fire and some bacon in the skillet. You've got the bread."

He didn't realize until Slocum was gone that his last sentence had been a jab. The Forebushes' bag of baked goods was at his side.

Breakfast was had, the last of the tack was mended, provisions were divvied out so that everybody was carrying an equal weight, the water was divided and shared, and Slocum, Forsythe, and Alba were finally on their own.

They dropped off the road at Alba's suggestion and began to wend their way across the plain, toward the point of Alba's last contact with Rafe Masterson.

"He is one tricky bastard," Juan said to Slocum. "He would sell his *mamacita* to a house of whores for a handful of beans and trade his papa into servitude for a drink of whiskey."

Slocum nodded. "He's mean, all right. I thought I had him up in Flagstaff. He and his gang took off to the southwest, into the San Francisco Peaks. Somewhere, over hard ground, they split up. Didn't know it until we got to softer ground, and by then it was too late. I was gallopin', gainin' ground, when somebody fired on me from across the gorge." He shook his head. It still got to him, even though it had been months ago. "That rat bastard shot my good horse right out from under me."

"*Lo siento mucho, amigo*," Juan murmured.

"Thanks," replied Slocum with a nod. "Killed him dead on the spot, then rode off without so much as a fare-thee-well. I hiked back down the mountain till I found an old trapper's cabin to hole up in. And then it began to snow. Snowed like a real son of a bitch, clear up to the cabin's roof!"

Slocum shook his head, remembering those icy nights with a palpable shiver. "I was trapped there for about two months before I could get out and climb down the mountain to a town. Which turned out to be only half a town at that," Slocum sneered.

"And why is that?"

"They didn't have no women, Juan!" Slocum blurted, as if this were cruel and unusual punishment, as if this offense were on a level with matricide and patricide.

It was, to his way of thinking, almost worse.

9

The cantina wasn't fancy, but then, San Diego wasn't a fancy town. Ships came, ships went, freight was loaded and unloaded, and the men went with the ships. Few stayed, outside of some Mexican farmers and shopkeepers, and the occasional errant gringo.

This was the cantina where most of the farmers spent their free time, along with those wayfarers who rode the trails instead of plying the waves. This day, most of the Mexican bar's patrons were Mexican, too. All, in fact, but one.

Rafe Masterson leaned forward over the bar. "Hey!" he called at the bartender, who was busy with customers at the other end. "Said I needed another beer! Cerveza!"

The barkeep acknowledged his order with a nod of his head but kept on pouring down at the far end of the bar.

"Goddamn it," Rafe growled. "Can't get no cruddy service at this cruddy bar!"

The man standing next to him said, "Give him the break, señor. He will get down to this end sooner or later."

"Who asked you?" Rafe snapped.

The man beside him—a farmer in town for the day, by the looks of him—jerked back involuntarily, then held up both hands to show they were empty. "Sorry, amigo," he said. "I was just trying to explain—"

"Shut the hell up!" Rafe barked, and the man turned away from him with a shrug. "A fine decision," Rafe grumbled at the back of the man's head. "Keep your shitty ass explanations to yourself from now on." He twisted his head. "Bartender!"

A hand shot toward him, seemingly from out of nowhere, and smacked a mug of beer down on the bar in front of him. "Cerveza, señor."

Rafe sneered, "'Bout time," and drank half the mug down. He swallowed and said, "Another," before taking a second drink that drained his glass.

"*Sí, señor*," said the bartender, shaking his head. He walked off toward the taps, carrying Rafe's glass.

Masterson wiped at his face with his hand. He might as well drink as much as he could hold. He wasn't planning on paying for it anyway.

While the barkeep walked down toward him, carrying his new beer, Rafe reached into his pocket and pulled out the letter.

"Cerveza, señor." The mug went *clunk* on the top of the bar.

Rafe waved the man off, saying, "Yeah, yeah . . . ," while he opened the letter he'd received that day, addressed to him at General Delivery. He already knew what it said. He just wanted to reread it and make sure his memory wasn't playing tricks on him.

The letter was from his old pal, Nash Ledbetter. They'd done some time together up in Kansas, and he'd met up with Nash again in Phoenix. Nash wouldn't have written him if the news weren't bad, and it was.

He scanned down until he found the part that interested him: *Do you know of a feller named Slocum? Didn't catch his first name, but he's a big guy, better than six foot with real dark hair. He was asking around town after you this week. Didn't look like he was going to give you a birthday present, either. Anyway, he headed out of town going west this morning. Was with the little gal from the whorehouse. Anyhow, since he was asking, I thought he might be on your tail. Thought you should know, Rafe. We went down to the canal this afternoon and I caught a string of catfish for supper . . .*

After that, Nash went off into his usual chatter, which Rafe didn't bother to reread. He did, however, check the letter for a postmark. It had been mailed about a week ago.

Rafe folded the letter back up and jammed it into his pocket, along with the envelope. A week ago. A week ago, he had been in Los Angeles, he thought. The chances that Slocum could find him out here were remote, that was for damn sure. But then, the chances that he would've shown up in Flagstaff—and carrying paper on Rafe—were pretty damned slim, too.

He swore under his breath, then grabbed his new beer and took one sip, then another. That damn Slocum! Why couldn't he just let the better man win? The better man, of course, being one Rafe Masterson.

He thought back to last time he'd seen Slocum. That was one helluva shot, even for him. Of course, he'd been aiming for Slocum, not his horse, but still . . .

He took another drink of beer. Even Slocum couldn't track him this far, through this country, not all the way to San Diego. The country was too rough and people too far apart. And Slocum was carrying that little brat from Kate's whorehouse, for reasons only God knew.

No, nobody could track him.

Nobody.

But an icy shiver ran along his fingers, up his arms, down his spine. Automatically, his hand went to his gun and he wheeled around.

There was no one there.

He holstered his weapon and muttered, "Son of a bitch is givin' me the creeps."

He took another drink of beer, then reconsidered. Maybe he should put a few more miles between them. Maybe, just in case. It'd be the wiser move, he thought, draining his beer. That Slocum was a tricky bastard. Rafe Masterson decided to stay over the night, then take off first thing in the morning.

That'd do it.

What had he ever done to piss off Slocum in the first place!?

"Nothin'," said Slocum, as the trio rode south through the desert. "I never set eyes on the horse-murderin' bastard until I tracked him into Flagstaff." He reined around a creosote bush, then came back, even with Alba. "Course, it was old paper I had on him. He was only worth $3,500 when it was printed. He's worth $5,000 now."

It seemed like the farther west he got, the more damage Masterson had done.

Alba nodded sagely, as if he could hear Slocum's thoughts. "It's good you trailed him to California, where he will bring more." Slocum started to glower, and Alba added quickly, "Of course, it is a great shame he had to kill your fine horse in the process."

"No shit," Slocum said, then swiveled in his saddle. "You still back there, Forsythe?"

Forsythe lazily waved a hand. He was about ten yards behind them, traveling at a walk. That Tennessee walker of his was pretty, all right, but Slocum would hate to be on him if they ever had to run for it. The fastest he'd seen that horse move was what they called a "rocking chair canter": all up and down and not much forward.

Come to think of it, he'd never tested Fleet's speed. Never had a call to. But now, mostly out of boredom, he said, "Let's let 'em run."

Alba barely had time to turn toward him and say, "What?" before Slocum was off and running.

Fast? Slocum was amazed! "You're named Fleet for a reason!" he shouted into the wind, and sank his spurs into the horse's flanks. The horse leapt ahead.

Slocum chanced a glance over his shoulder and saw the other two: Juan was nearly a quarter mile behind and riding all out; Forsythe was far behind—at a running canter, Slocum supposed. Gradually, he reined Fleet down to a walk, and a few moments later, Juan caught up with him.

"*Ay carumba!*" he said. He was out of breath himself, and Slocum had to laugh. "That is some real speed!" Alba went on, shaking his head. "Slocum, you could take him to the races and win every time!"

Slocum reached down and patted Fleet's neck. "I'll be damned if you ain't right, Juan. Didn't know he had it in him!"

"I will give you five hundred dollars for the horse," Juan said.

"Nope."

"Six hundred."

Slocum shook his head.

"All right. A thousand!"

"He ain't for sale, Juan," Slocum said, chuckling. "I'm gettin' to think he's a good one."

"You are the master of the understatement, my friend," Alba said, still shaking his head.

Just then, Forsythe cantered up beside them. He looked flustered, but he wasn't out of breath. His horse was, though.

"By God, Slocum," he said. "That is one fast Appaloosa you have there! They all have that much speed?"

Alba answered for him. "Not a horse in a million can run like that, Señor Forsythe!"

"I'm as surprised as anybody," Slocum admitted. He fiddled with his reins. "I just bought him over in Phoenix."

"You chose well," said Alba, nodding.

Slocum nodded. "Thanks."

Forsythe's mount was still blowing hard. But they were moving at a walk now. He'd cool down, eventually.

Alba guided them over to the west, toward the foothills. "Over this way," he said. "I last was fodder for his bullets in these hills."

Slocum gave a nod. "What's on the other side of 'em?"

"San Diego."

Slocum's brows arched. "San Diego? We that far south already?" He'd been to San Diego several times. Once, he'd just missed being shanghaied, he thought with a scowl. But then he smiled. They had a couple of nice brothels in San Diego . . .

Suddenly, Alba laughed, and Slocum said, "What?"

"You are thinking of women," Alba said. "It is on your face, Slocum. You have been to San Diego before, no?"

Slocum nodded. "Guilty as charged. On all counts. Madame Elena still have a place there?" He was thinking of a little Mexican gal from his last trek to San Diego. Boy, she was a firecracker!

"*Sí*, she does. We gave her some good business when we were there."

Slocum chuckled. "I 'magine you did."

"It is a nice thing to look forward to," Juan said. "We can celebrate catching Masterson there." He was grinning like a madman.

"What makes you think we can get him before we hit town?"

Alba shrugged. "With my guns and your luck—and your fast horse—nothing is impossible."

"You're an optimist, Juan. I like that. It's what's kept you alive and kickin' all these years."

Laughing, Alba threw his hands into the air. "At last, I am appreciated!"

They didn't find Masterson that day.

They made it halfway through the foothills, though. Slocum, tired of cooking, let Alba make supper. He was glad of it, too! Alba made them a pan of spicy fried rabbit and potatoes for a first course, then peach enchiladas for desert. Slocum knew he'd bought those canned peaches for a reason.

Later, they sat around the campfire smoking: Alba with his pipe, Slocum with a ready-made, and Forsythe, having forsaken his pipe, puffing on a ready-made he'd bummed from Slocum.

Alba was talking about the whores in San Diego again, which was making Slocum antsy. He figured he had no right to be thinking about loving when he had a job to do. Business before pleasure and all that stuff.

"When was the last time you ran into Masterson?" he asked, butting in. "I mean, when'd you last swap lead with him?"

Alba took a second to answer. Probably changing tracks from the whorehouse to the jailhouse, Slocum figured. Finally, Juan said, "The afternoon before we ran into you, my friend. Two days ago."

"Two days?" Slocum asked incredulously. Hell, Masterson could be in San Diego right now!

"*Sí,*" replied Juan. "It is only a half day's ride from here."

Slocum decided he'd been away from southern California for too long. He was losing his grip on where the hell entire cities were.

"This San Diego," interjected Forsythe, "it's on the coast, right?"

Slocum and Alba both nodded.

"Is there any chance our man might hop a freighter?"

"No way," answered Slocum. "He's from the Midwest."

Alba cocked his head. "This makes a difference?"

"That's what I mean, Slocum," insisted Forsythe. "It doesn't make a difference. He could have jumped a freighter and gone halfway up the coast already."

"Or down it," Alba reminded him, and Slocum grinned.

"Or down it," Forsythe repeated. "He could be half-way up—or down—the coast by now! I think we should ride tonight."

"Do you wish to handle this, or should I?" Alba asked Slocum.

Slocum sat forward. "I'll do it."

Forsythe looked confused.

"Do what? Let's ride!" Forsythe said, and leapt to his feet.

"Sit down, Forsythe," Slocum said, and stared at him until he did. "First off, we ain't gonna find him tonight. If he ain't made San Diego yet, he's likely holed up so tight, even the coyotes don't know he's there."

Forsythe raised his finger. "But—"

"No buts," Slocum said. "And don't try skippin' out on me again."

Forsythe opened his mouth, but Alba beat him to it. Which was a good thing for Forsythe, Slocum thought.

"Amigo," Alba began, "listen to Slocum. This man, Rafe Masterson, is as Slocum tells you. Do not worry. We will find him eventually. He cannot get away. No one gets away from John Slocum or Juan Alba."

He made a theatrical flourish with his arm, and Slocum broke out laughing, followed directly by Alba.

Forsythe shook his head sadly. "You two are as loony as a pair of, well, loons!"

"Relax, Forsythe," Slocum said between bouts of laughter. "We'll get him. The odds are on our side." He pounded Forsythe's knee. "Just don't try runnin' off in the night. He catches you alone, he'll kill you dead, sure as shootin'."

Alba nodded. "It is truth. Masterson would not hesitate to pick you off like a clay pigeon, Señor Forsythe. You must listen to Slocum."

Forsythe heaved a sigh.

Slocum patted his knee again. "Atta boy, Forsythe. You just do like you're told. Me and Juan are old hands at this. Your brother's killer's days are numbered, no matter how you look at it." His ready-made had gone out, and he lit a fresh one. "Another, Forsythe?"

Forsythe waved the pack away. "I am going to sleep now," he said.

Alba nodded. "We will pack up and ride early, no?"

"Right," answered Slocum.

"Right," echoed Forsythe, although with little gusto.

Later, Forsythe lay in his bedroll, still awake, still worrying.

He knew that they were going to lose Masterson, lose him most likely by being too late, or, very possibly lose him because they were too busy bickering among themselves.

And worst of all, he suspected that Alba knew. About him. He couldn't for the life of him give a concrete reason; surely it was nothing he had said or done. But Alba had a certain way about him, a way that said, "Stay away from me, you dirty fancy boy. Stay away, or I will kill you."

Not a word on the subject had passed between himself and Alba. Yet he knew the threat existed.

It made him nervous, very nervous.

10

Early the next morning, Slocum, Alba, and Forsythe rode out of camp and on through the foothills. But Rafe Masterson had ridden on from San Diego at the same time.

Rafe was headed southeast. He figured that he could make Mexico by the following afternoon if he didn't stop in that Arizona/Mexico border town. What was the name of it? He couldn't remember.

Hell, they were all the same anyway. There was a brothel and a cantina and not much else besides your usual lame-ass border-town sheriff.

No, he thought, he'd ride right past it and on down into Mexico. At least he'd be out of range of the U.S. Marshals. He'd killed another one just last week. That had been a nice shot: he'd picked him off from between two other riders at a distance of about two hundred yards. The marshal hadn't been at a dead run, like Slocum, but then, Slocum hadn't been so far out.

Milt Yardly had been the marshal's name. He'd seen him in Phoenix and been told—by Nash Ledbetter—that he was in the area. Fortunately for Rafe, he'd seen Yardly but Yardly hadn't seen him. Just what had brought him to California was anybody's guess, and Rafe didn't much care. As far as he was concerned, one less marshal was one less marshal, and it was all for the good.

He'd winged the rider in the lead, as well, although he figured he couldn't be blamed for missing—by then Marshal Yardly had hit the dirt from atop his horse, and the other two were already starting to scatter.

Oh, well.

He'd ridden off, leaving the other two to fire useless bullets at a man who wasn't there anymore. He smiled to himself.

So, Mexico was the place to be for right now. Well, either that or Canada, but who the hell in their right mind would want to run north, up into the ice and snow? It was just starting to warm up down here, for cripes sake!

Rafe had never been north, and so he was convinced that Canada held polar bears around every corner. And he was certain that all you had to do to find them was step a foot over the borderline.

He just might like to shoot himself one of those big, white brutes one day, but now wasn't the time for it. Right now, he only wanted to be certain his trail was free of marshals and bounty hunters and green kids lookin' to make a reputation.

The truth was, he was tired. He just wanted to rest for a while.

* * *

Slocum and his temporary partners finally rode down out of the foothills, and when they did, they could just see San Diego. It was still a trek, but Slocum was relieved.

Not as relieved as Forsythe, though. He let out a whoop when he first saw the place, and kicked his horse into a canter. Slocum and Alba had to gear up into a soft lope to keep even with him.

Upon their arrival in town, they went first to the marshal's office. Marshal Denver was the man's name, and he was the same officer who had been there on Slocum's last visit, two or three years ago.

"Slocum!" Denver exclaimed as the men slapped each other's backs. "By God! Never thought I'd see you again! How's it been going?"

"Catch you up in a second, Will," Slocum said. "First, I wanna introduce my partners. This here is Forsythe, and over there is Juan . . . Vega."

The marshal shook hands with both men, saying, "Any friend of Slocum's is a friend of mine."

Alba looked visibly relieved. He had asked Slocum not to mention his real name, and Slocum had nearly let it slip. But he covered it quickly, and the marshal was no wiser.

"We've got crimes to report," said Slocum. "Juan?"

Alba took a step forward. He adopted the stance of a peon and rolled his hat brim in his hands. "I wish to testify against Rafe Masterson, sir. He killed one of my friends on the other side of the foothills four days ago. His name was Julio Fernandez, and he leaves behind a wife and three children. Julio was killed up in the foothills by this Masterson."

"Well, I'll be damned," said the marshal. "Did you see him clear?"

"*Sí, señor.* I saw him very fine. He is a medium tall man, with brown hair and a mustache. And a long scar." Alba drew his finger up the side of his face. "He wounded another friend of mine, as well, but he has gone back to Arizona."

"You do anything to bring this on?" Marshal Denver asked.

"No. We were just riding along when he started shooting from above at us. We did nothing to provoke him, señor. *Nada.*"

The marshal sat behind his desk and pulled out some forms. He shoved two across the desk to Alba. "Can you fill those out for me, Señor Varga? Sorry. Señor Vega. If you don't write English, I can go get my deputy. He's Mexican, too, but he was raised in California," he added, as if this would explain everything. But he saw that Juan was already filling out the forms.

He turned toward Slocum and said, "You got any murders to report?" as if he were asking if Slocum had eaten any lunch yet.

"Nope," he said. He had no murders to report—and he hadn't had lunch, either, he thought.

"Well, you're the only one," the marshal said. "I had two young U.S. deputy marshals in here a few days back to report Masterson for killing their buddy. Attack from far off, as usual. Oh, and their buddy was with the marshals' office, too. Man named Yardly. You know him?"

When Slocum shook his head, the marshal went on, "They barely caught a glimpse of him, but it was Masterson. And I also hear he plugged a feller in a Los Angeles bar fight a few days before that. Reward's mountin' up faster than the Sacramento boys can keep up with."

"How much?" Forsythe said. He'd been silent up till now.

"Believe it's up to fifteen," said Marshal Denver, stretching his arms. "Be more after I turn this new information in."

Forsythe nodded.

Slocum said, "If you can take Arizona crimes, he killed my horse—at a dead run—tryin' to kill me."

Marshal Denver shook his head. "Sorry, Slocum. You gotta report that in Arizona. You out after him?"

Slocum nodded. "I am now."

"Good luck to you, then." He took the completed papers from Juan and thanked him, then rose.

His hand on the filing cabinet, he added, "I'd a lot rather see you fellers take him down—and take California for the cash reward—than have some deputies go out after him and get themselves killed in the process."

"Thanks, Will," said Slocum. "We'll do our best."

"Yes," said Alba, bowing and scraping.

"Thank you, sir," Forsythe said, and touched his hat brim. "It has been most . . . enlightening."

"You boys take care'a yourselves, hear?" the marshal said as they left.

Slocum said, "Back atcha!" as the door closed between them.

"Nice feller," commented Forsythe.

Juan Alba adjusted his sombrero. "You almost loused it up, Slocum."

"I know. Sorry."

Forsythe, seemingly oblivious, said, "Let's find us a whiskey!"

* * *

A few moments later, they went into Los Lobos Loco—
the first bar they came to. The place was mostly empty,
and Slocum began working the sparse crowd, asking
about Masterson.

He hit paydirt when the bartender said, "Yes. He was
in here yesterday afternoon. Well, early evening. And he
still owes me for cerveza!"

"When? He been here long? He still in town?" The
questions came fast and from every direction, confusing
the poor bartender.

"Hold it!" shouted Slocum, raising his hand. "Let me
ask the questions." He turned to the barkeep. "Yesterday
afternoon, you say. You remember about what time?"

The bartender shook his head. "Not the time, exactly,
señor, but it was nigh on to dusk. Is that good enough for
you?"

Slocum nodded. "Thanks, yes. Had he been in San
Diego awhile?"

The bartender shrugged. "A couple days. It might
have been more, but those were the days he came in
here."

"And is he still in town?"

"I do not know," said the bartender with a shrug. "He
hasn't been here today. Usually, he is here by now. If he
comes at all."

Slocum nodded, then dug into his pocket and gave
the man a couple of dollars for his trouble. "Any idea
where he was stayin'?"

"Could be Gomez's, up the street. Or Casa del Constanza, over a block. Depends on how much he likes the
ladies, also on how he is fixed for the *dinero*."

"Constanza's," said Alba, without thinking.

But Slocum figured he was most probably right. If Rafe Masterson could have stayed at a whorehouse, he surely would have.

He thanked the barkeep once more, then tossed back his whiskey. He said, "Let's go."

He dug into his pocket again and paid for the drinks, his companions' as well. And then, pulling Forsythe away from the last dregs of his beer and holding Alba back, he left the bar.

11

Masterson had, indeed, been staying at the cathouse for the past three days. They spoke to Constanza herself—a beautiful woman whom Slocum remembered from three years ago, and who remembered him.

After the requisite hugging and kissing and shaking of hands all around, Constanza told them that Masterson had been there. "Never again," she said, shaking her head. "He is the bad business. My poor Rhianna will not work again for weeks."

Forsythe shot to his feet. "Did he beat her?"

Slocum pulled him back down. "Nothin' you can do about it now. Just be still. When did he leave, Constanza? And which way did he go?"

"He left at about ten o'clock this morning, the pig. And he rode out to the south. Do you follow him to kill him?"

Slocum nodded yes.

"*Bueno.* I wish I could go with you and see him die."

Slocum stood up. "I'll be back and tell you all about it, Connie."

She said, "I hope so, Slocum. It is my prayer. But take care. This one, he is bad. He has killed before, and very many times, I think."

Slocum nodded. "We know, Constanza. We know, and we're prepared." He signaled to the other men, who also stood up. "Don't worry. We'll get him."

He heard Forsythe mutter, "All fifteen thousand dollars' worth," and glared at him.

"Sorry," Forsythe said, although he didn't look sorry at all.

In fact, he looked like he wanted nothing more than to dance a jig. *Well*, Slocum thought, *fat chance of that happening.*

He gave Forsythe a lot of credit for tracking Masterson this far—after all, his brother had been killed in Louisiana, for cripes sake—but some of his shit, Slocum just couldn't and wouldn't put up with.

Outside the front door, Forsythe looked like he was going to start in—one foot hitched up, his elbows crooked, and he readied himself to take a little hop to the side—when Slocum shouted, "Hold it!"

Forsythe froze. "What?"

"Just . . . whatever you were gonna do, don't do it, all right?"

Forsythe put his foot back down and straightened his arms. He looked disappointed. And angry.

"I don't see why we gotta follow your rules all the time. I thought this was an even split. Even all the way around!"

Alba stepped in, and just in time—Slocum was about

to slug Forsythe. "I beg you, Señor Forsythe, make yourself calm. Listen to Slocum. He knows what he is doing."

"I been listenin' to him for what seems like forever, and all I got so far is shot at, humiliated, and a sacka baked goods."

Slocum turned his face to hide the smirk he felt growing there. *Bitch, bitch, bitch . . .* he thought.

"Where do we go next?" Alba asked him. "Do we follow Masterson's trail?"

"Gotta stop and get grain first," Slocum announced. "Then we ride for the south. He's only been gone for about four hours. I say we take him before morning."

"May God be on our side," Alba said.

Forsythe said nothing.

Slocum was beginning to wonder if it was worth the trouble of hauling him around.

As they made their way south along the edge of the foothills, loping slowly so that Forsythe's horse could keep up, Slocum kept an eye peeled for any signs of their quarry's passing.

They were numerous. A snapped creosote branch here, a trampled aloe there. Masterson seemed unworried about being followed. He'd made no attempt to hide his tracks, to disguise his passing. Not that this country they were traveling over held many tracks. On the contrary. Most of it was baked to a hard crust that took no print, so that the only traces of Masterson were the freshly broken pieces of vegetation he left in his wake.

But it was enough. Enough to convince Slocum not only that they were on the right trail, but that they were gaining on him.

They might have Masterson before nightfall.

They'd better. Slocum was aching to get back to San Diego and Señorita Constanza. Señorita Constanza, especially. Come to think of it, *any* señorita. Any female of any kind—well, there *were* age limits: he drew the line somewhere.

If they didn't find Rafe Masterson pretty soon, he thought, he was going to have to find himself a goat. And then he laughed at the idea.

He wasn't *that* desperate yet!

Alba had fanned out to the right, and suddenly, he held his hand up, motioning to Slocum and Forsythe. They rode up next to him and reined in their horses.

Slocum saw it right away. The sparse grass was trampled where Masterson had stopped and reined this way and that, as if unable to make a decision. But then his trail took off again, this time to the southeast. Masterson was heading for Mexico, all right. He just wanted to make sure he didn't end up in Baja California.

Smart.

Forsythe's mount was blowing like crazy, lathered, and he looked near dead. Slocum and Alba exchanged glances, and Slocum said, "We'll walk for a spell, then we'll stop and have supper before we ride again. Okay?"

Alba, still looking at Forsythe's horse, said, "You are wise, Slocum."

And Forsythe, who immediately knew the reason for the slowdown was on his head, said, "Sorry, fellas. I shoulda traded him off when we were in San Diego."

"Don't worry about it," said Slocum. "He's yours, and you're used to him. A man just doesn't trade off a horse he likes."

Forsythe looked a little bit relieved, but not much. They rode on, at a walk.

After Forsythe's horse quit breathing so heavy, it was Alba who called a halt. He picked a place where a thin stream cut through the desert and where there were willow trees in between the cottonwoods along its bank. Spring flowers in yellow and purple dotted the greenery hugging the banks, too.

Slocum said it was the prettiest place he'd seen in a long time.

While he saw to the horses, Alba cut thick slices of ham and sandwiched them between pieces of bread, one sandwich per man.

"Will this be enough to hold you, Slocum?" he asked, after the big man had finished with the horses. He held out a sandwich so thick that Slocum wondered if he could fit it in his mouth for a bite.

"It'll do," he said, grinning. He took the sandwich in both hands, stretched open his jaws, and took a bite. "Good!" he said around the mouthful he was already chewing.

Forsythe handed him a cup of coffee. "To wash it down," he said.

Slocum grunted his thanks while he figured their situation. They'd have to start up into the hills pretty soon, and hills and canyons seemed to be Masterson's favorite places to shoot from. It didn't look good for them.

He scanned the horizon. Another hour or two, and they'd be up in the hills. He hoped that the hills were brief, with flatland on the other side. He hadn't been this way before.

Around it, yes. But not through it.

They finished eating at about four o'clock and were off again. But not for long. Alba spotted something off in the scrub and they all rode over to take a look.

A body had been hastily buried between the bushes, buried and cairned with rocks. They didn't dig it up. Slocum already had a pretty good idea who it was.

"Thus ends another U.S. marshal," he said, and wrapped string around the join of two pieces of wood to make a crude cross, which he planted at one end of the grave. He hoped it was the head.

"How do you know that?" Forsythe insisted.

"Because the marshal in San Diego said there were two of 'em, and they were trailin' Masterson. One'a the marshals dies, the other buries him. Masterson wouldn't have taken the time."

Alba said a simple prayer and crossed himself. Forsythe followed suit.

"Yeah, yeah," said Slocum. "Let's get movin'."

They followed the trail, which followed the stream. It was now three horses. Two being ridden and one being led, judging by the depth of the tracks. Rafe, followed by the marshal, who was leading the dead marshal's horse, Slocum reasoned. The ground was softer here, and he could see the tracks plainly, for the most part.

They rode gradually uphill, following not only the tracks, but the bed of the stream. It seemed to grow a little wider as they followed it inland, Slocum thought. The desert was like a sponge. He wondered if any of the water made its way across the state to the sea, or at least met another river that would carry it the rest of the way.

It didn't matter, not any of it, but at least it kept his mind occupied.

They hadn't moved out of a walk since they'd started out again after dinner, and Slocum decided they needed to put on some speed. For a while, anyway.

He said, "Let's move it up, boys, or he'll be in Bolivia before we make the Mexican border." He pushed his horse, and Fleet sprang into a soft gallop. Even then, he had to rein him in a little to keep pace with Alba. Forsythe was, as usual, far behind, riding his mount's up-down, up-down gait.

He wondered how a horse like Fleet had fallen into the hands of a drummer from Missouri. Had the drummer recognized his speed, or had he just ridden him from town to town, selling notions or whatnot? There was no way to tell.

The wind burnt his face and nearly took his hat before he realized he was going too fast. A glance over his shoulder told him that he had outdistanced the others, who couldn't even be seen on account of the hill's having crested. They were behind the hump, but he didn't know how far. He slowed up Fleet, who seemed to want to run some more, to run all out. But Slocum was having none of it. Rafe Masterson could be anywhere up here.

Slocum had gotten his wish. The land, after that slow rise and brief crest, had leveled out into a vast plain covered—well, as covered as a desert could be—in yucca, cholla, sage, and scattered boulders. Still plenty of places for a snake like Masterson to hide out and ply his trade. Especially since his trade seemed to be killing people.

Hell, thought Slocum with a snort. *Maybe it's his hobby. He's good at it, anyhow. And he seems to enjoy it, damn his eyes . . .*

He was still waiting for Alba and Forsythe to crest the rise behind him when the shot rang out. He only had time to note the graze on the crest of Fleet's neck before he grabbed his rifle, leapt from the saddle, and forced the horse down on its side.

"Sorry, Fleet," he muttered through gritted teeth. "You gotta be my shield for right now . . ."

Damn him to hell for tryin' to kill a second horse a'mine! he mentally raged.

He cocked his rifle, aimed it in the general direction from which the shot had come, and squeezed the trigger.

His shot was answered, almost immediately, and he took better aim for his second.

Then he heard a couple of slugs sing out not from the far rocks across the way, but from behind him and to the side. From the crest of the rise.

Rafe Masterson hunkered down behind a stand of jumping cholla, taking care not to get too close lest he end this shoot-out looking like a lady's pincushion. Another shot rang out from the first rider, cutting two connecting pads off the side of a prickly pear to his right.

He should have just kept on riding, he thought. Just dug his spurs into his mount and kept on going. He couldn't be certain it was Slocum, but the thought kept running through his brain. What if it was? What if he had managed to follow his trail all the way from Arizona to this little chunk of flatland in southern California? The shitheel! He'd be damned if somebody could do that to him!

He'd already knocked off two marshals today. One back at the stream, and the other lay sprawled not twenty feet from his current hiding place. That was the fate that awaited anybody who tried to track him, he thought.

He shouldn't have ridden back to make sure the marshal was dead. He should have just kept going.

He fired again, although he was firing blind now. Whoever was out there had laid his horse down—either that or Rafe had hit him—and was hiding behind the cactus. Somewhere.

He fired twice toward the place he thought the fellow was, then waited.

"I'll get you, you ring-tailed son of a bitch," he muttered, with a cruel glint in his eye. "I'll get you, if it takes me all day."

12

Two slugs sang past Slocum, long before the sound came, but he immediately fired back in kind. Behind him, Alba and Forsythe aimed and fired, also. He thought he saw something move, thought he saw a glimpse of something.

And then a horse burst up from the ground—a horse carrying a wounded man, a man whose right arm dangled uselessly at his side, flopping to the beat of the horse's gait.

Slocum mounted Fleet while the horse was still getting up, and took out after the rider. At a gallop, he stuck his rifle back in the saddle's boot and then, with windburnt fingers, pulled his Colt from its holster. He aimed at the figure on the horse, which was rapidly getting nearer.

He fired.

The rider, whose head had been turned to the side,

slumped forward and slid to the side, hitting the ground with a thump. After a few more strides, the horse stopped, too, blowing hard and sheeted with foam.

Slocum, keeping an eye on the downed man, rode to within ten feet of him before he swung down off Fleet. He kicked at the body with his toe. "C'mon Masterson, get up," he said.

No reply.

Just then, Alba rode up and slipped down from his horse. He joined Slocum. "He is dead?" he asked, hands propped on his hips.

"Looks that way," Slocum replied, this time using his boot to turn the body on its back. Rafe Masterson stared up into the sky, dead as a swamp log, and Slocum let out a sigh of relief. It was only then that he remembered the other marshal.

"Let's take him back to where he was shootin' from," he said, hauling Rafe up by his armpits and dragging him toward his horse. Alba was down off his horse and lent a hand, and they were just strapping Masterson to his saddle when Forsythe came up.

"Is he dead?" he asked, staring at the body.

"Far as we can tell," replied Slocum. He snugged up the rope around Rafe's knees, then secured it to the saddle's girth ring.

"Maybe not so dead as we thought," said Juan from the opposite side of the horse. Slocum felt the body twitch.

"Well, just rope him down good and take his weapons off him. I'll be damned if I'm chasin' him all over California again."

Alba nodded. "Is done."

Forsythe, who had yet to dismount, whined, "Why can't we just shoot him and get it over with?"

Slocum looked at him oddly. "Why waste the lead? State of California's already got the rope set aside, with his name on it. How come you're so bloodthirsty all of a sudden?"

Forsythe glowered. "He killed my brother. I told you."

"He killed a lot of people's brothers," Slocum said, then handed Masterson's reins up to the man from Louisiana. "Here. You lead him, Forsythe." Slocum jabbed his finger back toward Masterson's starting point.

Grudgingly, Forsythe took charge of the body while Slocum and Alba remounted. Slocum led them back toward the west, back to Masterson's shooting spot.

He slapped his horse on the neck and said, "Good boy, Fleet, good boy . . ."

The Appy, still raring to go, had barely broken a sweat.

Once they found Rafe's position, they also found the other marshal and his horse. The young marshal was dead. His horse was tethered behind a tall stand of prickly pear. Apparently, the boy had stopped to have some coffee, but Rafe had been waiting somewhere for him. Slocum scouted the countryside with his eyes. Rafe could have been anywhere, waiting.

The marshal hadn't had a chance, Slocum thought as he looked down at the boy's body. He'd been shot through the neck. He hadn't even pulled his gun.

Why hadn't he just turned back once his buddy had been killed? They both should have turned around and gone home once Rafe had killed the first marshal, up north. Slocum shook his head. What a waste of life.

But then, Rafe himself had been a waste of life from the moment he first drew breath. Slocum had half a mind to take Forsythe's advice and just make sure Rafe was dead.

When Slocum had asked the marshal in San Diego if Rafe Masterson was wanted dead or alive, he'd answered, "If I'd writ the posters, they woulda said 'Dead as a doornail,' period."

Slocum was inclined to agree with him.

"Pick up all the stuff from around the fire, Forsythe," he said, pointing to the fire that had barely started before burning out. "Put it in the marshal's pack."

He turned toward Alba. "And check the saddlebags for food and grain. It's almost dark now and we'll be needin' to stop for the night, but we can be back in San Diego by midday tomorrow even if we camp right here. Meantime," he added as he began gathering up the horses' reins, "we got a passel of sweaty horses that need to be walked out."

"Ah, thank you, my friend!" Alba said as Slocum walked off with the horses.

Forsythe, who'd barely got his foot clear of the leather before Slocum led his horse off, scowled. "Don't know why he's always takin' so much time with the horses," he muttered.

Alba heard him. He said, "Because the horses need the time, señor. Out here, a thing must have what is due to it, or it cannot benefit a man."

Forsythe cocked his head. "Y'know, even when you're talkin' English, I don't understand a word you're sayin' half the time."

Alba shrugged and went back to the saddlebags. He'd had good hunting so far, finding both grain and water.

But the real prizes were most of a roasted hen and a bag full of ripe purple grapes. He sat back and helped himself to the grapes. "These are the kind my brother makes into wine," he told Forsythe. He held out the sack. "Here. Try some."

Forsythe waved him off and dropped a few more odds and ends into the pile he was making for the marshal's saddlebags. He allowed himself another peek at the marshal, and shook his head. He was just a boy, really, just a boy of seventeen or eighteen with a tin badge on his chest. He was barely shaving, and he'd been shot through the neck. Probably died immediately.

Still, it was a shame. You only expected to see this kind of shenanigan during wartime, when the worst in men was the best you could hope for. Heaving a sigh, he began to search the ground again.

By the time Slocum finished walking the horses out and came back to camp, it was dusk and Juan had already started a fire and put the coffeepot on. Slocum didn't go up close right away. Masterson's gelding had walked too near a jumping cholla somewhere along the line, and after Slocum tied the horses, pulled their tack off, and made certain the area was free from those overactive cacti, he fed them and spent some time on Masterson's horse's legs with a pair of pliers. It looked like the gelding hadn't just gone too near; it looked like he'd trampled a whole mess of the cactus.

He checked Masterson, too. He was still alive, and still where he'd been left near the tethering spot for the horses.

He hadn't regained consciousness, and his breathing

was shallow. Slocum bent down to feel his face; it was ice-cold and clammy with sweat. He wouldn't last the night, Slocum thought. He'd be lucky to last the hour.

When Slocum finally came to the fire and sat down, he said, "I don't know why God invented jumping cholla. Far as I can tell, it's nothin' but a damn nuisance."

Juan nodded, settling a skillet filled with sliced ham on the fire next to another covered one. Forsythe asked, "What the devil's jumping cholla?"

Juan and Slocum looked at each other. Juan shrugged and said, "You can tell him."

"Gee, thanks," grumbled Slocum. But he went on, "It's a kind of cactus. I'd show you one, but it's too dark now. When any kind of critter—you included—passes too close, they shoot out spines."

Forsythe looked at him like he had lost his mind.

Alba spoke up. "It is true, Forsythe. They are sensitive to the heat from the bodies of animals and humans. I have never known any man to be killed by the plant, but I have known some that wished to never see one again." From the bag, he pulled out most of a cold chicken and began pulling it into pieces.

"I see," said Forsythe.

"No, you don't," said Slocum. "But you will." He pointed down at the back of Forsythe's calf. His pant leg was thick with spines. "Looks like you passed too close, too."

Forsythe, looking down, was horrified. "What do I do?! What do I do?!"

Slocum shook his head. "One, stop yellin'. Two, pull those suckers out. And three, toss 'em in the fire. Ain't gonna be nothin' much hotter than that around tonight."

Forsythe began to frantically pluck cholla spines from the denim of his leggings and to toss them in the fire.

Alba announced, "Coffee is ready."

Slocum helped himself to a cup, taking care not to put his hand in the path of Forsythe's fire-bound cactus spines. He escaped puncture for the most part, but after he replaced the coffeepot, he pulled a couple of spines out of the back of his hand.

"Chicken or ham?" asked Alba.

"Both," he replied.

A moment later, Alba handed him a plate with a chicken leg and thigh, a ham sandwich, and a serving of beans. "For desert, there is cake," he added.

"What kind?" Slocum asked around a mouthful of chicken.

Alba shrugged. "Brown," he said.

Chocolate, then. He wondered how in the world Forsythe could have been carrying a whole chocolate cake and not have mentioned it. But then, he was wondering a lot about Forsythe, lately.

The object of his musings sighed heavily. "I think I got 'em all," he said. "Lucky for me, they didn't go all the way through to the skin. Can I have some supper, please? Ham, if there's enough."

Slocum commented, "Quick recovery," while Alba fixed Forsythe's plate and handed it to him.

Forsythe took it, set it aside, and poured himself a cup of coffee. "You know, Alba, you're a pretty good cook." He sipped his coffee, then took a bite out of his ham sandwich.

Alba cocked his head. "You are just noticing this, señor?"

"Hell, he just didn't taste anythin' until now," Slocum muttered.

Alba laughed and shook his head. "The reward money. The knowledge of money coming, it makes everything better? Even the food?"

Forsythe gave out a lopsided grin. "I reckon so. Reckon so."

13

Morning came.

Slocum and Alba were up early. Forsythe came around shortly thereafter, and the first thing he did was to check Rafe Masterson for signs of life.

Slocum glanced over to see him kicking the body, kicking it viciously.

"Hey, Forsythe! Give it a rest!" he shouted.

"Not. Quite. Yet," Forsythe answered, punctuating each word with a kick to Masterson's ribs.

Slocum said, "He's dead already! Why you need to keep on hammerin' it home?"

Forsythe sent one last kick to the body's ribs, then ceased. "All right," he said. "I think I'm done now." He stared down at Masterson. "I think."

Slocum shook his head. Forsythe reminded him of a kid who had just killed a rattlesnake and kept on hitting it long after it was dead, "just in case."

"He only wishes to make sure," said Alba, grinning. "I will admit I woke in the middle of the night, dreaming bad dreams of Masterson. I even went to the body, to see if he still lived." Alba snorted through his nose. "He did not."

Slocum nodded. "Figured he'd croak last night when I brought the horses in." He changed the subject. "Breakfast about ready?"

"*Sí*. The coffee, she is ready now. You want a cup?" He reached for a cup, but Slocum held up a hand.

"I'll wait for everybody else," he said, watching Forsythe finally abandon the body and come toward them. Wanting to kill Masterson was a normal reaction for Forsythe—after all, he was avenging his own brother's death.

But killing him *after* he was dead? It left a bad taste in Slocum's mouth.

He decided that it was hitting Alba wrong, too. When Forsythe joined them and sat down at the fire, Alba moved away from him, almost imperceptibly.

Almost.

But it was there, and Slocum saw.

After breakfast, they saddled the horses, strapped Masterson's corpse across his saddle, roped the deputy across his, put most of the packs across the spare horse to lessen the load on their saddle horses, and set out to the west again.

They made San Diego late that afternoon and dropped the bodies with Marshal Denver. To say he was overjoyed was putting it mildly, but he wasn't so happy with the news of the deputies' deaths. Slocum took the body they had down to the undertaker's and drew the marshal a map to the other's grave. By five o'clock they had filled out the paperwork and the marshal gave them each a voucher.

Slocum was surprised. The reward had gone up to $21,000 when Marshal Dodge put the call in to Sacramento, and the reward paid to each of them was a third of the total: $7,000. It was too late to put it in the bank that day, so Slocum pinned his inside his shirt, then announced his intention of going to the barbershop for a shave and a bath.

The other two went along.

After a long, hot soak and a close, neat shave, they were all feeling fine as frog's hair, and retired to the nearest saloon.

Delgado's was its name, and it was a small Mexican cantina with a longish bar and four tables, three of which were vacant.

"*Tres cerveza*," said Slocum as he pulled out a chair at the first vacant table. "And keep 'em comin'."

The trio sat down. The beers arrived in short order and were swallowed down just as quickly. The bartender brought more. "You fellows looking for a little female company?" he asked hopefully as he set their beers down.

"Bet your ass, amigo," crowed Alba, pumped on the voucher in his pocket.

"Ditto," Slocum said.

Forsythe sighed, then asked, "Are they clean? I mean, disease-free?"

The bartender smiled. "The healthiest whores in the state."

Slocum muttered, "Yeah, sure," then in a louder voice, said, "Bring 'em on, amigo."

The bartender needed no further prodding. He turned

away, raised his arm, and motioned with it. Three girls, practically by magic, appeared at their table.

Apparently, the patrons in this joint had nothing to do with their choices from the menu of females. Slocum didn't give it much thought, though. A cute, little, brown-eyed señorita cozied up to him and slid herself onto his lap.

"Well, hello," he said, slipping his arm around her. "What's your name?"

"Maria," she said softly. "What is yours?"

As he told her, his friends' laps were being similarly filled. Well, similarly in sex, anyway. Forsythe made room for a green-eyed redhead, and Slocum grinned. Forsythe looked like a deer caught in the lamp of an oncoming train. On the other hand, Juan Alba—ever the handsome ladies' man—had pulled a very sophisticated Mexican beauty. And he looked like he had expected nothing less.

Well, good for him. Good for them all, as a matter of fact. Slocum turned his full attention to little Maria, the girl on his lap. She was a cutie, all right. Full-breasted and tiny-waisted, she was ripe for the plucking—seemed eager for it, too. Which, of course, was Slocum's favorite part.

After several beers and plenty of small talk, Slocum was ready. Alba and his girl had already left the table, but Forsythe and his redhead remained. And Forsythe still looked overwhelmed.

Well, to each his own, Slocum thought. And he was about to get his.

Maria led him upstairs, over the cantina, to her room. It turned out to be pretty nice—although that might have been just compared to Slocum's last few days in the desert. There was a wide, fresh bed, a chiffarobe, two chairs, and a table, and candles were burning on the bed's side tables.

Maria led him in with a wide grin on her face. "You like?" she asked.

"I like," he said, closing the door behind them. "I like it all."

He smiled, then kissed her long and deep. During the kiss, he slipped his hands up and down her narrow back. Her flesh was soft in the small of her back, and the swell of her hips was gentle but oh, so promising.

With practiced hands, he found the bow that cinched her waistband, untied it, and let her skirt fall to the floor. Then her petticoat, then her drawers. He gently pulled her blouse over her head, leaving her nude in his arms, while he realized just how much of a hurry he was in.

His actions sped up. He kicked off one boot, then the other, while his fingers feverishly pushed hers away and went to work at his belt buckle, then the buttons of his bulging trousers. It seemed only seconds before he had her on the table, with her knees hooked over his shoulders and him sinking into her.

She gasped as he pushed all the way inside; gasped and reached up for him. He was too busy pleasuring himself to notice. He plowed into her over and over, his hands knowing nothing but the hold they had on her hips, to steady her, to bring her closer; that, and the film of sweat that was forming on her skin, the sweat of passion.

She was pulling at him with her internal muscles now, as he grew even larger inside her. He felt himself on the brink, growing closer with each stroke, until he couldn't hold it back anymore—he tightened his grip on her hips, then pulled her toward him while he pushed into her for all he was worth. He exploded into her, and kept on for three more strokes before he collapsed on her chest.

His head pillowed on her slick-with-sweat bosom, he felt better than he had in days. Apparently she wasn't feeling too bad herself. He heard her whisper, "Slocum, you are *el tigre!*" before she sighed a sigh of contentment.

Still, he wasn't done. Not by a long shot. Slowly, he pulled out of her, then took off his shirt and his gunbelt before he scooped her up in his arms. She made a fluttery little sound as he hoisted her against his chest and kissed her lips again.

He laid her down on the bed, then joined her on it, and she wrapped her arms around him. "If you would like to go again," she whispered, "is only a dollar more. And I will wait until you are ready."

"Already ready," he said and grinned, guiding her fingers down to grasp him.

"You are!" she gasped. "How you do that?"

"Years of practice, honey," he said with a broad smile. "Years of practice."

He took her again, this time making certain that she came—twice—before he finished. After she caught her breath, she said, "Slocum, never . . . never has anyone . . . I have never felt that before! You make my blood into fire!"

He still felt full of vinegar. He whispered, "Like to feel that way again, Maria?"

"Yes!" she cried, eagerly. "Yes, I would like it very much!"

* * *

They didn't fall asleep until it was nearly light, and Slocum then slept till around ten. He got up carefully, so as not to disturb Maria.

While he dressed, he wondered why on earth she'd never had an orgasm before. She'd surely been working this bar for a while. Maybe nobody had ever tried to give her one.

Well, he figured he'd done his bit. She'd come six times altogether. At least, that he'd counted. She was making up for lost time. And so, in a way, was he.

He left the room quietly, latching the door behind him. First he had to go to the bank, and then he'd walk down to the stable to check the horses. Best of all, he wouldn't have to shoot anybody today!

He checked his shirt on the way downstairs to make sure he still had his voucher, which he did, then he walked up the street to the bank. It was small but adequate. He walked up to the cashier and said, "I want a hundred in cash, and the rest wired to my account in Tombstone." He whipped out his passbook.

The cashier was still staring at the voucher. "Y-you're one of the men who brought in Rafe Masterson?" he asked, slack-jawed.

"I am," Slocum answered. "You got a problem with that?"

"No! No sir! I-I was just wonderin', that's all."

"You'll likely have two more boys in here today with the same voucher. I didn't do it alone." He had, of course, but he'd made a deal. And, to his credit, he'd never once thought how nice it would be to have $21,000 all to himself.

Hell, he'd probably have just ended up giving most of it away to the first person he met with a good sob story. He wasn't much of a hand with hanging onto cash. That's why he'd started several savings accounts at different banks around the West. That way, if he ran low on money, he always had a cache nearby. Well, a few states or territories over, anyway.

And it had given him a new occupation: bounty hunter. Twice now, he'd hunted down the vermin that had robbed a bank his money was in, and collected the bounty. Once, he'd even recovered the bank's money.

The clerk had him sign a couple bank slips—one for the transfer and one for the cash received—and sent him on his way. He was just folding the hundred away when he practically ran into Alba, who was heading into the bank.

"Amigo!" Alba said. *"Que pasa?"*

"Just setting my money right," Slocum replied.

"I, too," said Juan. "I am having it sent to Dos Burros, in Mexico. I only hope that no one robs the stage while it is in transit."

Slocum laughed. If anyone was gonna rob that stage, it'd probably be Alba himself. He said, "Y'know, Juan, might be safer to just take the cash yourself. Can't think of anybody who'd be crazy enough to try to rob you!"

Alba thought this over, then nodded. "I think you are right, Slocum. I will take the cash."

"Might have to wait a couple'a days. They gotta get it from Sacramento to here first."

Alba shrugged, then smiled. "I can wait. I have found a most excellent whore in San Diego."

Slocum slapped him on the shoulder. "That's my man!"

"And you? You look like you have spent a pleasant night."

"That I did, Juan, that I did. Most satisfying."

The two men laughed.

Slocum said, "Well, I'd best get down to the stables and take a look at the horses. Just in case. Y'know."

Alba nodded. "Indeed I do. But keep in mind, Slocum, that Rafe Masterson is dead. You should know that. You have killed him yourself."

Slocum waved a hand. "Now, Juan. We weren't gonna discuss that."

"I know. But it is so obviously the case. I should not feel right, taking a full cut, but then," he added with a grin, "I am a thief. It is enough like stealing to make me happy."

Slocum grinned. "Aw, go turn in your voucher and quit your bitchin'."

Laughing, Alba ducked into the bank.

14

Embarrassed but sated, Forsythe quietly pulled on his clothes again. The redhead had been fine, he supposed. For a girl. But he was secretly anxious to get back to New Orleans, where he knew people who knew—and accepted—his private peccadilloes.

Last night's redhead had not been his first. No, she had been his second. The first was Lydia Garnier—little Lydia, he thought fondly—a daughter of a neighboring plantation owner. He'd been sixteen and she'd been fourteen, and she'd also been the prettiest girl he'd ever seen.

But his experience with her had been . . . disheartening. And he'd been called to war soon after. It was during the years he was fighting that he had discovered who and what he really was. It had been frightening at first. He'd never heard of such a thing! But it had felt right and natural for him from the beginning.

Back home, after the war and many years had passed, he had thought of himself as a knight, riding off into battle to avenge his brother. But actually, it hadn't been his brother who was killed by Masterson.

It had been Pierre, his lover. Pierre, a handsome, blond Frenchman and a first-generation export to America, who had had the bad sense to get himself into a poker game with Masterson. The rest was history.

Forsythe was no knight. He knew that now. He was a sniveling coward, a kicker of dead men, and a betrayer of friends.

He finished dressing, his head hanging like a dog's. He felt like a dog, a cowardly cur who had volunteered for more than he could handle and lived to regret it.

The voucher was in his pocket, though. It would not be enough. He had wanted to build Pierre a fine above-ground mausoleum, one where his body would be safe from Louisiana's insidious groundwater forever. He had wanted to have statues carved and a fine funeral with musicians playing and mourners mourning.

He could have that now, but then there would be nothing left for him, nothing to help him start a new life. Pierre would not have wished that for him. He did not want that himself.

He let himself out of the room, thinking all the time about what squalor these Westerners lived in. The red-head had actually been proud of the room in which he'd spent the night with her. He supposed that New Orleans had its share of rooms similar to this one, but that they were all deep in the Quarter, where nice people never saw them.

He still thought of himself as a nice person, and he was. Hadn't he helped Sister Florence raise money to build that new school? Hadn't he nursed that little Cajun girl back to health when everybody—doctors included—had said she was hopeless? Hadn't he stayed home with his parents long after he should have left, tending his sick mother?

And then God rewarded him by killing Pierre.

It was almost too much for him to handle, and he had to stop midway down the stairs to collect himself.

"Stop it!" he said to himself, under his breath. "Get a grip, Forsythe!"

At last, he focused himself and made his feet walk down the stairs. He would do what he had to do. He would go to the bank and transfer the money to his account in New Orleans. He would bid Slocum and Alba good-bye, and he would ride back to Louisiana, and he would *not* almost get himself lynched in El Paso again.

He shivered a little at that memory. Never again would he let himself be caught up in that game!

He gained the bar and decided to order a beer before he went to the bank. Hell, he'd order a whole breakfast if they had such a thing. He sat down at the first table at the foot of the steps, and a bartender, holding a pad and a pencil, appeared at his side.

"Would you like the breakfast, sir?" he asked, pencil poised.

It was close to noon, so Forsythe figured the man had to know he'd been upstairs with one of the girls. He said, "Yes, I would. What do you have?"

The horses were in a fine fettle when Slocum checked them. They'd been grained and groomed, and were all dozing peacefully in their box stalls. Slocum found the hostler and paid for another night's room and board for them. It wasn't that often that you found a city stable with as many box stalls available, and he figured the horses deserved nothing less for all the rough territory they'd been through these last few days.

He spent a little extra time with Fleet, talking to him quietly, stroking his dark neck and withers, telling him that he was glad he'd run across him, glad that he'd decided to make him his own.

The horse seemed happy with the arrangement, too, and buried his head in Slocum's broad chest.

"You're one'a those, are you?" Slocum said with a chuckle, and began to scratch the horse behind the ears. "Well, for any horse that's as fast as you, I reckon I can put up with a little head-rubbin' on my chest."

The horse began to close his eyes, and Slocum woke him back up again with a pat on the neck. "Easy there, Fleet. Do go tryin' to take advantage of me." He laughed and eased the horse's head away. "See you and your buddies after a bit."

He met Alba on his way out. "Reckon you're up to the same thing I was," he said. "I checked all the horses. They're doin' fine."

"Thank you, amigo," Alba said. "Still, I would like to take a peek for myself without giving offense?"

"None taken," replied Slocum with an understanding nod. If Alba had been down there first, Slocum would have been the one going in now.

He waited for Juan outside, leaning against the corral fence and staring out over the town. And before too long, here came Forsythe, headed right for him.

Slocum raised a hand as he neared. "Hey," he said.

Forsythe nodded.

"You been to the bank yet?"

Forsythe shook his head.

"You'd best go and take care of business. Alba's in there now, checking the horses."

Forsythe stopped. He said, "He is?"

Slocum nodded in the affirmative. "And I already been in and looked 'em over. They're all in good shape, and they been curried within an inch'a their lives."

Forsythe brightened. "Oh. Well, that's good news, isn't it?" He gave up on going to the barn and leaned against the fence, too, next to Slocum.

Slocum dug into his pocket for his fixings and began to roll himself a quirlie, saying, "Ain't you gonna go to the bank?"

"Telegraph office, and I've already been," Forsythe replied.

Incredulously, Slocum asked, "You wire that voucher all the way home to Louisiana?"

"Kinda," Forsythe said. "The cash'll be waiting for me when I hit New Orleans." He smiled a little, as if just the sound of the city's name cheered him. "And I'm takin' the train back. Know anybody who needs a nice Tennessee walker?"

"Not off the top'a my head," Slocum said, taking the first draw off his quirlie. He blew it out again and said, "Why don't you take him back with you? Seems like a nice horse to me. And he got you all the way out here. Halfway across a continent!"

Forsythe seemed to consider this, then said, "Y'know, you're right. I shouldn't just abandon him out here at the edge of the world, should I?"

"Now you're talkin'. And by the way, you never said. Does he have a name?"

"Certainly," Forsythe said with a nod. "It's Yancy."

"Yancy?"

"Yes, I know it's a man's name. But a little girl I know said he was as fancy as a cardsharp, and well, the name just stuck." Forsythe smiled.

"I'm inclined to agree with that little girl," said Slocum. "He is one fancy stepper."

"Here comes Alba," Forsythe said, pointing. "Shall we all go have a drink?"

"You got my attention," Slocum said, then hollered, "Hey Juan! You up for a beer?"

The trio walked to a new bar, which happened to be just down the street, and also happened to be next door to the undertaker's parlor. Slocum and Alba were each starting their second beers and Forsythe was still working on his first, when the batwing doors suddenly opened, and a man wearing a suit fell through the doors and onto the barroom floor.

Forsythe was the first one on his feet, and he went to the body in slap time. He announced, "He's alive!" and Slocum and Alba, along with several other bar patrons, crowded round.

"It's Sam Bristol!" said one of the onlookers.

"Who the hell is Sam Bristol?" asked Slocum, standing near the body's feet.

"Town undertaker," someone answered, and as Bristol's head was turned by those making ready to bring him around, Slocum recognized him.

"What the hell's goin' on around here?" Slocum muttered, genuinely puzzled.

"Get the doc, somebody," the barkeep ordered, and one

of the men shot out the door. "He's bleedin'," he added. "Somebody whacked him over the head but good."

Slocum saw the blood then, trickling down the back of Bristol's neck.

"He's still got a pulse," Forsythe reported. "Good and strong, too."

"He gonna be talkin' soon?" Alba asked. It would have been Slocum's next question.

Forsythe looked up. "Don't know how long it'll take him to come—"

The bartender dumped a full pitcher of water onto the undertaker's face, and Sam Bristol immediately came back to consciousness, sputtering incoherently.

"—around," Forsythe finished up, lamely.

As Bristol struggled to sit up and wipe the water from his vest and suit front, Slocum asked, "What the hell happened to you, man?"

"That damned Rafe Masterson!" Bristol barked. "That demon rose from the dead and tried to kill me!"

Most of the men present took a step back at Bristol's statement, but Slocum stepped forward and helped him to a chair. "Get him a beer," he said to the bartender.

"Make it a whiskey," said the sodden undertaker.

"Tell me what happened. From the beginning." Slocum wasn't a believer in spooks and haunts, and he knew there had to be a practical explanation.

From the corner of his eye, he watched Alba slip outside and head for Bristol's place of business. Good.

The bartender delivered a whiskey, as ordered, and after he drained it, Bristol began to talk.

15

It seemed that Bristol had waited until today to prepare Masterson for burial. This process, which was supposed to consist of sewing him into a shroud, was extended because he was famous. His clothes were removed—for resale—his hair was trimmed—for resale—and his slugs, rather, his slug, was taken out. Also with plans for resale.

The one that had broken his arm had passed clean through the bone and out the other side.

Bristol was going to make a killing on this burial. No pun intended, of course.

Slocum was surprised when he heard there was only one slug, but he held his peace.

Anyway, the doc happened to be at the undertaking parlor, so he did the honors. "Just one little slug," Bristol said, "in the back of the neck. It was wedged in the spinal column kinda funny. Don't believe I'd ever seen anythin' quite like it."

So the doc took the slug out carefully, so as not to scratch it, and Masterson began to bleed from the wound. Bleed? Even Slocum knew that dead men didn't bleed. But Masterson was bleeding nonetheless.

And then something happened that sent both the doc and the mortician jumping back a foot or two: Masterson spoke. A dead man talking, right there, in front of witnesses! It was shocking, the doctor swore. Also unheard of per the mortician.

Forsythe looked like he was about to jump right out of his boots. And Alba? Well, he looked kind of bored.

To make a long story short, the dead man got off the table, whacked them both upside the head, and that was the last either saw of him.

The doc had his theories on what had saved Masterson's life, but only Forsythe stayed around to listen. Slocum made for the stable to get the horses ready, and Alba ran up to the sheriff's office to tell Marshal Denver.

Slocum was right. Masterson's horse was gone, as was his tack. According to the stable hand, he had scooped out plenty of grain, too, and ridden off to the east without paying.

"You're goddamn lucky he didn't kill you," Slocum said gruffly as he saddled the second horse, that being Forsythe's. He'd already saddled Alba's.

Alba turned up just as he was starting on Fleet's tack. "I know I promised a few days' rest," Slocum said to the horse, "but I'm afraid I'm gonna have to break that promise." Fleet didn't look like he minded very much. In fact, he seemed eager to be off.

"Thank you for saddling my horse," Alba said.

"No problem," Slocum replied. He snugged up Fleet's cinch. "You seen Forsythe?"

"The same time you did. At the saloon."

"Damn it! Don't he realize we're workin' against the clock here?"

Alba tipped his head. "Maybe yes, maybe no."

Slocum twisted his head around. *"What?"*

"Maybe he no longer cares."

"Well, he has to care! He collected on Masterson, same as the rest of us. And now he has to go find him again, same as the rest of us. Shit! I shoulda just let him plug Masterson in the head when we thought he was dead!"

Alba nodded. "Yes, you should."

Slocum swung his leg over Fleet. "Do you got to be so goddamn agreeable all'a the time?"

Alba smiled. "Yes. You have not heard of us? The happy Mexicans?"

Slocum shook his head. "Aw, shut up, Juan."

"Sí, señor," said Juan, agreeably—too agreeably to make Slocum happy—and mounted up. "My pleasure is to serve you."

"Will you knock it off?"

Alba didn't answer him, just rode out of the stable and down the road, toward the saloon.

Grumbling under his breath, Slocum followed.

"I ain't comin'!" Forsythe said for the third time.

"Jesus! Why not?" Slocum growled. Juan leaned casually in the door frame.

"I've already been to see the elephant, Slocum. You, yourself, pronounced him dead. I'm not goin' to go off chasin' after some spook, and that's final!"

Slocum growled out some foreign sound of frustration and rage, and on his way out of the bar he kicked a table, breaking two of its legs in the process.

Alba turned to Forsythe. "Your horse, he is tacked up and on the rail. If I were you, I would be out of town when Slocum comes back."

Alba joined Slocum, who was still growling and grumping at the rail, and the two mounted up. Slocum asked, "East again?"

Alba said yes, and the two rocketed out of town.

"When we get back, I'm gonna kill him!" Slocum shouted into the wind.

"When we get back," Alba replied, "he will be gone."

Slocum reined in, and Alba followed suit. He said, "What d'ya mean, he'll be gone?"

"Just what I said. If you were him, would you not flee?"

"I ain't him."

"That much is obvious."

"Then why'd you go and—"

Alba suddenly raised his arm, pointing toward the southwest. "Look!"

Rafe Masterson's horse, bearing a wobbly rider with a blood-soaked back and a dangling arm, loped slowly through an opening in the brush, then vanished again.

Both Slocum and Alba set off without another word.

But Masterson was not alone. Unknown to Slocum or Alba, two of Rafe Masterson's gang, having heard that their boss had been caught and killed, had been making their way to San Diego to pay their last respects. They had been just a half mile out when their dead boss came galloping straight at them, shouting, "Go! Burn leather!"

They did, beating a nice path for their boss to follow as he galloped away from certain death at the hangman's noose.

But Slocum and Alba were bearing down faster.

Across the wide plain they galloped like lightning, their horses never putting a foot wrong, their course always true.

Fleet pulled ahead of Alba's mount just as the course began to wind uphill. A moment later a shot rang out: the outlaws, firing from above.

Slocum wasn't hit, but he grabbed his rifle, jumped off Fleet at a dead run, and rolled behind a thick stand of sage. Quickly, he brought his rifle to his shoulder, aimed, and fired.

A scream sounded from above, but the body that toppled down wasn't Masterson's. It was one of his men, and the corpse didn't stop bouncing and rolling through the cactus until it finally came to a halt, less than ten feet from Slocum.

It was enough to show Slocum that he was on the right track, insofar as his aim was concerned. He raised the rifle again and aimed to the side. He fired.

No body toppled this time, but he heard a loud whimper of pain and fired again.

Second time was the charm. Another body fell down the slope, this one stopping in front of a cactus about twenty-five feet out. He wasn't Masterson, either.

So all that was left was Masterson. And this time, Slocum was going to make *sure* he was dead.

Up the hill, tucked behind a boulder, slumped Rafe Masterson. So weak he could barely move, he was aware that he was losing too much blood, and that he had to make himself tie something around it to stop the bleeding. Although how he was going to tie something around his neck without choking himself to death was beyond him.

Still, he had to try.

With his one good arm—he had fallen from his horse on the other, and it had already felt broken—he managed to dig his bandanna out of his pocket and loop it around his neck. He simply held it in place. He couldn't do much more one-handed.

Slocum was still down there, still down there with that Mexican, although they hadn't fired since they'd killed Pete. If he didn't do something, they would sure as hell come up here looking for him.

He let go of the bandanna for a moment, then pulled his sidearm. It was almost too heavy for him to hold. With a mustering of much effort, he pointed the gun out toward the plain below and fired.

Back in San Diego, Forsythe made a deal for his horse down at the stable. Happily enough, the buyer was a traveling preacher, who would appreciate the horse's soft gaits and pleasant nature. Forsythe couldn't take Yancy with him. There was no room on the ship.

He'd booked passage on a sailing ship that would take him the long way around the horn and deliver him to New Orleans. He wasn't too happy about the long time in transit, but he could afford it, and there was absolutely no chance of him running into Slocum along the way. This gave him some comfort, although not the kind he needed.

He'd been torn over wanting to be out there with Slocum and Alba, finishing the job. He'd wanted to see it done up, right and proper.

But more than that, he'd just wanted it to be over with.

He had accomplished that much, anyway.

After Slocum and Alba left, the doctor had said that

he'd never seen such a thing, that it likely had something to do with the way the slug in Masterson's neck was positioned. That it was pressing on a nerve or something. It still made no sense at all to Forsythe. Probably not to the doc, either. It was just one of those things.

He went back to the bar and collected his things, then made his way down to the harbor and found his ship. He didn't count the masts, but there were many, and she was a big, imposing craft. Certainly big enough to weather the passage around the horn, he thought. He hoped.

Well, at least his horse was in good hands.

He marched up the gangway, got permission to come aboard, and got settled in his stateroom. He was told they'd leave that afternoon.

It couldn't be too soon for Forsythe.

When the shot came down from the top of the hill, it surprised Slocum for two reasons. First, he'd been sure that Masterson was lying up there dead as a doornail or at least passed out. Second, the shot hadn't come anywhere near them.

He exchanged looks with Alba, who raised his brows and shrugged his shoulders. Apparently, he was as puzzled as Slocum.

"Beginnin' to think that Forsythe had the right idea," Slocum said. "Just let him run for it and bleed to death in the process."

"No," responded Alba. "He did not have the right idea. And if there is any reward on these two," he added, waving a hand out toward the two bodies of the gang members, "we split it down the middle. Okay?"

Slocum managed a grin. "Deal. And if Rafe's alive when we find him—even if he looks dead—one of us puts a slug straight through his head. Just to make sure. 'Cause I ain't goin' through this again!"

"*Sí*," said Alba with a nod. "I do not wish to be chasing him through the desert forever, either."

Slocum set his mouth. And then heaved a sigh. "I'm goin' up there and flush him out. You cover me?"

Alba muttered, "You need to ask?"

"Right. And if I get myself killed, you contact Cain Doggett in Tombstone. He's got my will."

Alba's brow furrowed. "You will not die, Slocum. It is the rule. Slocum never dies."

Slocum put his hand on Alba's shoulder. "First time for everything, buddy." On hands and knees, he began snaking his way up the hill.

Shaking his head, Alba watched. Then he brought up his six-gun and began to shoot covering fire. Surely his friend had gone mad, talking like that! But he would do his best to make certain that the prophecy did not come true. Perhaps one of his bullets would hit home. Then they would have no more trouble from that devil Rafe Masterson!

16

Rafe let go of his neck cloth again long enough to fire a slug into the dirt. He could lift the gun no higher. His fingers and hands and feet were starting to go numb, and his eyesight . . . well, something was wrong with it.

Everything was blurry and swimming. That was, when it wasn't black.

He began to think that maybe he should just let himself be captured. Let the doc fix him up. Then escape again. He could do it. He'd done it before.

He fired another round into the dirt.

That oughta keep 'em scared.

At the first slug, Slocum flattened himself against the ground.

But no brush was disturbed, at least in his immediate vicinity. He waited a moment for Alba's covering fire to start again—he'd emptied the chamber, Slocum thought—and when it did, he started crawling up the hill again.

Up and up he went, slowly getting nearer and nearer to what he assumed was Masterson's perch. And then Rafe fired again.

But this time it was different. Instead of the sound ringing out accompanied by a slug slicing the air, it was followed by a dull thud, as if he were firing into the ground.

Odd.

Alba kept up his covering fire, but the returned fire wasn't in answer to his. It seemed random, as if the shooter didn't know where he was.

Or maybe the shooter didn't know where *Slocum* was.

He took heart and kept moving.

Alba paused to reload again, and Slocum dropped down on his belly. He was within ten feet of what he was certain was Rafe's hiding place, and he wanted to take no chances. Slowly, carefully, he pulled his Colt from its holster.

When Alba started firing again, he began to close the distance between himself and Rafe.

Alba's slugs were higher now, to account for Slocum's progress. Slocum came to the boulder behind which, unknown to him, Rafe sat, slumped and barely conscious.

Pistol first, Slocum edged around the boulder. Nothing. He crept a few inches farther, then a few inches more, and then . . . there was Rafe: passed out cold, his head resting on his arm.

Slocum didn't hesitate.

He aimed his pistol at the center of Rafe's forehead and pulled the trigger.

The result wasn't theatrical. A round hole appeared in the center of Rafe's forehead, and he jerked slightly, but that was all. The jerk could have been the last of his life exiting, or just the shock of the bullet disturbing an already dead body.

Either way, Rafe Masterson was gone.

Still staring at the body, Slocum called, "You can stop shootin', Juan."

Alba's gunfire ceased, and Slocum was suddenly aware of how quiet it was out here on the desert. It had never seemed so quiet before.

And then he heard Alba coming up the hill toward him. Heard him complain loudly when a jumping cholla got him.

Slocum allowed himself a smile. It was kind of refreshing, actually.

"Where are the horses?" Alba asked, from behind him.

Slocum pointed. "Likely over the ridge."

Alba grunted. "I will go and round them up."

He left, and Slocum sat down. He couldn't take his eyes off the man he'd had to kill twice. Stubborn son of a bitch! He said the same to Masterson, and damned if he didn't almost hear a reply.

He had his hand halfway to his gun before he realized it was Alba shouting at him, shouting that he had the horses in hand.

"Good!" Slocum yelled back.

When Alba reached him with the gunmen's horses, Slocum picked up Masterson's corpse and hoisted it over his saddle, and he made sure that he could stick his little finger into the dark hole in Rafe's forehead before he roped him across his horse.

Juan had the first of the other outlaws roped across the saddle by the time Slocum got down to him, and they put up the last one together.

Juan took off his sombrero and wiped his forehead with his sleeve. "I could use a cold cerveza about now," he said.

"Settle for water?" asked Slocum as he pulled out his canteen.

"For now," Alba replied, and took a drink. A long drink.

Slocum took the canteen back. "Jesus, Juan, you leave me any?"

"I hope so." At Slocum's raised brow, he added, "I am too old and too famous to be shot over a drink of water."

Slocum tilted back the canteen, and cool water rushed down his throat. "Too old, mayhap. Not too famous."

Together, the two men gathered up their own horses, watered them, mounted up, and at a soft jog, led the three corpse-bearing horses—also freshly watered—back toward San Diego.

They stopped at the marshal's office first and found him just preparing to leave. He saw them riding up and said, "Well, I'll be diggety damned! You fellers sure got the timing!"

Alba said, "Beg pardon?"

"Well, looks to me like you boys done brought in him that was already brought, plus two more! They part of his gang, come to break him out? That or go to the funeral, I mean."

Slocum said, "Somethin' like that. I'd give you their names, but they was too busy shootin' at us to hand 'em out."

"Tsk, tsk," Marshal Denver said with a shake of his head. "Ain't it sad how downright rude some of our outlaws is gettin'?" He lifted the first man by the hair. "This one's Pete Somethin'-or-other. Ain't worth much, but it's better than pocket change." He went to the next body. "Andy Cowl. Same on the reward, maybe a little more or less. Too bad Toby Keith wasn't with 'em. He'd have brought you another grand each. I take it you're splittin' this two ways and not three?"

"How'd you know that?" Slocum asked.

"Small town. News travels fast," the marshal said as he ushered them into his office. "Also Doc Kellerman's been ridin' that high-steppin' strutter of his up and down Main Street all afternoon. Seems he bought him off your fancy friend. Who, I understand, took passage on a ship that headed south outta here about a half hour ago."

He set a stack of paper in front of both Alba and Slocum, then nudged over an inkwell and two pens. "Go to it, fellas. I'm gonna take your boys here on down to the undertaker."

He paused a moment, then added, "If he'll have 'em."

Slocum finished up his paperwork, then turned to Alba. "You remember the name you put on the first papers. What was it? Vargas?"

Alba didn't look up. "Vega," he said, and signed the last paper with a flourish. "I am now five hundred dollars richer, as are you, Slocum. I should take up this bounty hunting. There appears to be more money in it than robbing stages."

Slocum laughed. "You gotta get yourself on the right side of the law first, or the first time you haul somebody in, they'll be collectin' the reward on you!"

Alba shrugged. "*Sí,*" he said. "I am better off sticking to who I am."

"Yeah," said Slocum. "It'd likely take you two months a'Sundays just to get Wells Fargo off your back."

Alba nodded, although not at all sadly. He said, "They are . . . how do you say? Tenacious. Tenacious but stupid. That is it."

"Well, you wanna wait for the vouchers or come back later?"

"Later. I am in no hurry."

"Good." Slocum pushed his chair back and stood up. "I'm in the mood for a drink. I believe I owe you one, too. And I gotta pay Maria."

The two men straightened their paperwork and started to leave, but the marshal pushed the door in before they could open it. "Leavin' so soon?" he asked.

"You were takin' so long with the bodies, we thought they came back to life on you," Slocum said with a chuckle.

The marshal scowled. "Think you're real funny, don'tcha? But you're nothin' compared to that damn Bristol, our undertaker. I ain't never seen such a case of the heebie-jeebies in all my born days! You'd think Masterson was gonna come to life all over again!"

"Well, he did it once," said Slocum, "but I don't think he's gonna pull it off twice. Not with that slug in the middle of his forehead."

"I pointed that out," said the marshal grimly. "Still didn't believe me. I had to take out my gun and shoot the body through the temple to satisfy him." And then he grinned. "Made him promise not to try to dig either slug out to sell, too."

Alba nodded and smiled.

Slocum clapped the marshal on the shoulder. "Atta boy, Will."

The marshal snorted in reply, then said, "If you boys want your money, I can give you each a voucher right now. All right?"

Both Slocum and Alba agreed readily.

Slocum had no more than lowered his knuckles from Maria's door when it opened, exposing Maria in all her spangles.

She looked surprised to see Slocum and put a hand to her mouth.

"It's all right, honey," he said. "I just came to pay you. Was in such a hurry this mornin' that I plumb forgot!" He didn't go into the whole story. Time had taught him that it was easy to lie to whores.

She opened the door and let him in, and he gave her $50, despite her protests that it was too much. "For this, you could have me for a week!" she said, staring down at the cash.

"I'd settle for one more night," he said and grinned. "But only if you'll let me take you to dinner, too."

"Señor Slocum, I—"

"Good, good," he said, cutting her off. "You ready to go, Maria? And I'd appreciate it if you'd hold off on the señor part."

She nodded her head obediently, then beamed. "A real dinner? With forks and napkins and a waiter?"

"Whatever you want, baby doll."

"There is a place, a place I have always wished to go. It is called the Cloisters. May we go there?"

"Wherever you want, Maria," he replied, although he was beginning to worry that the fifty bucks he had left wasn't going to be enough. But he'd made a promise, and he wasn't about to go back on his word.

Proudly, she led him down the street, turned two corners, and they were at the Cloisters. He had to admit that he'd never seen such a fancy place, not even in San Francisco. A waiter met them at the entrance and said, "Two, sir?"

Slocum nodded, and the waiter bowed, then ushered them inside. The place was bright with gaslights, and the waiter showed them to a curtained table along one side. After he seated them, they were brought glasses of water and menus.

The latter had Slocum a bit leery. There were no prices on them.

But the food they ordered was past wonderful! They had a bottle of wine each—hers was white, and his was red. Maria had a whole crab, Slocum a steak—what they called a grand filet mignon—and he had never had such a tender, toothsome piece of meat in his life! The side dishes were nothing to scoff at, either. Slocum had long, skinny-cut fried potatoes called *pomme frits*, Maria had a side of fried clams, and they both shared fresh-baked bread and a huge green salad with raspberries in it and some kind of red dressing.

For desert, they each had a wedge of something called cheesecake, drizzled with chocolate sauce.

Slocum felt full as a tick and as satisfied as a sow in an orchard full of ripe peaches.

And when he pulled out his money to pay, the tab was only $20!

He paid it gladly and left the waiter a $5 tip.

He was a happy man.

17

"What do you like to do?" Slocum asked as they started to walk back to the cantina.

Maria looked as if she didn't understand him, so he tried again. "I mean, on your days off. What do you like to do?"

"Oh! I like to eat, as you have just seen," she said with a blush. "I like to walk down to the harbor and look at the ships. They are beautiful, with the tall masts and the giant sails. Sometimes, I have Jorge make me a sandwich, and I go for all day."

"Jorge?"

"The bartender at the cantina."

"Ah." Slocum nodded.

Just then, as they were approaching the mouth of an alley, a shabbily dressed man, gun drawn, leapt out to block their path. Drunkenly he said, "Your money or your life, mister!"

Maria clapped her hands over her mouth and through them sputtered a hysterical "*Madre de Dios!*"

After a moment, Slocum said, "Go sleep it off, buddy."

The drunk frowned. "Said your money or your life. Mean it."

Slocum nodded. "I'm sure you do, friend, but you have to remember to load your gun before you start makin' threats with it."

The man tipped the barrel of the gun up, as if he could make certain it was loaded by looking down the business end, and Slocum took advantage of the situation by slugging him right square in the jaw. The man crumpled on the spot, going down in a heap.

"Pleasant dreams, buddy," muttered Slocum, and, like a gentleman, he escorted Maria around the unfortunate drunk and up the street.

Slowly, holding hands, they followed the path they had taken to get them down to the restaurant. En route, they passed Consuelo's Café, where they peeked in a window to spy Juan and his sultry señorita partaking in an enchilada dinner.

Slocum rapped on the glass to get Juan's attention, then waved. Juan waved back before he returned his attention to his señorita.

Finally, they found themselves at the door to the cantina. Slocum held the door wide for Maria, and she walked in like a lady. Even Jorge, the bartender, took a second look at her. She was a new Maria!

It was amazing what a good dinner and a little gentlemanly treatment could do to make a woman feel like a woman.

Or a whore feel like a princess.

Slocum grinned to himself as he walked her through the crowd to the stairs. He stopped at the first step and signaled to Jorge. "Bring us a bottle of champagne and a couple'a glasses soon's you can, all right?" he said, and the bartender nodded.

Forsythe's redhead was traveling solo tonight, but seemed to have picked out a sailor at the back table. She was twining herself around him, and he was grinning like an idiot.

Slocum followed Maria's delectable backside as it swished the rest of the way up the stairs, then down the hall to her room.

There was no place like home, he thought with a smirk.

Slocum heard Juan and his woman stumble up the steps at least two hours later. While he and Maria had been sipping champagne and howling with the wolves, it seemed that Juan and his woman had been guzzling the vino, period. The slam of their bedroom door was followed by several whoops, hollers, and throaty giggles.

Slocum had to smile. Maria was passed out in the crook of his arm, a victim of multiple orgasms, and grinning in her sleep. He should grab some shut-eye, too, but every time he thought he was just dozing off, another thud or giggle or bark of laughter came from the room next door.

He couldn't blame Juan, though. It had been a rough couple of days for the both of them. They both deserved some time to whoop it up.

Funny, but he hadn't spent his time that way. Instead

of carousing, he'd taken a girl to a nice restaurant—a *really* nice restaurant!—and walked her home like a gent. Of course, he'd screwed her silly once he got her there, but still . . .

Hell, maybe he was getting old.

Addled in the brain, more like.

He sure wasn't up to his old hijinks, that was for certain. He used to be able to hit six bars and have three women in one night of celebration.

Used to. That was the operative phrase.

Well, he'd been young then, and riding the owlhoot trail. Young, on the dodge, and filled with the optimism and verve of youth.

Today, he'd told Juan what to do in case he died. He'd never done that before. It had never even occurred to him to mention it before. But it had today. Maybe he was getting too old for this game. Maybe he should retire, settle down.

But then Maria rolled halfway over in the crook of his arm, pillowing her head on his shoulder with a small, satisfied sigh.

And he thought, *Me? Retire? Not by a long shot. I'm still young! Hell, I'm still livin' easy! I got a lot of bounties comin' my way, goddamn it!*

And he had a lot of damsels out there, just waiting to be rescued. And quite a few more who *didn't* want to be rescued.

Either way, he was happy to oblige . . .

He fell asleep with a smile on his face.

The next morning, he met Alba downstairs for breakfast. He seemed in quite a chipper mood, and Slocum didn't need to ask why. He and his lady friend had been thumping and bumping around next door all night long. Well, every time that Slocum woke up, that was.

"Later, you wish to go to the bank with me?" Alba asked around a mouthful of flapjacks.

Slocum took a drink of coffee, then grinned. "Why? You afraid to go by yourself? Afraid they'll recognize you?"

Alba chuckled. "Any other man, I would shoot for saying that, my friend."

"So you're takin' me for protection. Or distraction," Slocum added.

"*Sí,*" Alba said with a shrug. "You are handy. Take no offense."

Slocum shrugged. "None taken."

After breakfast, they strolled up to the bank, where the clerk recognized them right away. "Mr. Slocum! Mr. Vega! What can we do for you today?"

Slocum pulled out his voucher, followed by Alba. "Don't suppose there's any chance'a just cashing these in?" said Slocum.

The clerk stared at the vouchers for a moment. "I believe we can do that for you," he said, much to Slocum's surprise.

"Well, hot damn!" he whispered to Alba as they endorsed their vouchers. "A bank that actually has some money!"

"It is lucky no bank robbers are in town," Alba whispered archly.

"Oh, shut up," Slocum replied just as the clerk reappeared.

"You want this in cash? Is that correct, gentlemen?"

the teller asked. "I only ask because you'll carry that much money at your own peril. Once the bank has paid you, that's the end of its responsibility."

Alba turned his back and made a face, but Slocum said, "We understand. Thanks for your concern."

They took their money—$500 each, in crisp $100 bills—and left the bank with Slocum pinning his share inside his hat. It made a satisfyingly thick wad, doubled and secured with a safety pin. Slocum finally felt at ease.

The first thing he did was lead Alba to the tobacconist's shop, where he bought himself two packs of readymades and Alba got several of those long, thin, black cigars he liked to smoke. Enjoying a smoke, they walked up to the livery to check the horses. All was well, although Slocum mourned the loss of that stupid, fiddle-fronted Tennessee walker of Forsythe's. He almost missed Forsythe, too, although he was loath to admit it.

After the livery, they stopped in at the undertaker's. This time, he'd gotten right on with his business: the bodies, all three of them, were leaned upright in their coffins outside on the walk. Each had a sign hanging around his neck to identify him, but Rafe's was especially long.

It said, "Rafe Masterson. Killed by Slocum, Vega, and Forsythe. Rose from the dead, and was killed again by Slocum and Vega. If it please the Lord, may he stay dead this time. Amen. Burial today, 6:00 pm, Old Cemetery."

Slocum didn't know if it was a notice, a prayer, or a plea. He asked Alba, "Where's the Old Cemetery?"

"I think it is the one south of town. The one where they bury the 'undesirables.'"

"Sounds like the place," Slocum said. At least

Masterson wouldn't be resting next to a schoolmarm. "They bury the dogs and horses out there, too?"

Alba looked over at him. "No, the children bury their pets in the plot next to the good people's cemetery. And Slocum," he added, looking at him oddly, "horses would be too big to bury."

Slocum laughed, even though he had buried many a horse in his time. Sometimes, it was all you could do. That or cremate them.

They came to the marshal's office, and Slocum stuck his head in the door. But nobody was home. He closed the door again, shrugging his shoulders. "Guess the marshal went out to dig up the other marshal. The dead one, I mean. Man's been underground already for a few days." He made a face just thinking about it. "That'll be a closed coffin."

"*Sí.*"

"They say at the bank when you could expect to get your money?"

"Yesterday they said four days. So now it should be three."

Slocum nodded. It was pretty swift service for a state bank. But then, most states and territories didn't have the railroad system enjoyed by California. Anyway, not most of the ones west of the Mississippi.

"Tell me, Slocum," Alba began, "why are you interested in how long my money takes to get to me? Do you plan to rob me?"

The question was so unexpected that Slocum burst out laughing. "Do . . . do I plan to *what*?"

Alba was laughing, too. "You should have seen your face, amigo!"

18

Slocum felt a good deal richer that night. It was amazing what $500 in his hat could do for a fellow's ego! Well, $400. He'd given Maria another hundred to pay for her exclusive company for the rest of his time in town, and she was thrilled. They had talked a little that afternoon, and he'd learned that she had a younger sister whom she was trying to keep out of the life.

The girl lived with the sisters at the local nunnery, and went to school there, too, for which Maria paid them $30 per month. It was the same as a cowhand's monthly salary, and often, she said, it was all she could do to make it, what with Jorge's boss taking half her money. Slocum immediately took her down to the bank and had her put the hundred in an account in her name only—he told her he wanted her to have a little nest egg, something to fall back on in case times got tough.

She gratefully accepted his offer and took him to the

convent to meet her sister, who turned out to be only twelve years old. Maria's mother had died in childbirth with Conchita. Up until then, she'd also been a hooker, who had worked a hard life down by the docks. She'd left the two girls alone and without a cent.

It was obvious the girls had different fathers. Maria was half-white by the looks of her, with a black Irish twinkle in her soulful brown eyes. The little girl, Conchita, had light hair—surprisingly, almost blond—and a sparkle in her green eyes—a sparkle that was amazing to find in a little one who'd had such a rough and ungainly start in life.

After meeting her, Slocum was torn. He wanted to help them out, but most of his money was now in Tombstone. After he walked Maria back up to the cantina, he went down to the bank again and arranged a transfer from his Tombstone account in the amount of $5,000 directly into Maria's newly opened account in San Diego.

He'd done it hastily, but he felt good once he'd done it. $5,000 would get her and her sister out of San Diego, buy them a house, and get it set up. It would also let them live a life of leisure for several years, or until Conchita decided what she wanted to do, or until one of them landed a husband.

Two girls could live very nicely on $5,000, if they watched their p's and q's.

At six o'clock, he walked down to the Old Cemetery, and found just what Alba had described—the place for the bodies of "undesirables." Most of the graves were unmarked, save for the occasional wooden cross or middle-sized rock. One of the latter bore the clumsily carved name "Bill Latner."

The new graves had been dug, and the grave diggers sat to the side beneath a palo verde, smoking cigarettes and waiting to fill them in again.

Nobody joined in Undertaker Bristol's parade to the burial site, but half the town, including Juan, was waiting to watch the dirt cover up Rafe Masterson's ugly face for good and all.

Bristol seemed surprised by the turnout, but handled it like a master. He opened the coffins again so that everyone could have a last look—and be certain that the outlaws were going in the ground. The crowd seemed pleased by this, and they cheered when Rafe Masterson's coffin was opened and also when the first shovelfuls of dirt hit the lid.

It seemed Rafe had been universally disliked.

Of course, Bristol was stuck with burying them all in their coffins—he had to, or be found out for the cheapskate he was—but Slocum thought he handled it pretty fair for a man who was watching a small fortune get buried, right before his eyes.

Slocum stayed until the last shovelful of dirt was patted into place, until the last grateful citizen had shaken his hand in gratitude, and until even the grave diggers had left.

Alone, he stood, silhouetted by the setting sun and staring down at Rafe Masterson's final resting spot.

"I'll be damned if you can get out of this one, you son of a bitch," Slocum muttered, then spat on the grave before he turned to walk back to town.

It was a satisfied Slocum who treated them all—Juan and his lady, too—to supper at the cantina. He couldn't wait to tell Maria that she had a much bigger nest egg than she had thought, but it would have to wait. He didn't want the whole cantina to know, and he especially didn't want her boss to find out.

He didn't trust pimps, period.

Any man who made his living off the backs of women was dirt, in his book. Although he didn't mind the madams so much. At least they'd lived the life themselves and could commiserate with the girls. And sometimes, like back in Phoenix, they'd sleep with a client just for old time's sake.

Bless the ladies, every one of them.

After dessert, they hung around the bar for a few hours more, drinking champagne—also on Slocum—and listening to Juan's stories of his boyhood in Mexico. He had some good ones, like the one in which, when he was eleven, he was cornered by a Mexican grizzly bear and only escaped by skittering up a treacherous cliff (called "The Rocks of Death" by the locals—according to Juan) and slipping into a narrow crevice some sixty feet above the ground.

Unfortunately, the bear managed to follow him up, and Juan had to wait the grizzly out. For a long day and a half.

"It was a good thing you had water on you," said Slocum when Juan finished the story.

"*Sí*," said Juan with a nod. "If not, I could be there until this very day, forever an eleven-year-old skeleton." He sighed, then smiled. "But I would be a very good-looking one."

The girls giggled behind their hands.

Slocum shook his head. The night wasn't getting any younger. He pushed back his chair. "Well, it's nigh on near ten. Think I'll take myself upstairs." He held out his hand. "And you, Maria?"

"It is late," she said demurely. "I will accompany you."

She rose, too, and together they mounted the stairs, leaving Alba and Rosa, his woman, behind. Juan winked at him as he climbed the stairs. And he remembered, just then, that he'd have to get himself back to Miss Katie's in Phoenix and let Blossom know that she wouldn't have need to fear Rafe Masterson and his goddamn knife again. Nobody would have to.

Chuckling and shaking his head, Slocum continued upward.

Upstairs, Slocum closed Maria's door behind them and latched it. "Maria, honey, I got somethin' to tell you first."

Her skirt dropped to the floor, and she stood waiting in her pantaloons and blouse.

He motioned toward the chair. "You better sit down."

She sat, but she said, "What on earth could you have to tell me that is so important I must be seated?" She twisted her head quizzically.

He sat down across from her, on the edge of the bed. "Honey," he said, "I just wanted to tell you that you are officially retired."

Her brows knitted. "Slocum? I do not understand."

"This afternoon I went to the bank—"

"I know," she said, nodding. "I was with you, remember? You opened an account for me and put in one hundred U.S. dollars. You are very kind, and I am most grateful, my Slocum!"

"Yes, I know," he said, taking her hand. "But I went

back again. I transferred more money to your account. Enough for you and little Conchita to go somewhere and buy a house. Somewhere you won't have to work on your back anymore, and where Conchita will never have to."

Maria's mouth was hanging open rather stupidly and he said, "Maria? Honey?"

She sputtered, "I didn't . . . You put . . . I . . ." And then she collapsed in sobs—deep, heart-wrenching sobs that were infectious enough that Slocum shed a tear or two, as well.

"How . . . how . . . how much?" she finally got out.

"Five thousand," he said, and when she burst out in a new flood of tears, he dropped down to the floor and took her into his arms. "It's all right, Maria, it's all right. I got more than that for bringing in Masterson. This way, we can both be all right."

She looked up at him, her eyes brimming with tears. "You will be all right, too?"

"Sure! And I'll have the great pleasure of knowing that you and your sister are safe and taken care of. Some of us fellers think about stuff like that, you know." He grinned at her.

And she stopped crying so much. She shook her head. "No, not so many. I am twenty, and I have made my living like this ever since I was thirteen. No one has ever . . . ever . . ."

He wrapped her in his arms again and thought of her when she was thirteen, just a kid. She should have been playing jump rope or hopscotch instead of . . .

He didn't want to think about it.

It was on her mind, though. "I thank you, Slocum. I thank you for myself, but most of all for my little Conchita, who will now have a chance. Perhaps she will do well in marriage."

"She's sure pretty enough," said Slocum with a smile. "Smart as a whip, too."

"*Sí*. It is why I worry about her so. She needs to meet nice boys who will respect her. She needs to dance and be happy."

"And so do you, Maria. All those things and more for the both of you. Find yourself a nice place in a new town. Make nice, new friends. Be happy."

That evening, Forsythe found himself spending his second night aboard the *Sea Witch*, sailing south about a mile from the coast. The ship, he decided, had been misnamed. It should have been the *Sea Bitch*. It seemed that every ten minutes or so, he was racing up the stairs and across the deck to the rail, to heave up what precious little remained of his dinner.

His dinner from three nights ago, that was.

A steward had told him that this would pass, and had given him some pills for it, but he hadn't taken one yet. He remembered the trouble Fan had gotten into with those heroin pills, and he hadn't a clue what was in these.

None of the other passengers seemed to suffer a similar malady. He'd met them at supper—which he'd thrown up roughly three hours ago—and there were only five. Mr. and Mrs. Parkington, an elderly couple from Boston who were just returning from a long vacation to see China; Mr. and Mrs. Burke, bound for Maine, who had been visiting Mr. Burke's interest in a shipping company up in Seattle; and Tom Hinds, who was traveling alone. Hinds was from Kentucky.

And he looked, to Forsythe, like a real candidate.

Meaning that he thought Hinds was a fellow homosexual.

But he was destined not to learn any more this evening. Besides him, the only ones awake on the *Sea Witch* were a few crewmen. And they all looked to be straight.

Well, time would tell, he thought to himself. He stood erect, still hanging onto the rail, and stared out across the black waters.

Time would tell.

At a little after midnight, Slocum sat in the chair where Maria had sobbed. His feet were propped on the bed where she now slept, while he watched the end of his ready-made glow in the dark.

She had been like fine wine before, but tonight she had been . . . transcendent. Her breasts seemed riper, her hips shook like thunder, her hands were everywhere. Like the finest champagne, she had bubbled and fizzed and buoyed him up far beyond any normal heights. She'd been the finest music any man ever had the pleasure to hear, the most beautiful painting ever painted.

The breeze from the open window caressed her skin on its way to softly tickle the hairs on his legs and belly. The night air was cool, and it felt good.

He wondered where Maria would choose to buy her house. Would she stay near the sea or go farther inland? He sort of hoped she'd go over to Arizona, where she'd be handy, but that was just his self-absorption talking.

Shame on me, he thought with a grin. Once he rode out of town, Maria was strictly off-limits.

Unless, of course, she . . .

No. Strictly off-limits.

He ground out his cigarette, took the last gulp of what was left of their champagne, then eased himself into the bed slowly and quietly, to avoid waking her. In her sleep, she made a happy little purring sound and curled up next to him like a kitten.

He smiled. He'd done the right thing.

And after all, it was only money.

19

The next morning, Alba woke early. Seven o'clock is too early for a man who has a woman like Rosa in his bed, even if she is only rented, he thought.

But he couldn't go back to sleep, no matter how hard he tried, and so he quietly got up, dressed, and crept downstairs.

Downstairs wasn't open yet. There was no one behind the bar, the front door was locked, and there was nobody to fix him breakfast. Dejected, he pulled out a chair at one of the tables and sat down. He could outwait anybody.

He didn't have to wait long, though, before he heard the sound of boots from overhead, boots trying to tiptoe without much success. He waited while the bootsteps came to the head of the stairs, then started down them. When the body attached to the boots turned the corner of the stairway, he looked up and was surprised to find Slocum. He had expected to see one of the bartenders.

He lifted a hand. "Good morning, my friend. I did not expect to see you so early."

Slocum came forward and sat himself in the opposite chair. "You ain't the only one." He ran hands up his face, then under his hat to comb his hair. "Couldn't sleep."

"A common problem, it would seem." Juan's eyes searched the back bar again, with the same result as last time. There was nobody there. He sighed.

"Where is everybody?" Slocum asked. He seemed to have just noticed the problem. "I was sorta lookin' forward to breakfast."

"I fear it will not come soon," Juan said.

Somebody rattled the front door, and both men jumped. The glass-paned outer doors showed the faint ouline of a small person, very slender and dressed in pants. Slocum could not tell the sex for certain, though. The figure was too petite to be a boy, but yet there were the pants . . .

The door rattled again.

Slocum raised a brow. He said, "Somebody wants a drink pretty damn bad."

"*Sí,*" replied Alba. He stood up and started toward the doors. They were locked, but he had just remembered that these were the kind of doors you could unlock from the inside, if you knew how. And he did.

When he reached the doors, he bent to get a closer look at the left-hand knob. As he'd thought, there was a small button next to the knob, a button that would slide up or down. Right now, it was in the down position. He shoved it up with his thumb, something clicked, and the door on his right swung outward just a hair.

He grabbed the knob and pushed it the rest of the way outward to find . . . a girl?

While he scratched his head, she pushed past him and walked on into the cantina. She halted abruptly in the center of the floor. She was staring at Slocum. And he was staring back.

Slocum's brows knitted. "What the hell are you doin' down here?"

The girl's spine stiffened. "I'm looking for Mr. Forsythe."

"You're a little late. He's gone."

The girl wavered, just a touch, and Alba could see enough of her face to see her eyelashes flutter. Then she gathered herself. "Where's he gone to?"

Slocum leaned back in his chair and pulled out his pack of ready-mades. Out came a sulfur-tip, too. He flicked the match to light with a quick stroke on his jeans, then said, "Dunno. He hopped a ship, probably bound for the Horn, about three, four days ago." He lit his ready-made and took a long draw, expelling the smoke in two long jets from his nostrils.

The girl slumped, her shoulders drooping with what Alba assumed to be disappointment. She whispered, "Bound for the Horn?"

"Yeah," Slocum replied casually, between drags on his smoke. "You know. The south end of South America? Then up north again, I guess. Goin' home to Louisiana."

Suddenly, the girl crumpled to the floor. She was out cold by the time Alba and Slocum reached her.

"What the hell goes on?" Alba muttered as, together, they lifted her to a tabletop. "Slocum? Who is this *muchacha*?"

"This *muchacha* is one Miss Fannie Forebush. Me and Forsythe escorted her out here from Phoenix." He removed his vest and rolled it up to pillow her head.

"Seems like she didn't wanna stay put at her aunt and uncle's."

On the table, Fannie groaned. She was coming around already.

"Fan?" Slocum said, patting her cheek. "Fan, you in there?"

The girl's eye's slitted open. She murmured, "Mr. Forsythe?"

Slocum rolled his eyes, and Alba began to wonder if there was any story behind this. Slocum spoke again. "Fan, it's Slocum. Slocum, Fan. Forsythe ain't here, remember?"

She blinked a few times. "Slocum. Slocum, I'm sorry. I didn't remember there, for just a second. He's gone away, to go round the Horn, right?"

Slocum nodded in the affirmative, and Fan sighed, "Oh, he's so brave!"

Alba rolled his eyes and leaned back in his chair. This girl had just told him everything by saying nothing. And poor Señor Forsythe! He knew Slocum well enough to know him for a man who liked grown-up women.

But Forsythe? If he had been a fancy boy—as Alba suspected—well, Alba couldn't imagine what Forsythe had been put through, coming out from Arizona with Fannie. Alba couldn't hold back a laugh, but he was able to cover his mouth in time and disguise it as a cough.

Slocum recognized it for what it had been, though, and scowled at him. And that scowl told him the rest of the story—Slocum hadn't known about Forsythe. He hadn't had a blessed clue!

Now Alba *really* felt like a good laugh, but he didn't dare tempt that scowl again. He very simply kept his mouth shut. In fact, he stuck a lit pipe in it to help him disguise his glee.

He looked at the girl again. She was lean and gawky, and just sitting up. She had brown hair and eyes, and a face that held a promise of beauty that had not yet arrived. Perhaps in another year or so, he thought, she would grow into those cheekbones and full lips. But for now, she was just a gawky little girl wearing cast-off men's trousers.

By the time that Jorge showed up and made them all some breakfast, Slocum had gotten most of the whole story out of her.

She been pining away up in Palos Verdes since they'd dropped her off; pining for the trail, pining for campfire cooking, pining for Slocum and Forsythe.

He figured he could just cut that down to "pining for Forsythe."

Some kids were just too damn precocious for their own good.

Too bad they weren't so good at lying about it.

She hadn't told her aunt and uncle that she was leaving. She'd just pulled up stakes in the middle of the night and gone. Stupid move. She was lucky she hadn't been raped and killed while she was out there, following the stage route, just in the hopes that she might find Forsythe.

"You might just as easily have found Masterson," Slocum said to her.

"But I didn't," she said, and crammed another bite of eggs into her mouth.

Slocum just shook his head. Now he supposed he'd have to take her back up north before he could head east.

Damn it anyway. He'd been planning to leave today, and now it looked like he'd be leaving, all right, but in the wrong direction.

He supposed the first order of business, though, was to get up to the telegraph office and wire Fan's folks. They must be worried sick.

He didn't tell Fan, though. He figured she'd likely pitch a fit.

And he was right. After they finished breakfast, he and Alba walked her down the street. But the instant she realized they were headed for the telegraph office, she bolted.

Alba caught her. He snaked out a hand and caught her up by the arm almost before she realized what was happening.

Slocum—feeling older and slower than he wanted to think about—said, "Thanks," and opened the door to the telegraph office. He held the door wide. "Inside, missy."

Alba had to give her a little shove before she did it.

Inside, Slocum sent the wire: "FOUND FAN IN SAN DIEGO STOP BRINGING HER BACK STOP SHE'S FINE STOP SLOCUM STOP."

Short and to the point. Slocum paid the telegrapher and exited, with Fan and Alba bringing up the rear. She was still sulky, and Alba still had a grip on her arm. Slocum started to mention her injury, but then realized it was the other shoulder.

He decided to keep his mouth shut.

They walked back up to the cantina, where Slocum would pick up the last of his things and say good-bye to Maria.

But when they arrived, Maria was just coming out. Her

bags, hurriedly packed, were sitting on the walk, and she was dressed for travel.

She smiled a grin at Slocum. *"Buenas dias!"* She looked like the world was her oyster.

And it probably is, thought Slocum. And then he began thinking about the way that money changed everything. Money. There was nothing, almost, that it couldn't fix. Well, it couldn't fix disease. Or natural calamities. Or the will of God.

Aw, shit, he thought with a scowl. *Who the hell needs it, anyway?*

He did, he realized. He needed it for whores and whiskey, anyhow. And people like Maria and her sister did, for one reason or another. Not everybody could live off the land. Not everybody wanted to.

Stop thinkin' about it, he told himself. Why did he go off on these tangents in the first place? Nobody cared, not really.

"Slocum?"

He turned toward Maria's voice. "What, honey?"

"You looked strange for a little time. Are you all right?" Worry twitched at her brow.

Slocum laughed. "I was just waxin' philosophical, Maria." He leaned against the front of the cantina. "Have you decided where to go yet?" He figured if she hadn't, he could make a few suggestions.

But she said, "Yes! I have, Slocum. Conchita and myself, we go north to Los Angeles, where the weather is not so hot and where we have friends. They will let us stay with them until we find a place of our own." She grinned like she had just solved all the problems of the world, single-handed.

And Slocum grinned back, happy that she still had some innocence left.

Behind him, Alba's voice, tense with anger, said, "You will excuse us, Slocum? It is time for Miss Fan to go inside."

"Sure." He watched while Alba disappeared through the batwing doors with a struggling Fannie, then he heaved a sigh. Give him a gun battle in the desert any day!

He walked Maria to the stage depot, where she was to meet Conchita, and along the way he picked up Spots off the rail. Dropping him at the stable, he ordered him up full rations and a box stall. He quickly checked on Alba's pinto and his Appy while he was there, too.

The pinto was fine, but the Appy looked a little off, which worried him. He told the hostler he'd be back, and wondered what the hell else was going to shit in his coffee today.

He found out down at the stage depot.

He was watching the northbound stage pull up to the depot. He held Conchita's hand. She was sure a cute little thing! And she was delighted about the stage and the trip, which would take her to Los Angeles to start a new life—one without nuns and one with, hopefully, lots of new playmates.

"Here it comes!" she shouted. "Here it comes, Maria, Mr. Slocum!"

"Calm yourself, Conchita," said Maria, although her own hand was tightening on Slocum's other arm.

Slocum chuckled as the stage slowed and stopped down the walk from them. He bent to pick up Maria's bags, then suddenly stood erect.

Maria said, "Slocum? What is it?"

He shushed her, keeping his eyes on the open coach door. Max Furling had just climbed down the steps, and he was followed in a matter of seconds by Toby Keith. The two remaining members of Rafe Masterson's gang. It was obvious to Slocum that the gang had split again and was trying to rendezvous in San Diego.

Max and Toby weren't going to be happy to learn what had happened to their friends.

But then, Max and Toby together were worth $1,700 in Arizona. Maybe they were worth more out here . . .

Max and Toby walked south down the street, away from Slocum, and they never saw him. He doubted they'd recognize him anyway. He put Maria and Conchita on the stage while the depot employees switched teams, leading the old team down the alley to the barn and leading out a freshly harnessed four-in-hand of matched bays. They were attached to the stage's traces in no time, and then, just like that, Maria was gone. All that was left was Conchita's little arm, stuck out the window and waving good-bye as the stage and its cargo disappeared into the distance.

He felt a little pang, but it didn't last long.

He set off, not north to meet up with Alba and Fan, but south, down the street, tagging along on the path that Max Furling and Toby Keith had taken.

20

Slocum had no more than turned the corner when he caught sight of Max and Toby again. They had stopped a couple of blocks west, down toward the sea, and were talking to some fellow on the sidewalk.

Slocum stood, slowly lighting a ready-made and eyeing the little group. He had no wish to hurry things along. Not yet.

While he watched, the man Max and Toby had at first been speaking to was replaced by a second, then a third. They were standing outside a bar, and it was pretty clear that the townsfolk weren't providing the kind of information the outlaws liked. Slocum half expected somebody to turn around and point him out as one of the men who'd delivered their three friends into town for burial—one of them twice.

Nobody pointed at him, though, and eventually the two men started back up the street. Slocum slipped into the mouth of an alley until they passed, then slipped out again just in time to see them turn south, a block up on Main.

They were going to the Old Graveyard.

And Slocum kept on following.

This would have been a lot easier with Alba to back him up, he thought—wishing, for just a second, that he'd drummed Juan from the cantina to help. But then again, no. Somebody had to keep an eye on Fannie. And he'd just as soon take a chance on being shot than sign up for babysitting duty.

Not any sooner than he had to, that was.

They were almost at the end of the street now, almost to the graveyard.

When Max and Toby walked through the graveyard's crude gate, Slocum stopped and watched. They had managed to find the graves, which Slocum knew had only been tagged with bits of cloth attached to a wire. If the townsmen they'd talked to hadn't told them about Slocum, they knew now. The tags were the signs that had been hung around the corpses' necks by the town undertaker, each one announcing the buried party's name and his cause of death.

Shit.

Eventually, the outlaws left the cemetery and started coming back up the street. Seeing that they were approaching on his side of the street, Slocum quickly stepped into the mouth of an alley and pulled his Colt. His back pressed to the side of the building nearest them, he waited.

He didn't have to wait there very long. It seemed only moments until he heard the double boot strides approaching, then watched the two men cross the alley in tandem.

He waited another moment before he emerged on the sidewalk behind them, with his gun raised.

"Hey, Max! Toby!" he called in a cheerful voice, and they both stopped, then did a slow turn toward him.

Toby reacted first, starting to pull his pistol when he was only halfway turned. The sound of his shouted "Bounty hunter!" was clipped short. Slocum fired before Toby could pull his gun all the way around.

And once Toby was dead, Max Furling stood not knowing what to do.

"Empty your hand," Slocum said, and Max acted like a pet dog. Numbly, he dropped his pistol, which went *clunk* on the boardwalk. Slowly, his eyes never leaving Max's, Slocum knelt and picked up the gun. He said, "You got others on you?"

Max shook his head. He acted as if he were in shock, which was something you didn't see every day. Usually, captured owlhoots went down like wounded cougars—scrappy, and just as deadly, until the end.

Slocum said, "Pick him up." He indicated Toby Keith's body with one quick flick of his gun barrel.

Max's mouth began to move, but Slocum cut him off. "I said, pick him up. You're gonna drag him up the street for me."

Max bent to drag Toby up by his arms. Now, Max wasn't what Slocum would have called a big man, but Toby looked to have missed quite a few campfire calls. Max was able to lift him under the armpits to drag him backward. Toby's gun fell from his lifeless fingers.

When Max's eyes flicked toward the sound, Slocum

barked, "Leave it," and Max did. Slocum motioned again with his gun barrel. "Go on. Up the street."

Max began to move backward, dragging his partner's body. Slocum stuck Max's pistol in his belt and bent to grab up Toby's.

They continued, slowly, up the street. The sidewalk emptied before them as they made progress. As they approached, shoppers, businessmen, and on-leave sailors alike scattered and began to form a straggling, unorganized, gaping band in their wake.

Slocum heard the mutters from behind him.

"It's him! It's Slocum!"

"Who's the dead one?"

"What happened? Did you see?"

The murmurs grew to a clamor as they neared the marshal's office. They made enough noise that Marshal Denver opened the door and came outside, then down the street toward Slocum.

"What ya got for me today, Slocum?" he said, breaking out into a premature smile.

"Toby Keith and Max Furling," Slocum replied, without breaking the eye contact with Max, who was visibly tiring. Slocum made a small movement with his gun hand. "Stop."

Max halted, allowing the body of his dead partner to drop a little.

"No shit?" asked the marshal, even as he stepped in to move Max away from the body and quickly pat him down. At least Max had been a man of his word: the marshal came up empty.

"Step away from him," he told Max, then hollered out to the crowd, "Hey, somebody go tell the undertaker to pick up this body!" He drew his gun and then he pulled out a pair of handcuffs. "Thanks, Slocum. I'll take it from here."

Finally, Slocum relaxed a little. He didn't put his Colt away, though, until the marshal had Max Furling cuffed and steered toward the jail. His head down with an exhaustion he couldn't explain, Slocum dogged the marshal and his prisoner up the walk.

After all the paperwork was done, Slocum went back down to the cantina. He figured that Alba was going to start their reunion plenty pissed. But he also knew that once he gave him what was in his pocket, Juan would brighten up quite a bit.

He smiled to himself a little as he pushed open the saloon doors and proceeded inside.

He didn't spot Alba or Fan right away, though. Several men (who he assumed had been in the crowd behind him, earlier) came up to shake his hand or offer him a beer.

He didn't see Alba until he was almost to the stairs; he and Fan were at the rearmost table in the place, and Alba still had a grip on her arm.

"The stage, she took a long time to come in," Juan said sarcastically, as Slocum walked toward him. He didn't rise to greet him, either. Slocum could tell he was plenty angry about being left with the girl. Well, he had a right to be.

Slocum glanced at her. She was scowling.

"Hello, Fan," he said as he pulled out a chair, sat down, and began to dig in his pocket.

She didn't answer, just stared daggers at the bar behind him.

Slocum's digging fingers found their mark, and he

pulled the papers out of his pocket. "I see nothin' has much changed," he said, then handed Alba a new voucher for half the reward on Max Furling and Toby Keith. The reward was higher than in Arizona, as Slocum had suspected, and he presented Alba with a voucher for $1,200.

Alba looked at the paper, and his eyebrows shot up. "I am indeed in the wrong business!" he said as a smile of abject delight spread over his face. "Slocum, how?"

Slocum shrugged his shoulders, ordered a couple of beers for him and Juan (and a sarsaparilla for Fan), and told the tale. While he was telling them the story, he realized that he still had to go back and check on Fleet, but he finished the telling to the end, anyway.

During the talk, he'd been stopped a few times by people listening behind his back or at nearby tables. Somebody even asked for his autograph! They'd also ordered lunch, and Fan was enough taken by the story that Alba let go of her arm in time for her to take advantage of a thick roasted turkey sandwich.

"And so, why the voucher made out to me, amigo?" asked Juan.

Slocum was full of shrugs today, and he gave one to Juan. "Partners," he said.

"But I did not even go to the depot, Slocum. I did not even see these men!"

"You babysat," Slocum said, and gave Fannie a wink. He was feeling quite a bit better, now that he had the last of the damned Masterson gang taken care of, and also a thick beef sandwich in his belly.

Surprisingly, Fan returned his wink and said, "That's excellent, Mr. Slocum!"

"Thank you, Miss Fan," he answered with a bow of

his head. Maybe he could learn to like her? "By the way, I took your horse down to the livery and set him up. Which reminds me," he said, pushing his chair back and standing up again, "I've gotta go back down there and see to something."

Alba waved the voucher at him. "So this is mine? I can cash it?"

"Thanks for seeing to Spots," Fan chirped. "I woulda gone myself, but somebody had hold of my arm." She threw a glare at Alba, which was returned only by a sly, lady-killing smile. "For hours and hours!" she added.

"You're welcome, Fan," Slocum replied, and ignored the "making faces" game currently going on between her and Alba. Slocum should be paying attention, he knew, but Juan had a kid about her age down in Mexico. In fact, Juan was a papa several times over. "And yes," he added, switching his attention to Alba, "you can cash it."

"*Muy bueno, mi amigo!* No paperwork?"

"Not a scrap." He turned to leave and bumped straight into one of the men who'd congratulated him on his way in. Without a word, the man shoved one of those damn dime novels into his hand along with a pencil. It was *Slocum and the Big Roundup*. He signed his name on the front cover and handed it back, also without a word.

The man, hugging his book to his chest, began to sputter effusively, but Slocum didn't stick around for it. As he headed out the door he heard the man say, over the crowd, "The writer described him as a man of few words! Just wait till I get back down to the bakery and tell them that the famous Slocum didn't speak to me!"

Chuckling under his breath, Slocum headed down to the stable.

*   *   *

When he got there, another look at Fleet and a long conversation with the hostler revealed that exactly nothing was wrong, other than that the horse was pouting. Lack of exercise, Slocum figured, and ordered a turn-out for him.

Juan arrived at the bank moments after Slocum got there, and both men presented their vouchers. Slocum had his money wired to the Tombstone bank, while Alba requested his in cash. The clerk complied—and then asked Alba whether he'd like his $7,000 today.

"It has arrived already?" Alba asked enthusiastically.

"Yessir, just a few minutes ago."

"Yes, thank you, I would like it now," Alba said. He was likely amazed that the bank was offering money for free, Slocum thought. And the $1,200 still to come was a helluva lot of cash per hour for babysitting. "All of it," Juan added.

The clerk pushed a slip of paper toward him. "Just fill this out and sign here."

Slocum held back a chuckle. Juan was so excited that he almost forgot to sign for the cash with his false name. At that, Slocum had to cough to fight back the raucous bellow he found rising up his throat.

He succeeded, but it was a close call.

And then he remembered.

"Who's got Fan?"

Alba must have heard the panic rising in his voice, because he said, "Calm down, Slocum. I left her with Jorge, at the cantina."

Slocum's brows furrowed. "He trustworthy?" Slocum had known a lot of Jorges at a lot of cantinas. Too many, in fact, for him to trust this one.

Juan patted him on the back. "Relax. He is trustworthy because he knows I will give him ten dollars to get Miss Fan back in the exact same condition that she was in when I left." Alba grinned. "She will be fine, Slocum."

The clerk was back with Alba's money in hand, and Alba turned toward him while he counted it out.

Alba rode out later that afternoon with little fanfare, and Slocum was left with a girl he was supposed to take back but couldn't. At least, not today. Last time he'd checked, Spots was snoring in his stall.

So Fan stayed the night over at the hotel, in a room a couple of doors down from Slocum, and rose early the next morning with dishonest—or, at least, sneaky— intent. She snuck from the hotel and had made it half- way down to the stable when Slocum—who had already had breakfast, checked the horses, and had a nice little conversation with Forsythe's redhead—stepped out of the shelter of an alley and stopped her dead in her tracks.

After her shock at first seeing him when she thought she'd been so clever, she was sufficiently cowed to fol- low him back to the hotel, where he bought her break- fast and began to tell her what the redhead had told him.

"You know, you don't pick the client," he said as she attacked her flapjacks. "He picks you, and you gotta do what he says."

"Why are you tellin' me all this?" she asked, between bites.

"Because I think I know why you ran out on your aunt and uncle. And I'm seein' your whole life run out ahead of you, like a fairy-tale magic carpet. Except it ain't no fairy tale, Fan."

She wrinkled her brow. "Huh?"

He tried again, except this time, he was more graphic

in his details of the thing she was about to do to her life, and how to easily avoid it. "Besides," he added, "the man you're throwin' everything out the window for is gone, and he don't even like girls. You hear me, Fan? He don't even like girls!"

She heaved a little sigh, as if what he spoke of wasn't even possible. He knew just how she felt, actually. The redhead's story had shocked him down to the boots of his soul.

"It's the truth, honey," he said in a lower voice. "You coulda asked him yourself if you'd got here a few days earlier," he lied, "but you got here now, so I'm tellin' you now."

She began to cry.

Later, when they were out on the trail, she began to get hold of herself. The sobs, which at one time had grown to great heaves, were down to the occasional whimpering hiccough. Slocum thought she finally believed him. He'd walked her up to the cantina after breakfast and let the redhead have a talk with her, too.

He figured that the latter had finally convinced her. He found it sort of hard to believe, too. How could he not have known? Why, he'd spent most of the nights on the trail with Forsythe not even three feet away! He shook his head almost imperceptibly. How could anybody . . . how could any man consider women without wanting them? That's what he couldn't figure out.

"Slocum?" the girl said in a peep.

"What, hon?"

"Slocum, I believe you." She sniffed again.

"Sorry, honey."

She said, "So just don't talk about it again, all right? I just can't picture, I mean, I just can't figure . . ."

"All right, Fan."

From then on out, the trip went much smoother. So far as Slocum was concerned, it was almost pleasant. By the time they reached her new hometown and rode out to her aunt and uncle's place, everything was pretty normal. Well, pretty normal for a man traveling with a thirteen-year-old kid of the female variety.

Slocum lifted his hat and dipped his head in a little bow. "I'd admire to stop and have the noon meal, ma'am. Thank you in advance!"

Mary Forebush was smiling and as sweet as last time he'd been through, but he didn't envy Fan the tongue-lashing he knew was coming her way. He supposed he'd best have a word or two with Fan's uncle, as well.

He did. He supposed that he'd done the right thing in telling him, but he didn't expect the reaction it inspired. Very few of the men who had called Slocum a liar were still breathing, but he left Fan's uncle alive. And he rode out, without waiting for Aunt Mary's meal or to say a last good-bye to Fannie. He just wanted to get clear of the whole mess as fast as he could.

And he did.

A few days later, he and Fleet arrived at the ferry where they could cross back into Arizona. The ferry was a welcome sight, but the gunshots that rang out from across the river weren't. Slocum dived down to the ground behind a water trough and pulled his gun. He'd have rather had his rifle, but it was in Fleet's boot, and he wasn't going to chance catching the horse to grab the rifle off his saddle.

He had thrown himself to the ground right next to the ferryman—who had headed for the horse trough, too— and Slocum asked, "Who the hell is that?"

The ferryman shook his head, then pulled off his hat to slap it against his leg. "It's that danged Ruben Clifford, that's who. He's always comin' round when he's drunk. Always shootin' up the store! Ain't we got enough woes already?"

Slocum didn't know about—or much care—what their woes were. He just wanted the fellow across the river to stop shooting so that he could get on his way.

Two hours later he was still pinned down, along with the ferryman, and the water trough had sprouted several leaks. A little stream poured from the trough to Slocum's hat and to the ground, further muddying his knees.

"Shit!" he shouted. "Why don't you just fall over like a regular drunk?"

He ducked when the next few slugs came across the river, and one of them created another leak in the trough—this time above the ferryman.

"Oh, fine!" the man sputtered. "He's bad enough when he's on just a regular toot, but you gotta come along and antagonize him!"

"Hell, I didn't do anything to him!" Slocum shouted over the gun noise. The man across the river was on a real toot, all right. Slocum sent two more slugs his way.

Abruptly, the shooting stopped.

Slocum chanced a peek over the edge of the trough. He could see nothing.

An old man, the one Slocum remembered buying the oranges and heroin from, came out of the store and stood on the porch. "You're clear!" he bellowed through his cupped hands.

Ruben Clifford, the ferryman told him, must have finally passed out. Slocum didn't think there was much love lost between them.

Slocum loaded his horse on the ferry, then crossed the river. About halfway across, he asked, "Does he ever wake up and start shootin' again?"

"A little late to be askin' that," said the ferryman, whose name, he had learned during their time in the dirt together, was Bob. "No, never has. But there's a first time for everything."

"Great," Slocum said, and sat on the bench.

When they gained the other bank and pulled the ferry into its wooden stall, he led Fleet off and up the bank. "That's quite a welcome wagon you got there," he said to the old man.

The man crossed his arms, tilted his head, and said, "Not no more."

When Slocum made it to the store, the ferryman hard on his heels, he finally saw Ruben Clifford. He was sprawled in the dirt, and he was sure enough dead. There was a round hole high on one side of Clifford's forehead and a bigger one low in the back of his skull.

Slocum had been the only one firing back at him. It was his kill, all right.

He leaned back against the horse rail and sighed, "Shit. Hope he wasn't kin to either of you fellers."

"He wasn't kin to no one that I know of. But they'll be glad to see him up to Half Moon Crossin'," said the storekeeper.

"Oh, they will," echoed Bob. "That they will."

Slocum's face perked up. "Why? He wanted?"

Bob, the ferryman, nodded. "Oh, yeah." The shop-keeper nodded his agreement.

Slocum said, "How much?"

Bob scratched the back of his head. "It was a couple hundred, last I heard."

The storekeeper cut in, "But that was afore he killed Jason, wasn't it, Bob?"

Bob finally said, "I believe that there's the case. Killin' somebody would have added somethin' to it, all right. You gonna claim the reward?" he asked Slocum.

As if there was any other option. Slocum said, "This man got a horse?"

And within the hour, Slocum was riding north, lead-ing Ruben Clifford—a thirty-ish, unwashed trail hand, wanted for killing Jason Somebody—behind him on Ruben's chestnut, fiddle-fronted mare.

"I don't get it," Slocum muttered as he rode along, leading the horse. "Lately, people just keep comin' up to me askin' to be killed."

But at least the man would bring him a little more money, and he wouldn't be shooting up any more un-suspecting travelers. As for Slocum, he wouldn't have to explain himself to some sheriff.

It's not so bad, he thought, *livin' the life I chose.*

He smiled a little.

No, it wasn't so bad.

Not so bad at all.

Watch for

SLOCUM AND THE FOUR SEASONS

377th novel in the exciting SLOCUM series
from Jove

Coming in July!

THE MANY-SPLENDORED
FISHES OF THE ATLANTIC COAST
INCLUDING THE
FISHES OF THE GULF OF MEXICO,
FLORIDA, BERMUDA, THE
BAHAMAS
AND THE CARIBBEAN

408 FISHES IN FULL COLOR

by Gar Goodson

Illustrated by Phillip J. Weisgerber

•

Graphic Design and Cover by Robert Shepard

•

Published by Marquest Colorguide Books
Palos Verdes Estates, California

INTRODUCTION

Although written primarily as a fishwatcher's guide, this book is also aimed at catching the interest of those who have never looked beneath the surface of the sea. West Atlantic reefs are a fishwatcher's paradise, as evidenced in these pages. There is no other experience in the world quite like a diver's first tour of an underwater reef. Whether in temperate waters or tropical coral reefs, one finds an unforgettable realm of oceanic blue, teeming reef fish colonies, towering, mysterious reef formations, brilliant sea grass and algae beds, all glistening and sparkling in the sea-filtered sunlight. No special diving skills, exotic equipment or deep water dives are required to make a tour of the reefs. Most of the fishes shown here can be seen while snorkeling on the surface over shallow water reefs (5 to 20 foot depths) with a face mask, snorkel tube and swim fins. The ability to swim is all that is required. See page 202 for diving tips for beginners.

This guidebook is designed for the fishwatcher; that non-technical, curious person, whether casual tourist-swimmer, skin or SCUBA diver, fisherman or aquarist who seeks to know more about the abundant and beautiful marine life of the West Atlantic. No special knowledge of fishes is required to comprehend this book other than a general understanding of fish anatomy. The illustration at right identifies the parts of a fish.

I have sought to be as accurate as possible in describing in words and pictures 378 West Atlantic fish species, with particular focus on those commonly sighted by divers, taken by fishermen or collectors, or found in the marketplace. For each fish family I have provided information, when known, about behavioral and breeding patterns, color variations, attack and defense behavior and other distinguishing characteristics. For each fish species I have provided the common name in English, the Spanish common name (in parentheses), the scientific name, maximum size (total length), salient characteristics of the fish, range and edibility. One hundred and eighty-two of the 378 species described here, including virtually all of the common food and game fishes, have a Spanish common name. It is hoped that this will make the book helpful to Spanish-speaking, as well as English-speaking fish-watchers.

To assist the reader in visualizing the vast West Atlantic, and to aid in locating the range of specific fishes, I have provided maps of the area on pages 203 and 204. The West Atlantic is shown from Labrador to Brazil, along with a more detailed map of the Gulf of Mexico, Florida, the Bahamas and Caribbean areas. Of special interest to fishwatchers are the underwater parks. The John Pennekamp Coral Reef State Park in the Florida Keys (see page 204) is highly recommended for beginning divers and experienced aquanauts. The State of Florida has declared 75 square miles of splendid coral reef as an underwater park where no spear fishing or taking of reef animals is allowed. Buck Island near St. Croix in the U.S. Virgin Islands was declared a national monument by President Kennedy in 1961 because of the magnificent barrier reef surrounding the eastern half of the island. A remarkable underwater snorkeling trail has been provided for fishwatchers (see page 204). It is my hope that this book will encourage the establishment of many new underwater parks, trails and reefs throughout the West Atlantic.

A final and important objective of this book is to remind the coastal states of the U.S., and the islands of the West Indies, of the magnificent and highly perishable resource that lies just off their shores. New measures of conservation and reef management are critically needed. Most of our coral reefs are now still intact, but these fragile structures can be seriously damaged or destroyed

THE PARTS OF A FISH

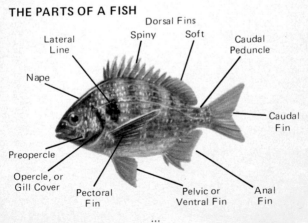

Dorsal Fins
Spiny Soft
Lateral Line
Caudal Peduncle
Nape
Caudal Fin
Preopercle
Opercle, or Gill Cover
Pectoral Fin
Pelvic or Ventral Fin
Anal Fin

by overfishing, careless coastal and harbor developments, landfills, sewage, industrial wastes and careless divers, fish collectors and fishermen. The recent butchering of Florida's coast by an army of bulldozers is a prime example of the danger threatening littoral zones throughout the West Atlantic.

The establishment of city, state and national underwater parks and preserves is a key step in reef preservation. Fishes and other creatures of the sea need not be hunted to extinction or driven from their habitats. They are fascinating, beautiful animals to study and admire, deserving of our care and concern. The wilderness question is especially applicable to the reefs of the West Atlantic. Will we have to tell our grandchildren about the wilderness that was, and the underwater world of the reefs that used to be? Or can we preserve these frontiers, so that they can find them as we did, and experience the same joy and admiration?

I am especially indebted to Dr. Camm C. Swift, Associate Curator of Fishes at the Los Angeles County Museum of Natural History. His years of experience in the study of Florida and other West Atlantic fishes, his careful review of these pages prior to presstime, and his counseling and recommendations as to areas of research were invaluable aids in the preparation of this book. I am also indebted to Mssrs. J. E. Bohlke and C. G. Chaplin for their monumental work "Fishes of the Bahamas and Adjacent Tropical Waters," to Mr. J. E. Randall for his excellent "Caribbean Reef Fishes," to Mssrs. W. A. Starck and R. H. Chesher for their comprehensive work on Florida's Alligator Reef, to W. Beebe and J. Tee-van for their "Field Book of the Shore Fishes of Bermuda and the West Indies," and many others too numerous to mention here. Acknowledgements to these and many other authors whose works were valuable in compiling this book are made in a detailed bibliography and list of reference reading on page 191. Special appreciation is also due to Mr. R. Stuart Johnson, Vice President and Manager of the California First Bank in Manhattan Beach, California for his counseling in the considerable financing required to produce this book, and to Robert D. Kennedy for his willing assistance in the timetaking process of editing and review.

CONTENTS

SEA BASSES AND GROUPERS

Striped bass, striper, rock, rockfish *Morone saxatilis* To 5 feet. Prime target of surf fishermen on both east and west coasts of the U.S., this splendid bass is sought for its tenacious fighting ability, its striped beauty and its excellence as a table fish. The rod and reel record is 72 pounds on 50 pound line. A temperate bass of the Percichthyidae family, the striped bass in anadromous like the salmon, migrating up streams to spawn. **Range:** St. Lawrence River to Florida and through the Gulf of Mexico to Louisiana. **Edibility:** excellent.

The West Atlantic is especially favored in having a splendid array of basses and groupers. They include some of the finest food fishes, and range in size from the tiny, brilliant basslets through the colorful hamlets to the large and magnificent striped, speckled and spotted groupers. The handsome striped bass excited the admiration of the early colonists to New England over 360 years ago. Captain John Smith wrote: "The basse is an excellent fish, both fresh and salte. They are so large, the head of one will give a good eater a dinner, & for daintinesse of diet they excell the Marybones of Beefe."

☐ Groupers and seabasses (family Serranidae) are bottom dwellers. They either sit on the bottom in caves or reef crevices or roam across the bottom. Many of them have large, gaping mouths indicating their carnivorous feeding habits. The identification and classification of the serranids has been and continues to be a difficult task. This is due in part to the fact that many basses, like their cousins the wrasses, are highly changeable in sex and coloration. Groupers are accomplished quick-change artists,

1

adept at changing their colors to match their background. They can flash from spots to stripes, blotches, bars or solid colors as they move from coral to rock to sandy bottom. Many species show a distinct difference in color with depth. Fishes taken from deeper waters have much more red coloration. This highly developed ability to change coloration protects them from larger predators, and enables them to prey effectively on smaller fishes.

☐ Some groupers seem to change their coloration wildly at feeding time. In writing about the Indo-Pacific cerise grouper (*Variola louti*), the aquarist Graham Cox states that "when at rest, it is an uninspiring russet-brown with a hint of blue spots scattered over its body. If a small, live fish is introduced into the tank, a miraculous change in appearance occurs. Almost imperceptibly at first, then with gathering momentum, the fish's whole body becomes suffused with an indescribable shade of red. Small islets of sapphire-blue radiate a strange glow as the fish's body pulsates with light a few seconds before the 'grouper lunge.' After capturing the fish, the grouper's colors subside until the next mealtime."

Black sea bass *Centropristis striata* To 22 inches. A very popular bottom fish among sport fishermen along the Atlantic coast, from southern Massachusetts to northern Florida. Two closely related species, *C. philadelphica* (rock sea bass) and *C. ocyurus* (bank sea bass) range from South Carolina south thru the Gulf of Mexico. Although related to the striped bass, this sea bass is exclusively marine, never venturing into rivers or streams. An excellent food fish with fine, white flaky flesh. Averaging 1½ to 3 pounds it will run occasionally to 5 pounds. **Range:** southern Massachusetts to northern Florida. **Edibility:** excellent.

Nassau grouper (cherna criolla) *Epinephelus striatus* To 4 feet. This beautifully colored fish is the least wary and most friendly of all the groupers. If once offered food, it will return again and again to pester divers for handouts. It is most like the red grouper in appearance, but has much bolder stripes , a black spot or saddle at the base of the soft dorsal, and notched dorsal spines (the red groupers' dorsal is smooth). A notorious color-changer, the Nassau grouper can blend perfectly into any background, from pale white to solid black. A very important food fish in the West Indies. **Range:** North Carolina and Bermuda south to the 'hump' of Brazil, including the Gulf of Mexico. **Edibility:** good.

Speckled hind, calico grouper *Epinephelus drummondhayi* To 20 inches. Distinctive for being the only grouper covered with small white spots on the body and all fins. One of the smaller groupers, it is rather rare over its range. **Range:** Bermuda, South Carolina, and Florida, including the Gulf of Mexico. **Edibility:** good.

Snowy grouper, golden grouper, (mero, cherna) *Epinephelus niveatus* To about 2½ feet. Young are easily recognized by the pearly white dots on body. Over 15 inches, these dots begin to fade. Large adults move well offshore to 1500 feet depths and take on a coppery gold coloration with up to 18 dark stripes on the sides. **Range:** New England to southeastern Brazil, including the Gulf of Mexico. **Edibility:** good.

☐ The sexual life of the serranids is even more surprising. Some are functional hermaphrodites: certain species of *Serranus* and *Hypoplectrus* basses are both male and female at the same time. Most groupers mature first as females and produce eggs. Later in life they reverse sex to become functioning males, which then fertilize the young females. The term "grouper" is usually applied to the larger basses belonging to the genera *Epinephelus* and *Mycteroperca*. It is a misnomer, since most large sea basses live solitarily in reef holes, crevices and burrows. They do not swim together in groups or aggregations. Serranids range in size from a few inches to 8 feet in length and 1000 pounds in weight. In the West Atlantic the largest grouper (the jewfish) attains a weight of 800 pounds. In the Indo-Pacific there have been accounts of divers being stalked and swallowed alive by giant groupers. Some groupers, especially the Nassau grouper, become quite tame after repeated contacts with divers. Some of the smaller forms of serranids and serranid allies, including the hamlets (*Hypoplectrus* species), soapfishes (Grammistidae) and fairy basslets (Grammidae) are included here, although their precise classification and even their inclusion with the serranids is not agreed upon by all ichthyologists.

Red grouper (cherna Americana, mero, cherna de vivero) *Epinephelus morio* To 3 feet. The most abundant species of the genus, this handsome grouper is heavily fished from Virginia to Texas. Easily separable from other groupers by the elevation of the second dorsal spine, and green eyes. Highly changeable in color. Can easily be mistaken for the Nassau grouper, which see. **Range:** New England and Bermuda to Brazil, including the Gulf of Mexico. **Edibility:** good.

Red hind (cabrilla, tofia) *Epinephelus guttatus* To 1½ feet. The common grouper of Florida, the Gulf of Mexico and the West Indies, ranging north to North Carolina. Easily hooked or speared close inshore and on offshore banks. Party boats take this fish off the bottom using large cut baits. Can be mistaken for the rock hind, but the red hind has no large black spots on the back. **Range:** Bermuda and North Carolina to Brazil, including the Gulf of Mexico. **Edibility:** good.

Rock hind (cabra mora, mero cabrilla) *Epinephelus adscensionis* To 1½ feet. This splendid grouper is very common in the West Atlantic. It is often seen over rocky bottoms in shallows of 10 feet of water or less. Can easily be confused with the red hind, but note the 4 to 5 large black spots along the dorsal, and the black saddle spot behind the soft dorsal. It is a more wary fish than the red hind, and more at home in inshore water turbulence. **Range:** New England and Bermuda to southeastern Brazil, including the Gulf of Mexico. **Edibility:** excellent.

5

Jewfish (guasa mero) *Epinephelus itajara* To 8 feet. This is the giant sea bass of the Western Atlantic. A record 7 foot jewfish was taken off Florida that weighed 680 pounds. Makes its home in large caves, coral crevices, sunken wrecks and under ledges, and when hooked, heads straight for its burrow. **Range:** Bermuda and Bahamas to southeastern Brazil, including the Gulf of Mexico. **Edibility:** excellent.

Mutton hamlet (cherna, guaseta) *Epinephelus afer* To 1 foot. A strange little seabass, closely related to the groupers, but more often a resident of sea-grass beds, rather than reef holes and crevices. Also distinctive for the stout spine on its cheek (covered by skin) possessed by no other grouper. (Previously known as *Alphestes afer*.) **Range:** Bermuda, Bahamas and Florida to Argentina. **Edibility:** good.

Warsaw grouper, black grouper (garrupa negrita, guasa mero) *Epinephelus nigritus* To 6 feet. Another monster of a grouper distinguishable from the jewfish by its brown color and its long dorsal spines (the jewfish has short dorsal spines). One of the best fighters of the groupers, usually found in deep, offshore water. Common along the Northern Gulf of Mexico. **Range:** Massachusetts to Brazil including the Gulf of Mexico. **Edibility:** good.

Marbled grouper *Epinephelus inermis* To 3 feet. A rare grouper taken occasionally off southern Florida. Said to be a secretive fish, prone to dart for reef caves and grottos when alarmed. Young are dark brown with scattered white spots. (Previously known as *Dermatolepis inermis*.) **Range:** southern Florida and the West Indies to Brazil. **Edibility:** fair.

Coney (guativere, corruncha) *Epinephelus fulva* To 1 foot. The coney exhibits a number of color phases, including the bi-color phase shown (thought to be an excitement phase), the golden phase, and the common phase, when the fish is a solid, dark reddish-brown. Note the two distinct spots just behind the soft dorsal and two more spots on the lower jaw, very evident in all color phases. (Previously known as *Cephalopholis fulva*.) **Range:** Bermuda, Bahamas and southern Florida to Brazil, including the Gulf of Mexico. **Edibility:** good.

Graysby (enjambre, cuna cabrilla) *Epinephelus cruentatum* To 1 foot. Another color changer capable of switching its ground color from pale white to brown, and even occasionally taking on a banded pattern not unlike the Nassau grouper. The best identifiers are the 4 or 5 distinct spots at the base of the dorsal fin. *Petrometopon cruentatum* is a synonym. **Range:** Bermuda, Bahamas and Florida to Brazil, including the Gulf of Mexico. **Edibility:** good.

Yellowmouth grouper (abadejo) *Mycteroperca interstitialis* To 30 inches. Distinctive for its yellow mouth, faint brownish body marblings and the narrow yellow margins on virtually all fins. Popular with sport fishermen. Juveniles are sharply bi-colored—dark above and white below. **Range:** Cape Cod, Bermuda, Bahamas and Florida to Brazil. **Edibility:** good.

Scamp, salmon rockfish (abadejo, cuna garopa) *Mycteroperca phenax* To 2 feet. Though rare, the scamp is considered the finest food fish of all the groupers. Similar to the yellowmouth grouper but the brown spots on the scamp tend to run together to form hazy bands, and the fins are spotted. **Range:** Cape Cod to Florida; common in the Gulf of Mexico and in the southern Caribbean. **Edibility:** excellent.

Gag, black grouper *Mycteroperca microlepis* To 3 feet. An excellent game and table fish, the gag is distinctive for the tiger stripes radiating from the eye, and the vague, scrawled body markings. It is often taken with the red grouper along Florida coasts. Many fishermen locate grouper reefs by trolling a plug just over the bottom and tossing a buoy overboard when a gag hits the lure. **Range:** Atlantic and Gulf Coast of U.S. to Brazil. **Edibility:** excellent.

Tiger grouper (bonaci gato) *Mycteroperca tigris* To 30 inches. Easily recognized by its bold 'tiger' stripes and the trailing tags that large individuals develop on the dorsal, anal and caudal fins. Often encountered near-shore at depths from 10 to 30 feet. Like the yellowfin, the tiger grouper will rise from 50 foot depths to take a surface lure. **Range:** Bermuda, Bahamas and Florida to northern coast of Brazil, southern Gulf of Mexico. **Edibility:** good.

8

Black grouper (bonaci arara, aguaji) *Mycteroperca bonaci* To 4 feet. An excellent sportfish, this grouper is notable for its size (often exceeds 50 pounds and has been reported to reach 180 pounds) and its ability to change color. It can change to a dark reddish gray, to a solid black, or it can flash to a very pale coloration. Note narrow orange margins on pectoral fins. **Range:** Massachusetts, Bermuda, Bahamas and Florida to southeastern Brazil, including the Gulf of Mexico. **Edibility:** good.

Yellowfin grouper, black grouper (bonaci de piedra, bonaci cardinal, cuna) *Mycteroperca venenosa* To 3 feet. Often confused with the closely related black grouper, the yellowfin has definite broad yellow margins on its pectoral fins. This fish is adept at changing its color, from solid black to near-red to pale green, as the background requires. **Range:** Bermuda, Bahamas and Florida to Brazil, including the Gulf of Mexico. **Edibility:** good, but large yellowfins may be toxic in ciguatera-prone areas. See page 39.

Comb grouper (cuna negra) *Mycteroperca rubra* To 30 inches. A common grouper in the southern Caribbean, this fish has bold markings when young. As the fish matures, the markings fade and become less distinct. Also, occurs in the eastern Atlantic from the Mediterranean to the Congo. **Range:** West Indies to Brazil, including the Gulf of Mexico. **Edibility:** good.

9

Sand perch (bolo) *Diplectrum formosum* To 1 foot. These little seabasses will excavate a burrow in the reef bottom which they use until they have outgrown it. Highly changeable in color, they can switch their pattern from vertical bars (when at rest) to longitudinal stripes (when moving). **Range:** North Carolina, Florida, the Bahamas to Uruguay, including the Gulf of Mexico. **Edibility:** good.

Lantern bass *Serranus baldwini* To 2½ inches. Often found in seagrass beds, as well as around rocks, coral rubble and shell fragments from the shoreline to 250 foot depths. Individuals from deeper water are suffused with much more red and yellow. **Range:** The Bahamas, and Florida to Surinam. **Edibility:** poor.

Chalk bass *Serranus tortugarum* To 3½ inches. A tiny, deepwater basslet, this little fish has been seen at depths from 40 to 150 feet hovering in small groups over patches of coral rubble. It has been taken at depths of 1320 feet. Appears to be a plankton feeder. **Range:** southern Florida, Bahamas and the West Indies to Honduras. **Edibility:** poor.

Harlequin bass *Serranus tigrinus* To 4 inches. This spotted beauty is a common basslet found from the shoreline out to 120 feet. Fond of seagrass beds, coral and rocks, the harlequin bass feeds mainly on crustaceans. **Range:** Bermuda, Bahamas and southern Florida to Yucatan. **Edibility:** poor.

Orangeback bass *Serranus annularis* To 3½ inches. This brilliant little seabass is not seen by many divers since its preferred depth range is 100 to 200 feet. It is frequently seen in pairs, swimming close to the bottom. **Range:** Bermuda, Bahamas and south Florida to Brazil. **Edibility:** poor.

Belted sandfish *Serranus subligarius* To 3 inches. Lives at moderate depths off the coasts of southern U.S. Has been taken in such varying locales as Beaufort, North Carolina, Charleston and Pensacola. This fish became famous for its reproductive powers when an isolated belted sandfish in an aquarium fertilized its own eggs. **Range:** see above. **Edibility:** poor.

Swissguard basslet, peppermint basslet *Liopropoma rubre* To 3½ inches. Unfortunately this brilliant beauty is a very shy, secretive fish, living deep in the recesses of reef caves and crevices, thus it is rarely seen by divers. When placed in an aquarium, it may be weeks before this fish will venture out of hiding. Found over a depth range from 10 to 140 feet. **Range:** Bahamas, Florida Keys to Curacao and Yucatan. **Edibility:** poor.

Candy basslet *Liopropoma carmabi* To 2 inches. Quite similar to the Swissguard basslet, and with the same, secretive habits. Note the differences in coloration and striping. Also, the candy basslet has no spot on the anal fin, and the two spots on the caudal fin lobes are clearly separated by blue lines. **Range:** Bahamas, Puerto Rico, Barbados, Bonaire and Curacao. **Edibility:** poor.

Ridgeback basslet, cave bass *Liopropoma mowbrayi* To 3¼ inches. Not previously recorded from the U.S. until W.A. Starck sighted one of these elusive cave dwellers on Alligator Reef off the Florida Keys. Lives in caves and crevices at depths of from 100 to 180 feet. **Range:** Bermuda, Bahamas, Florida Keys, Puerto Rico and Curacao. **Edibility:** poor.

Tobaccofish (guatacare de canto) *Serranus tabacarius* To 6½ inches. The light portions of this fish may vary from bright yellow to pale white. Sometimes it is suffused with rose-red tints, other times with olive. A solitary fish, it ranges from 3 to 250 feet. **Range:** Bermuda, Bahamas and south Florida and throughout the West Indies. **Edibility:** poor.

12

Butter hamlet (vaca) *Hypoplectrus unicolor* To 5 inches. The hamlets are small seabasses distinctive for their often lavish coloration, and for their deeper, foreshortened, almost snapper-like body profile. They tend to slink, catlike, about the reef in a deliberate manner, as though stalking other fishes. Even though many of the hamlets were first described by the Cuban ichthyologist Felipe Poey y Aloy in 1852, very little is known about them to date. Many of them are quite rare, and some of them are found only at 100 to 140 foot depths.   The butter hamlet is quite common in the Florida Keys, and Cervigon reports that it is abundant off Western Venezuela, but it appears to be fairly rare in the Caribbean. **Range:** Bermuda, Bahamas, Florida to Brazil. **Edibility:** poor.

Blue hamlet *Hypoplectrus gemma* To 5 inches. This rare hamlet, a splendid iridescent blue animal, is so far reported only from Florida, although it is probably more widespread. Starck reports that it is common at Alligator Reef in the Florida Keys. **Range:** southern Florida. **Edibility:** poor.

Barred hamlet, banded hamlet (vaca) *Hypoplectrus puella* To 6 inches. This is the most common hamlet, often seen picking stealthily about shallow reefs, especially in the West Indies. Scientists of the Tektite II Program found it to be very common at Lameshur Bay in the Virgin Islands, and Starck lists it as "occasional" at Alligator Reef in the Florida Keys. **Range:** Bermuda, Bahamas, Florida Keys, Gulf Coast of Florida, West Indies. **Edibility:** poor.

Golden hamlet (vaca) *Hypoplectrus gummigutta* To 5 inches. Apparently a deep-water hamlet. Bohlke and Chaplin report one individual taken at 120 feet in the Exumas, Bahamas. Poey found it to be fairly common around Cuba. **Range:** Bahamas, Cuba, Jamaica, Dominican Republic. **Edibility:** poor.

14

Yellowtail hamlet *Hypoplectrus chlorurus* To 5 inches. Distinctive for its dark body with the bright yellow caudal fin. Reported from the West Indies, Venezuela, and from the southern Texas coast, where it was found around shallow, rocky wharves. **Range:** see above. **Edibility:** poor.

Shy hamlet (vaca) *Hypoplectrus guttavarius* To 5 inches. A beautiful little seabass, apparently very shy, which has been taken only in the Bahamas, Florida Keys and in scattered locales in the West Indies. Poey reported it to be fairly common off Cuba. **Range:** see above. **Edibility:** poor.

Yellowbelly hamlet (vaca) *Hypoplectrus aberrans* To 5 inches. So far recorded from the Florida Keys and the West Indies. Tektite II scientists observed a few of these at Lameshur Bay, Virgin Islands. **Range:** Southern Florida and the West Indies. **Edibility:** poor.

Indigo hamlet (vaca) *Hypoplectrus indigo* To 5½ inches. A blue version of the barred hamlet, so far taken from the Bahamas, Florida, Cuba, Haiti, Jamaica and off Honduras. **Range:** see above. **Edibility:** poor.

Black hamlet (vaca) *Hypoplectrus nigricans* To 6 inches. Differs from other hamlets in its dark bluish-black coloration and in the longer pelvic fins of adult fishes. Can be mistaken for a damselfish when seen on the reef. **Range:** Bahamas, Florida, West Indies. **Edibility:** poor.

16

Fairy basslet, royal gramma *Gramma loreto* To 3 inches. The fairy basslets (Grammidae family) are small, brilliantly colored allies of the groupers and seabasses. Five species are known from the tropical Western Atlantic. Two of the most attractive and best known are the fairy basslet and the blackcap basslet. Favorites of aquarists and rare fish fanciers, they are spectacular showpieces for any aquarium. The fairy basslet is usually found hiding in caves, holes or under ledges over a depth range from a few feet to 200 feet. Bohlke and Chaplin report it is common everywhere in the Bahamas. Groups of 2 or 3 to a dozen or more cluster in the same cave. **Range:** Bermuda and the Bahamas through the Caribbean to Venezuela. **Edibility:** poor.

Blackcap basslet *Gramma melacara* To 4 inches. So far known only from the Bahamas and the islands off British Honduras, this lovely magenta-hued basslet is exceedingly abundant at 100 and 200 foot depths, where it is found under overhangs and in crevices of the extremity of the offshore bank. **Range:** See above. **Edibility:** poor.

Creole fish (rabirubia de lo alto) *Paranthias furcifer* To 11 inches. A handsome, flame-colored fish which, like the creole wrasse and blue chromis, is often seen in small schools high in the water column, feeding on the tiny plankton that swarm about the reef. Note the 3 bold white spots along the back. **Range:** Bermuda and southern Florida to Brazil, including the Gulf of Mexico. **Edibility:** fair.

Greater soapfish (pez jabon) *Rypticus saponaceus* To 13 inches. The soapfishes (family Grammistidae) are small, bass-like fishes named for the suds-like mucus they produce when they are caught or handled. In some species (*Rypticus saponaceus* is one) this mucus is toxic, perhaps serving to ward off predators. **Range:** Bermuda, Bahamas and Florida to Brazil, including the Central American coast. **Edibility:** poor.

JACKS, POMPANOS, PERMITS, SCAD

Horse-eye jack (ojo gordo) *Caranx latus* To 2½ feet. Often confused with the crevalle jack, but easily distinguished by the large eye, black dorsal fin, yellow tail, and numerous other characteristics. Often enters fresh water. An inquisitive, bold jack, the horse-eye will approach a diver closely. Occasionally implicated in ciguatera poisoning in the West Indies. Young have 6 body bands. **Range:** New Jersey and Bermuda to southeastern Brazil, including the Gulf of Mexico. **Edibility:** good—see above.

Pound for pound the offshore jack fishes of the Carangidae family are the fastest, most voracious fishes of the sea. They are deep water fishes that range the ocean in roving predaceous schools. Frequently they will sweep in over the reefs to feed on resident fishes. Jacks depend on their speed of attack to kill. Their speed and tenacity provide a real challenge to the fisherman that hooks one. It is the toughest fighting fish for its size known. The jack will rarely break out of the water, but takes punishing runs and dives for deep water, and never gives in until it is completely exhausted. Even small juvenile 4 to 8 inch jacks are dauntless fighters.

☐ West Atlantic jacks display a wide range of body shapes and sizes. The roving offshore jacks include the moderately deep-bodied jacks of the genus *Caranx*, the amberjacks (*Seriola*), the cigar-shaped scads (*Decapterus*)

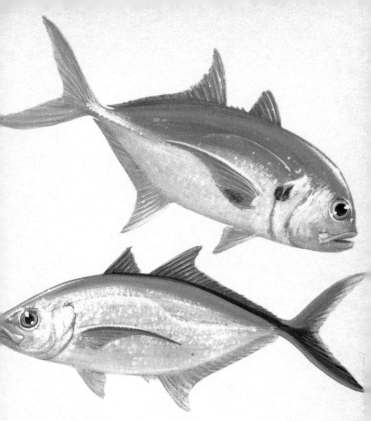

.Bar jack, skip jack (cibi mancho, cojinua) *Caranx ruber* To 2 feet. The bar jack is the most common West Indian jack, frequently seen by divers over the reefs. It is a splendid fish to see underwater. In the sunlight the sky blue bar bordered by black along the dorsal fin base gleams like a ribbon of blue neon. Young to 5 inches have about 7 dark bars on body. **Range:** New Jersey south to Bermuda, Bahamas, Florida, through Antilles to Venezuela, including the Gulf of Mexico. **Edibility:** good — excellent when smoked.

Crevalle jack, common jack, cavally (caballa, jiguagua, jurel, toro) *Caranx hippos* To 3½ feet. An abundant jack, valuable as a food fish, especially in Central American markets. Smaller fishes are said to be good eating, but individuals over 1½ feet are reported to be dark and almost tasteless. A fierce, stubborn and tenacious gamefish, a 20-pounder may take an hour to land on light tackle. **Range:** Nova Scotia to Uruguay including the Gulf of Mexico. **Edibility:** see above.

20

and the rainbow runner (*Elagatis*). The deep-bodied and compressed pompanos, permits and palometas (*Trachinotus* and *Alectis*), and the highly-compressed and high-browed lookdowns (*Selene*) are for the most part inshore fishes that feed on mollusks, small fishes, sea urchins and crustaceans found over sand flats, reefs and mud bottoms. These fishes make excellent eating. Some of the larger offshore jacks, including the amberjack, almaco jack, yellow jack, horse-eye jack and black jack are suspected of carrying ciguatera poisoning, especially large adults of these species. Where the fish poisoning problem is serious, as in certain West Indian locales, hungry natives will not take large adults of these fishes as a gift. (See "Ciguatera Poisoning," page 39).

☐ The bar jack is one of the most common jacks, often seen by divers around inshore reefs and jetties. It schools seasonally in enormous shoals of thousands of fishes, called 'passing jack' in the Bahamas. An excellent game fish and one of the best eating of the *Caranx* jacks is the blue runner. Schools sweep in over the reefs occasionally to feed on smaller fishes, but rarely linger. The colorful amberjack is a large fighting jack that dwells well off-

Blue runner, hard-tailed jack (atun, caballa) *Caranx fusus* To 2½ feet. This fish and the crevalle jack are the most abundant jacks of the eastern seaboard of the U.S. Also very common in the Gulf of Mexico. Divers often see them hovering singly, in pairs or pods around reefs, docks and jetties. Young have 8 vertical bands across body. Previously known as *Caranx crysos*. **Range:** Nova Scotia to southeastern Brazil, including the Gulf of Mexico. **Edibility:** good.

Yellow jack (cibi amarillo, cojinua) *Caranx bartholomaei* To 3 feet. Occasionally confused with the blue runner and bar jack, but the yellow jack is usually suffused with yellow (fins and body), lacks the spot on the gill cover of the blue runner, and has no dorsal-to-tail bar like the bar jack. Tiny ¾ inch young have 5 body bars. **Range:** New England to the hump of Brazil, including the Gulf of Mexico. **Edibility:** fair to good. A market fish in the West Indies, occasionally implicated in ciguatera poisoning.

Black jack (cibi negro) *Caranx lugubris* To 3 feet. An unusual jack in many respects, this rare fish is reported to be world-wide in tropical waters, principally from isolated or offshore islands. It is a sport fish of some importance off the Bahama Banks. **Range:** circumtropical—in the West Atlantic from Bermuda and the Bahamas to southeastern Brazil, including offshore in the Gulf of Mexico. **Edibility:** implicated in ciguatera poisoning in the West Indies and the Indo-Pacific. Larger fish are more toxic.

22

African pompano, Atlantic threadfin (flechudo) *Alectis crinitus* To 3 feet. Not a true pompano, this carangid is closely related to the Indo-Pacific threadfin, *Alectis ciliaris.* The illustration shows the surprising difference between a small juvenile and a large adult. So different in appearance are the two that adults were once mistakenly classed as a separate species, *Hynnis cubensis* (the "Cuban jack"). A fine game fish, usually taken by trolling. **Range:** Massachusetts to Brazil, including the Gulf of Mexico. **Edibility:** fair.

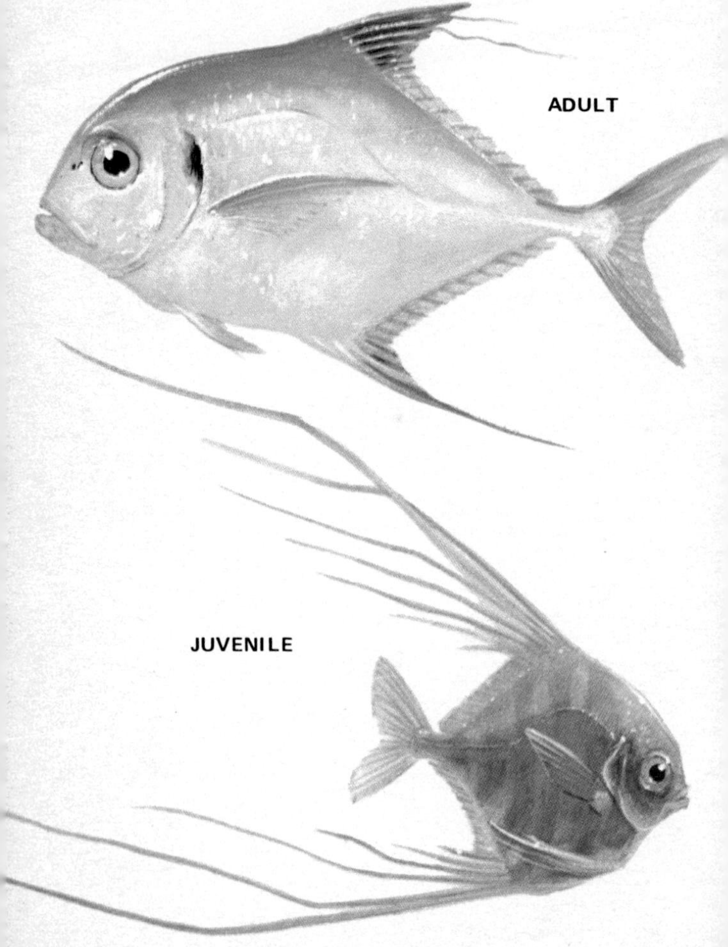

ADULT

JUVENILE

23

shore in fairly deep water. It sounds with speed and power and is a popular game fish. The rainbow runner is a rare but respected game fish that roams the open water. It is a solitary fish, swift and restless, that puts up a ferocious fight when hooked. As it dies, its brilliant rainbow colors fade to dull grey.

☐ Permits and pompanos often root close inshore for the mollusks and crustaceans that are a major part of their diet. They are very flighty, nervous fishes, hard to hook. Anglers often despair, after seeing hundreds of permits and pompanos on a fishing trip, of landing or even hooking a single fish. The African pompano is an exotic member of the Carangidae family, with long trailing threads that stream from its dorsal and anal fins. It was once assumed that only juveniles sported the long streamers, and the threads shortened with age. Numerous adult fishes from 1½ to 2 feet long have been taken, however, with threadfins almost as long as the juveniles. Most juvenile jackfishes display bold or light vertical bars (as shown by the juvenile African pompano) which fade as the fish matures.

Florida pompano, pompano *Trachinotus carolinus* To 2½ feet. Epicures proclaim this fish to be the very finest food from either fresh or saltwater. The flesh is firm, flaky and flavorsome. An excellent gamefish on light tackle, pompanos are extremely nervous, unpredictable and panicky when stalked. Rooting close inshore for mollusks and crustaceans, they may show anglers a tail or flank, then bolt. Young are much like adults in form. Adults are very similar to the adult permit. **Range:** Massachusetts to Brazil, including the Gulf of Mexico. Most abundant off Florida and in the Gulf of Mexico. **Edibility:** see above.

24

Atlantic permit, round pompano (young) *Trachinotus falcatus*
To 3 feet, 9 inches. Young permit, previously called "round pompano," and thought to be a separate species, are now recognized to be juveniles on their way to becoming adult permit. The juvenile and adult phases of the fish are so dissimilar, as illustrated, that it is easy to see why they were first assumed to be different species. Much like the pompano, the permit is the angler's delight and agony. They are very wary, skittish fishes that can wear down nerves by their unwillingness to take a baited hook. It may require from 30 minutes to 3 hours to land a large permit on light tackle. While not as succulent as the pompano, the permit is a fine food fish. **Range:** recorded from both sides of the Atlantic. In the west Atlantic from New England to Brazil, including the Gulf of Mexico. **Edibility:** excellent.

ADULT

JUVENILE

Palometa, gafftopsail pompano, longfin pompano *Trachinotus goodei* To 15 inches. This is the most graceful and striking of all the carangids. To be circled again and again by a school of 25 to 50 palometas is an exhilerating experience for a diver and one that is quite common, especially in the West Indies. It is an abundant fish in clear water along sandy, exposed shores, where it feeds on small fishes, mollusks and crustaceans. Occasionally feeds in the company of the threadfin and the sand drum. It is often confused with the young permit, but the palometa has 4 distinct bars on its side that the permit lacks, and the dorsal and anal fins are much longer than those of the permit. Long known as *T. glaucus.* **Range:** New England, Bermuda, Bahamas and Florida south to Argentina, including the Gulf of Mexico. **Edibility:** good.

Lookdown (jorobado) *Selene vomer* To 1 foot. Juveniles have long, flowing fins and may be confused with the young African pompano, but the eye of the pompano is much closer to the mouth (one eye diameter or less) than that of the lookdown. A closely related fish, *Vomer setapinnis*, the moonfish, has the same range as the lookdown, and is quite similar in appearance. **Range:** Massachusetts and Bermuda to Uruguay, including the Gulf of Mexico. **Edibility:** excellent.

26

Greater amberjack (coronado) *Seriola dumerili* To 6 feet. This roving offshore predator is the largest and most common of the Atlantic amberjacks, and is a prime target of the charterboat fisheries of Florida, the Carolinas and the Gulf of Mexico. A record 5 foot 11 inch fish was taken from the Bahamas that weighed 149 pounds. Usually taken trolling at or near the surface, but has been taken bottom fishing at 180 feet. Two-inch young have 5 body bands, which begin to fade at 8 inches. **Range:** circumtropical; in the West Atlantic, from Massachusetts to Brazil, including the Gulf of Mexico. **Edibility:** fair, but in the West Indies is second only to the barracuda in causing ciguatera poisoning (see page 39).

Almaco jack (coronado) *Seriola rivoliana* To 32 inches. A popular sport fish, especially in the West Indies and Bermuda. The color is variable, and at times the almaco jack appears quite like the amberjack, including a brassy stripe from nose to tail. It is a deeper-bodied fish, however, with much longer dorsal and anal fin lobes than the amberjack. Young display 5 or 6 dark body bands. Previously known as *Seriola falcata*. **Range:** New Jersey and Bermuda to Argentina, including the Gulf of Mexico. **Edibility:** fair,

Rainbow runner (salmon) *Elagatis bipinnulata* To 4 feet. A rare and wide-ranging species and an esteemed game fish when taken on light tackle. A record 3 foot 11 inch runner was taken off Hawaii. **Range:** circumtropical in warm seas. In the West Atlantic from Massachusetts to Venezuela, including the Gulf of Mexico. **Edibility:** excellent.

27

Leatherjacket (zapatero) *Oligoplites saurus* To 1 foot. Leatherjackets are schooling fishes usually found along sandy beaches, inlets and bays. They possess sharp dorsal and anal spines capable of inflicting injury if carelessly handled. **Range:** Massachusetts to Uruguay. **Edibility:** poor.

Mackerel scad (antonino) *Decapterus macarellus* To 1 foot. The *Decapterus* genus scads all possess a detached finlet behind both the dorsal and anal fins. The mackerel scad is an offshore fish, occasionally seen schooling over the outer reefs. Due to its small size, it is usually ignored by anglers. It is important as a bait fish either salted or frozen. **Range:** Nova Scotia to the hump of Brazil. **Edibility:** good.

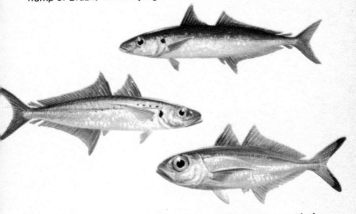

Round scad (chuparaco) *Decapterus punctatus* To 1 foot. An offshore schooling fish, occasionally taken inshore in beach seines. Primarily used as a bait fish, it is not sought by anglers, although it reportedly has a good flavor and is often sold in fish markets. **Range:** Nova Scotia to Brazil, including the Gulf of Mexico. **Edibility:** good.

Bigeye scad, goggle - eye jack *Selar crumenophthalmus* To 16 inches. This scad is a popular food fish and is often found in West Indian markets. Also popular as a live bait fish. Occurs on outer reefs in large schools. **Range:** circumtropical; in the Western Atlantic, from Nova Scotia to Rio de Janeiro, including the Gulf of Mexico. **Edibility:** good.

28

TUNAS AND MACKERELS

Bluefin tuna, thon (atun azul) *Thunnus thynnus* To 14 feet.
The giant of the mackerel family and among the largest of all
fishes. A 1,600 pound, 14 foot tuna was taken off New Jersey.
One of the world's gamest animals, it has been described as "a
living meteor" when hooked. A 125 pound bluefin has been
known to fight an angler for 7 hours, and tow a small boat 20
miles offshore. In the first 3 months of life the bluefin averages
13 inches and 1½ pounds. Within 14 years it will reach 105
inches and 700 pounds. Worldwide in distribution, bluefins
range the West Atlantic from Newfoundland to Puerto Rico and
the Gulf of Mexico. Fishes tagged off the Bahamas have been
captured in Norway, indicating transatlantic migration. **Range:**
see above. **Edibility:** good.

For spectacular big-game fishing, and for fishermen who
don't mind hard work, a good spot to be is Cat Cay in
the Bahamas when shoals of great bluefin tuna pass in
migration from early May to June 15. Vast schools of
200 to 800 pound tackle busters make their crossing in
the shallows near the Gulf Stream dropoff, crowding together in incredible numbers. These magnificent blue-
water predators are heading for their summer feeding
grounds in the North Atlantic, to feed on herring off
Nova Scotia, and the ling, whiting and butterfish off
New York and New Jersey coasts. Battling a 500 pound
bluefin is no job for an amateur, and spectacular struggles
between man and tuna are waged in the shallows of Cat
Cay. Smaller but no less fascinating struggles are waged
throughout the Gulf of Mexico, the east coast of the U.S.,
Bermuda, the Bahamas and throughout the Caribbean
with other fighting representatives of the Scombridae,
the tunas and mackerels.

29

Yellowfin tuna, Allison's tuna (atun) *Thunnus albacares* To 7 feet. Although some sport fishermen still insist that Allison's tuna is a distinct species, fishery biologists have concluded that the large tuna with very long, trailing yellow dorsal and anal fins are merely adult specimens of the well-known yellowfin tuna of both the Atlantic and Pacific. Splendid gamefishes, they are sought by anglers in the West Indies and the Gulf of Mexico north to Maryland and New Jersey. They average 20 to 120 pounds. The largest yellowfin, taken in Hawaii, was 6 feet, 10½ inches, weighing 266½ pounds. **Range:** world-wide in tropical waters. In the West Atlantic, from New England to the Gulf of Mexico, and throughout the Caribbean to Brazil. **Edibility:** good.

☐ The scombrids are fork-tailed, heavily-muscled fishes built for a roving, predaceous existence at the ocean's surface. They prey on smaller fishes, and tuna-wise boat captains keep their eyes peeled for the flocks of screaming, diving sea birds which feed upon the smaller fishes and squid driven to the surface by the pursuing tuna. When a school is sighted, the captain runs the boat across the head of the school, slows to a few knots, and live anchovies and other tuna bait fish are thrown overboard to keep the tuna circling.

☐ All of the tunas and most of the mackerels are popular shore and offshore game fish because they are very fast swimmers that strike hard and pull hard, preferring to run and sound down deep, rather than to twist and battle the hook. The thrill of tuna fishing is the long drawn out battle of sheer weight. Frequently the fisherman never sees the fish until it is hauled up, completely exhausted, alongside the boat. The little tuna, bonito, skipjack and blackfin tuna are small tuna favorites of West Atlantic fishermen for their splendid fighting qualities and food value. Another favorite in the big game fish class is the yellowfin tuna, a magnificent fighter that reaches 300 pounds in weight, although the average taken is 40 to 50 pounds.

☐ The wahoo is a long, slender mackerel also known for its fighting prowess. Acclaimed for its excellent flavor, the wahoo is a circumtropical fish, taken throughout the Caribbean and Gulf of Mexico. The king mackerel is a prime favorite of West Atlantic offshore fishermen. The king is a voracious feeder and will hit a trolled bait with considerable shock and power. Kings run the year around in Florida, with the biggest runs coming to southern Florida in the winter months. In Texas, Louisiana and Mississippi waters, kings run in the late spring and throughout the summer. The Spanish mackerel and cero are excellent food fishes, targets of shore and offshore fishermen from Florida to Texas, and from Massachusetts to Rio de Janeiro. Experienced gulf coast fishermen say that the Spanish mackerels will run when gulf water temperature reaches 75° or more. These runs hit Texas waters around Easter Week each year and continue to run along Texas, Louisiana and Mississippi waters for about five

Albacore, longfin tuna (albacora, atun) *Thunnus alalunga* To 4 feet. Rare in the West Atlantic, except for the Bahamas and Cuba, the long-finned albacore is occasionally taken by sport fishermen well offshore. A popular gamefish reaching 90 pounds in weight. The average caught is about 20 pounds. The most valuable of all the tunas for canning, and the only one that can be labeled as "white meat tuna." **Range:** world-wide in all tropical seas; in the West Atlantic from New Jersey to Puerto Rico, including the Gulf of Mexico. **Edibility:** excellent.

31

months. Spanish mackerels and ceros are caught from beachfront piers and jetties, and occasionally even by surf casting. More frequently, however, they are caught a few miles offshore, particularly where swirling currents carry small fishes away from the protection of coral and rock reefs. Tunas and mackerels are excellent eating when fresh, but the oily meat deteriorates very quickly in tropical heat. Always drain the blood away immediately after landing—preferably into a bucket, and not overboard (unless you want a school of sharks on your trail). Freezing these fishes is not recommended, due to the high oil content. They should be eaten fresh. Cases of food poisoning in the tropics are common from eating spoiled tuna and mackerel.

Blackfin tuna (albacora) *Thunnus atlanticus* To 3 feet. A small dark-colored species, the blackfin is an excellent food fish, and many are taken in Cuba's commercial fishery. Commonly hooked by offshore anglers in Florida and the West Indies. A favorite food of the blue marlin. **Range:** Cape Cod to Brazil. **Edibility:** good.

Atlantic bonito, little tunny (bonite) *Sarda sarda* To 3 feet. Huge, voracious schools roam the West Atlantic, hot in pursuit of squid, mackerels, menhaden, and alewives. Anglers looking for bigger game find that even 4 to 8 pound bonito are furious fighters. Often called "skip jacks" and "horse mackerels." **Range:** St. Lawrence River to Argentina, including the Gulf of Mexico. **Edibility:** poor.

32

Skipjack tuna, striped tuna, bonito (bonito oceanico, cachoretta, barrilete) *Euthynnus pelamis* To 3 feet. Skipjacks have been observed in schools of over 50,000 fishes. They prey voraciously on squid, fishes and crustaceans. A record skipjack taken in the Bahamas was 3 feet 3 inches, weighed 39 pounds, 15 ounces. **Range:** world-wide in warm seas; in the West Atlantic, from Cape Cod to Leeward Islands, including the Gulf of Mexico. **Edibility:** good.

Little tunny, false albacore, bonito (bonito chico, barrilete) *Euthynnus alletteratus* To 4 feet. Popular east coast and Gulf Coast sport fishes; anglers gear up for the little tuna in summer and fall, when schools are abundant around inlets, bays and beaches. The average taken is 5 to 8 pounds, and rare 35 pounders have been recorded. An important West Indian market fish. **Range:** New England, Bermuda, Bahamas to Brazil. **Edibility:** good.

33

Spanish mackerel (caballa, sierra) *Scomberomorus maculatus*
To 4 feet. When a silvery, gold-spotted projectile grabs a trolled
bait from a Florida charter boat and then leaps 10 feet into the
air to begin a furious fight, the fish is a Spanish mackerel. Commercial fishermen use aircraft to spot schools off Florida and
the Gulf and take nearly 10 million pounds per year. Menhaden
are their favorite food. **Range:** Maine to Brazil, including the
Gulf of Mexico. **Edibility:** excellent.

Cero, painted mackerel (caballa, pintada, sierra) *Scomberomorus
regalis* To 3½ feet. Another splendid leaper and fighter, the cero
is often confused with the Spanish mackerel. The two very similar mackerels can be distinguished by the body markings. The
cero has a series of dot-and-dashed gold lines from pectoral fin
to tail while the Spanish mackerel has large definite spots from
pectoral fin to tail. A beautiful fish, occasionally appearing in
large schools off Florida and through the West Indies. **Range:**
Cape Cod to Brazil, including the Gulf of Mexico. **Edibility:**
good.

34

King mackerel, kingfish (carite, sierra conalera, caballa)
Scomberomorus cavalla To 5 feet. The largest of the
Spanish mackerels, this magnificent fish may vault out of
the sea when hooked and leap 25 feet in the air before starting a long, furious battle. Anglers use trolled spoons, fish and
squid to land these fighters. At times, more than 100 boats may
be concentrated over a large school of kings. **Range:** North
Carolina to Brazil, including the Gulf of Mexico. **Edibility:** good.

Frigate mackerel *Auxis thazard* To 2½ feet. Like the little
tuna, this fish may school inshore in summer and fall, but its appearance is irregular. It is not highly valued as food, but is often
used as bait. Averaging one to three pounds, it can reach 10
pounds. **Range:** world-wide; in the West Atlantic, from Cape
Cod to Brazil. **Edibility:** poor.

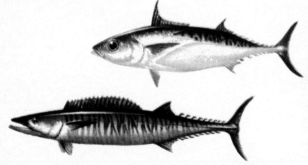

Wahoo (peto, bonito negro) *Acanthocybium solanderi* To 7 feet.
This famous fighter takes off so fast on its initial run that light
tackle fishermen must pursue it full throttle to prevent their
lines from being stripped. If it can be checked, the wahoo provides a breathtaking battle of 30 foot leaps, soundings and long
runs. Rare over its range, the wahoo often swims solitarily about
Florida and West Indian reefs and in blue water. **Range:** all
tropical seas; in the West Atlantic, from Maryland to Venezuela,
including the Gulf of Mexico. **Edibility:** excellent.

35

SNAPPERS

† **Gray snapper, mangrove snapper** (pargo prieto, caballerote) *Lutjanus griseus* To 2½ feet. Like most of the lutjanids, the gray snapper is highly changeable in color—sometimes very pale, sometimes very dark, often tinged with red or olive, sometimes covered with bars or blotches. The broad oblique stripe through the eye, like that of the schoolmaster, is usually apparent, but not always. Common inshore in such habitats as coral reefs, rocky outcroppings, piers, and wrecks. Especially fond of mangrove sloughs, earning the name "mangrove snapper." **Range:** Massachusetts south to Bermuda, Florida and the Bahamas to southeastern Brazil, including the Gulf of Mexico. **Edibility:** excellent.

Snappers are well-known for their excellent food quality. They are sought after by every manner of fisherman's bait and underwater spear technique. Probably because of this popularity, snappers are the wariest of game fishes. Many West Atlantic fisherman swear that snappers are not only able to think, but they frequently out-think the fisherman. Because of this wariness, and because of their preference for the deeper reefs, large snappers are not often seen by the casual diver. Smaller representatives of many species, especially the schoolmaster, mahogany and yellowtail snappers, are common off most shallow reefs.

□ The carnivorous snappers of the Lutjanidae family are closely related to the grunts. Both have the characteristic sloping head and shovel-nosed appearance known as the "snapper look." Although primarily marine in habitat, some lutjanids, such as the dog and gray snappers, readily enter brackish and fresh water. Snappers are numerous in the headwater springs of the Homosassa and other rivers along Florida's west coast. Shallow mangrove areas provide ideal nursery grounds for many snappers. Although most of the lutjanids shown here are shore snappers, a few, such as the red, blackfin and silk snappers are deep-water fishes. These and a few other closely-

Schoolmaster (pargo amarillo, caji) *Lutjanus apodus* To 2 feet. The commonest and most familiar snapper on tropical West Atlantic reefs. The schoolmaster is virtually everywhere—coral reefs, particularly elkhorn coral stands, rocky bottoms, tide pools, turtle grass, marl and mangrove-lined tidal creeks. Juveniles are brilliantly striped in yellow like bumble bees. **Range:** New England, Bermuda, Bahamas, and Florida to Brazil, including the Gulf of Mexico. **Edibility:** good.

Mutton snapper (pargo, pargo criollo, sama) *Lutjanus analis* To 30 inches. A very handsome snapper, distinctive for its reddish fins, blue markings around the eye and the bold spot beneath the soft dorsal fin. Can be confused with the mahogany snapper underwater, but the mahogany lacks the grayish-green barred markings found on the sides of the mutton snapper. Prefers protected bays, tidal creeks, bights, and mangrove sloughs, where it feeds on fishes (especially small grunts) and crustaceans. **Range:** Massachusetts south to the Bahamas and Florida to Brazil, including the Gulf of Mexico. **Edibility:** excellent.

related species are the magnificent food fishes that populate the well-known "snapper banks" of the Gulf of Mexico. The banks lie in water up to 800 feet in depth. The Pensacola area is rich in snapper banks, as is the Texas

Lane snapper (biajaiba, manchego, raiado) *Lutjanus synagris* To 15 inches. A splendid fish with about 8 golden stripes running from nose to tail. Like the mutton snapper, has a subdorsal blotch, but it is hazy and less distinct. Note yellow anal and ventral fins and light olive vertical body bars. **Range:** Carolinas, Bermuda, Bahamas and Florida to southeastern Brazil, including the Gulf of Mexico. **Edibility:** excellent.

Dog snapper (jocu, pargo colorado) *Lutjanus jocu* To 3 feet. The pale triangle under the eye is distinctive. Not common anywhere, the dog snapper (named for the enlarged fang-like teeth at front of upper jaw) is found around deep reefs, submerged wreckage and rocky inshore areas. Often taken around Key West, Florida in fall and winter. **Range:** New England to Brazil, including the Gulf of Mexico. **Edibility:** good, but large dog snappers in certain areas may carry ciguatera poison. Check with local fishermen.

coast and Florida's east coast, especially St. Augustine and Cape Canaveral. Most snappers feed heavily on crustaceans. The large species, such as the cubera and dog snappers, are fish-eating carnivores, and are occasionally implicated in ciguatera fish poisoning.

CIGUATERA FISH POISONING

While quite rare, ciguatera is a particularly unpleasant type of food poisoning to be avoided at all costs. In certain areas at certain seasons of the year, ciguatera has been detected in such carnivores, herbivores and detritus feeders as snappers, barracuda, certain species of surgeons, groupers, jacks and moray eels. Frequently larger individuals are found to be toxic, especially barracuda, jacks and cubera and dog snappers, while smaller fishes of the same species are free of ciguatera. In the Bahamas and through the West Indies, fishes on the steep windward side of a small island may be highly toxic, while those of the same species on the shallow leeward side are perfectly edible. The first symptom is usually a tingling feeling of the mouth, lips and throat, occurring in from 1 to 30 hours after the fish is eaten. Extreme weakness, muscular pains, aches, nausea and diarrhea may follow. A mortality rate of 7 percent has been reported. If you are fishing in a strange area, and you catch and plan to eat any of the fishes named above, check first with the local population, especially local fishermen, as to the edibility of the fish. In most cases and in most areas throughout the West Atlantic, the fishes will be perfectly safe to eat.

Cubera snapper (cubera) *Lutjanus cyanopterus* To 3½ feet. Said to reach weights of 100 pounds, this is the largest of all the snappers. A very strong fighter, it is taken along submarine ledges off Cuba and Florida in 60 to 120 foot depths. **Range:** New England to the hump of Brazil, including the Gulf of Mexico. **Edibility:** good, but large individuals in certain areas may carry ciguatera toxin. Check with local fishermen.

Mahogany snapper (ojanco) *Lutjanus mahogoni* To 15 inches. Appears to the diver as a pale, almost white snapper with a distinct black subdorsal blotch. As on the mutton snapper, this blotch tends to be large on young fishes, smaller on large adults. Found in small aggregations around coral reefs and over rocky bottoms. **Range:** Carolinas and Bahamas to Venezuela. **Edibility:** excellent.

Red snapper (pargo guachinango, pargo colorado) *Lutjanus campechanus* To 30 inches. So popular and succulent is this fish that it is marketed whole, head and all, to insure against substitution. Fishes that have often been "disguised" and sold as red snapper include gray, blackfin and silk snappers, red groupers, yellowfin and black grouper, gag, scamp, snook and doubtless many others. Occurs in vast schools over deep snapper banks. Twelve million pounds of red snapper are caught on handlines each year. Juveniles to 1 foot have a subdorsal spot, which fades on adults. This is the *Lutjanus blackfordi* and *Lutjanus aya* of previous literature. **Range:** Cape Hatteras south to Yucatan, including the Gulf of Mexico. **Edibility:** excellent.

Silk snapper (pargo de lo alto) *Lutjanus vivanus* To 30 inches. Another deep water snapper, very common on snapper banks (200 to 800 foot depths) of the Gulf Stream and the Gulf of Mexico. Often confused with the red snapper, but easily distinguished by its bright yellow eye, deeply forked tail, and yellowish body lines and markings. Silk snappers up to 1 foot have a black subdorsal spot like the mutton snapper, but this disappears as the fish matures. **Range:** Carolinas, Bermuda, and Bahamas to Venezuela, including the Gulf of Mexico. **Edibility:** excellent.

Blackfin snapper (sesi, sesi de lo alto) *Lutjanus buccanella* To 20 inches. A moderately deep water snapper, usually taken from 120 to 400 foot depths. The only snapper with a distinct black blotch at the pectoral fin base. Quite common around Cuba. Juveniles are frequently seen at 20 to 60 foot depths. **Range:** Carolinas and Bermuda south to Venezuela, including the Gulf of Mexico. **Edibility:** good.

Vermilion snapper (cagon) *Rhomboplites aurorubens* To 20 inches. A common snapper on deeper reefs and over hard bottoms, often caught with the red snapper on the snapper banks of the Gulf of Mexico at 90 to 200 foot depths. **Range:** Carolinas, Bermuda and Bahamas to southeastern Brazil, including the Gulf of Mexico. **Edibility:** excellent.

Yellowtail snapper (rabirubia) *Ocyurus chrysurus* To 30 inches. In a class by itself, the yellowtail snapper is a lovely, active fish to see in its yellow and blue attire, a fine fish to catch with tenacious fighting ability, and an excellent fish to eat. A common snapper that prefers open water over the top of the reef. Usually feeds at night on small fishes, benthic crustaceans and plankton. **Range:** New England, Bermuda, Bahamas and Florida south to Brazil, including the Gulf of Mexico. **Edibility:** excellent.

Black snapper (arnillo) *Apsilus dentatus* To 18 inches. A handsome dusky black snapper with a violet tinge. Even the inside of the mouth is black. A deep water, offshore fish said to be common and a good market fish around Cuba. Recently reported from U.S. coasts; Starck states that it is "rare, offshore," at Alligator Reef in the Florida Keys. **Range:** Bahamas, Florida through the West Indies. **Edibility:** good.

42

GRUNTS

White grunt (ronco arara, corocoro) *Haemulon plumieri* To 18 inches. A lovely fish, probably the commonest and most important food fish of all the West Atlantic grunts. May be seen in dense aggregations by day at the edges of patch reefs and over any suitable bottom, usually in 20 feet or less of water. The inside of the mouth is blood-red. Engages in "kissing" displays. Distinguishable from the French and blue-striped grunt by the striped head and checked scale pattern on body. Coloration is changeable with a broad, dusky bar sometimes visible on mid-side of body, sometimes not. **Range:** Chesapeake Bay, Virginia, Bermuda, Bahamas, Florida and Gulf of Mexico to Brazil. **Edibility:** excellent.

In spite of their unlovely name, many of the West Atlantic grunts are brilliant, gold - striped, shimmering fishes. Grunts are virtually everywhere off Florida, Bahaman and Caribbean reefs, hovering in small groups or massing in great schools. Large schools of French, smallmouth or bluestriped grunts are often seen to stream like a river of gold between coral heads, and even a small school of cottonwicks, white grunts or porkfishes is a joy to behold. Closely related to the snappers, the grunts are also noted for their excellence as food fishes. Early settlers in the Florida Keys virtually subsisted on a diet of "grits and grunts," and today they still form an important part of the fisherman's catch. Although generally considered small panfish, many grunts attain one and a half feet (Spanish, bluestripe, white grunts) and two feet (margate and black margate) in length.

☐ Grunts, of the family Pomadasyidae, are so named because of the sounds they produce by grinding their pharyngeal teeth together. The adjacent air bladder amplifies the sound, and agitated grunts can be quite noisy when they are taken from the water. Most grunts have mouths that are bright orange-red on the inside. Certain of these (the French, white and bluestriped grunts) are known for their unique "kissing" behavior, where two grunts will face and push each other with open mouths. Hans Fricke theorizes that, like the purplemouth moray which opens its brilliantly-colored mouth to ward off aggressors, red-mouthed grunts utilize the same technique to frighten off other grunts who threaten their territory. The young of most of the grunts shown here all look very much alike, with black lateral stripes and a black spot at the base of the caudal fin, as shown for the French grunt, porkfish and black margate.

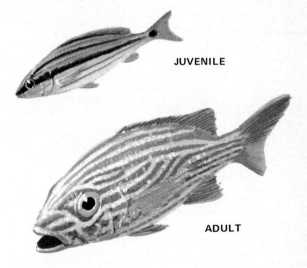

JUVENILE

ADULT

French grunt (condenado, corocoro) *Haemulon flavolineatum* To 12 inches. Another very common grunt, beautifully marked and highly visible gathered into large, shimmering aggregations by day, often by the thousands. At night they range out over sand and grass flats to feed on benthic invertebrates. Mouth red. Engages in "kissing" displays. Swims occasionally with the white grunt. **Range:** Bermuda and South Carolina to Brazil, including the Gulf of Mexico. **Edibility:** excellent.

44

Bluestriped grunt (ronco amarillo, corocoro) *Haemulon sciurus*
To 18 inches. Although it appears similar to the white and
French grunts when seen on the reef, the bluestripe is distinctive
for its bold blue and gold stripes on head and body, and its
dusky soft dorsal and caudal fins. Often encountered swimming
with the white grunt. Mouth red. Engages in "kissing" displays.
A common grunt on Florida and West Indian reefs. **Range:** Bermuda and South Carolina to southeastern Brazil, including the
Gulf of Mexico. **Edibility:** good.

**Margate, white margate, sail-
or's choice** (ronco blanco, jal-
lao) *Haemulon album* To
26 inches. This excellent food
fish, the largest of the grunts
was named after the English
seaport by early Bahaman settlers who came from Margate.
Frequently seen in small groups
around low corals, gorgonians,
rocky areas and shipwrecks.
The adult color phase is shown
here. Also has a subadult color
phase with no stripes, body
pearly gray, soft dorsal and caudal fins black. **Range:** Bermuda, Bahamas, south Florida to
Brazil. **Edibility:** excellent.

Smallmouth grunt (arara) *Haemulon chrysargyreum* To 9
inches. A reef-dwelling grunt
often seen in small aggregations
by day hugging the reef. At
night, like other grunts, it may
forage hundreds of yards from
reef shelter. The mouth is red.
Feeds on copepods, amphipods,
ostracods and shrimps. Quite
similar to the striped grunt, but
the smallmouth grunt has all
yellow fins and bolder body
bars. **Range:** Bahamas and
Florida south to Brazil. **Edibility:** fair.

45

Cottonwick (jeniguana) *Haemulon melanurum* To 12 inches. Not a common fish but a handsome sight to see because of its bold, scissor-like dorsal and tail stripes and the bandit-like mask which usually conceals the eye. Some fishes lack the eye stripe. The cottonwick shuns murky water, and seeks clear water, both inshore and offshore. Inside of mouth is red. **Range:** Bermuda, Bahamas, and south Florida to Brazil. **Edibility:** fair.

Sailors choice (ronco blanco, corocoro) *Haemulon parrai* To 14 inches. Similar to the margate, but with a more distinct scale pattern accentuated by spots, and a larger eye. Feeds largely at night, taking small fishes and mollusks. Juveniles are common inshore over grass beds; adults move offshore to school in open areas of the reef. **Range:** Bahamas, south Florida to Brazil. **Edibility:** excellent.

Caesar grunt (ronco carbonero) *Haemulon carbonarium* To 15 inches. Another reef-dweller, often seen in small schools near coral heads and rocky areas. Similar to the bluestriped grunt under water, but lacks blue stripes and all fins are dusky. Mouth pale red. **Range:** Bermuda, Bahamas and south Florida to Brazil. **Edibility:** good.

46

Tomtate (jeniguano, cuji) *Haemulon aurolineatum* To 10 inches. One of the slimmest and smallest of the grunts, fond of schooling over sea grass and sand flats at relatively shallow depths (30 feet or less). Easily identified by the two yellow stripes on the side and the black blotch at the base of the tail. Although most juvenile grunts have a black spot at the tail base, the tomtate is one of the few that retains this blotch into adulthood. Mouth is red inside. **Range:** Cape Cod, Massachusetts, Bermuda, Bahamas, Florida, and the Gulf of Mexico south to Brazil. **Edibility:** fair.

Black grunt (ronco prieto, corocoro) *Haemulon bonariense* To 11 inches. Quite like the sailor's choice, but with the spots on the scales arranged into oblique stripes running across the body. Also note all-white fins and black tail. A rover, it is found around coral reefs, seagrass and algae beds and mud bottoms. **Range:** southern Gulf of Mexico and Cuba to Brazil. Rare in West Indies but common in the southern Caribbean. **Edibility:** good.

47

Spanish grunt (corocoro) *Haemulon macrostomum* To 17 inches. Much like the caesar grunt, but distinctive for the bold, dark stripes running from head to tail. The mid-lateral stripe from eye to tail is especially visible. Also note dusky belly, yellow pectoral fins, yellow-tinged caudal, dorsal and anal fins. Mature adults average about 1 foot in length. Inside of mouth is red. A bottom feeder, it prefers clear water around coral reefs. **Range:** Florida Keys south through West Indies to Brazil. **Edibility:** excellent.

Latin grunt (ronco raiado, chere-chere) *Haemulon steindachneri* To 10½ inches. Well-named for its latin distribution, this grunt occurs on both coasts of tropical America from the Gulf of California to Panama, and in the Atlantic from Santa Lucia to Brazil. Quite common on the Brazilian coast and in the southern Caribbean, though rare through the West Indies. Said to be extremely abundant around Mazatlan, Mexico. **Range:** see above. **Edibility:** good.

Striped grunt (ronco) *Haemulon striatum* To 11 inches. At one time thought to be quite rare, but now recognized to be a grunt with a preference for moderately deep water (over 40 feet). Walter Starck reports it to be abundant at Alligator Reef in the Florida Keys. Juveniles have a single mid-lateral stripe running from the eye to a dark blotch at the base of the tail. **Range:** Bahamas, Florida and Gulf of Mexico south to Brazil. **Edibility:** fair.

Porkfish (sisi, catalineta) *Anisotremus virginicus* To 14 inches. A brilliant, handsome grunt, not at all common over its range. It is rare in the Bahamas and was finally introduced to Bermuda. Abundant around Florida, especially the Keys, and has been photographed there in large magnificent schools, occasionally swimming with the white grunt. Young porkfishes pick parasites from the bodies of other fishes. **Range:** Bermuda (introduced), Bahamas, and Florida south to Brazil. **Edibility:** good.

ADULT

JUVENILE

49

Black margate (pompon) *Anisotremus surinamensis* To 2 feet. The margates are the largest of the grunts. This fish is often seen either solitary or in small groups of 2 or 3. Favors inshore rocky bottoms, caves or the larger patch reefs where it feeds on crustaceans, fishes and sea urchins. **Range:** Florida, Bahamas, Gulf of Mexico south to Brazil. **Edibility:** good.

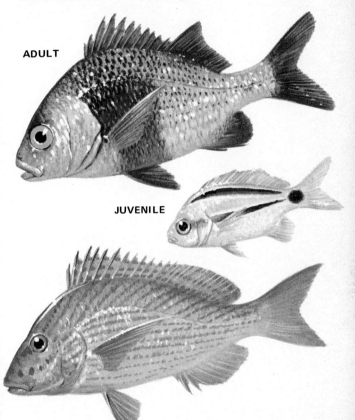

ADULT

JUVENILE

Pigfish, hogfish, sailor's choice *Orthopristis chrysoptera* To 15 inches. Ranging from Long Island south to Bermuda, Florida and through the Gulf of Mexico to the Rio Grande, the pigfish is a popular game fish and an excellent pan fish. Large numbers are taken along the Carolina coast. The *Orthopristis* genus grunts differ from the *Haemulon* grunts in their smaller mouths, more developed anal fins and less-developed dorsal spines. **Range:** see above: **Edibility:** good.

GOATFISHES

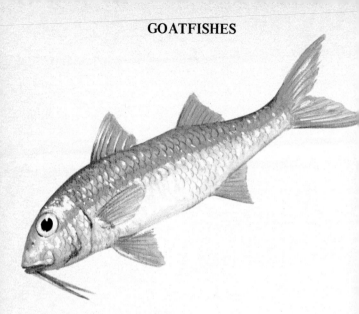

Yellow goatfish (salmonete amarillo) *Mulloidichthys martinicus*
To 15½ inches. The broad yellow stripe from eye to tail is al-
most always evident. Often seen swimming lazily in huge aggre-
gations over the reefs. Appears to be a night feeder. **Range:**
Bermuda, Bahamas and Florida to Brazil, including the Gulf of
Mexico. **Edibility:** good.

Goatfishes are the bottom grubbers of the reef, and their
distinctive characteristic is their long, tactile and highly
sensitive barbels under the chin, with which they work
constantly and busily over the bottom, probing for small
crustaceans and worms. They frequently work alone,
other times in groups of 2 or 4, other times they form
into great schools for short migrations across the reef. A
vast school of yellow goatfishes is a many-splendored
sight to see, like a shimmering curtain of gold. Goats are
very welcome sights to fishermen too, since they are excellent food fishes. The ritual spawning of goatfishes is
typical of the process of birth on the reef. A pair of goatfishes will swim together in steep loop-the-loop circles up
to the surface of the water, discharging sperm and eggs
as they ascend. If the male ejects too soon, or the female
ejects a fraction of a second too late, thousands of eggs

Spotted goatfish (salmonete colorado) *Pseudupeneus maculatus*
To 11 inches. Distinctive for the 3 large blotches on the body,
but this fish is a color-changer. When swimming the blotches
may disappear from the fish, then re-appear when settling to the
bottom. This is the goatfish usually seen rooting about sand and
mud bottoms for the invertebrates that are its main source of
food. Wrasses, rays and other fishes often follow the rooting
goatfish, to snap up morsels missed in the search. **Range:** New
England to Bermuda, the Bahamas and Florida south to Brazil,
including the Gulf of Mexico. **Edibility:** good.

perish. Although generally most eggs are fertilized, only
a small portion of the fry ever reach maturity. They are
quickly consumed by larger fishes. Many West Atlantic
fishes mate in the same way. Each of them must produce
hundreds of thousands of eggs, simply to assure that
enough are fertilized and mature to continue the species.
The eggs and fry are not wasted however. They become
part of the plankton mass which feeds other creatures of
the reef, thus assuring the survival of all species. Goats
are also noted for their ability to change color to match
their background. There is a surprising difference between their daytime and nighttime colorations. Goatfishes are members of the Mullidae family, and they are
surmullets, not to be confused with the true mullets,
which belong to the Mugilidae family.

52

DRUMS, CROAKERS, SEATROUT, WEAKFISHES

Weakfish, spotted sea trout, squeteague (corvina) *Cynoscion nebulosus* To 2½ feet. More U.S. anglers seek weakfish on both the Atlantic and Gulf coasts than any other sport fish. Called weakfish because the mouth and flesh are tender, they gamely respond to trolling, casting and stillfishing. Two closely related species range from Texas to Florida (*C. nebulosus*) and from Florida to Nova Scotia (*C. regalis*). Average 3 pounds; reach 15 pounds. **Range:** see above. **Edibility:** good.

Drums, croakers, roncadores, corvinas, redfishes, channel bass, seatrouts, squeteagues, weakfishes, spots, lafayettes, kingfishes, whitings—members of the large and varied family Sciaenidae are called by many names, but nearly all of them share a common characteristic—they are the noisiest fishes of the sea. Early submarine commanders were at first astounded to hear the "boop-boop-boop-boop" of schools of croakers, suspecting that enemy craft were near. Later they found they could hide the sound of their own engines behind the din of the croakers. In Chesapeake Bay, an important spawning area, the croaker cacophony begins to increase in the evening, reaches a crescendo of sound before midnight, then tapers off to near silence. Their message, if any, is still understood only by other croakers, but it is theorized that it plays an important part in courtship activity. The sound is made by vibrating special muscles attached to the air bladder, which amplifies the sound much like a guitar when a string is plucked. A few sciaenids lack air bladders (kingfishes, whitings) but they are able to produce sound by grinding their teeth together.

☐ Croakers and drums are dear to the hearts of shore fishermen. They frequent warm turbid bays and estuaries—easily accessible to anglers—where they browse for shrimps, oysters, crabs and other crustaceans. Most of

Silver seatrout, silver trout, squeteague (corvina) *Cynoscion nothus* To 12 inches. Occurring from Chesapeake Bay to Florida and throughout the Gulf of Mexico, this small seatrout is related to the weakfish. It prefers open ocean more than its relatives, moving into shore in the winter months. A similar relative, the sand seatrout (*C. arenarius*) ranges from Florida's west coast to Texas and south to Mexico's Gulf of Campeche. **Range:** see above. **Edibility:** good.

Southern kingfish, whiting (corvina, lambe) *Menticirrhus americanus* To 15 inches. Occasionally divers will see this handsome, silvery fish resting or feeding on sand bottoms, quite near shore. Surfcasters bait with shrimp and hook them off sandy beaches. Four similar species range the Atlantic and Gulf coasts of the U.S. The southern kingfish *M. americanus* ranges from New York to Argentina and to the Northern Gulf of Mexico. The northern kingfish, *M. saxatilis* occurs from Maine to Florida. The Gulf kingfish, *M. littoralis* extends from Virginia to Florida and through the Gulf of Mexico. The minkfish, *M. focaliger* is restricted to the Gulf of Mexico. **Range:** see above. **Edibility:** good.

them make excellent eating and many wage a dogged struggle once they are hooked.

☐ Sciaenids are easily recognized by their two separate dorsal fins, two anal spines and a rounded snout. Also, the lateral line extends out onto the caudal fin, as in the snooks. Some croakers have barbels on the chin with which they probe sandy bottoms for crustaceans, worms and mollusks. Divers do not often encounter croakers due to their preference for sedimentary bottoms and turbid, brackish water. Occasionally a solitary, silvery black mottled kingfish is found resting on the bottom, and various drums may be seen probing the sand with their barbels.

☐ The fishes of this family are largely restricted to continental coastlines, with very few species reaching islands. With a few exceptions, none of the drums and croakers shown here are found around the islands of the West Indies, and this is true the world over. The smaller and more remote an island is from the mainland, the less like-

Red drum, channel bass, redfish (pescado colorado) *Sciaenops ocellata* To 4½ feet. Favorite of surf fishermen, the red drum swims with the weakfish, striped bass and bluefish in a hard-fighting team that attracts anglers from New Jersey to Texas. Four to six pound red drums are good eating, but over 15 pounds the flesh is coarse and stringy. Rod and reel record: 83 pounds. **Range:** Cape Cod to Florida and across the Gulf of Mexico to Texas. **Edibility:** see above.

Black drum (roncador, corvina negra) *Pogonius cromis* To 4½ feet. One of the largest food fishes on our coast; a 146 pound black drum was taken at St. Augustine, Florida. Sluggish fishes, they browse lazily in coastal shallows, probing with their sensitive barbels for crustaceans and mollusks. The loudest of the drummers, both males and females drum raucously, especially at spawning time. **Range:** Massachusetts to Argentina, including the Gulf of Mexico. **Edibility:** fair.

Silver perch *Bairdiella chrysura* To 1 foot. Fond of bays and estuaries, the silver perch is an excellent panfish (though small, averaging ¼ pound) and schoolboys and shore anglers from New Jersey to Texas fish for them actively. They are superabundant in Chesapeake Bay. Bottom fishing with small shrimp, clam, or worm is most effective. Most active in summer. **Range:** Cape Cod to Texas. **Edibility:** good.

Sand drum (petota) *Umbrina coroides* To 1 foot. One of the few drums that ranges from the U.S. coast through the West Indies to South America. Favors sandy beaches in shallow water where it swims with mojarras, palometas and threadfins to feed on crustaceans dislodged by the surf. Plain silvery when swimming, it can put on 7 vertical body bars when at rest. **Range:** Chesapeake Bay and Bahamas to Brazil, including the Gulf of Mexico. **Edibility:** good.

Reef croaker (caimuire) *Odontoscion dentex* To 1 foot. As its name implies, this croaker and the four *Equetus* genus drums (see following) are reef dwellers with a different life-style than that of other drums and croakers. The reef croaker may be seen in small aggregations hiding in reef crevices by day. It emerges at night to feed on crustaceans and small fishes. **Range:** Florida Keys to Bahia, Brazil. **Edibility:** fair.

High hat, striped drum (obispo) *Equetus acuminatus* To 9 inches. Juveniles of this species and other *Equetus* drums are incredible little creatures to see on the reef. All have extremely elongated dorsal, ventral and tailfins, and they resemble tiny, lovely oriental kites floating languidly in the blue tides. Adults and juveniles are often seen during the day in small groups hiding in or hovering near coral reefs, rock ledges, or rocky outcroppings in mixed sand and seagrass beds. At night they leave their hideaways and poke about the sand flats in search of food. Formerly known as *Equetus pulcher*, this fish is now the official "high hat." **Range:** South Carolina, Bermuda, Bahamas and Florida south through the Lesser Antilles. **Edibility:** poor.

ly it is to have sciaenids. Hawaii has not a single drum or croaker. One reason for the dependence of sciaenids on continental waters is their need for estuaries for breeding the young. A number of sciaenids have developed a completely freshwater existence.

Cubbyu (obispo) *Equetus umbrosus* To 9 inches. This drum is almost identical to the high hat, *Equetus acuminatus*, in all respects except for the blackish dorsal, caudal, anal and ventral fins. Some authorities still consider this fish to be simply a dark-tinged subspecies of *Equetus acuminatus*. The name-swapping between some of the *Equetus* genus drums is based on the recommendation of George C. Miller, and has been recognized by the American Fisheries Society. It is all quite confusing to the average fishwatcher and aquarium keeper, but the explanation is as follows: the fish known as the "striped drum" *Equetus pulcher*, is now recognized as the "high hat," *Equetus acuminatus*. The fish formerly known as the "cubbyu," *Equetus acuminatus*, still retains the common name "cubbyu," but the scientific name has changed to *Equetus umbrosus*. So far as is known, the cubbyu's life style and habitat are quite similar to the high hat. The cubbyu is reported to be "occasional" at Alligator Reef, Florida by Walter Starck, and is common off Florida's West Coast. **Range:** uncertain—see above. **Edibility:** poor.

☐ Unique among the drums and favorites of aquarists are the beautifully striped species of the genus *Equetus*, the high hat, cubbyu, striped drum and jackknife fishes. These lovely drums, unlike other sciaenids, are reef dwellers. They are secretive by day, and are typically found either solitary, in pairs or small groups, hiding under rock ledges or in reef crevices. They are completely at home on the reef, do not depend on estuarine waters to spawn, and consequently are found throughout the West Indies to Central and South America.

Spotted drum (obispo) *Equetus punctatus* To 11 inches. Originally thought to be extremely rare, this shy drum was observed by scientists in Tektite I and II Man-in-the-Sea Programs and by Starck and Davis to be very secretive, hiding deep in reef crevices by day, but emerging at night to forage boldly for crustaceans, polychaetes and gastropods. Similar to the jackknife fish, it is easily distinguished by the dark-colored and spotted dorsal and tail fins, and the multiple (rather than single) body bars. A very striking and impressive aquarium fish. **Range:** Florida, Bahamas through Greater Antilles. **Edibility:** poor.

Jackknife fish (obispo) *Equetus lanceolatus* To 9 inches. A beautiful animal, both on and under the reef and in the aquarium. The elongated first dorsal fin is even more impressive in juveniles, and the fin is used almost like an antenna by all the long-dorsal-finned *Equetus* genus drums. In the aquarium the spine is erected like a warrior's lance if the fish is startled, threatened or frightened, and at feeding times. It serves effectively as a deterrent to predators, since, with the fin erected, the little drum is very difficult to swallow. The Spanish name "obispo" (bishop) likens the long dorsal fin to the high pointed hat of a bishop. **Range:** Carolinas, Bermuda and Bahamas to the hump of Brazil. **Edibility:** poor.

59

Spot, goody, lafayette (chopa blanca) *Leiostomus xanthurus*
To 14 inches. Small, but one of the tastiest panfishes of the sea,
the popular spot feeds close inshore on crustaceans, worms and
mollusks.   Abundant one year, scarce the next; anglers lower
bloodworms from anchored boats to catch the spot. Commercial
fishermen of Norfolk, Virginia and South Carolina land much of
the nearly 10 million pounds annual catch. **Range:** Cape Cod to
Florida and across the Gulf Coast to Texas. **Edibility:** excellent.

Atlantic croaker (roncador, corvina, blanca) *Micropogon undula-
tus* To 20 inches. From Cape Cod to Texas, anglers pursue the
croaker or "hardhead" bottom fishing over sandy bottoms, where
the fish probes with sensitive barbels for worms, crustaceans and
mollusks.   Exceedingly abundant on the Gulf Coast. **Range:**
Massachusetts to Mexico. A closely related species, *M. furnieri*,
ranges through the West Indies to Venezuela. **Edibility:** good.

PORGIES, SEA BREAMS, CHUBS, SPADEFISHES

Spot porgy, silver porgy, spottail pinfish (San Pedra) *Diplodus holbrooki* To 1 foot. A sociable, active fish of the surf zone and near-shore reefs, the spot porgy swims peaceably in the company of chubs, mojarras, threadfins and croakers. **Range:** South Florida, Bahamas throughout Caribbean. **Edibility:** fair.

A familiar and pleasing sight to divers in Southern Florida, the Bahamas, and the Caribbean is the brilliant and sparkling spot porgy, also known as the spottail pinfish or silver porgy. Easily identified by the large round black spot on the tail, these silvery beauties may be seen singly or in schools of from 10 to 30 fishes, often in the company of chubs and sea breams. Porgies, of the family **Sparidae**, are related to the grunts, and they look somewhat like a cross between a round-headed snapper and a grunt. They are not often seen by divers, partly due to their extreme wariness. Many porgies are bottom dwellers and some range out to 250 ft. depths. Shellfish are a major part of their diet and they are equipped with powerful incisor and molar-like teeth to crush and grind shells. Though occasionally seen around rocks and coral reefs, they are not reef dwellers. If attacked, they rely on their speed and agility to outdistance pursuers, rather than hiding in reef crevices. In general, porgies are excellent food fishes.

☐ Chubs, of the family Kyphosidae, are also known as rudder-fishes because of their habit of following in the wake of ships. Bermuda chubs are especially fond of trailing ships, and have been known to follow them for hundreds of miles into the West Atlantic. Chubs are plant-feeding fishes that are often caught on hook and line. They are excellent game fishes that fight powerfully when hooked, but they are poor food fishes and are usually released when caught. They often school along with porgies, especially the spot porgy, which they superficially resemble.

Jolthead porgy (bajonado) *Calamus bajonado* To 2 feet. The largest of the porgies, the jolthead reportedly got its name from the way it "jolts" or shakes mollusks loose from rocks and pilings with its powerful jaws. A splendid table fish with firm, moist, white flesh. **Range:** Rhode Island south to Bermuda, Bahamas, Florida to Brazil, including the Gulf of Mexico. **Edibility:** excellent.

Saucereye porgy (pez de pluma) *Calamus calamus* To 16 inches. A very rapid color-changer, this fish can go to striped or blotched coloration in a twinkling. Young are found in seagrass beds; adults over the reefs. Has been taken from near-shore to 250 feet. **Range:** North Carolina, Bermuda, Bahamas and Florida to British Honduras, including the Gulf of Mexico. **Edibility:** good.

62

□ One of the most impressive sights in the underwater world is a large school of spadefishes. These magnificent fishes (family Ephippidae), reaching lengths of 3 feet, seem curious about divers, and have been known to circle the diver, literally walling him in by a silvery, moving cylinder of spadefishes. They have a vast range, from Massachusetts to Brazil. Recently introduced to Bermuda, they seem to be doing well there. They are virtually omnivorous, with a special craving for shellfish.

Red porgy (guerito) *Pagrus sedecim* To 20 inches. This is a deepwater porgy that is often taken along with red snappers on the snapper banks of Florida from Pensacola south. Numerous red porgies are also taken by commercial fishermen in bottom trawls fished off the coast of the southeastern United States. **Range:** New York to Argentina including the Gulf of Mexico, but not the West Indies. **Edibility:** good.

Sheepshead porgy (pez de pluma) *Calamus penna* To 18 inches. Ranges from near shore to 270 feet. A bottom fish, it may flash to a barred coloration when it is on or near the bottom. **Range:** Bahamas and Florida to Brazil, including the Gulf of Mexico. **Edibility:** good.

Grass porgy, shad porgy *Calamus arctifrons* To 10 inches. A small porgy, rather common in shallow water seagrass patches on both coasts of Florida and in the eastern Gulf from Louisiana to Florida. Though small, it is valued as a good panfish. **Range:** see above. **Edibility:** good.

Sheepshead, convict fish (sargo) *Archosargus probatocephalus*
To 3 feet. A popular game and food fish, especially in Florida.
Like most of the porgies, the sheepshead is a very suspicious,
wary quarry, fond of lurking in holes and crevices. They feed
on mollusks, crabs and barnacles which they noisily scrape off of
rocks and pilings with their strong incisor teeth. **Range:** apparently restricted to continental coastlines, *A. probatocephalus* occurs from Nova Scotia to Florida and through the Gulf of Mexico to Yucatan, and a similar subspecies, *A. aries* occurs from
British Honduras to Brazil. **Edibility:** excellent.

Pinfish, sailor's choice, pigfish, bream (chopa spina, sargo) *Lagodon rhomboides* To 14 inches. Ranging from Cape Cod south to Florida and throughout the Gulf of Mexico to Yucatan, this brilliant active little fish is extremely abundant, especially in the southern part of its range. Shore fishermen regularly take home strings of pinfish, and find them to be excellent eating. **Range:** see above. **Edibility:** good.

Sea bream (chopa amarilla, salema) *Archosargus rhomboidalis* To 13 inches. This handsome porgy and the pinfish are quite similar shallow-water fishes, and are often confused by Florida fishermen. They may be separated by noting the deeper body of the sea bream, and the blackish spot, larger than the eye, behind the gill cover. Formerly known as *A. unimaculatus*. **Range:** Florida through the West Indies to Brazil, including the Gulf of Mexico. **Edibility:** good.

64

Scup *Stenotomus chrysops* To 18 inches. Abundant on the east coast of the U.S., this popular and excellent table fish is called scup in New England, porgy in New York, maiden, fair maid and ironsides in Chesapeake Bay, and porgy again in the Carolinas. Anglers bait the hook with shellfish, anchor over sandy bottoms, and reel in scup by the score. A very similar scup, *S. caprinus*, replaces *S. chrysops* in the Gulf of Mexico. **Range:** *S. chrysops*, Nova Scotia to Florida; *S. caprinus*, South Carolina south through the Gulf of Mexico. **Edibility:** good.

Spadefish (chirivita chiva) *Chaetodipterus faber* To 3 feet. Found around reefs, piers, wrecks and bridges, and common around offshore oil platforms in the Gulf of Mexico. Large schools of up to 500 spadefishes are occasionally seen off Bimini. Tiny all-black juveniles drift motionless near shore, mimicking leaves, mangrove pods and floating trash, as does the tripletail. **Range:** New England, Bermuda (introduced), Bahamas, Florida to southeastern Brazil, including the Gulf of Mexico. **Edibility:** good.

65

Bermuda chub (chopa, morocoto) *Kyphosus sectatrix* To 30 inches. These fishes appear as silvery or steel gray to the diver on the reef. On close inspection, the yellow markings and fine striping become visible. Some fishes in a small school will flash to a white-spotted coloration on occasion, especially when chasing other fishes. **Range:** both sides of the Atlantic; in the West Atlantic from New England to Bermuda, the Bahamas and Florida to Brazil. **Edibility:** variable—sometimes quite good; other times very poor.

Yellow chub (chopa) *Kyphosus incisor* To 26½ inches. Very like the Bermuda chub, but the yellow stripes on this fish are more pronounced, as are the yellow head markings. Both the yellow and Bermuda chubs are plant feeders, usually found over rocky bottoms, seagrass beds and coral reefs. Both are powerful fighters when hooked. **Range:** both sides of the Atlantic; in the West Atlantic from New England, the Bahamas and Florida to Brazil. **Edibility:** variable—sometimes quite good; other times very poor.

ANGELFISHES

JUVENILE

INTERMEDIATE

ADULT

French angelfish (chirivita, cachama negra) *Pomacanthus paru*
To 1¼ feet. The French angel is a splendid fish to see on the reef.
Juveniles are occasionally seen stationed at a coral head, picking
and cleaning parasites from larger fishes. Many inch-long French
juveniles have bright blue borders on their ventral fins and a blue
spot on the anal fin. French angels may be distinguished from
gray angels by their more rounded tails (especially in the young).
The adult french angel is a much darker fish than the gray, has
golden edges to the body scales, and a yellow bar at the base of
the pectoral fin. **Range:** both sides of the Atlantic. In the
Western Atlantic, from the Bahamas, Florida and the Gulf of
Mexico to southeastern Brazil. **Edibility:** poor.

67

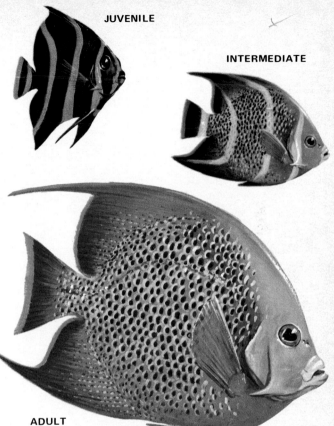

JUVENILE

INTERMEDIATE

ADULT

Gray angelfish, black angelfish (chirivita, cachama blanca) *Pomacanthus arcuatus* To 2 feet. This impressive fish appears to be the hardiest of the West Atlantic angelfishes—stragglers have been taken as far north as New York. The yellow pectoral fins and the square-cut tail separate it from the French angel, which it superficially resembles. Juveniles are beautifully colored with yellow stripes on a black body. French and gray angelfish juveniles are so alike that it is extremely difficult to distinguish between them. Probably the best identifier is the tail fin—the French angel juvenile has a more rounded tail fin, while that of the young gray angel is usually more truncate and rectangular. **Range:** New England to southeastern Brazil, including the Gulf of Mexico. **Edibility:** poor.

The most vividly beautiful fishes in the West Atlantic, without doubt, are the dazzling angelfishes. The black and gold brilliance of the rock beauty, the regal splendor of the queen and blue angels, the French angel with its jet-black body speckled with gold, and the more subdued beauty of the gray angel bring joy to the fishwatcher wherever they are seen. Not content with one brilliant color phase, each of these fishes has juvenile and intermediate color stages that rival the adult, as shown on these pages.

□ Closely related to the butterflyfishes, the angelfishes (family Pomacanthidae) are so like the butterflies that they are frequently classed in the same family. They differ from the butterflies in having a strong, sharp spine at the lower edge of each gill plate. Perhaps because of this extra weapon, which they use to good effect in battle, angelfishes seem a bit more aggressive than the more timid and retiring butterflies. Angelfishes are frequently seen in pairs, and they are very sensitive about their territory. They will defend it stoutly against all comers.

Cherubfish, pygmy angelfish *Centropyge argi* To 2¾ inches. This pygmy member of the angelfish family was first described in 1951 from a single Bermudan specimen taken in 1908. In 1952 another was found in the stomach of a snapper off Yucatan. No more were found until 1959, when members of the Miami Seaquarium staff netted a number of cherubfishes off Bimini. Since then alert divers have encountered numerous others in the Bahamas and elsewhere. Walter Starck reports it as "occasional" at Alligator Reef, Florida. They appear to be more common in water over 100 feet in depth. **Range:** Bermuda, Bahamas, south Florida, West Indies, Gulf of Mexico. **Edibility:** poor.

☐ West Atlantic angelfish species vary in size from the dainty cherubfish reaching 2¾ inches to the magnificent gray angelfish which grows to 2 feet. Most angels feed heavily on invertebrates, principally sponges and tunicates, but algae is also an important part of their diet. Juvenile angelfishes have feeding habits quite different from those of adults. Some juveniles have been seen stationed at coral reef "cleaning stations," where they pick parasites from larger fishes who come for the service. Angelfishes are not numerous in the West Atlantic, and they can be (and have been) completely eliminated in certain easily accessible diving locales. Their curiosity and boldness makes them easy targets for thoughtless spearfishermen and fish collectors.

Rock beauty (vaqueta de dos colores, cachama medio luto) *Holacanthus tricolor* To 1 foot. Adults are conspicuous and unmistakable and a delight to see. Although they are not abundant anywhere, they are fairly common in the West Indies. Bright orange-yellow juveniles might be confused with the 3-spot damselfish (page 78) except the damsel has 3 spots (one on the tail) instead of 2. **Range:** Florida to southeastern Brazil; stragglers reach Georgia and Bermuda. **Edibility:** poor.

JUVENILE

ADULT

Queen angelfish (isabelita, cachama de piedra) *Holacanthus cili-*
aris To 1½ feet. This gaudy, magnificent animal can be almost
inconspicuous in its natural habitat among the blue and yellow-
dappled sea whips, sea fans and corals. Can easily be confused
with the blue angelfish, but adult blues lack the regal corona
spotted with blue over the eye. Queens also have all-yellow tails
and pectoral fins while blue angels have blue pectoral and tail
fins with only the outer edges yellow. **Range:** Bermuda and Bahamas to Brazil, including the Gulf of Mexico. **Edibility:** poor.

Juvenile queen and **blue angels** are quite difficult to distinguish.
They all have yellow pectorals and yellow tails, and whitish-blue
stripes on the sides which vary greatly with growth. Usually, the
second bold blue bar on the body of the young queen angel is
curved, while on the young blue angel it is more straight as
shown. Under about 2 inches, both queen and blue angel juveniles have the basic pattern of 3 light blue body bars on a dark
body. As the fish grows, the bars first increase in number, then
gradually disappear.

JUVENILE

ADULT

71

Blue angelfish *Holacanthus bermudensis* To 1½ feet. This fish has a splendor of its own—a more subdued version of the queen angel. The queen and blue angelfishes apparently freely interbreed, resulting in hybrid forms which are intermediate in color. This led to much confusion in the description and naming of the blue angelfish. It was previously known as *H. isabelita*. The name *H. townsendi* is based on a hybrid specimen between the queen and blue angelfishes. **Range:** Rare in the Bahamas, but common in Bermuda, and Florida. Ranges through the West Indies and the Gulf of Mexico. **Edibility:** poor.

JUVENILE

ADULT

BUTTERFLYFISHES

Bank butterflyfish *Chaetodon aya* To 5 inches. A fairly rare deepwater butterflyfish distinctive for the high, strong dorsal and anal fin spines, long snout and bold oblique bars transversing its body. This fish seems to inhabit deep, offshore reefs and much colder water than most butterflyfishes. **Range:** Reported from North Carolina, Georgia, and taken in the Gulf of Mexico from hard offshore bottoms east of the Mississippi delta in five (rare) to 25 fathoms. Also a sighting reported in the "Flower Gardens" coral reef off the Galveston, Texas coast. **Edibility:** poor.

Much like a marine butterfly, the butterflyfish flashes in yellow and black-banded beauty around West Atlantic coral reefs. The foureye, spotfin and banded butterflies are quite common throughout the tropical Western Atlantic and the Gulf of Mexico. They prefer coral reefs, but can be found around almost any rock formation, singly or in pairs, rarely in schools. Many butterfly species characteristically pair off at an early age (2 to 3 inches in length). The pair seem almost inseparable, and follow each other around as though attached by a string. The two fishes rigorously patrol their territory, and will defend it fearlessly against aggressors—especially other butterflies. Since butterflies do not raise their young, it has been a source of debate as to why they pair off, apparently for life. Hans Fricke theorizes that this is a means of guarding against faulty cross-breeding between species, thus insuring the purity of the breed.

☐ The chaetodonts are disc-shaped fishes with small mouths set with bristle-like teeth (chaeta = bristle, odont = tooth). Some, like the longsnout butterfly, have forceplike snouts for picking small invertebrates from coral crevices. West Atlantic butterflies range in size from 3½-inch species like the longsnout butterfly to the spotfin butterfly, which reaches 8 inches.

☐ Although seemingly fragile and defenseless against the numerous predators of the reef, butterflyfish are able to survive by their rapidity, agility and defensive shape and coloring. They rarely stray far from the sheltering reef, and their narrow bodies fit easily into cracks and holes in the coral. If cornered, they lower their heads and spread their dorsal and anal spines, presenting the attacker with a difficult, prickly meal to swallow. Further, as

JUVENILE

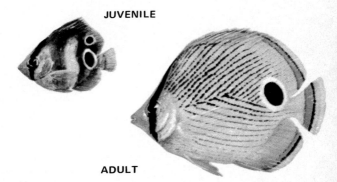

ADULT

Foureye butterflyfish (isabelita) *Chaetodon capistratus* To 6 inches. The most common butterflyfish in the West Atlantic. This fish occurs in large numbers in the Bahamas and is abundant throughout the Caribbean. Juveniles have two eye-spots, and indistinct vertical body stripes that fade as the fish matures. **Range:** New England south through the Lesser Antilles, including the Gulf of Mexico. **Edibility:** poor.

Spotfin butterflyfish (isabelita) *Chaetodon ocellatus* To 8 inches. Easily identified by the small black dot on the outer edge of the soft dorsal fin, and the larger dusky spot on the inner edge of the soft dorsal fin. This butterfly undergoes a surprising change of color at night when all chaetodonts enter into a state of torpor. Broad, dusky dark bands appear on the body, and the large, pale spot on the soft dorsal becomes dark black. **Range:** New England south to Brazil, including the Gulf of Mexico. **Edibility:** poor.

JUVENILE

ADULT

Longsnout butterflyfish *Prognathodes aculeatus* To 3½ inches. Another deepwater butterflyfish, the longsnout is said to be the most common butterflyfish at depths over 100 feet. Nevertheless it has been sighted in the shallows (once in 3 feet of water) in such Caribbean locales as the Virgin Islands, Leeward Islands and Curacao. Its long snout enables it to pick invertebrates from coral crevices. Also feeds on the tubefeet of sea urchins, the tentacles of tubeworms, and various small crustaceans. **Range:** Florida and the Bahamas south through the Lesser Antilles, including the Gulf of Mexico. **Edibility:** poor.

shown in these illustrations, all West Atlantic butterflies possess a dark stripe or patch passing through and concealing their eyes. Some also have a false eye spot or "ocellus" located near the tail. Current theory holds that this false eye spot is designed to fool predators. The false eye spot is usually larger than the real eye, thus confusing the attacker as to the size of its prey, and the location of the head of the butterfly. Thus when the attacker lunges at the wrong end, the wily butterfly makes its escape to a nearby crevice.

Banded butterflyfish (isabelita) *Chaetodon striatus* To 6 inches. Strikingly banded in black at all stages. The young are especially so and make attractive aquarium inhabitants. Next to the four-eye butterfly, this is the commonest of West Atlantic butterfly-fishes. **Range:** Both sides of the Atlantic; in the West Atlantic from New Jersey to southeastern Brazil, including the Gulf of Mexico. **Edibility:** poor.

Reef butterflyfish (isabelita) *Chaetodon sedentarius* To 6 inches. This fish is fond of deeper water, thus it is rarely seen by divers. Walter A. Starck reports it is common at Alligator Reef, in the Florida Keys. Juveniles are almost identical to adults, except for a single small spot on the soft dorsal surrounded by a white ring. **Range:** Bermuda (rare) and the Bahamas; North Carolina to southern Florida, and the eastern Gulf of Mexico and the Caribbean. **Edibility:** poor.

DAMSELFISHES

ADULT

JUVENILE

Yellowtail damselfish (morocota) *Microspathodon chrysurus* To
6 inches. Both adults and juveniles of this species are truly splendid animals, unmistakable with their bright blue or white spots
set like rhinestones across their bodies. Adults seem capable of
paling their body color from black or dark blue to brown, russet
or violet. A common fish on coral reefs. The young are often
seen among the blades of yellow stinging coral (*Millepora*). Feeds
on algae and organic detritus, coral polyps and other invertebrate
animals. Juveniles have been seen picking at the bodies of larger
fishes in search of parasites. **Range:** Bermuda, the Bahamas and
Florida to northern coast of South America, including the Gulf
of Mexico. **Edibility:** poor.

Occasionally divers are ferociously attacked by a dusky
little 4-inch fish that dashes from its coral cranny and in-
sistently rushes the intruder, sometimes nipping lightly
at the diver's arms, legs or fins. This tiny reef marauder
is the damselfish, one of the most courageous and pugnacious residents of the coral reef. Damsels will fearlessly
attack large barracuda, jacks, parrotfishes or anything that

threatens their coral home. The pomacentrids, or damsel-fishes, are small, tropical fishes distinguishable from most other marine species in having only one nostril on each side of the snout (instead of the usual two). They range in size from 2½ to 10 inches, and inhabit inshore reefs and tidepools over depths from 5 to 50 feet. Some range out to 180 foot and greater depths.

□ Most pomacentrids spawn on the bottom, and unusual mating behavior has been reported among some species. The male fish sets up a strongly defended territory on a section of rock, and begins a series of invitations to passing females indicating that he is ready to spawn. When an egg-bearing female sees him making his looping motions over his territory and accepts his invitation, she is led to the cleared area. Some species of male damsels have been heard to emit a distinct churring sound—brrrrr—during spawning. It is deduced that this sound is an im-

ADULT

JUVENILE

Threespot damselfish *Pomacentrus planifrons* To 4½ inches. Though tiny, this fish is one of the most consistently aggressive animals in the world. It will fearlessly attack large jacks, groupers, barracuda, crabs, even divers and TV cameras which venture near its territory. Yellow juveniles are easy to identify, with their bright yellow jackets and three-spot markings. They are likely to be confused only with the juvenile rock beauty (see page 70). Adult threespots are dusky and dark, and quite similar to numerous other adult damsels, including the dusky, beaugregory and cocoa damsels. The fairly deep, rounded body and yellowish tinge are good identification aids for the adult threespot. **Range**: Bermuda, Bahamas and southern Florida south through the Caribbean. **Edibility**: poor.

portant component of mating, without which the female would not lay eggs. Once she has deposited all her eggs, the male fertilizes them with his spawn; the female is chased from the nest, and the male continues his looping mating signals. When several females have deposited their eggs he takes total responsibility, fanning the eggs with his fins to oxygenate them, and guarding them ferociously against all predators. Large fishes and even skindivers have been chased and routed by worried male damsels. His vigil ends when the eggs hatch and the tiny damsels are left to fend for themselves on the vast, teeming reef.

ADULT

JUVENILE

Dusky damselfish (leopoldito) *Pomacentrus fuscus* To 6 inches. Adults are fond of mixed sand and rocky tidepool areas. I have found areas of tumbled rocks close to shore where virtually every large rock was closely guarded by a pugnacious little dusky damsel. Young are brilliant little fishes as shown, bright blue with the distinctive orange wash running across the nape and into the dorsal fin. It is often difficult to distinguish an adult dusky damsel from the very similar adult cocoa, beaugregory or threespot, but if the fish is almost entirely dusky bluish-blackish-brown with little hint of yellow, it is probably a dusky damsel. Note the small black spot at the upper edge of the pectoral base. **Range:** Bermuda, Bahamas and Florida through the Caribbean, including the Gulf of Mexico. **Edibility:** poor.

Beaugregory *Pomacentrus leucostictus* To 4 inches. The young beaugregory is a lovely, ubiquitous animal, common in calm, shallow tidepools, rock, sand and seagrass bottoms of a few inches in depth out to coral reefs over 20 feet deep. As they grow, they become uniformly dusky, much like the other dusky damsels, except for the tail, which remains relatively pale. They retain the blue spots on the nape and dorsal and the dark spot on the soft dorsal well into adulthood. As they age, these features disappear completely. One aid to identification is the torpedo shape of the beaugregory—it is the most shallow bodied fish of the genus. It has no spot on the tail base. **Range:** Maine to Bermuda, the Bahamas, Florida and the Gulf of Mexico and throughout the Caribbean to the hump of Brazil. **Edibility:** poor.

JUVENILE

ADULT

ADULT

JUVENILE

Cocoa damselfish *Pomacentrus variabilis* To 4¼ inches. One of the non-aggressive damsels, the cocoa swims peaceably about its home range, picking and plucking at the coral or bottom. The cocoa damsel is not as common as the previous three fishes, but neither is it a rare fish. The problem of trying to distinguish between adults and juveniles of the *Pomacentrus* genus damsels becomes evident when comparing the cocoa damsel with the last three species. They all have striking similarities, and it takes a sharp eye underwater to separate them. The cocoa damsel is not deep-bodied like the threespot damsel, and there is on most fishes (not all) a pronounced spot on the tail base of both young and adults. It might be confused with the dusky damsel, but the adult cocoa is more suffused with yellow than the dusky adult. **Range:** Bahamas and Florida to Brazil, including the Gulf of Mexico. **Edibility:** poor.

Bicolor damselfish *Pomacentrus partitus* To 4 inches. Fairly common on isolated patch reefs at depths of from 25 to 75 feet, and can be seen occasionally in shallow water. One was taken from a depth of over 1200 feet off Puerto Rico. Male bicolors guard egg clusters anchored to the substrate by filaments, and they can be quite pugnacious when on guard. **Range:** Bahamas and Florida and throughout the Caribbean. **Edibility:** poor.

Honey gregory, honey damselfish *Pomacentrus mellis* To 2½ inches. A rare and striking fish that seems to retain the same coloration in all phases of growth. Because of its pattern of violet lines and dots, the honey damsel might be mistaken for the cocoa or beaugregory juveniles, but both of these fishes possess a blue wash over nape and dorsal that the honey gregory lacks. No spot at base of tail fin. One of the smallest of the damsels. **Range:** Bahamas and Florida through the West Indies to Venezuela. **Edibility:** poor.

Blue chromis *Chromis cyaneus* To 5 inches. Look for this splendid fish in the blue water above the deep outer reefs and patch reefs. Mixed with clouds of blue chromis you will often find brown chromis and the wrasse that mimics the blue chromis, the creole wrasse (see page 96). These fishes feed on the zooplankton floating in the water column, and they can be seen picking copepods, one by one, from the passing water mass. **Range:** Bermuda, Bahamas, and Florida south through the Caribbean. **Edibility:** poor.

Brown chromis, yellow-edge chromis *Chromis multilineatus* To 6 inches. Very like the blue chromis in all respects save color, and the two fishes often swim together in large aggregations over reefs, picking plankton (mostly copepods) from the water mass. Note the dark blotch at the base of the pectoral fin, and the white spot behind the soft dorsal fin. *Chromis marginatus* is a synonym. **Range:** Bermuda, Bahamas and Florida south through the Lesser Antilles. **Edibility:** poor.

Yellowtail reeffish *Chromis enchrysurus* To about 4 inches. A deep-bodied fish quite similar in shape to the sunshine fish (see following), but with 2 violet stripes near the eye and a distinctive yellow tail. Fairly rare in shallow water, but quite common at 90 to 130 foot depths. **Range:** Both coasts of Florida; in the Gulf of Mexico it prefers deepwater reefs and hard bottoms from Pensacola, Florida south. **Edibility:** poor.

Sunshine fish, olive damselfish *Chromis insolatus* To 4 inches. The only green damsel in the West Atlantic, the juvenile sunshine fish is a brilliant animal, lime green or bright yellow above, dull olive below. As the fish matures, this bicolor pattern fades, and the damsel becomes olivaceous overall. A deepwater fish, it ranges from 50 to 160 feet off the Florida Keys, where Walter Starck finds it in abundance. In the Bahamas it has been taken at depths from 35 to 180 feet. Tends to stay close to the bottom, feeding on plankton. Often swims with the purple reeffish. **Range:** Bermuda and the Carolinas, Bahamas and Florida, south through the Lesser Antilles. **Edibility:** poor.

Purple reeffish *Chromis scotti* To 4 inches. Another deepwater damsel closely related to the sunshine fish. The purple reeffish is iridescent blue as a juvenile, purple-blue or dull blue as an adult. The deepwater chromis damsels have rounded, short, stubby bodies and only slightly-forked caudal fins that suits their bottom-dwelling existence. The high water chromis damsels (blue and brown chromis) on the other hand have more slender, streamlined bodies and deeply forked tails that enable them to maneuver rapidly in the shifting water mass high over the patch reefs. **Range:** reported from Bermuda, Florida and the eastern Gulf of Mexico from Pensacola south. **Edibility:** poor.

Night sergeant *Abudefduf taurus* To 10 inches. If you dive off any rocky inshore area such as a rock jetty or pier, you may find a few schools of night sergeants, peering cautiously out from their grottos. They prefer turbulent water, the shallower the better—I have found quite large night sergeants in as little as 2 feet of water. They are wary and evasive and since they are primarily herbivorous, they rarely take a fisherman's hook. **Range:** Florida, Bahamas and the Gulf of Mexico south to the Central American coast. **Edibility:** fair.

84

Sergeant major (petaca) *Abudefduf saxatilis* To 7 inches. The familiar sergeant major is found almost everywhere—over all kinds of bottoms from coral to sand to sea grass beds to rocky tide pools and dock pilings—eating with the most catholic of tastes—from anemones and tunicates to zooplankton, small fishes, algae and fisherman's bait. When guarding its egg patch from voracious wrasses, the adult male becomes dark bluish in color—so blue that at times the vertical body bars are almost obscured. **Range:** New England to Uruguay, including the Gulf of Mexico. **Edibility:** fair, but usually too small to warrant the effort.

SEE GUIDE MAPS TO WEST ATLANTIC,
Pages 203 and 204

SEE TIPS FOR FISHWATCHERS,
Page 202

To convert inches and feet to millimeters,
see metric conversion table, Page 193.

WRASSES

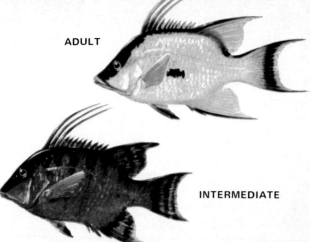

ADULT

INTERMEDIATE

Hogfish (el capitan, peje perro, pargo gallo) *Lachnolaimus maximus* To 3 feet. Unmistakable at all growth stages. Capable of various color changes from pale to mottled to banded, and from light grey to brick red. Aptly named, the hogfish is well-designed for rooting for food with its long snout. Large individuals have been observed rooting deep 6 to 9 inch holes in sand flats in search of mollusks, crabs and crustaceans. A popular food fish. Large 20 to 25 pound hogfish are now quite rare in some areas, owing to predation by spearfishermen. **Range:** North Carolina and Bermuda to Venezuela, including the Gulf of Mexico. **Edibility:** excellent.

If you see a small, gaudy, cigar-shaped fish pushing itself busily about the reef with its pectoral fins, you are watching a member of the wrasse (Labridae) family. West Atlantic wrasses occupy a variety of habitats. The blackear wrasse and the little green dwarf wrasse like sea grass beds where they hide easily in the blades of turtle grass. Razorfishes prefer sandy bottom or sea grass areas where they can dive quickly for cover. The creole wrasse swims with its look-alike, the blue chromis, high above the deeper patch reefs. Hogfishes (*L. maximus*) roam across open bottoms and sand flats where they feed on sea urchins and root happily for mollusks, crustaceans and worms. Most of the smaller cigar-shaped wrasses prefer the coral reefs and fan or sea-whip covered rocky flats.

Two exceptions are the bluehead and the slippery dick, which seem to move easily in virtually all habitats.

☐ Many wrasses have the curious habit of burying themselves in the sand at night, and aquarium watchers are frequently surprised to find that a tank filled with wrasses by day will be completely barren at night—they are all tucked away sleeping in the bottom gravel. Closely related to the parrotfishes, the wrasses have many characteristics in common with the parrots. Many West Atlantic wrasses spin themselves a gelatinous cocoon "nightgown" for protection while sleeping at night, as do certain parrotfishes.

☐ The colors of the labrids are astonishing in their beauty and variety. They glisten with gem-like spots, flecks, blotches, stripes and bars. Like the parrotfishes, the wrasses almost defy classification due to the startling color changes that occur as the fish mature. To add to the confusion, sex-related changes occur that can change a female to a male, and possibly a male to a female.

Spanish hogfish (loro gallo) *Bodianus rufus* To 2 feet. Not abundant anywhere, but not uncommon over reefs of 10 to 100 foot depths. Lovely jewel-like juveniles (quite similar in coloration to the fairy basslet, page 17) are occasionally seen working their cleaning stations, picking parasites from large jacks, groupers, and other predators. **Range:** Bermuda, Bahamas and Florida to Brazil, including the Gulf of Mexico. **Edibility:** good.

87

□ Certain young juvenile wrasses become sexually mature as small as 1½ inches, and mate in groups. Group mating usually begins with upward spawning rushes by an egg-laden female. She is followed by numerous young males, all of whom assist in fertilizing eggs. A certain number of the males, and apparently some sex-reversed females, become terminal-phase supermales, emerging in brilliant hues of blue, green, red or yellow, and sporting flowing, lyre-like tails. These supermales tend to mate and spawn individually with one or more females. Dominant supermale wrasses of some species set up "harems" on the reef of from 4 to 10 females and actively mate with all members of the harem. If the supermale dies or is dispatched by a predator, the largest female in the harem changes into a supermale, and assumes the dominance and mating duties of the harem. On the larger reefs, the bluehead wrasse has a mating system whereby several dozen large supermales set up spawning territories in a restricted area of the reef. Each guards his area strongly against younger male wrasses. Each day near midday, females come to this area and select the largest and most brightly-colored supermale for mating. Large supermales often spawn more than 40 times a day, and in high population areas, 100 times a day is not unusual. Small wonder that bluehead wrasses are so numerous.

Spotfin or Cuban hogfish *Bodianus pulchellus* To 9 inches. Quite similar in many respects to the Spanish hogfish, except for the coloration. Juveniles are cleaner fishes, like the Spanish hogfish. Up to 2 inches in length, young are all yellow with part-black dorsal fins. Rare in less than 50 feet of water and has been taken at 360 foot depths. **Range:** South Carolina, Bahamas, and Florida to Lesser Antilles. **Edibility:** poor.

SUPERMALE

ADULT FEMALE OR MALE

INTERMEDIATE

JUVENILE

Bluehead *Thalassoma bifasciatum* To 6 inches. One of the most successful fish in the tropical West Atlantic, representatives of this species seem to be everywhere. Their brilliant yellow bodies dart in and out of coral reefs, rocky flats, reef sand and sea grass habitats. The name "bluehead" is a misnomer, since only the terminal phase male, constituting about 4% of the population, has a blue head. Adult females, adult males and juveniles are yellow-jacketed with a midlateral stripe or bar, as illustrated. In seconds these wrasses can flash from a broad midlateral stripe to a row of squarish blotches or bars, possibly to match their background. Yellow individuals have been seen to pick parasites from other fishes, and a recent observer found a large male bluehead cleaning another fish. **Range:** both sides of the Atlantic; in the West Atlantic, from Bermuda, Bahamas and Florida to Curacao, including the Gulf of Mexico. **Edibility:** poor.

☐ In size, West Atlantic wrasses vary from small species that attain a maximum length of 3 inches up to bull males of other species that reach 3 feet in length. Their flesh is generally soft and pasty, unattractive as food—with two exceptions. The hogfish, which grows to 3 feet, and the Spanish hogfish, reaching 2 feet, are considered excellent eating and are prize catches for fishermen.

☐ In the tropical West Atlantic the brilliant little juvenile Spanish and spotfin hogfish wrasses turn their home base coral heads into cleaning stations, and larger fishes come and often wait in line to be cleaned. Bluehead wrasses, juveniles and adults, have also been seen picking parasites off other fishes. It is an incredible sight to see these tiny wrasses fluttering about the fins, gills, and even into the mouths of huge jacks and groupers, predators that could easily dispatch them with a single gulp. Other fishes and

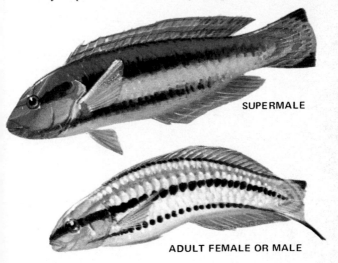

SUPERMALE

ADULT FEMALE OR MALE

Slippery dick (loro verde) *Halichoeres bivittatus* To 9 inches. One of the most abundant species of the genus, occurring in such diverse habitats as coral reef, sea-whip covered rocky flats, shallow reef and reef-sand areas. They feed mainly on crabs, sea urchins and mollusks. Easily distinguished by the two broad dark stripes on the sides of the body in virtually all phases. **Range:** North Carolina and Bermuda south to Brazil, including the Gulf of Mexico. **Edibility:** poor.

invertebrates that engage in symbiotic cleaning relationships with larger fishes include the neon goby and the sharknose goby (see page 167); and the scarlet lady and banded coral shrimps (see pages 189-190). One opportunistic fish, the wrasse blenny (see page 169), has gone to great lengths to mimic the bluehead cleaner wrasse. Thus it enjoys the same immunity from predation as the cleaner wrasse without having to work for it.

Yellowhead wrasse *Halichoeres garnoti* To 8 inches. Supermales, adult females and males and juveniles are quite unmistakable and distinct from other wrasses. Note the vividly blue-striped juvenile. A common inshore wrasse, but has been taken from 160 foot depths. **Range:** Bermuda, Bahamas and Florida to southeastern Brazil. **Edibility:** poor.

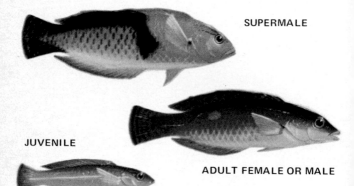

SUPERMALE

JUVENILE

ADULT FEMALE OR MALE

Rainbow wrasse, painted wrasse *Halichoeres caudalis* To 7 inches. This deep-dwelling wrasse is rarely seen by divers due to its preference for 90 to 240 foot depths. Note the black "ear" similar to the blackear wrasse. In the Gulf of Mexico it has been taken over deep reefs from Pensacola south and from the central Texas coast. **Range:** Florida, Greater Antilles and the Gulf of Mexico. **Edibility:** poor.

Clown wrasse *Halichoeres maculipinna* To 6½ inches. Both adult males and females and the splendid supermale are brilliantly painted in circus colors. A handsome fish to see on the reef, and voracious clown wrasses are common in many areas of the tropical West Atlantic. **Range:** North Carolina and Bermuda, Bahamas, and Florida to Brazil. **Edibility:** poor.

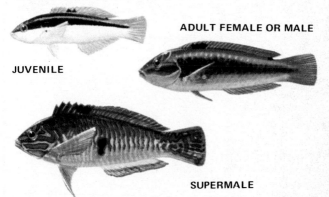

ADULT FEMALE OR MALE

JUVENILE

SUPERMALE

Blackear wrasse *Halichoeres poeyi* To 8 inches. Look for this wrasse in seagrass beds where it blends in perfectly with the blades of turtle grass. The black "ear" spot behind the eye is distinctive at all stages. Shown is the supermale and the yellow juvenile. Adult females and males appear very like the supermale, except they lack the red markings on the tail and have more subdued red spots and markings on the green body. **Range:** Bahamas and Florida to Brazil. **Edibility:** poor.

JUVENILE

SUPERMALE

92

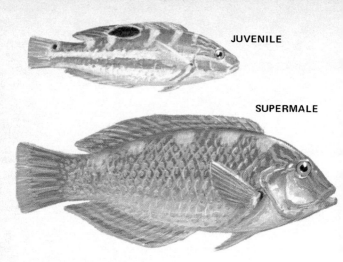

JUVENILE

SUPERMALE

Puddingwife *Halichoeres radiatus* To 20 inches. The big super-male is unmistakable with its blue-green spots, stripes and worm-like scrawls. Smaller adult females, males and juveniles are almost totally different in coloration, but also unique. The 5 white spots just below the dorsal, broken by from one to two black blotches are distinctive, and present at all phases except the fully-grown supermale. **Range:** North Carolina, Bermuda, Bahamas, and Florida to Brazil. **Edibility:** poor.

Painted wrasse *Halichoeres pictus* To 6 inches. The painted wrasse is a coral reef species that stays well off the bottom, often swimming with bluehead and clown wrasses. The supermale is unmistakable. Younger males and females have two light brown stripes from nose to tail. Tiny juveniles are pale with a single lateral dark stripe. **Range:** Bahamas and Florida to the Lesser Antilles. **Edibility:** poor.

ADULT FEMALE OR MALE

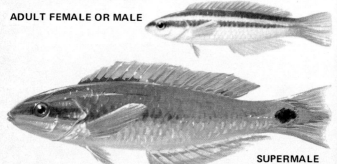

SUPERMALE

93

Yellowcheek wrasse, yellowback wrasse *Halichoeres cyanocephalus* To 6 inches. An attractive yellow and blue striped wrasse not often seen by divers due to its preference for the deeper reefs. It was recently discovered (1965) off the American coast. Walter Starck reports that it is "frequent" at Alligator Reef, Florida. **Range:** uncertain. **Edibility:** poor.

Rosy or straighttail razorfish *Hemipteronotus martinicensis* To 6 inches. Most razorfishes possess compressed, razorlike heads, shaped almost like the prow of a ship. Since they burrow constantly into the gritty reef sand and gravel, a narrow forehead is a distinct asset. Shown is the adult male. Females are pale with a rosy stripe from eye to tail. **Range:** Bahamas to Venezuela, and west to Yucatan. **Edibility:** poor.

Green razorfish *Hemipteronotus splendens* To 4½ inches. If while diving you see a large-headed fish dive straight for the sand and disappear, that will be a razorfish. Longley at Tortugas found that green razorfishes always return to the same hiding place in the sand. They do not build nests, however, like the pearly razorfish. The adult male fish is shown. **Range:** Bermuda, Bahamas and Florida to Brazil. **Edibility:** poor.

94

Pearly razorfish *Hemipteronotus novacula* To 15 inches. Much like the sand tilefish, this fish burrows into the sand and builds a nest of coral fragments to which it returns if threatened by a predator. Also very adept at diving into the sand if alarmed. **Range:** the Carolinas, Bahamas and Florida to Brazil, including the Gulf of Mexico. **Edibility:** poor.

Cunner *Tautogolabrus adspersus* To 15 inches. The cunner is closely related to the tautog and these two fishes often swim together over much the same range. It is the northernmost of all the West Atlantic wrasses, ranging from Newfoundland to Chesapeake Bay. Young display blotches and dark bars. **Range:** see above. **Edibility:** good.

Tautog, blackfish, oysterfish *Tautoga onitis* To 3 feet. Ranging from Nova Scotia to South Carolina, the tautog is most abundant from Cape Cod to Delaware Bay. They are sluggish fishes, and divers often find them reclining on a rocky bottom or retreating reluctantly a few feet ahead. It is popular with anglers, and is taken to some extent in pots, traps and trawls. **Range:** see above. **Edibility:** good, but not extensively eaten.

Creole wrasse *Clepticus parrai* To 1 foot. This wrasse schools with and mimics the blue chromis damsels in open water around the deeper patch reefs. It can be distinguished from the damselfishes by its heavier body, broader tail and purple coloration. It also stubbornly swims with its pectoral fins in typical wrasse fashion. **Range:** North Carolina and Bermuda, the Bahamas and Florida south through the West Indies. **Edibility:** poor.

Dwarf wrasse *Doratonotus megalepis* To 3 inches. The smallest of the West Atlantic wrasses, this little fish is quite common over its range, yet rarely seen. It lives in shallow seagrass beds, and can change its coloration to exactly match its turtle grass background. **Range:** both sides of the Atlantic; in the West Atlantic from Bermuda, the Bahamas and Florida south through the Lesser Antilles. **Edibility:** poor.

PARROTFISHES

JUVENILE

ADULT FEMALE AND MALE

SUPERMALE

Queen parrotfish (vieja) *Scarus vetula* To 2 feet. So different are the male and female queen parrotfishes that earlier fish experts assumed that they were two different species and gave the name *Scarus gnathodus* to the female. The queen parrotfish has been seen to occur in "harems" of three or four females to one supermale, grazing together like cows and a bull. Known to envelop themselves in cocoons at night. For identification of the supermale, note the distinct markings on the nose, pectoral fins and tail, and the lunate tail. **Range:** Bermuda, Bahamas and Florida throughout the Caribbean to Venezuela. **Edibility:** poor.

If you dive off any shallow coral reef as the tide is coming in you are likely to encounter dozens of gaudy parrotfishes. They swarm in over the reef in blue-green, grey and rust-colored waves, grazing like guernsey cows through the coral. Many parrots are large, bulky fishes and they must wait for high tide to flood the close-packed coral reefs to give them room to maneuver and feed. They are single-minded, gentle creatures of habit, and they have their set patterns of travel. Occasionally I have come nose-to-nose with a large parrotfish in a narrow defile, and I had to back off respectfully to let it pass. They are not easily deterred from their feeding routes, and they seem to regard the curious diver with tolerance and some irritation for interrupting their non-stop, movable feast.

☐ Although closely related to the carnivorous wrasses, parrotfishes are herbivores of the Scaridae family. They are named for their gaudy colors and parrot-like beaks with which they bite away chunks of coral, leaving distinct beak-marks on the reef. In their constant quest for food, they are highly efficient recycling mechanisms. As they graze algae off the reefs, they turn coral and rock

ADULT FEMALE AND MALE

SUPERMALE

Rainbow parrotfish (guacamaya) *Scarus guacamaia* To 4 feet. One of the largest and most impressive of West Atlantic parrotfishes. Experiments at Bermuda indicate that this fish may use the sun for navigation. It traveled a considerable distance from its nocturnal home cave to feed by day and returned at evening in the same way, on a direct course to its cave. **Range:** Bermuda, Bahamas, and Florida south to Argentina. **Edibility:** poor.

into fine sand. They extract the algae by crushing the rock-hard coral with powerful plate-like pharyngeal teeth located in the back of the throat, then pass this stony rubble down an apparently cast-iron digestive tract. Due to their set patterns of travel and their almost constant defecation, they leave mounds and floors of fine sand and undigested coral rubble throughout the reef.

☐ Recent interest and knowledge of the scarids, speeded by the advent of scuba diving, has revealed that parrotfishes undergo dramatic color changes as they mature and, like the wrasses, sex changes as well. Most species mature through three different color phases, including juvenile, adult and "terminal phase" colorations. Male and female adults often share the same color pattern, but some males, as well as certain sex-reversed females, will

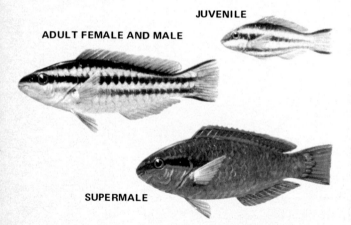

JUVENILE

ADULT FEMALE AND MALE

SUPERMALE

Princess parrotfish (pez loro) *Scarus taeniopterus* To 13 inches. The lavishly colored supermale seems to glow at times in red, blue and green neon. Much confusion has resulted from the close similarity in coloration between this fish and the mottlefin parrotfish, both supermales and females. Note the differences in the tail fins and the positions of the stripes around the eye. On the females, note the difference of the white striping on the head. On both females and juveniles, note the distinctive dark margins on the tail fin of the princess parrotfish. Known to produce cocoons at night. **Range:** Bermuda, Bahamas and Florida throughout Caribbean. Due to the confusion between the princess and mottlefin parrotfishes, the precise distribution of both species is uncertain. **Edibility:** poor.

mature into large terminal phase "supermales," sporting gaudy peacock colors and long, flowing tails. The reasons for these changes and the processes by which they occur are not well understood, but it is a subject of intense study in ichthyological circles. This startling new information has brought chaos to the inexact science of giving scientific names to the parrots. Of some 350 species of parrotfishes previously recorded throughout the world, a recent study reduced this number to 80 species, and many of these are in doubt. On-going studies continue to demonstrate that various fishes previously considered to be different species were actually male and female, or juvenile and adult specimens of the same fish species.

☐ The considerable difference between male and female parrotfishes is clearly illustrated here by the queen, stoplight and redband parrots. In general, it is safe to say that most of the brilliant blue, green, red and lavishly-striped and mottled parrots are adult terminal-phase males, while most of the dull grey, green red or brownish-colored

SUPERMALE

ADULT FEMALE AND MALE

JUVENILE

Mottlefin or striped parrotfish (bullon) *Scarus croicensis* To 11 inches. Mottlefin is a particularly good name for the supermale of this species, since one of the key features that distinguishes it from the princess and queen parrotfish supermales is the blue mottling or marbling evident on all of the vertical fins. Also distinctive for the blue edges on the tail fin. Known to produce cocoons at night. **Range:** Bermuda, Bahamas, Florida south throughout the Caribbean, including the Gulf of Mexico. **Edibility:** poor.

100

parrots are females or immature males. Juvenile parrots 1½ to 4 inches long of most of the tropical West Atlantic species are colored a light grass green, grey or mottled green-brown, with various stripes, spots, bars and other markings across the body that differ according to the species.

□ Parrotfishes vary greatly in size. West Atlantic species range from the rosy parrot that attains an adult size of 4½ inches to the blue and rainbow parrots that reach 4 feet in length. It is a very impressive sight, when diving on the reef, to see a few 4 foot parrots browsing slowly among the coral heads. There have been reports of some Indo-Pacific parrots attaining lengths of 6 feet, and scattered claims of massive old bull males reaching 12 feet in length and 6 feet in depth. Even more strange, Jacques Yves Cousteau tells of seeing huge bumphead parrotfishes (*Bolbometaponmuricatus*) charging at high speeds and smashing their curious, bumper-like heads into the reef to dislodge pieces of coral, which they would then munch contentedly in the manner of most parrots.

JUVENILE

ADULT FEMALE AND MALE

SUPERMALE

Blue parrotfish (loro azul, guacamaya) *Scarus coeruleus* To 4 feet. Both adult males and females are usually an even cerulean blue, but are capable of phasing to a mottled blue and black pattern to match the background. Large supermales develop the characteristic hump on the forehead. Beebe and Tee-Van report sighting a vast school of thousands of blue parrotfishes at 30 feet off Bermuda, all headed down and out toward open sea. **Range:** Virginia and Bermuda south to Brazil. **Edibility:** poor.

Another remarkable characteristic of certain parrots and a few wrasses is their habit of laboriously fabricating a mucous cocoon or "sleeping bag" around themselves before bedding down in the coral at night. Some species take 30 minutes to produce the cocoon at night, and another 30 minutes to break out of it in the morning. How and why the cocoon is made is a mystery. One theory postulates that the mucous cocoon serves to protect the sleeping fish from such night predators as moray eels, which depend on their keen sense of smell to locate their prey.

□ Tropical West Atlantic parrots are divided into two main genera—the genus *Sparisoma* and the genus *Scarus*. *Sparisoma* parrots have the 'beak' of the upper jaw en-

Midnight parrotfish, indigo parrotfish *Scarus coelestinus* To 30 inches. I spotted my first midnight parrotfish at Cozumel, Mexico and was so impressed that I followed it for 10 or 15 minutes while it munched algae off rocks and coral. A truly beautiful animal. Color is the same at all growth stages. **Range:** Bermuda, Bahamas and Florida to Brazil. **Edibility:** poor.

Emerald parrotfish *Nicholsina usta* To 1 foot. A wide-ranging parrotfish, found along the east coast of the U.S. from New Jersey to Florida, the Gulf of Mexico and the Greater Antilles to Brazil. Seems to prefer sea grass beds, but has been taken from close inshore to 240 foot depths. **Range:** see above. **Edibility:** poor.

Rosy parrotfish, slender, many-tooth or bluelip parrotfish *Cryptotomus roseus* To 4½ inches. This cigar-shaped little parrotfish is quite wrasse-like in shape and habits. Prefers grassy areas, tidal canals, turtle grass beds. Shown is the adult male. In the aquarium has been observed at night wrapped in a mucous cocoon and buried in the sand with only its head protruding. **Range:** Bermuda, Bahamas, and Florida to Brazil. **Edibility:** poor.

Redband parrotfish (pez loro) *Sparisoma aurofrenatum* To 11 inches. A much smaller fish than the stoplight, but has many similarities. The supermale can be distinguished from the stoplight supermale by the more squarecut tail, with black outer margins, the two black spots surrounded by yellow behind the eye, and the black spot at the base of the pectoral fin. The redband female and young are easily identified underwater by the white blotch or saddle just behind the dorsal fin. **Range:** Bermuda, Bahamas and Florida to Brazil. **Edibility:** poor.

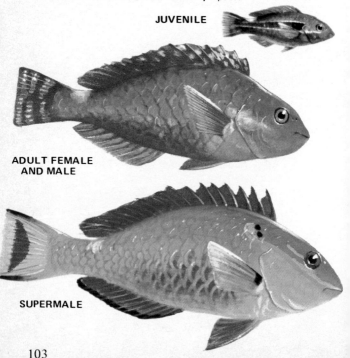

JUVENILE

ADULT FEMALE AND MALE

SUPERMALE

closed by the beak of the lower jaw when the mouth is closed. This condition is reversed in the genus *Scarus*, where the upper 'beak' encloses the lower. Some of the *Scarus* parrots occasionally sleep in cocoon nightgowns (the rainbow, blue, princess and striped parrots), while others do not. *Sparisoma* parrots apparently do not spin cocoons. The rosy parrotfish of the genus *Cryptotomus* is smaller and more wrasse-like in shape and habits than any of the other parrots shown here. The rosy parrot not only spins a cocoon sleeping bag at night, but like the wrasses also buries itself in the sand, apparently for double protection.

ADULT FEMALE AND MALE

JUVENILE

SUPERMALE

Stoplight parrotfish (macho—loro verde; hembra—loro colorado) *Sparisoma viride* To 21 inches. Supermales are distinguished from the similar redband parrot by their lunate, flowing tails and the distinctive gold spot at the upper corner of the gill cover. The harlequin-garbed red-bellied female and immature male are lovely animals to see on the reef. Even the tiny juvenile stoplight is a handsome spotted fish. **Range:** Bermuda, Bahamas and Florida to the hump of Brazil, including the Gulf of Mexico. **Edibility:** poor, but a market fish in Puerto Rico.

104

Redtail parrotfish (loro verde, cotoro verde) *Sparisoma chrysopterum* To 18 inches. This fish moves easily from coral reef to rocky areas to seagrass beds, and is a great color changer, adept at matching its background. Usually it is a very mottled gray-green fish and usually (but not always) with a red tail. Look for the distinct black spot at the pectoral fin base and the white saddle behind the dorsal fin on mature males and females, as well as on striped and spotted nondescript young. **Range:** Florida and the Bahamas to Brazil. **Edibility:** poor, but eaten in Puerto Rico.

ADULT FEMALE AND MALE

SUPERMALE

Bucktooth parrotfish (pez loro) *Sparisoma radians* To 7½ inches. Another expert color-changer, the sea-grass-dwelling bucktooth has an infinite variety of mottlings, patches, blotches and stripes to match any background in sea-grass, sand or rocky substrate. Shown is the mature male. Females and young males lack the bold black markings of the mature males, and have a light blue spot at the pectoral fin base (instead of black and a light blue margin on the gill cover. **Range:** Bermuda, Bahamas and Florida to Venezuela, including the Gulf of Mexico. **Edibility:** poor.

105

Yellowtail parrotfish (pez loro) *Sparisoma rubripinne* To 18 inches. The yellow-tailed females and young males are very common close inshore. Their nondescript, mottled coloration aids them in eluding predators by expertly matching their background. Large supermales were originally thought to be a separate species, *Sparisoma axillare*. **Range:** Massachusetts, Bermuda, Bahamas and Florida to Brazil. **Edibility:** poor.

**ADULT FEMALE
AND MALE**

SUPERMALE

CARDINALFISHES

Bigtooth cardinalfish *Apogon affinis* To 4½ inches. At night this cardinalfish moves up to occupy the same plankton feeding area high in the water column vacated by the diurnal blue and brown chromis damselfishes. It is called "bigtooth" because of the large, distinct canines in its jaws. During the day it frequents dark caves, overhangs and hollow coral heads at depths of 50 feet or more, thus it is rarely seen by divers. **Range:** Bahamas and Florida Keys to Venezuela. **Edibility:** poor.

As dusk descends over the reef, and after all of the day-light-active fishes have retired to their reef holes and crevices for the night, there is a short period of calm and inactivity. One by one, like sentries on guard duty, the cardinalfishes appear. These large-eyed, nocturnal fishes are tiny, seldom over 5 inches in length. But they are so numerous and occupy such a variety of habitats that they are virtually the masters of the night reef. The bigtooth cardinalfishes rise from reef holes and bottom crevices high in the water column to occupy the same stations vacated by the chromis damselfishes. The conchfish, a tiny cardinal that hides during daylight hours in the mantle cavity of the queen conch, comes boldly out at night to forage across the reef bottom. The whitestar cardinalfish, a reef hole and cave dweller by day, moves very little at night, feeding quite near its daytime habitat. These mini-masters of the night reef occupy the same stations vacated by various fishes active only during the day. All of them feed on zooplankton in the tides that sweep the reef, and their shift-like day-night activity assures that each fish species has its turn to feed, without overcrowding.

□ So it is that the cardinalfishes (Apogonidae family) are not usually seen by the daylight diver unless he searches the darker areas of the reef. A sharp eye will discover some of the more common cardinalfishes (the barred cardinal or the flamefish) sharing a dark reef hole or burrow with a few squirrelfishes or sweepers. Like most night-roaming fishes, the cardinals are handsomely colored in tones of red or bronze. This dark coloration allows them to forage at night without being seen, while their large eyes are adept at spotting zooplankton on the darkened reef.

□ Certain West Atlantic cardinalfishes have been observed sheltering close to starfishes and sea anemones, apparently for protection from predators. The freckled

Flamefish *Apogon maculatus* To 4 inches. A beautiful, flame-red little fish, one of the most familiar and common cardinals over (and under) West Atlantic reefs. Frequently seen in shallow water floating in the mouths of caves and crevices. Males have been seen carrying eggs in their mouths. **Range:** New England, Bahamas, Bermuda and Florida to Brazil, including the Gulf of Mexico. **Edibility:** poor.

Whitestar cardinalfish *Apogon lachneri* To about 2½ inches. This fish is well-named, for the tiny white spot on the back seems to gleam starlike in the 35 to 200 foot depths preferred by the whitestar. Also taken occasionally in 12 feet of water. **Range:** Bahamas and southern Florida to Venezuela, including the Gulf of Mexico. **Edibility:** poor.

Barred cardinalfish *Apogon binotatus* To 5 inches. A fairly common cardinalfish, reported by Bohlke and Chaplin as being abundant in the Bahamas, and by Walter Starck as frequent at Alligator Reef, Florida. It seems to be capable of changing its color from pale salmon to dark red. Longley working in the Tortugas noted that when over a light background the fish switches instantly to the pallid color phase. Ranges in depth from nearshore to 160 feet. **Range:** Bermuda, Bahamas and Florida to Venezuela. **Edibility:** poor.

Belted cardinalfish *Apogon townsendi* To 2½ inches. A brilliant and iridescent little cardinal, distinctive for the very broad band near the tail with black vertical margins. Younger fish display only the black marginal stripes of this band, which gradually fill in with pigment to become one band, as the fish matures. Taken from near-shore to 90 foot depths. **Range:** Bahamas and Florida to Venezuela. **Edibility:** poor.

109

Twospot cardinalfish *Apogon pseudomaculatus* To 3½ inches. Somewhat like the flamefish, but notable for being the only cardinal in our area with a small black spot near the tail. A deep water fish ranging from 50 to over 1300 foot depths. A mouthbrooder. **Range:** New England, Bermuda, Bahamas and Florida south to Brazil, including the Gulf of Mexico. **Edibility:** poor.

Freckled cardinalfish *Phaeoptyx conklini* To 3½ inches. There are three closely-related species of distinctively spotted or freckled West Atlantic cardinalfishes that have recently been placed in the genus *Phaeoptyx*. They include the freckled cardinalfish shown here, the sponge cardinalfish (*P. xenus*) and the dusky cardinalfish (*P. pigmentaria*). Due to their spotted coloration, they are often difficult to distinguish underwater. All three species appear to have unusual preferences in the selection of habitats—the sponge cardinal seeks shelter during the day in the central cavity of cylindrical sponges, while the dusky cardinal has been seen sheltering in or near the spines of sea urchins. The freckled cardinalfish has been observed off the Florida Keys hovering around the basket starfish *Astrophyton muricatum* when it is expanded at night. **Range of all three cardinalfishes:** Bahamas and Florida to Venezuela. **Edibility:** poor.

cardinalfish has been observed off the Florida Keys hovering around the basket starfish, *Astrophyton muricatum*, when it is expanded at night. Although cardinalfishes do not have immunity from the stinging tentacles of sea anemones, recently the bridle cardinalfish, *Apogon aurolineatus*, and the sawcheek cardinalfish, *Apogon quadri-*

110

squamatus (not shown), were sighted sheltering closely to the deadly tentacles of Caribbean sea anemones. Apparently the protection from predators offered by the host outweighs the danger of being stung and eaten by the anemones. Most cardinals are mouthbrooders that take their eggs into their large mouths for incubation. In most cases, but not all, it is the father who takes this responsibility. The eggs are usually contained in a compact ball, and may number tens of thousands. This very close care and nurturing of the developing eggs, compared with other fish species which allow the eggs to drift with the ocean tides, assures that many more cardinalfishes hatch and grow to maturity.

Conchfish *Astrapogon stellatus* To 3 inches. This rather drab little fish lives as a commensal within the mantle cavity of the live queen conch *Strombas gigas*. As many as five conchfish have been taken from a single conch. They remain in the conch by day, and emerge at night to feed on shrimps, sea lice and other crustaceans. What service they provide to the conch, if any, is not known. The single row of dots running back from pectoral fin to tail is distinctive. **Range:** Bermuda, Bahamas and Florida Keys to Brazil. **Edibility:** poor.

Punctate cardinalfish *Astrapogon puncticulatus* To 3 inches. Closely related to the conchfish, this cardinal is so similar that the two were thought to be the same fish until recently. This fish has never been found in a queen conch, however, and seems to prefer dead shells, rocks and holes in the reef. For differences, note the more pronounced lines radiating from the eye of the punctate and the lack of the distinct line of dots found on the conchfish. **Range:** Florida and the Bahamas to Venezuela. **Edibility:** poor.

SQUIRRELFISHES, SOLDIERFISHES

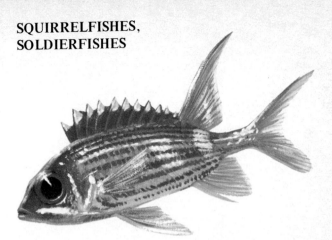

Squirrelfish (candil) *Holocentrus rufus* To 12½ inches. Ranges from shore to about 100 foot depths. Note white spots at tips of dorsal fin spines. This fish and the longjaw are distinctive for the elongated upper tail fin lobes. **Range:** Carolinas, Bermuda, Bahamas, Florida throughout Caribbean. **Edibility:** good.

The holocentrids, commonly known as squirrelfishes or soldierfishes, are primarily nocturnal animals with large, squirrel-like eyes and red coloration. During the day most of the squirrels hide in or near their crevices on the reef bottom. They become active at night, when their dark red hues make them almost invisible, and their keen eyes enable then to forage across the dark reef for shrimps, crabs and other crustaceans. They are very rough, spiny, prickly fishes, not attractive meals to bigger fishes, and most squirrels possess a sharp spine at the base of the gill cover with which they can inflict painful, sometimes poisonous wounds. Most squirrels are not much used for food due to their small size and spiny bodies. The blackbar and cardinal soldierfishes do not have the spiny, prickly bodies of other squirrels and are good food fishes, although rather small in size (to 8½ inches).

☐ Although noted for their shyness during the daytime hours, the secretive squirrels are not difficult to locate for the sharp-eyed diver. Longjaw squirrels are commonly seen by day lurking in or near their reef holes, often in the company of a few blackbar soldierfishes, cardinalfishes, bigeyes or sweepers. Certain West Atlantic squirrels have been found to be rather noisy fishes, much like the croakers. Scientists of the Tektite II Man-In-The-Sea Project recorded a surprising array of squirrelfish sounds, ranging from staccatos and chirps (by the longjaw squirrel) to quacks and a "squeaking door sound" (by the longspine squirrelfish). Their reasons for making these sounds is still not clear, but they may be a component of aggressive action, flight or courtship activity.

Longjaw squirrelfish (candil) *Holocentrus ascensionis* To 2 feet. Quite common, often seen skulking about outer patch reefs. Note greenish dorsal fin, longer upper lobe of tail fin. **Range:** New York, Bermuda, Bahamas, Florida to Brazil, including Gulf of Mexico. **Edibility:** good.

Reef squirrelfish (candil) *Holocentrus coruscus* To 5½ inches. Inhabits coral and rock reefs from shore to 75 foot depths. Note distinctive black spots between first few dorsal fin spines. **Range:** Bermuda, Bahamas, Florida through Lesser Antilles to Venezuela. **Edibility:** poor.

Dusky squirrelfish (candil) *Holocentrus vexillarius* To 6 inches. A common inshore species, found hiding about coral reefs, rocky outcroppings, tidepools. Note black spots between dorsal fin spines. **Range:** New Jersey, Bermuda, Bahamas and Florida through Caribbean, including the Gulf of Mexico. **Edibility:** poor.

Longspine squirrelfish (candil) *Holocentrus marianus* To 7 inches. Prefers 50 to 200 foot depths. Note very long third anal fin spine. **Range:** Carolinas, Bahamas through the Caribbean. **Edibility:** poor.

Cardinal soldierfish (candil) *Plectrypops retrospinis* To 5 inches. A secretive fish, preferring patch reefs over 30 to 80 foot depths. A uniformly red fish. **Range:** Bermuda, Bahamas, Florida through the Caribbean. **Edibility:** poor.

Blackbar soldierfish (candil de piedra) *Myripristes jacobus* To 8½ inches. Occasionally seen by divers drifting just inside reef holes and crevices. A handsome fish. **Range:** both sides of Atlantic. In West Atlantic from Bahamas and Florida to Brazil, including the Gulf of Mexico. **Edibility:** good.

BIGEYES, SWEEPERS AND BOGAS

Copper sweeper, glassy sweeper *Pempheris schomburgki* To 6 inches. **Range:** Bermuda, the Bahamas and Florida to Brazil. **Edibility:** *poor.*

Sweepers of the family Pempheridae are cave and crevice dwellers by day, and it is a real delight to discover a small school of these handsome coppery fishes peering out of their grotto. They make strange bobbing movements as they float, caused by vibration of their pectoral fins. Juvenile copper sweepers are tiny, glassy, transparent beauties with opercles and organs of the body cavity glittering iridescent silver with copper and blue reflections. The vertebrae are heavily pigmented with red and black. The iris of the eye is powdered densely with golden bronze and the lips are lemon yellow. William Beebe and John Tee-Van repeatedly sighted a large school of several thousand sweeper juveniles, all barely an inch long, transparent and floating six fathoms down in an open grotto off Bermuda. The "glassy sweeper" gets its name from this juvenile phase. As the fish matures, it assumes the coppery color shown in this 5-inch adult.

☐ Bigeyes, also known as catalufas, are nocturnal fishes like the sweepers, squirrelfishes and cardinalfishes, and they are occasionally found by day sharing a reef cave or grotto with these fishes. Like the squirrels, the bigeyes (family Priacanthidae) are most active at night when they actively stalk such prey as small fishes, crustaceans and polychaete worms, as well as zooplankton in the night

115

tides. They are not entirely nocturnal, however. Investigations show that the stomachs of bigeyes often contain fresh food items during daylight hours.

Glasseye, glasseye snapper *Priacanthus cruentatus* To 1 foot. **Range:** circumtropical; in the West Atlantic, from Bermuda, Bahamas and Florida to Brazil. **Edibility:** fair.

Bigeye *Priacanthus arenatus* To 15 inches. **Range:** both sides of the Atlantic; in the West Atlantic from New England and Bermuda to Argentina, including the Gulf of Mexico. **Edibility:** fair.

☐ Bogas, or bonnetmouths are small, open-water school-ing fishes of the family Emmelichthyidae. They are very fast swimmers, difficult to catch, and they seem to prefer 30 to 150 foot depths, thus little is known of their life cycle. They possess very protrusible upper jaws (hence the name "bonnet mouth" used in the West Indies) well-adapted to plankton feeding. Great schools of bogas appear occasionally off the Cuban coast, usually in the month of December.

Short bigeye *Pristigenys alta* To 11 inches. **Range:** New Eng-land, Bermuda, Florida south through the Antilles, including the Gulf of Mexico. **Edibility:** fair.

Boga, bonnetmouth *Inermia vittata* To 9 inches. **Range:** Ba-hamas and Florida to Venezuela. **Edibility:** fair.

MOJARRAS, TRIPLETAILS, HAWKFISHES

Yellowfin mojarra (mojarra de casta) *Gerres cinereus* To 15 inches. **Range:** both Atlantic and Pacific Coasts; in the West Atlantic, from Bermuda, the Bahamas and Florida to Brazil, including the Gulf of Mexico. **Edibility:** fair.

Mojarras, of the family Gerridae, are familiar fishes to divers in the West Indies since they are often hovering nearby, especially over sandy bottom, shallow water areas. They are curious fishes, and their large, jet-black eyes set in pale, silvery bodies seem to follow the diver about the reef. They feed on such small invertebrates as worms, mollusks, crabs and shrimps, which they dig out of the sand with their protrusible mouths. They are adept at changing color, and their bodies can flash from silver over sandy bottom to striped green-brown over weedy areas.

☐ The tripletail is so-named for the extended lobes of the dorsal and anal fins, giving it the appearance of having three tails. Tripletails, of the family Lobotidae are found in brackish and fresh water inlets as well as in inshore reef environments. These fishes have the surprising ability, especially as juveniles, of "playing dead," apparently to deter predators. They turn sideways and float on the surface, and manage to look very much like dead leaves floating on the water. They are fished, especially in warmer months, around docks and jetties, buoys and wrecks.

☐ Hawkfishes of the family Cirrhitidae, get their avian name from their habit of perching in the branches of coral heads or in rocky crevices, and swooping rapidly on smaller fishes and crustaceans. Hawkfishes will sit for hours in motionless vigil, punctuated by sudden dashes for food. Although numerous species of hawks are common in the Indo-Pacific, only one species is known from the tropical Western Atlantic—the red-spotted hawkfish. It is a common sight to see this red-speckled predator sitting boldly out in the open or nestled in a coral clump, waiting for a meal to swim by.

Redspotted hawkfish *Amblycirrhitus pinos* To 3½ inches. **Range:** Bahamas and Florida south through the Antilles to Central America. **Edibility:** poor.

Tripletail (viajaca de la mar) *Lobotes surinamensis* To 40 inches. Usually dark brown in color, but pale, greenish and cream yellow individuals have been taken. **Range:** circumtropical; in the West Atlantic, from New England, Bermuda, the Bahamas and Florida south to Argentina, including the Gulf of Mexico. **Edibility:** good.

TARPON, BONEFISHES, LADYFISHES, HERRINGS, SHAD

Tarpon (sabalo) *Megalops atlantica* To 8 feet. **Range:** both sides of Atlantic; in the West Atlantic from Nova Scotia to Brazil, including the Gulf of Mexico. **Edibility:** poor.

A June moon may mean one thing to lovers, but for the compulsive tarpon fisherman it has a gravitational pull equal to or greater than the attraction of star-crossed lovers, or the lure of Las Vegas to the gambler. There is no other game fish in the world that provides such an explosive, dynamic reaction to being hooked as the tarpon. Dedicated anglers leave families and jobs for the awesome experience of hooking into 40 to 125 pounds of chrome-plated violence. Tarpon havens abound throughout Florida, the Bahamas, the Caribbean and the Gulf of Mexico. One mecca for tarpon fishermen is Florida's Boca Grande.

☐ At a time known to fishermen as the "big tides," when the moon reaches its first full phase in June, it strikes a position with relation to earth and sun that causes the waters of Charlotte Harbor to race out rapidly through Boca Grande Pass, carrying with it millions upon millions of baitfishes, shrimp, crabs and other crustaceans into the hungry mouths of waiting tarpon, massed in silvery phalanxes for their summer onslaught on the Gulf Coast. The scene above water is even more chaotic, as 30 to 40 boats jockey into position for their onslaught on the tarpon. In spite of all the preparation, many a beginner has literally been known to "freeze" when the great white ghost approaches the boat. And when 3 to 6 feet of fury explodes from the water, any angler can be easily unnerved.

☐ Tarpon, of the family Elopidae, have no real food value, and out of consideration for the nobility of this lordly fish, few people ever kill one. They are usually released to strike another day. A peculiar characteristic of the tarpon is the habit of "rolling" on the ocean's surface. Tarpon have a lung-like gas bladder and the rolling helps them take in atmospheric air. One angler tells of a fishing trip in a primitive lagoon in the outback of Yucatan. When he asked the Mexican charterboat captain if there were any fish in the lagoon, the captain motioned him up the mast. When he climbed to the top of the mast, he gulped hard. He saw fishes rolling as far as the eye could see—literally miles of tarpon rolling in silvery splendor. A number of 200 pound tarpon have been taken by fishermen, but the record is an 8 foot giant that weighed an estimated 340 pounds.

☐ Tarpon and bonefishes are among the most primitive of living bony fishes. Both have a long, deeply forked tail and a single dorsal fin of soft rays. Bonefishes of the family Albulidae are targets of the light tackle game fishermen. They combine a wariness that can unnerve the most patient angler with incredible speed and power when hooked. Large expanses of water around the Florida Keys, the Bahamas, the Gulf of Mexico and numerous islands of the Caribbean consist of wide stretches of shallow-water flats, varying from white ocean sand to shallow creek beds to thick turtle-grass and mangrove-choked bays and sounds. This is bonefish country, and skiff fishermen pole patiently, stalking "bones" through polarized sunglasses. Even a modest-sized bonefish will make the line disappear from the spool so fast when it strikes that beginning anglers are often left with a snapped and empty line before they realize that the bone has come and gone. Only the permit approaches the incredible long-run capacity of the wily bonefish. Closely related to the tarpon, the ten-pounder or ladyfish of the family Elopidae occurs around the world in tropical seas. It, too, is a resident of shallow, brackish lagoons. The ladyfish also leaps and struggles when hooked, but is a pale shadow of a fighter compared with the bonefish or tarpon.

121

☐ To see a school of sardines, anchovies or herrings move through the underwater world is to see a perfectly coordinated *corps de ballet*—hundreds, even thousands, of silvery projectiles moving through the water as a single unit, in perfect unison and beauty. All of the herrings of the family Clupeidae are noted for their oily flesh. Economically they form one of the world's most important groups of food fishes, not just for man, but as a vast food reservoir for larger fishes. Other important members of the clupeid family include the menhaden, which is used extensively to produce fishmeal, the shad and the alewife, found from Nova Scotia to Florida. Anchovies, of the family Engraulidae, look and act much like small, round herrings with one important difference. All of the 100 or so species of anchovies are instantly recognizeable by their small, shark-like lower jaw set far back on the underside of the head. Anchovies are tremendously valuable as food for humans, as well as for live and frozen bait. Their greatest abundance is in tropical marine waters.

Bonefish (macabi) *Albula vulpes* To 3½ feet. **Range:** worldwide in tropical seas; in the West Atlantic from New England to southeastern Brazil, including the Gulf of Mexico. **Edibility:** poor.

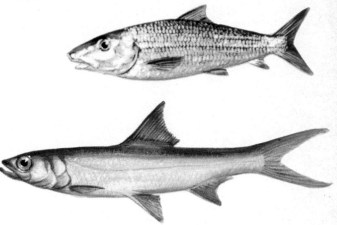

Ladyfish, tenpounder (matezuelo real) *Elops saurus* To 3 feet. **Range:** New England to Brazil, including the Gulf of Mexico. **Edibility:** poor.

Atlantic thread herring (machuelo) *Opisthonema oglinum* To 12 inches. **Range:** New England and Bermuda to southeastern Brazil, including the Gulf of Mexico. **Edibility:** poor.

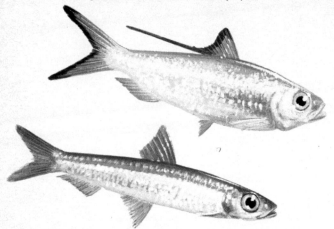

Dwarf herring *Jenkinsia lamprotaenia* To 3½ inches. **Range:** Bermuda, Bahamas and Florida to Venezuela, including the Gulf of Mexico. **Edibility:** poor.

Redear sardine (sardina) *Harengula humeralis* To 9 inches. **Range:** Bermuda, Bahamas and Florida to Brazil, including the Gulf of Mexico. **Edibility:** good. Used for food and bait throughout West Indies.

Dusky anchovy (anchoa) *Anchoa lyolepis* To 3 inches. **Range:** Greater and Lesser Antilles, and the Gulf of Mexico. **Edibility:** good. Also used extensively as fishermen's bait.

American shad, white shad *Alosa sapidissima* To 30 inches. The anadromous shad lives most of its life at sea. Spawning brings them into rivers each year. They have suffered heavily from dams, pollution and overfishing. **Range:** St. Lawrence River to Florida. A very close relative, the hickory shad (*A. mediocris*) ranges from the Gulf of Maine to Florida, and is more dominant in southern waters. **Edibility:** American shad—excellent; hickory shad—poor (roe is excellent).

Alewife *Alosa pseudoharengus* To 14 inches. Very similar to the shad and menhaden, but with a larger eye. Formerly of substantial commercial importance, it is much less so today. The meat is bony and of poor quality. The roe is excellent. **Range:** Labrador to Florida. **Edibility:** see above.

Atlantic menhaden *Brevoortia tyrannus* To 18 inches. An important commercial fish, over 2 billion pounds were taken in the U.S. in 1960, used mostly for animal and poultry feeds. Also used heavily as a chum and bait fish. **Range:** Nova Scotia to northern Florida and the Gulf of Mexico. **Edibility:** poor.

124

COBIAS, SNOOKS, SEA CATFISHES

Cobia (bacalao) *Rachycentron canadum* To 6 feet.
Range: world-wide; in the West Atlantic, from New England, Bermuda, the Bahamas and Florida south to Argentina, including the Gulf of Mexico. **Edibility:** good.

Cobias are roving, predaceous fishes that range the Atlantic from Massachusetts to Argentina. They are found well offshore, and inshore around inlets, bays and mangrove sloughs, where they feed on crabs, shrimps, fishes, and squids. Gulf Coast charterboat fishermen react strangely when the cobia, or ling is sighted. They thump the sides of the boat, splash water with rods and oars, ring bells, or turn the boat in tight, noisy circles. This activity would frighten off most fishes, but the cobia seems to need excitement and noise to get into a feeding mood. At the peak of the noise-making a pair of cobia may suddenly explode into action and take the bait for a series of 70 or 80-yard runs. Ten to 15 pound cobia are frequently caught from beach piers. Twenty-five to 30 pound fish are caught in marginal offshore waters. Big 50, 60 and 70 pound giants may be had in the offshore blue. One 5' 10" cobia was taken off Virginia that weighed 102 pounds. The cobia, of the family Rachycentridae, occurs around the world in warm waters.

☐ Snooks or robalos of the family Centropomidae are shovel-nosed fishes frequently found inshore in mangrove sloughs and river mouths. While snorkeling near shore in 3 feet of water off Pompano Beach, Florida, I poked my nose into a rock grotto and came eyeball-to-eyeball with a 3 foot snook. I am not sure who was more surprised, but the snook came bursting out of the grotto over my right shoulder to disappear in a froth of bubbles and snook wake.

☐ Four species of snook are known from the Caribbean and a fifth from the Gulf of Mexico. The common snook shown here grows to be the largest in the West Atlantic, reaching 4½ feet in length. It is an excellent food fish, with delicate, white flaky flesh, not unlike that of the striped bass.

☐ The sea catfish, or "hardhead," which ranges from Cape Cod to the West Indies and throughout the Gulf of Mexico, gets a very low rating as a gamefish. The gafftopsail catfish, however, is gaining a sizeable following on the Gulf Coast as a fine gamefish and an excellent food fish (the flesh is white, firm and tasty). In Texas it has acquired the nickname "tourist trout," and when the gafftops are running, people who live hundreds of miles

Snook (robalo) *Centropomus undecimalis* To 4½ feet. **Range:** South Carolina to Brazil, including the Gulf of Mexico. **Edibility:** excellent.

126

inland swarm to the coast for the action. Veteran Gulf Coast anglers say that when the gafftops make their initial appearance each spring as the water begins to warm, the Spanish mackerel, king mackerel, cobia (ling) and pompano will not be far behind. Both the sea and gafftopsail catfishes belong to the Ariidae family, and they are mouthbrooders, like the cardinalfishes. The male fish carries from 50 to 60 large (½" to 1" diameter) eggs in his mouth until they hatch some 9 weeks later. Even after they hatch, he nurtures them in his mouth for an additional two to four weeks, until they are about 3" long and ready for independence. During this entire 11 to 13-week period, the male catfish goes without food.

Sea catfish, hardhead (bagre) *Arius felis* To 1½ feet. **Range:** Cape Cod south through the Antilles and throughout the Gulf of Mexico. **Edibility:** poor.

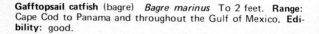

Gafftopsail catfish (bagre) *Bagre marinus* To 2 feet. **Range:** Cape Cod to Panama and throughout the Gulf of Mexico. **Edibility:** good.

127

BLUEFISHES, TILEFISHES, REMORAS

Bluefish, tailor, snapper (anchoa) *Pomatomus saltatrix* To 4 feet. **Range:** world-wide in tropical and temperate seas. **Edibility:** good, but spoils quickly. Must be eaten fresh.

Bluefishes are fast-moving, schooling fishes with a reputation for bloodthirsty feeding habits that outstrip those of the jacks and barracuda. Not unlike the vicious piranha, the bluefish is an animated chopping machine that continues to slaughter other fishes, apparently for the pleasure of killing. The bluefish, of the family Pomatomidae, is a favorite with fishermen, both shore and offshore, for its fighting quality and its excellent taste. Young juveniles, often called tailors or snappers, are common inshore. One characteristic by which bluefishes may be distinguished from similar fishes is the black blotch at the base of the pectoral fin.

☐ The sand tilefish is an interesting, industrious animal with a unique talent for constructing burrows around the reef. Scientists of the Tektite I and II Man-In-The-Sea Projects observed and documented the bird-like nest building activity of the tilefish. The fish first excavates a trench in the sand bottom of the reef, over which it constructs intricate walls and a roof of coral debris and shell fragments. Here the fish hovers, just a few inches off the bottom, plunging headfirst into its burrow when disturbed. In one experiment, Tektite divers marked and then scattered from 500 to 600 fragments of a tilefishes'

128

burrow. Upon returning, the tilefish began putting his house in order. Within 8 days he had rebuilt his burrow, using 460 of the original coral and shell fragments.

☐ The common tilefish is another interesting member of the family Branchiostegidae. First introduced to the New England market in 1879, this tilefish was an immediate commercial success. Shortly after, disaster struck the vast tilefish schools that ranged from New England to the Virginia Capes. Millions of dead tilefish were reported, and one ship sailed through 150 miles of them. Estimates of mortality ranged up to 1½ billion fish. Scientists explained that unseasonal Arctic gales and ice had suddenly chilled the water, making it too cold for the tilefish. It was 10 years before any more tilefish were taken, and then only 8 individuals were caught. Gradually, however, the fish reestablished itself, until recently, when 1,238,500 pounds were taken.

☐ The remora or sharksucker is the well-known hitchhiker of the sea. By means of a laminated disc on the top of its head, the remora clamps itself firmly to almost any available host and takes a free ride. Sharks are popular hosts, but remoras are not fussy. They are found attached to whales, marlin, groupers, rays, boats, timbers and other floating objects. Various species of remoras ap-

Sand tilefish (blanquillo) *Malacanthus plumieri* To 2 feet. **Range:** Bermuda, the Bahamas and South Carolina to Brazil, including the Gulf of Mexico. **Edibility:** fair.

pear to be always associated with the same kind of host. Some species are found only on billfishes, while others are at home only on barracudas. Incredibly, remoras have been used as "living fishhooks" by various primitive tribes the world over. A line is tied to the tail of the remora and it is thrown overboard in the vicinity of a large turtle. When it attaches itself to the turtle, fishermen play the turtle near to the boat, and it is captured. The Arawak Indians of southern Cuba, Venezuelan Indians, Australian aborigines and numerous other tribes used the remora in this ingenious way.

Common tilefish *Lopholatilus chamaeleonticeps* To 2½ feet. **Range:** Nova Scotia to the Gulf of Mexico. **Edibility:** good.

Sharksucker, remora, suckerfish (pegador) *Echeneis naucrates* To 3½ feet. **Range:** circumtropical; in the West Atlantic, from New England and Bermuda to Uruguay, including the Gulf of Mexico. **Edibility:** poor.

BARRACUDA, SILVERSIDES, MULTS AND THREADFINS

White mullet, black mullet, fatback, jumper (lisa blanca, liseta)
Mugil curema To 3 feet. **Range:** both sides of the Atlantic; in
the West Atlantic, from New England to southeastern Brazil, including the Gulf of Mexico. **Edibility:** good.

Vast, silvery clouds of silversides and mullets school, race
and leap in Western Atlantic coastal shallows, providing a
movable feast for such predators as barracuda, jacks,
mackerel and man. The torpedo-shaped mullet ranks as
a leading food fish in Florida, where it is called the "black
mullet." They are so rich in oil they can be fried in their
own fat. Also called "fatbacks" and "jumpers," mullets
are expert at leaping out of the water to escape nets,
predators, and seemingly just for the pure joy of jumping.
At certain times of the day, coastal shallows, bays and inlets are often alive with leaping mullets. Members of the
family Mugilidae, mullets are bottom grubbers, fond of
sucking up mouthfuls of bottom sand and filtering out
small plants and animals. Since they are basically herbivorous, they rarely take a hook unless it is baited with
bread or dough. They are frequently caught in nets.

☐ Silversides (family Atherinidae) are named for their
brilliant, flashing lateral stripe, and they share with mullets such characteristics as divided dorsal fins, pelvic fins
placed in the middle of the abdomen, small, weakly-
toothed mouths and tasty, oily flesh. Often scooped out
of the sea and cooked over spits on the beach, they pro-

131

vide such delicious fare that Mexican and Caribbean gourmets call them *pescado del rey*, "fish for a king." Strangely for schooling fishes, silverside fry start life shy and antisocial. Studies at New York's American Museum of Natural History indicate that quarter - inch hatchlings avoid each other. Half-inchers may aggregate a few seconds, but avoid meeting head-on. At three-quarters of an inch, 10 fry may assemble in a ragged formation. From then on they school easily and with increasing discipline. A well-known relative is the California grunion silverside (*Lueresthes tenuis*) which rides waves ashore to mate and spawn on the beach.

☐ Nothing is more disconcerting to the diver than the specter of a 1 or 2 foot barracuda following closely and watchfully as the diver makes his rounds of the reefs. In Florida and Caribbean waters, the "friendly" barracuda (family Sphyraenidae), is almost inescapable in some areas. The wise diver soon gives up trying to chase them away (they quickly return anyway) and welcomes them along as companions on his tour. They are quite harmless and seem content to follow the diver curiously, as though waiting for a handout. Most of the recorded attacks by the "ferocious" barracuda occurred when the fish was speared, boated or trapped, at which time most fishes will bite anything. Some barracuda attacks have occurred in murky water, when visibility was poor, and

Fantail mullet (lisa) *Mugil trichodon* To 18 inches. **Range:** Bermuda, Bahamas and Florida to Brazil, including the Gulf of Mexico. **Edibility:** good.

Smallscale threadfin (barbudo) *Polydactylus oligodon* To 16 inches. **Range:** Bahamas and Florida to Brazil. **Edibility:** good.

presumably the fish mistook an arm or leg for a small fish. Divers wearing shiny metal objects would do well to remove them in the presence of barracuda. They have been known to strike at shiny objects, apparently mistaking them for the flash of a small fish's side or belly. Although adult barracuda tend to be solitary hunters, smaller ones have been observed in schools, herding smaller fishes into compact groups. They will cut a swath through the group, snapping at and killing their prey by the score. Then they return and eat the stunned or maimed fish at their leisure. Barracuda are excellent game fish, capable of providing all the battle a sport fisherman can handle. Small barracuda make excellent eating, but large ones in the West Indies rank with the amberjack in causing ciguatera poisoning (see page 39).

☐ Threadfins of the family Polynemidae are much like mullets, but the unique pectoral fins are split into two parts, the lower of which is composed of 7 or 8 threadlike rays. Threadfins probe into sand and mud bottoms with these rays, and they probably serve both tactile and chemoreceptor functions. The mouth is under a pronounced, pig-like snout. They are beautiful silvery fishes when seen underwater, often swimming with sand drums and palometas over sandy beach areas.

Great barracuda (picuda) *Sphyraena barracuda* To 10 feet. Rare over 5 feet. Contrary to popular belief, attacks by barracuda on man are very rare. **Range:** world-wide; in the West Atlantic, from New England to Brazil, including the Gulf of Mexico. **Edibility:** small fish (2-3 pounds) good. Larger fish may carry ciguatera toxin (see page 39).

133

Southern sennet (picudilla) *Sphyraena picudilla* To 18 inches. This small barracuda and the similar "guaguanche" (*S. guachancho*) are reported to be good eating, and have not been implicated in ciguatera poisoning. **Range:** *S. picudilla:* Bermuda, Bahamas and Florida to Uruguay. *S. guachancho:* New England to Brazil, including the Gulf of Mexico. **Edibility:** see above.

Hardhead silverside, blue fry *Atherinomorous stipes* To 5 inches. **Range:** Bahamas and Florida to Brazil. **Edibility:** good.

Reef silverside, blue fry *Allanetta harringtonensis* To 3 inches. **Range:** Bermuda, Bahamas, Florida through the West Indies, including the Gulf of Mexico. **Edibility:** good.

CODS AND HAKES

Atlantic cod *Gadus morhua* To 6 feet. **Range:** Arctic seas south to Virginia. **Edibility:** excellent.

These cold and temperate water bottom fishes are vitally important to the world's food supply and they support huge, centuries-old fisheries on both sides of the Atlantic. The profitable codfish pulled Europeans across the North Atlantic by the shipload to settle New World shores. So paramount was the common cod to the settlers of New England that it was placed on the colonial seal of Massachusetts. Its popularity as a basic food fish has not diminished. The Grand Banks off Newfoundland and the coastal shelves of Greenland still attract the fishing fleets of the world in search of succulent, nutritious cods and hakes. Fishermen take nearly 150 million pounds of haddock every year, making it a leading East Coast food fish. The annual commercial take of pollock, another member of the cod family, is nearly 10 million pounds. Commercial fishermen use large trawling nets, set lines, seines and gill nets. Because the flesh keeps so well, dried and salted cod may be shipped to any part of the world.

Haddock *Melanogrammus aeglefinus* To 44 inches. **Range:** Greenland to Virginia. **Edibility:** excellent.

☐ Almost all of North America's 24 species of cods and hakes are marine fishes. Members of the family Gadidae, they are omnivorous and they roam sand and rock bottoms 100 to 1500 feet down, preying in voracious packs upon crustaceans, mollusks, fishes, worms and vegetation. Codfishes and their relatives may be distinguished by the "cod look," partly due to the fact that the ventral fins are placed ahead of the pectoral fins, often under the throat. They all possess soft-rayed fins, usually without spines.

Pollock *Pollachius virens* To 3½ feet. **Range:** Gulf of St. Lawrence to Virginia. **Edibility:** excellent.

Silver hake *Merluccius bilinearis* To 3 feet. **Range:** Gulf of St. Lawrence to South Carolina. **Edibility:** good.

Red hake, squirrel hake *Urophycis chuss* To 2½ feet. **Range:** Gulf of St. Lawrence to North Carolina. **Edibility:** poor.

136

FLATFISHES

Ocellated flounder *Ancylopsetta quadrocellata* To 10 inches. **Range:** Maryland to Florida and the Gulf of Mexico. **Edibility:** good.

If you see what appears to be a flying carpet with fins and a white underside rippling about the reef, gliding to the bottom to disappear into the sand, you are watching a flatfish. The flatfishes include many of the world's tastiest and most valuable food fishes, such as the sole, flounder, halibut, sanddab, turbot, and plaice. All flatfishes begin life much like any other symmetrical fish, with an eye on either side of the head. Within a few days, however, one eye starts migrating toward the other, and soon both eyes are close together on the upper side of the animals' body. The mouth becomes strangely twisted, and the dorsal fin grows forward on the fish, almost reaching the mouth. These unusual developments prepare the fish for its bottom-dwelling existence. Within a few more days, the young flatfish sinks to the ocean bottom, where it spends the rest of its life lying on its blind side (which is usually white), with the eyed side up. American flatfishes are separated into two broad categories. One of these includes the Bothidae and Pleuronectidae (flounders, halibuts, whiffs, sanddabs and soles), the other is the Soleidae and Cynoglossidae (broadsoles and tonguefishes). The Bothidae are left-eyed flounders (so called because their eyes are on the left side of the head) and the Pleuronectidae are right-eye flounders. Most flatfishes have a remarkable facility to change their colors to match the bottom. Their excellent camouflage is aided by their ability to quickly bury themselves in the bottom sand and they are extremely difficult to locate by an untrained eye. Most are carnivorous fishes that dash out of hiding to gobble down smaller fishes and crustaceans. They range in size from only a few inches to great, flat 10-foot giants weighing 700 pounds. Biologists recently discovered an unassuming little sole in the Red Sea (*Pardachirus marmoratus*) that appears to carry a highly effective shark repellent. Repeated tests demonstrate that sharks refuse to bite the sole, and the fish is being closely studied to see if the repellant can be isolated for use by man.

BOTHIDAE – LEFT-EYE FLOUNDERS

Peacock flounder (arreves) *Bothus lunatus* To 18 inches. **Range:** Bermuda, Bahamas and Florida to Brazil. **Edibility:** good.

Bay whiff *Citharichthys spilopterus* To 8 inches. **Range:** New Jersey to Brazil, including the Gulf of Mexico. **Edibility:** fair.

Southern flounder *Paralichthys lethostigma* To 2½ feet. **Range:** North Carolina to Texas. **Edibility:** good.

138

Summer flounder *Paralichthys dentatus* To 2½ feet. **Range:** Maine to South Carolina. **Edibility:** good.

Eyed flounder (arreves) *Bothus ocellatus* To 6½ inches. **Range:** New York and Bermuda to Brazil, including the Gulf of Mexico. **Edibility:** poor.

PLEURONECTIDAE — RIGHT-EYE FLOUNDERS

Winter flounder *Pseudopleuronectes americanus* To 1½ feet. **Range:** Labrador to North Carolina. **Edibility:** excellent.

SOLEIDAE — SOLES

Naked sole, zebra sole (arreves) *Gymnachirus melas* To 6 inches. **Range:** Massachusetts to Bahamas, Florida and the Gulf of Mexico. **Edibility:** poor.

Hogchoker *Trinectes maculatus* To 9 inches. **Range:** Massachusetts to Panama and the Gulf of Mexico. **Edibility:** poor.

CYNOGLOSSIDAE — TONGUEFISHES

Caribbean tonguefish *Symphurus arawak* To 2 inches. **Range:** Florida Keys and throughout Caribbean Sea. **Edibility:** poor.

140

SURGEONS, TANGS

ADULT

JUVENILE

Blue tang (sangrador azul)
Acanthurus coeruleus To 1
foot. Great clouds of brilliant
blue tangs are common over West
Atlantic reefs. Note the lemon yel-
low juvenile. Pre-adults may be part blue and part yellow. Blue
fishes with yellow tails are common. Separable from the ocean
surgeon and doctorfish by the white sheath on the caudal spine.
Range: New York, Bermuda, Bahamas and Florida to Brazil, including the Gulf of Mexico. **Edibility:** poor.

If, while diving around coral heads, you are suddenly engulfed in a vast, indigo-blue cloud of fishes, you have met
the magnificent blue tangs of the West Atlantic. Large
schools of blue tangs, doctorfishes and ocean surgeons
are common off West Atlantic reefs, and they cover a
wide range from Massachusetts to Brazil and the Gulf of
Mexico. To see one or two hundred of these fishes rising
in an indigo-blue or pale gray storm from a coral head is
a feast for the eyes. The surgeonfishes of the Acanthuridae
family, frequently called tangs or doctorfishes, are so-
named for the scalpel-like spine on either side of the body
just in front of the tail. The spine may be more aptly
compared with a switch-blade knife, since in most surgeons the blade is hinged and lies flat along the body in a
sheath. When called into play, the blade flicks out and

points forward, and by repeatedly sideswiping another fish, the surgeon can cause serious injury. Careless fishermen who are unaware of the blade can receive nasty cuts when handling the resourceful tang. The beginning diver need not worry about being attacked by hordes of surgeonfishes. The tang, or for that matter, any fish, will rarely attack a creature larger than itself. The usual object of attack is another fish, often of the same size and species, that acts as though it may threaten the hold of the first fish on its section of reef or "territory." In its natural reef habitat, the tang has but to give a warning flick of its tail toward an intruder fish, which invariably withdraws. In an aquarium, however, where there is no place to hide, an overly aggressive surgeon can do considerable damage to its tankmates. Like parrotfishes, tangs are herbivorous, continually searching out and cropping the reef algae. A large school of tangs may swoop down on a small coral head and leave it practically bare of algae. They are not much esteemed by fish gourmets because of the strong odor and savor of the flesh.

Ocean surgeon (sangrador) *Acanthurus bahianus* To 14 inches. Quite similar in appearance to the doctorfish, and the two are often seen swimming together in feeding aggregations, but the ocean surgeon has a more lunate tail, and no bars on the body. **Range:** New England, Bermuda, Bahamas and Florida to the hump of Brazil, including the Gulf of Mexico. **Edibility:** poor.

Doctorfish (sangrador) *Acanthurus chirurgas* To 13½ inches. The doctorfish, like all surgeons, is highly changeable in color, and it can change from deep brown to pale coloration depending on background and lighting. May be easily mistaken for the ocean surgeon, but note the vertical body bars and the more rectangular tail. **Range:** New England, Bermuda, Bahamas, Florida to the hump of Brazil, including the Gulf of Mexico. **Edibility:** poor.

142

TRIGGERFISHES AND FILEFISHES

Queen triggerfish, old wife (cochino) *Balistes vetula* To 2 feet. Unmistakable with its blue-striped head and long, trailing fin filaments. A very intelligent, aggressive animal with a special fondness for sea urchins, particularly *Diadema.* A reef dweller, it also ventures into sand, seagrass and rubble habitats. A good food fish, called "turbot" in the West Indies due to its resemblance to the flatfish when skinned. **Range:** both sides of the Atlantic; in the West Atlantic from New England to southeastern Brazil, including the Gulf of Mexico. **Edibility:** see above.

A close look at the triggerfish of the Balistidae family shows it to be a fascinating, attractive animal with a perky disposition and a peculiar "hide and lock" defense mechanism. Probably because they are such slow swimmers, triggers have developed a number of protective devices. When attacked or frightened, the trigger dives straight for a hole or crevice in the coral and erects its large first dorsal fin, which is locked in place by the second sliding dorsal spine or "trigger." Thus wedged into its hole, there is no way a predator can remove the trigger and it is usually left alone.

☐ Although seemingly grotesquely configured, with their eyes almost in the center of their bodies, the carnivorous triggers are perfectly designed to prey upon prickly crustaceans, mollusks and echinoderms. Triggers are one of the few animals that can attack a spiny sea urchin with impunity. Since their eyes are so far back in their heads, safe from the spines, they can bite the urchin's spines off with their sharp teeth, throw the urchin on its back, and feast on the soft underbelly. Another technique learned by the intelligent trigger to obtain food is the art of using water as a tool. The queen triggerfish has been seen to blow jets of water at the base of a strolling sea urchin, until it is finally bowled over by the force of the jets. Once on its side, the urchin becomes a meal for the hungry trigger. The bodies of triggers are covered with hard, plate-like scales, forming a flexible yet solid armor. The tails of some species are equipped with rows of spines, and they are adept at side-swiping and tail-whipping an enemy.

☐ Very noticeable in balistids is their ability to rotate the eyes independently, enabling them to observe two different scenes at once. They swim by undulating the soft dorsal and anal fins languidly, bringing their tail into action only when speed is required.

Gray triggerfish (cucuyo) *Balistes capriscus* To 1 foot. Found either singly or in small pods over reefs, rocks and hard bottoms. Rare in the West Indies, but more common around Bermuda and higher latitudes. **Range:** Nova Scotia to Argentina, including the Gulf of Mexico. **Edibility:** fair.

Ocean triggerfish *Canthidermis sufflamen* To 2 feet. A large grayish fish, at times almost white, often seen cruising singly over offshore reefs near drop offs to deep water. **Range:** New England south through the Lesser Antilles, including the Gulf of Mexico. **Edibility:** good.

Sargassum triggerfish *Xanthichthys ringens* To 10 inches. One of the most abundant West Indian reef fishes at depths of over 100 feet. Rarely encountered in shallower depths. Juveniles have been taken in floating clumps of sargassum weed. **Range:** uncertain, but thought to be circumtropical; in the West Atlantic, from the Carolinas, Bermuda and the Bahamas south to Venezuela. **Edibility:** poor.

Black durgon *Melichthys niger* To 1½ feet. Common in some areas, such as Bimini and the Bahamas, fairly rare in others. Prefers clear water outer reefs at depths of 50 feet or more. A striking fish. **Range:** circumtropical, in the West Atlantic, from the Bahamas and Florida to Brazil. **Edibility:** poor.

□ The filefishes of the family Monacanthidae are very closely related to the triggerfishes. They are distinguished by the fact that their first dorsal spine is located well forward, usually over the eye, while on the triggerfish the first dorsal spine is placed well in back of the eye. Filefishes also have much narrower bodies than the triggers and possess a skin that is almost file-like (hence the name), compared to the plate-like scales of the triggers. A common sight on West Atlantic coral reefs is a pair of white spotted filefishes, picking and fluttering about the reef. As with the butterflyfishes, it is not known whether these are always male and female fishes, but they seem very closely attached.

145

Whitespotted filefish *Cantherhines macrocerus* To 17 inches. Often seen in pairs fluttering daintily about the reef. Limited data indicates that these pairs are male and female fishes. Feeds on such unlikely fare as sponges, hydroids, stinging coral, gorgonions and algae. **Range:** Bermuda, Bahamas and Florida to Brazil. **Edibility:** poor.

Orangespotted filefish, taillight filefish *Cantherhines pullus* To 7½ inches. Distinctive for the orange spots across the body and the 2 white spots at top and bottom of the tail base. Fairly common. When threatened it erects its formidable first dorsal spine. **Range:** New England, Bermuda, Bahamas and Florida to Brazil, including the Gulf of Mexico. **Edibility:** poor.

Fringed filefish *Monacanthus ciliatus* To 8 inches. Look for this filefish hiding (often head down) in beds of turtle grass. An expert color-changer, it can skillfully blend into its sea grass background. **Range:** Newfoundland to Bermuda, Bahamas and Florida to Argentina, including the Gulf of Mexico. **Edibility:** poor.

Pygmy filefish, speckled filefish *Monacanthus setifer* To 7 inches. The adult male (shown) has the second dorsal ray prolonged into a filament. Highly changeable in color to match surroundings. **Range:** North Carolina, Bermuda, Bahamas south through the Caribbean, including the Gulf of Mexico. **Edibility:** poor.

Slender filefish *Monacanthus tuckeri* To 3½ inches. Unique due to its slender body, this little filefish has been found over seagrass, patch reefs, rock and sand bottoms, and hiding among gorgonian fronds. **Range:** Carolinas, Bermuda, Bahamas and Florida through the Antilles. **Edibility:** poor.

Orange filefish (cachua perra) *Aluterus schoepfi* To 1½ feet. Distinctive for the tiny orange spots peppered across the body. Found in a variety of habitats, appears to feed on algae and seagrasses. **Range:** Nova Scotia south to Brazil, including the Gulf of Mexico. **Edibility:** poor.

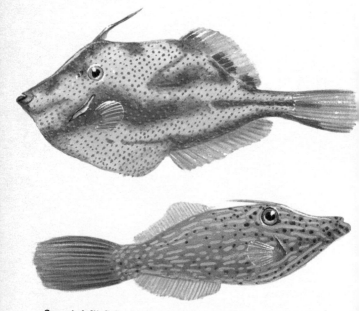

Scrawled filefish *Aluterus scriptus* To 3 feet. Notable for its large size, brilliant blue markings and broom-like tail. Often seen drifting along, head downward, surveying the bottom for food. Known to eat stinging coral, algae, gorgonians, sea anemones and tunicates. **Range:** circumtropical; in the West Atlantic, from Massachusetts to Brazil, including the Gulf of Mexico. **Edibility:** poor.

PUFFERS, PORCUPINEFISHES AND TRUNKFISHES

Bandtail puffer (tambor)   *Sphoeroides spengleri*   To 1 foot. Common in seagrass beds but also found over patch reefs, sand and coral rubble, usually in shallow water rarely over 25 feet deep. The row of round black spots from chin to tail is distinctive. **Range:** New England, Bermuda, Bahamas and Florida to Brazil, including the Gulf of Mexico. **Edibility:** poor, viscera may be poisonous.

Checkered puffer (tambor)   *Sphoeroides testudineus*   To 10 inches. A bright-eyed puffer with an orange iris, common in seagrass habitats, mangrove sloughs, and found over a variety of shallow-water reef and sand bottoms. **Range:** New England, Bahamas and Florida to Brazil, including the Gulf of Mexico. **Edibility:** poor, viscera may be poisonous.

When threatened by a predator, a puffer fish sucks in a bellyful of water and almost instantly becomes three times larger. The hungry predator, realizing that the fat little puffer is now too big to fit in its mouth, looks elsewhere for a meal. When removed from the water by curious humans, puffers use the same defense, gulping air instead of water and producing angry grunting noises.

As a result, they frequently become lampshades or mantlepieces in seaside restaurants and the homes of marine collectors. The organs and sometimes the flesh of certain puffers contain a deadly poison, tetrodotoxin. Although it has wide medical application, the poison can kill quickly if eaten, and puffer food poisoning is fatal in 60 percent of the cases. Even so, puffers are eaten with great relish in Japan, in a dish called *fugu*. Fortunately the dish is prepared very carefully by certified *fugu* cooks, and fatalities are rare.

□ The sharp-nosed puffers of the Canthigasteridae family are common in the tropical West Atlantic, and may be distinguished by their long, pointed snouts. They are dainty little fishes, rarely exceeding 4½ inches in length. The common puffers, Tetraodontidae family, differ from the sharp-nosed puffers in having short, rounded snouts and more rounded, uniform bodies. The common puffers also grow to be considerably larger than sharp-nosed puffers. The checkered puffer shown here reaches 10 inches, and the bandtail puffer attains 1 foot. The common puffers (genus *Sphoeroides*) are most often implicated in cases of tetraodon poisoning.

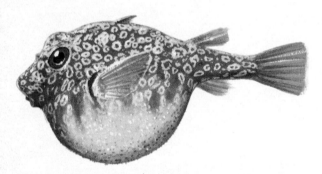

Southern puffer (tambor) *Sphoeroides nephelus* To 1 foot. Shown inflated, this is the common inshore puffer of Florida, occasionally straggling to Alabama and Mississippi shores. Matures at 5 inches. **Range:** Bahamas and Florida to Brazil, including the Gulf of Mexico. **Edibility:** poor, viscera may be poisonous.

149

□ The porcupinefishes and burrfishes of the family Diodontidae are also adept at puffing themselves up when disturbed. They reach lengths of 2 feet, and it is a strange sight to see a puffed-up, spine-covered basketball with eyes and fins, paddling furiously about the reef. Of the four spiny puffer species shown, the species of *Diodon* have the longest spines, which fold back against the body when not inflated. The *Chilomycterus* species possess spines that are 3-rooted and always rigidly erect.

□ The trunkfishes include the boxfishes and cowfishes of the family Ostraciidae. For protection against predators, these odd, fascinating little animals are enclosed in a solid, bony box with holes for the eyes, mouth, fins and vent. Their movements on the reef are curious, almost like miniature helicopters as they maneuver their rigid, boxed-in bodies with the aid of tiny, fluttering pectoral fins and tail. They are such slow swimmers that they can easily be approached and studied by divers. Some trunkfish species are known to discharge a toxin into the water when under stress. This poison, named ostracitoxin, will kill other fishes in aquaria and bait tanks, even after the trunkfish is removed. Strangely, it will even kill the trunkfish.

Caribbean puffer (tambor) *Sphoeroides greeleyi* To 6 inches. This puffer is often found in shallow turbid water habitats over mud bottoms, and occasionally on shallow sand bottoms. **Range:** Greater and Lesser Antilles to Brazil. **Edibility:** poor, viscera may be poisonous.

Sharpnose puffer *Canthigaster rostrata* To 4½ inches. Occurs in a variety of habitats, including coral reef, seagrass beds, mixed sand and rock and rocky tide pools. Prefers seagrass tips, but also eats sponges, crustaceans, mollusks and sea urchins. **Range:** both sides of the Atlantic; in the West Atlantic, from Bermuda, the Bahamas and Florida throughout the Caribbean, including the Gulf of Mexico. **Edibility:** poor.

150

Spiny puffer, barred spiny puffer, balloonfish *Diodon holocan-thus* To 20 inches. This puffer may be distinguished from the very similar porcupinefish by the large black blotches on its back. The illustration shows a typical spiny puffer in a relaxed cruising mode, with his spines tucked away. **Range:** circum-tropical; in the West Atlantic, from the Bahamas and Florida to Brazil, including the Gulf of Mexico. **Edibility:** poor, viscera may be poisonous.

Porcupinefish, spotted spiny puffer *Diodon hystrix* To 3 feet. Here is a spiny puffer in the inflated mode. May be distinguished from the barred spiny puffer (above) by the numerous small spots on its body, with no blotches. Bohlke and Chaplin report spearing a large female porcupinefish in the Bahamas which was swimming with a smaller male fish. The male companion refused to leave his mate, and swam around close by while she was on the spear. **Range:** circumtropical; in the West Atlantic, from New England to southeastern Brazil, including the Gulf of Mexi-co. **Edibility:** poor, viscera may be poisonous.

Striped burrfish *Chilomycterus schoepfi* To 10 inches. Very common along Carolina and Florida coasts. This puffer has been seen to aid its forward movement by expelling jets of water through its gill openings: "jet propulsion." **Range:** New England, the Bahamas and Florida to the hump of Brazil, including the Gulf of Mexico. **Edibility:** poor.

Web burrfish *Chilomycterus antillarum* To 1 foot. This fish lacks the stripes of the striped burrfish, and instead has numerous lines in a network pattern on its body, along with large dark round spots, usually 3, on each side. **Range:** Bahamas and Florida to Brazil. **Edibility:** poor.

Smooth trunkfish (chapin) *Lactophrys triqueter* To 1 foot. The smallest of West Atlantic trunkfishes. Has been seen to eject a jet of water from its mouth into the sand to expose the worms, crabs and other crustaceans that are a major part of its diet. **Range:** New England, Bermuda, the Bahamas and Florida to Brazil, including the Gulf of Mexico. **Edibility:** poor.

Buffalo trunkfish (chapin) *Lactophrys trigonus* To 18 inches. Often found in sea-grass beds, and highly changeable in pattern and color. Will make grunting noises when taken from the water. **Range:** New England, Bermuda, the Bahamas and Florida to Brazil, including the Gulf of Mexico. **Edibility:** considered an excellent food fish in the West Indies, but has been implicated in ciguatera poisoning.

Spotted trunkfish (chapin) *Lactophrys bicaudalis* To 16 inches. Trunkfishes are fascinating aquarium fishes, but their ability to release toxins that kill other fishes should be noted. Bohlke and Chaplin report that Bahaman fishermen will not keep the smooth or spotted trunkfishes in their live-wells, due to the toxin. **Range:** Florida Keys and the Bahamas to Brazil, including the Gulf of Mexico. **Edibility:** poor.

Scrawled cowfish (toro) *Acanthostracion quadricornis* To 1½ feet. The commonest and most wide-ranging trunkfish in the West Atlantic, highly changeable in coloration. Often found in seagrass beds. **Range:** New England, Bermuda, the Bahamas and Florida to Brazil, including the Gulf of Mexico. **Edibility:** poor.

Honeycomb cowfish (toro) *Acanthostracion polygonius* To 1½ feet. Unaccountably, until recently, this fish and the scrawled cowfish were thought to be the same species. This is the least common of West Atlantic trunkfishes. Primarily a reef-dweller. **Range:** New Jersey, Bermuda, the Bahamas and Florida to Brazil. **Edibility:** poor.

153

SCORPIONFISHES

Spotted scorpionfish (rascacio) *Scorpaena plumieri* To 17 inches. A common fish found over shallow water coral reefs and rocky bottoms. When alarmed it spreads its pectoral fins and displays its brilliant black and white axillary coloration, thus warning off predators. **Range:** New England to Brazil, including the Gulf of Mexico. **Edibility:** good.

This bizarre, fascinating family of fishes has been given more names than any other fish in the world, including scorpionfish, turkeyfish, zebrafish, dragonfish, tiger and lionfish, cardinal scorpionfish, rockfish, firefish, cobrafish and probably numerous others. It is a family to which many of these names do apply, due to its fearless nature, its poisonous spines, and the odd appearance and lifestyle of its members. Most if not all scorpionfishes are poisonous, and should never be handled without a net or other protective device. Such names as "scorpion" and "cobrafish" come from the venomous potential of the dorsal, anal and ventral fin spines, which can give the careless fisherman, diver or aquarist a very painful puncture wound. In the West Indies, the two largest species (the spotted scorpionfish and the barbfish) are highly valued as food.

☐ The scorpaenid (mail-cheeked) fishes are so named because of the bony plates under their eyes, and they include several hundred species world-wide. Their lumplike or rocklike appearance and improbable appendages would seem to be the antithesis of what a streamlined fish configuration should be, but the scorpionfish is well-designed for its job. It is a master at camouflage, and it waits quietly and patiently in an algae-covered crevice, frequently hanging upside down, where it looks almost exactly like part of the reef. When a small fish or crustacean comes to examine the algae-like appendages which dangle from its face, the scorpion engulfs the intruder with surprising rapidity.

□ They make fascinating pets for aquarium owners, but let the buyer beware when buying the scorpionfish. One report tells of an aquarist who inadvertently grabbed and was punctured by a scorpionfish. He immediately felt shooting pains in his arm, and eventually fell to his knees. After a tourniquet was applied he was rushed to a nearby hospital, where injections put him on the road to a speedy recovery. The Indo-Pacific lionfishes (*Pterois*) can inject venom that is extremely painful, but usually not fatal. The Indo-Pacific stonefishes (*Synanceja*) possess a venom so powerful that an agonizing death can occur shortly after a puncture. West Atlantic scorpionfishes, fortunately, are not deadly. The wounds they inflict, while extremely painful, are not serious if carefully cleaned and treated to prevent infection.

Barbfish (sapo) *Scorpaena brasiliensis* To 14 inches. The barbfish seems to favor continental waters rather than islands, and occurs from inshore shallows to 300 foot depths. Scorpionfishes can inflict painful wounds with their poisonous spines. Great care should be exercised in handling them. **Range:** Virginia to Brazil. **Edibility:** good.

Plumed or grass scorpionfish *Scorpaena grandicornis* To 7 inches. Distinctive for the large cirrus or "horn" sprouting over its eye. Found over seagrass beds, grassy bays and channels. **Range:** Bermuda, Bahamas and Florida to Brazil. **Edibility:** poor.

Reef scorpionfish (sapo) *Scorpaenodes caribbaeus* To 5 inches. This is a common little scorpion over inshore reefs throughout the Caribbean, but it is such an expert at camouflage, it is rarely seen. **Range:** see above. **Edibility:** poor.

ANGLERFISHES, TOADFISHES, GURNARDS, SEA ROBINS, DRAGONETS, LIZARDFISHES

Sargassumfish *Histrio histrio* To 6 inches. Found in floating clumps of seaweed, these masters of disguise are almost invisible to all but the keenest eyes. They are so voracious and cannibalistic, they will devour their own kind in an aquarium, no matter how much food is available. **Range:** circumtropical, including the Atlantic, Pacific and Indian Oceans; in the West Atlantic, from New England to Brazil, including the Gulf of Mexico. **Edibility:** poor.

The anglerfishes of the Pediculati (or "little foot") order are similar to the scorpionfishes in lifestyle, and even more bizarre. Like the scorpionfishes, the anglerfishes spend most of their time sitting motionless on the bottom, trying to appear as rocklike and inconspicuous as possible. Most of them are formless, lump-like fishes endowed with warty, prickly skins and an expert talent for catching their food with the aid of movable fishing rods which they erect over their mouths when hungry. A curious smaller fish unwise enough to investigate this curious baited fishpole is sucked into the mouth of the anglerfish with such speed that the human eye cannot follow its movement.

157

☐ The frogfishes of the family Antennariidae are excellent anglers and very adept at camouflage. They are voracious fishes, and when angling is poor they have been known to actively stalk other fishes. They commonly swallow fishes longer than their own bodies. Of 45 species worldwide, 9 are recorded from the West Atlantic. Batfishes (family Ogcocephalidae) are batshaped anglers commonly seen sitting quietly on sandy bottoms blending nicely with their surroundings. If prodded, they lurch awkwardly for a few feet and return quickly to their motionless vigil position. They eat small mollusks and crustaceans, and their lure apparently is not often used in feeding.

☐ Lizardfishes of the family Synodontidae are voracious carnivores also fond of sitting motionless on the bottom. They may even bury themselves in the sand until only their eyes protrude. When a smaller fish draws near, they dart upward, lizard-like, to engulf their prey in a cavernous mouth lined with fine, sharp teeth.

Ocellated frogfish *Antennarius ocellatus* To 15 inches. Easily recognized by the 3 large, ocellated spots and the short "fishing pole." All frogfishes are highly voracious, and will devour anything within reach. They are not recommended for aquaria. **Range:** North Carolina, Florida and the Bahamas to Venezuela, including the Gulf of Mexico. **Edibility:** poor.

☐ Toadfishes of the Batrachoididae family are slow-moving bottom dwellers equipped with large mouths lined with sharp teeth. They are shallow-water opportunists, quick to take advantage of any available habitat. They are often found clustered sociably in beer cans, sewer pipes, discarded shoes and other debris. They are pugnacious and quick to bite, especially at spawning time, from June to July.

☐ The colorful sea robin (family Triglidae) "walks" across the bottom on three pairs of detached lower pectoral rays, feeding chiefly on small crustaceans and mollusks. The largest members of the sea robin family reach 3 feet in length and are considered excellent eating in some areas. The flying gurnard, sometimes confused with the sea robin, also has long, expandable pectoral fins like the sea robin. It too, "walks" across the bottom on foot-like pelvic fins, using short pectoral rays to probe the sand for food. When alarmed, it spreads its enormous and colorful pectoral fins. Gurnards are members of the family Dactylopteridae and feed mostly on crustaceans and occasionally, small fishes. Dragonets of the family Callionymidae are small, often brightly colored fishes with broad, flattened heads. The lancer dragonet is a bottom dweller usually found in coral reef or coral rubble areas.

Longlure frogfish *Antennarius multiocellatus* To 4½ inches. Similar to the ocellated frogfish, but with a longer lure and more spots, less well-defined. All frogfishes are highly changeable in color, able to match virtually any background. **Range:** Bermuda, Bahamas and Florida to Venezuela. **Edibility:** poor.

Splitlure frogfish *Antennarius scaber* To 4½ inches. Note the divided illicium or "fishing pole" for which this fish is named. An accomplished color-changer, it can phase from pale gray to brown to reddish to solid black. This frogfish will inflate itself, balloonlike, with water, as do the puffers, if roughly handled. **Range:** New Jersey, Bermuda and Bahamas to Brazil, including the Gulf of Mexico. **Edibility:** poor.

Lancer dragonet, coral dragonet *Callionymus bairdi* To 4½ inches. Found in seagrass beds and coral rubble areas. Also seeks protective shelter under longspine sea urchins. The male (shown) has an elevated first dorsal fin; females do not. **Range:** Bermuda, Bahamas and Florida through the Antilles, including the Gulf of Mexico. **Edibility:** poor.

Polka-dot batfish, redbellied batfish (murcielago) *Ogcocephalus radiatus* To 11 inches. An odd, sluggish animal, easily caught by hand. Found over sand bottoms, seagrass, mud and coral rubble. The belly of adults is orange-red. **Range:** Bahamas, Florida and the Gulf of Mexico. **Edibility:** poor.

Gulf toadfish *Opsanus beta* To 10 inches. Toadfishes have been found nesting in tin cans and old shoes. They will snap at anything going by their burrow. Approached by divers, they croak irritably. **Range:** Bahamas, Florida and the Gulf of Mexico. A very similar relative, the oyster toadfish, *Opsanus tau*, is found from Maine to Florida. **Edibility:** poor.

Inshore lizardfish, galliwasp (lagarto) *Synodus foetens* To 18 inches. Named for its alert, lizardlike head, this fish is a master of camouflage. It waits motionless to ambush crustaceans and small fishes. **Range:** Cape Cod to Brazil. **Edibility:** poor.

Flying gurnard *Dactylopterus volitans* To 18 inches. Not really a flyer, the gurnard is a bottom-dweller that, when threatened, will spread its enormous blue-spotted pectoral fins, making it a difficult meal to swallow. **Range:** New England, Bermuda, Bahamas and Florida to Argentina, including the Gulf of Mexico. **Edibility:** poor.

Northern sea robin *Prionotus carolinus* To 10 inches. In some ways similar to the related flying gurnard, this fish is distinctive for having its 3 lower pectoral fin rays developed into finger-like tactile organs. The sea robin creeps over the bottom on these rays, picking, probing and overturning stones in search of food. Noisy fishes, they croak like frogs, especially at spawning time. **Range:** Maryland to Florida and the Gulf of Mexico. **Edibility:** considered a delicacy in some parts of the world, but rarely eaten in our area.

162

TUBEMOUTHED FISHES

If you should glance back while diving and see a two-foot length of brown garden hose peering over your shoulder, don't panic. It's merely one of the curious and friendly trumpetfishes that are quite common off West Atlantic coral reefs. They are astonishing fish to see, as they stare back at you with their large, independently-movable eyes set at the front of slender, luminous, tube-like bodies. Trumpetfishes are specialists at following larger fishes (and even divers) about the reefs, using them as stalking horses to allow the trumpetfish to prey on unsuspecting smaller fishes. A curious fish is sucked up in one quick intake of the vacuum-like snout.

Lined seahorse (caballito de mar) *Hippocampus erectus* To 5½ inches. Shown in rare red coloration phase. **Range:** Nova Scotia to Argentina, including the Gulf of Mexico. **Edibility:** poor.

☐ The tubemouthed fishes (order Gasterosteiformes) consist of two sub-orders: one includes the seahorses and pipefishes; the other contains the trumpetfishes and cornetfishes. The tubelike snout is one characteristic that all tubemouthed fishes have in common. They are all masters at vacuuming up their food by rapid intakes of water. Most of them possess a partial or complete armor of bony plates, and most of them demonstrate curious spawning behavior where the female deposits her eggs in a brood pouch or patch near the tail of the male fish. The impregnated father then incubates the eggs and ejects them live into the sea some 8 to 10 days later. West Atlantic tubemouthed fishes range in size from tiny adult pipefishes of one inch to huge adult cornetfishes reaching 6 feet in length.

☐ Cornetfishes are quite similar to trumpetfishes except for the blue-spotted coloration and the long filament extending from the tail. Most pipefishes and seahorses are sargassum and seagrass dwellers that are usually so well camouflaged in their weedy environment that they are rarely seen by divers. Shown here is the lined seahorse, the common seahorse of the Atlantic coast. Its usual coloration is ashen gray with delicate black and white lines and reticulations. Occasionally lined seahorses are discovered that are brick red in color. They are very rare, and one of these is illustrated. Although quite different in appearance, seahorses and pipefishes are very closely related—so closely, in fact, that seahorses are actually pipefishes with curled-up tails and horse-like tilted heads. Recently an unusual creature, the pipehorse, was identified that is intermediate between a pipefish and a seahorse. Its head is slightly cocked from the body and it has a prehensile tail, as shown below. It is extremely rare, and has so far been collected only in Bermuda and the Bahamas.

Gulf pipefish *Syngnathus scovelli* To 18 inches. **Range:** eastern Florida through the Gulf of Mexico. **Edibility:** poor.

Trumpetfish (corneta) *Aulostomus maculatus* To 3 feet. **Range:** Bermuda, Bahamas and Florida south to the hump of Brazil, including the Gulf of Mexico. **Edibility:** poor.

Bluespotted cornetfish (corneta) *Fistularia tabacaria* To 6 feet. **Range:** both sides of the Atlantic; in the West Atlantic, from New England and Bermuda to Brazil, including the Gulf of Mexico. **Edibility:** poor.

Pipehorse *Amphelikturus dendriticus* To 3 inches. **Range:** very rare in collections, thus far known only from Bermuda and the Bahamas. **Edibility:** poor.

BLENNIES, GOBIES, JAWFISHES

Yellowhead jawfish *Opistognathus aurifrons* To 4 inches. A particular favorite of aquarists because of its pale, delicate coloration and its preoccupation with keeping its burrow clean and tidy. On the reef it lives in colonies at moderate depths (10 to 100 feet). When not policing and bulldozing around its burrow, its usual posture is hovering gracefully 6 to 8 inches over its burrow, tail down, revolving slowly while snapping zooplankton from the passing water mass. **Range:** Bahamas, Florida and through the West Indies. **Edibility:** poor.

Most of the sharp-eyed, active little fishes that are seen darting into crevices, hovering around holes or squatting on coral branches are blennies, gobies or jawfishes. Blennies may be recognized by their single continuous dorsal fin, while gobies have dorsals that are separated into two distinct segments. The majority of the blennies are carnivorous or omnivorous bottom dwellers, and many blennies have unusual crests, fringes or "eyebrows" decorating their heads. A wide range of diversity in anatomy and behavior exists among the fifteen or more families of blennies. The West Atlantic species shown here include the combtooth or scaleless blennies (family Blenniidae) and the scaled blennies or klipfishes (family Clinidae).

☐ Gobies (family Gobiidae) are among the smallest fishes of the sea, and West Atlantic species range from ½ to 3 inches when adult. The tiniest vertebrate animal known is a Philippine goby, *Pandaka pygmaea*, which is full grown at less than half an inch. All gobies possess a sucking disk under the forward part of the body which they use skillfully to anchor their tiny bodies to coral or rocks in the surge zone. Most gobies are not seen by divers since they are small, usually hidden and well camouflaged. The well-known neon goby, however, displays its brilliant colors around large stands of brain coral, where it sets up cleaning stations to relieve large fishes of parasites. Most gobies lay elongated eggs attached by stalks to rocks and coral, and they guard their eggs until they hatch, both parents usually sharing in the duty.

□ Jawfishes, of the family Opistognathidae, are fascinating but secretive blenny-like fishes which live in burrows on the reef bottom. They are usually seen hovering or "tail standing" just outside their crater-like burrows. When danger threatens, they dart into their burrows, tail-first, until only the head protrudes. They make excellent aquarium pets because they are such active, industrious animals, fascinating to watch. The jawfish always seems busy with household chores—chasing intruders away from its burrow; excavating and cleaning its tunnel in the sand or crushed coral bottom; dashing about and wrestling bits of rock and shell over to the burrow; spitting sand and aggregate like a miniature bulldozer.

Spotfin jawfish (traganavi) *Opistognathus macrognathus* To 8 inches. Easily recognized by the bold ocellated spot on its dorsal fin. Reluctant to leave its burrow, this fish peers out warily from its nest, or hovers over it, fins fluttering. A colony of jawfishes is pandemonium, as each fish tries to steal stones from its neighbor's burrow, amid much mock battling and threat display (but very little real biting). **Range:** Florida and throughout the Caribbean to Venezuela. **Edibility:** poor.

166

Greenband goby *Gobiosoma multifasciatum* To 1½ inches. A brilliantly - colored shallow water goby that prefers limestone bottoms, and is often discovered in tide pools. It has been found in live sponges off Curacao and among dead coral branches and the spines of sea urchins around Puerto Rico. **Range:** Bahamas south through the Antilles. **Edibility:** poor.

Rusty goby *Quisquilius hipoliti* To 1½ inches. A common goby over rocky areas and coral reefs to a depth of 420 feet. Note the bright orange spots on all vertical fins, and the prolonged second dorsal spine. **Range:** Florida and the Bahamas south to Venezuela. **Edibility:** poor.

Neon goby *Gobiosoma oceanops* To 3½ inches. A popular aquarium fish, this goby sets up cleaning stations on the upper surface of large brain corals. Larger predatory fishes come and often wait in line for the parasite-picking services of the neon goby. Distinctive for the brilliant neon-blue lateral stripe. In some instances, pairs have spawned in home aquaria. **Range:** Florida Keys, West Indies and the southwestern Gulf of Mexico. **Edibility:** poor.

Sharknose goby *Gobiosoma evelynae* To 1½ inches. Distinctive for the shark-like mouth set well back from the snout. Occasionally seen in pairs atop large coral heads. Like the neon goby, a well-known cleaner of larger fishes. Two almost identical cleaner gobies, *G. evelynae* and *G. genie* are known from the West Indies. **Range:** *Gobiosoma evelynae:* Bahamas, Puerto Rico, through the Lesser Antilles; *Gobiosoma genie:* Bahamas and Grand Cayman Island. **Edibility:** poor.

Crested goby *Lophogobius cyprinoides* To 3 inches. The crested goby seems to prefer brackish and silty inland bays and tidal creeks, and is abundant around the mangrove swamps and bays of West Florida. In Bermuda it has been found living in brackish inland lakes. **Range:** Bermuda, Bahamas and Florida through the West Indies, including the Central American coast. **Edibility:** poor.

Redlip blenny *Ophioblennius atlanticus* To 4¾ inches. It's hard not to like this comical little blenny in the aquarium, with its grinning red lips and bright eyes that seem decorated with eyelashes. A herbivore, this fish is superabundant on West Indian reefs. **Range:** North Carolina south through the West Indies. **Edibility:** poor.

Hairy blenny (guavina) *Labrisomus nuchipinnis* To 8 inches. Distinctive for the cowlicks over each eye, and for being one of the largest of the West Atlantic blennies. Encountered in rocky areas, sand and seagrass, it is highly changeable in color, from pale to near black. **Range:** Bermuda, Bahamas and Florida south to Brazil including the Gulf of Mexico. **Edibility:** poor.

Molly miller (chivato) *Blennius cristatus* To 4½ inches. Crests, ridges and fringes on the head are helpful identification marks for many of the blennies, and the molly miller is well-endowed with a crest and cirri. A common blenny over shallow, inshore rocky areas. **Range:** Florida to Brazil, including the Gulf of Mexico. **Edibility:** poor.

Wrasse blenny *Hemiemblemaria simulus* To 4 inches. This amazing blenny has gone to great lengths to mimic the bluehead wrasse, *Thallasoma bifasciatum* (see page 89). The resemblance to the bluehead is almost perfect through 3 distinct color phases from juvenile to adult (yellow phases only, not the adult super-male bluehead). The blenny even swims with the yellow blueheads, copying their swimming motions and appearance in every respect. Since the blueheads, due to their parasite-picking activities, are virtually immune from predators, the wrasse blenny enjoys all the privileges of this immunity without having to work for them. A sharp-eyed fishwatcher will note that the wrasse blenny has a more pointed snout than the bluehead wrasse. **Range:** Florida and the Bahamas. **Edibility:** poor.

Yellowface pikeblenny, sand pikeblenny *Chaenopsis lim-baughi* To 3 inches. Usually encountered in clear water areas on coral rubble bottoms or sandy areas near coral reefs. A closely-related species, the bluethroat pikeblenny (*Chaenopsis ocellata*) lives in worm tubes in shallow water grass beds. **Range (both species):** Florida south through the West Indies. **Edibility:** poor.

Sailfin blenny *Emblemaria pandionis* To 2 inches. Only the male fish sports the high sail-like dorsal fin. Females and immature males are light tan with tiny, scattered light spots and dark flecks. **Range:** Florida, the Bahamas and Puerto Rico to the Central American coast. **Edibility:** poor.

169

NEEDLEFISHES, HALFBEAKS, FLYING FISHES

Redfin needlefish (agujon) *Strongylura notata* To 2 feet.
Range: Bermuda, Bahamas and Florida through the Antilles.
Edibility: good.

The leaping, gliding, skittering, sailing needlefishes, half-beaks and flying fishes are all members of the order Synentognathi, and they are true masters of life at the ocean's surface.

☐ If you have never stood at the rail of a fishing boat and seen a houndfish leaping after a smaller fish, then you have a treat in store. Looking very much like jet-propelled gleaming silver javelins, these 2 to 5 foot fishes can execute a series of high-speed twisting, turning, diving and re-surfacing leaps across 100 feet of water that once seen is never forgotten. They are quite possibly the fastest fishes in and out of the water. Like living arrows, leaping houndfishes sometimes impale boaters with their beaks.

☐ The needlefishes (family Belonidae) of which the houndfish is the largest member, are voracious predators and use their tremendous agility and swept wing speed either to attack smaller prey with their fearsome, slashing jaws, or to escape from larger predators. They are protectively colored for life at the surface, with green or blue backs and silvery white sides and belly. Thus their needlelike shapes are extremely difficult to discern either from the surface or from below. Their dorsal and anal fins are placed opposite each other, just in front of the V-shaped tail. If you shrink a needlefish by about 1 or 2 feet and remove the long upper jaw, you have a half-beak. Halfbeaks (family Exocoetidae) are ancestors of the flying fishes and some of them can glide 40 feet.

☐ Passengers on ocean liners never tire of watching the "bluebirds of the sea," flying fishes (family Exocoetidae), as they scull violently with their tails, taxiing to attain flight speed. They spread their pectoral fins, glide a few seconds, then splash back into the sea. At night, open illumined port holes on ships bring an occasional flying fish soaring inside. A one-pounder in flight can deal a man a knockout punch. Flight speeds of 35 miles per hour have been clocked, and flights have been timed as long as 13 seconds.

Houndfish (agujon) *Tylosurus crocodilus* To 5 feet. **Range:** both sides of Atlantic; in the Western Atlantic, from New England and Bermuda to Brazil, including the Gulf of Mexico. **Edibility:** good—in spite of the greenish-colored bones!

Timucu (agujon) *Strongylura timucu* To 2½ feet. **Range:** Florida and the Bahamas south to Brazil. The closely related Atlantic needlefish, *S. marina*, ranges from New England south through the Caribbean. **Edibility:** good.

Atlantic flying fish *Cypselurus heterurus* To 16 inches. **Range:** both sides of the Atlantic; in the West Atlantic, from the St. Lawrence to Brazil, including the Gulf of Mexico. **Edibility:** fair.

Ballyhoo *Hemiramphus brasiliensis* To 15 inches. This halfbeak ranges both sides of Atlantic; in the West Atlantic from New England to Brazil, including the Gulf of Mexico. **Edibility:** poor.

MORAYS, CONGER EELS, SNAKE EELS

Manytooth conger eel (congrio) *Conger triporiceps* To 3½ feet. **Range:** Bermuda, the Bahamas and Florida to Brazil. **Edibility:** good.

Garden eel *Nystactichthys halis* To 20 inches. **Range:** Florida and the Bahamas south through the West Indies. **Edibility:** poor.

On a population basis, the most numerous reef animals throughout the West Atlantic are the eels of the Anguilliformes order. Due to their secretive nature, however, and their daytime concealment in reef caves and crevices, their great abundance is not evident to the casual observer. The largest and most conspicuous family of eels is the Muraenidae, or moray. The moray can and will bite with vicious, fang-like teeth. Since it almost always remains well anchored to its reef hole with its powerful tail, it is a very formidable fighter. Morays are not particularly aggressive toward larger animals, even with all their power. Most of the recorded instances where morays have attacked humans occurred when the moray was caught by a fisherman, or when a diver put a hand into its cave.

Green moray (morena verde) *Gymnothorax funebris* To 6 feet. **Range:** New England, Bermuda, the Bahamas, Florida south to Brazil. **Edibility:** fair—eaten in the West Indies.

☐ Recent contacts between divers and morays indicate that these eels can be almost puppy-like. They will emerge from their caves and gently take food from a diver's bare hand. Although the moray opens and closes its mouth constantly, making it appear vicious and aggressive, these mouth movements are the moray's way of breathing by pumping water across its gills. It feeds almost exclusively on small fishes, octopus and crustaceans. The moray has an acute sense of smell, and will forage across the reef at night hunting for small, wounded or sleeping fish. A current theory holds that certain wrasses and parrotfishes wrap themselves in a mucous cocoon before sleeping at night as a protection against marauding morays and other predators. It is postulated that something in the mucous cocoon hides the scent of the sleeping fish from the hungry moray. Morays are eaten in the West Indies and many other parts of the world, but several species have proved to be poisonous, with fatalities resulting in about 10 percent of the cases recorded (see page 39, ciguatera poisoning).

☐ Conger eels of the Congridae family are easily distinguished from morays by their usually prominent pectoral fins (morays do not have pectoral fins). When the conger eel moves, it is truly poetry in motion as undulating ripples flow down the fins and the body snakes gracefully through the water. Congers have strong jaws, but lack the long, canine teeth of the morays. Garden eels are a subfamily of the congers (family Heterocongrinae), famous for their burrowing habits and the "eel gardens" they produce when many have their burrows in one patch or "garden." Snake eels (family Ophichthidae) are also burrowing eels named for their long, cylindrical snake-like bodies. Although sea snakes do exist in various tropical seas, there are no sea snakes in the West Atlantic. Mistaken reports of sighting "sea snakes" in our area are probably due to seeing the fairly common snake eel. These eels do not live in permanent burrows as do the garden eels, but they burrow easily through bottom sand and gravel, forward or backward. Some species may be seen moving freely about the reef and shore by day, notably the brilliant gold-spotted snake eel, one of the most attractive eels of the tropical West Atlantic. Their eyesight is very bad (they hunt by smell), thus they are quite harmless and may easily be observed as they pick and probe their way around sand and seagrass areas.

Purplemouth moray *Gymnothorax vicinus* To 4 feet. **Range:** both sides of the Atlantic; in the West Atlantic, from Bermuda, the Bahamas and Florida to Brazil. **Edibility:** fair.

Spotted moray (morena pintada) *Gymnothorax moringa* To 4 feet. **Range:** both sides of the Atlantic; in the West Atlantic, from north Carolina, Bermuda, the Bahamas and Florida to Brazil, including the Gulf of Mexico. **Edibility:** fair—eaten in the West Indies.

Blackedge moray *Gymnothorax nigromarginatus* To 2 feet. **Range:** South Carolina and Florida south through the Antilles, including the Gulf of Mexico. **Edibility:** fair.

Chain moray *Echidna catenata* To 3 feet. **Range:** both sides of the Atlantic; in the West Atlantic, from Bermuda, the Bahamas and Florida to Brazil. **Edibility:** fair.

Goldentail moray *Muraena miliaris* To 2 feet. **Range:** Bermuda, Bahamas and Florida south through the Antilles. **Edibility:** fair.

175

Viper moray *Enchelycore nigricans* To 3 feet. **Range:** Bermuda, Bahamas and Florida south through the Antilles. **Edibility:** fair.

Goldspotted snake eel *Myrichthys oculatus* To 3 feet. **Range:** both sides of the Atlantic; in the West Atlantic from Bermuda, the Bahamas and Florida south to Brazil. **Edibility:** poor.

Shrimp eel *Ophichthus gomesi* To 2½ feet. **Range:** South Carolina and Florida south to Brazil, including the Gulf of Mexico. **Edibility:** poor.

Sharptail eel *Myrichthys acuminatus* To 3 feet. **Range:** Bermuda, the Bahamas and Florida south through the Antilles. **Edibility:** fair.

MARLINS, SAILFISHES, SWORDFISHES AND DOLPHINS

Blue marlin, Cuban black marlin (aguja de casta, espadon) *Makaira nigricans* To 15 feet. To 2,000 pounds; average 200 - 400 pounds. **Range:** world-wide in warm and temperate seas; in the West Atlantic, from Cape Cod and New York south to Uruguay, including the Gulf of Mexico. **Edibility:** good.

White marlin (aguja blanca) *Tetrapturus albidus* To 160 pounds; average 50-60 pounds. **Range:** Nova Scotia to Brazil, including the Gulf of Mexico. **Edibility:** poor. Release when caught.

The majestic billfishes are the most sought after of all the big game fishes—the true fighting aristocrats of the sea. Perhaps no other area in the world offers such a variety of habitats, such a range of excellent billfishing as the West Atlantic. Blue water fishermen comb the Gulfstream from New York to Bermuda and Bimini, and from the famed banks of the Bahamas to the rich billfish grounds off Puerto Rico. They sit patiently in deck chairs awaiting the strike of the leaping, fighting blue marlin, the sailfish and the valiant white marlin from the coast of Maryland to the marlin fishing grounds around Jamaica, through the Antilles to Venezuela, throughout the Gulf of Mexico and down the Central and South American coast to Uruguay.

□ The principal targets of all this activity are the representatives of two fish families: the Istiophoridae, comprising the marlins and sailfishes, and the Xiphiidae, or swordfishes. Billfishes all possess a sword or bill—a bony projection from the upper jaw—that is apparently used in subduing smaller fishes. They use the sword as a club to maim their victims as they rush through a school of mackerel or similar smaller fishes. Small squadrons of sailfishes have been seen to herd schools of smaller fishes into compact balls, then slash their way through them, killing and eating in well-coordinated teams. The West Atlantic's special attraction for big game fishermen is the abundance of the splendid blue marlin. The big blue is taken off New England, North Carolina, the Florida Keys, the Bahama Banks and the abundant billfish grounds off Puerto Rico and Jamaica. The blue marlin attains a weight of 2000 pounds, although the average taken is between 150 and 400 pounds. The largest blue marlin taken by sport fishermen was a 1,085 pound fish caught off Hawaii in 1972. It was disqualified for record because more than one angler handled the line.

□ Atlantic white marlins are the special favorites of many blue water fishermen because of the spectacular, twisting acrobatics they perform when hooked. All marlins are impressive fighters, noteworthy for their individuality in fighting compared to other game fish. Some marlins will fight the hook to the surface, twisting and tail-walking, while others will sound deep, which means a long, tedious battle. They are sought more for their fighting spirit than for their strong and oily flesh. More and more conservation-minded fishermen are releasing billfishes and other game fishes after boating them, so that they can provide additional sport for those who come after.

☐ A much smaller billfish is the Atlantic sailfish, a strikingly beautiful animal with a huge, fan-like dorsal fin. The sailfish is such a popular gamefish off Florida's east coast that the annual Invitational Masters Angling Tournament held at Palm Beach each January results in close to 200 sailfishes being caught and released in a 5-day period. Both the white marlin and sailfish are taken along the Gulf Stream, in the Gulf of Mexico, the Bahamas, Puerto Rico, Jamaica and through the Windward and Leeward Islands to Venezuela. The broadbill swordfish rivals the shark in both size and strength. It exceeds 1000 pounds in weight and 15 feet in length, although the average caught is about 250 pounds.

☐ Dolphins or dorados of the Coryphaenidae family are beautiful, active fishes that range all warm seas. They are common in the tropical West Atlantic and are taken by offshore fishermen all year, although they are most numerous from May to December. When prevailing winds blow quantities of sargassum weed, dolphin frequently accompany it. Their favorite prey seems to be flying fishes. The terrific speed of the dolphin enables it to flush the flying fishes like quail, catching them as they fall after a fumbling start or a full flight. Because of its valor and strength as a fighting game fish, and its excellent meat, the dolphin is hunted by man the world over. It is a gorgeous fish when caught, with iridescent shades of purplish-bluish gold, sea green and emerald. When death occurs, however, it quickly becomes plain gray in color. The name "dolphin" is confusing, since it is applied to this fish and to the porpoise, which is an aquatic mammal. The two totally different animals can be separated by remembering that the dorado dolphin is a water-breathing fish, while the porpoise dolphin is an air-breathing cetacean closely related to the whales.

Sailfish (pez vela, aguja de abanico) *Istiophorus platypterus* To 10 feet. To 141 pounds; average 30-50 pounds. **Range:** world-wide; in the West Atlantic, from Rhode Island to Brazil, including the Gulf of Mexico. **Edibility:** poor. Release when caught.

Longbill spearfish (aguja) *Tetrapturus pfluegeri.* To 50 pounds; average 15 to 30 pounds. **Range:** New Jersey to Venezuela, including the Gulf of Mexico. **Edibility:** poor. Release when caught.

Swordfish (espadon, pez espada) *Xiphias gladius* To 15 feet. To 1182 pounds; average 250 pounds. **Range:** world-wide; in the West Atlantic, from Nova Scotia to Brazil. **Edibility:** excellent.

Dolphin, dorado *Coryphaena hippurus* To 5 feet. To 75 pounds; average 4 to 25 pounds. A closely related fish, the pompano dolphin (*Coryphaena equisetis*) is almost identical to the dolphin, except it has a deeper body, longer ventral fins, and reaches only about 30 inches in length. **Range (both species):** world-wide in warm seas; in the West Atlantic, from Nova Scotia and Bermuda to Brazil, including the Gulf of Mexico. **Edibility:** good.

SHARKS AND RAYS

Great white shark
(jaqueton) *Carcharodon carcharias* To 25
feet. Average: 16-18
feet. Record 2071 pounds.
Range: world-wide in warm and temperate seas; in the West Atlantic, from Newfoundland to Brazil. **Edibility:** good.

For the interested swimmer who considers skin or scuba diving as a sport, probably one of the greatest fears is the shark attack. Popular misconceptions engendered by movies, TV, books and newspaper stories contribute to the image of this brute of the sea as being literally waiting offshore to pounce on anyone who enters the water, especially in tropical seas. Yet actual shark sightings around shallow reefs are rare, and incidents of attacks on humans off most of the world's beaches are extremely rare. According to figures gathered by Jacques Yves Cousteau, out of countless millions of swimmers, divers, surfers and fishermen who enter the world's oceans, only about 50 shark attacks occur each year. This compares with about 125 people who are killed by lightning each year in the U.S., and 50 to 75 people who die from insect stings in the U.S. alone. Thus, fear of shark attack off most of the world's beaches is totally unwarranted.

☐ Most sharks are not reef-dwelling fishes, but they make occasional visits to the reefs to feed on resident fishes. Divers who spear or maim fish may attract sharks to their area by the low frequency vibrations and scent trails that emanate from the wounded fish. All sharks can be

181

Oceanic whitetip shark *Carcharhinus longimanus* To 13 feet. **Range:** Long Island to Barbados, including the Gulf of Mexico. **Edibility:** poor.

Shortfin mako shark (tiburon, carite) *Isurus oxyrinchus* To 12 feet. **Range:** world-wide in tropical seas. **Edibility:** excellent.

dangerous, without exception, including small nurse sharks. The wise diver gives them a wide berth. Only a very uninformed diver would grab a shark by the tail, no matter how small. Occasionally divers and beach-goers are badly bitten while engaging in this risky sport.

☐ Sharks and rays of the Elasmobranchi group of fishes are distinct from all of the foregoing bony fishes because their skeletons are composed of cartilage instead of bone. Of some 250 shark species inhabiting the seas of the world, about 30 species have been recorded from the West Atlantic. The tiger shark is easily identified by the indistinct vertical bars and spots along its sides. The largest tiger shark ever taken was an 18 foot animal caught off Cuba. The great white shark is an offshore species, undoubtedly the most dangerous animal in the sea. Fortunately there are very few records of the great white shark in the West Atlantic.

□ Nurse sharks are commonly seen on West Indian reefs, often lying motionless on the bottom. Lemon sharks, reef, bull, blacktip, whitetip, silky and hammerhead sharks are some of the more common West Atlantic sharks. Like the nurse shark, both the lemon and reef sharks are capable of lying motionless on the bottom. Two roving offshore sharks are the mako and the blue sharks. The mako, a close relative of the great white shark, is a favorite of fishermen because of the spectacular leaps and tireless fight it provides when hooked as well as for its tasty flesh. The names "sand shark" and "mako" are often mistakenly given by fishermen to any of various species of sharks in the West Atlantic. *Odontaspis taurus* is the true sand shark, and it ranges from Maine to Brazil. The true mako is a fast-swimming offshore species, *Isurus oxyrinchus*, possessing a very pointed nose. It ranges worldwide in all tropical seas.

Tiger shark (alecrin, tintorera) *Galeocerdo cuvieri* To 25 feet. Average: 10-13 feet. Record 1382 pounds. **Range:** world-wide in warm seas; in the West Atlantic, from New England to Uruguay, including the Gulf of Mexico. **Edibility:** poor.

Lemon shark *Negaprion brevirostris* To 11 feet. **Range:** both sides of the Atlantic; in the West Atlantic, from New Jersey to Brazil, including the Gulf of Mexico. **Edibility:** good.

Blacktip shark (tiburon galano) *Carcharhinus limbatus* To 8 feet. **Range:** world-wide in warm and temperate seas. In the West Atlantic from New England to Brazil. **Edibility:** poor.

Bull shark *Carcharhinus leucas* To 10 feet. **Range:** worldwide in all warm seas; in the West Atlantic, from New York to Brazil, including the Gulf of Mexico. **Edibility:** poor.

Silky shark *Carcharhinus falciformis* To 10 feet. **Range:** both sides of the Atlantic; in the West Atlantic, from North Carolina to Trinidad. **Edibility:** poor.

Sand tiger shark, sand shark (dientuso) *Odontaspis taurus* To 10½ feet. **Range:** Maine to Brazil, including the Gulf of Mexico. **Edibility:** poor.

Reef shark (tiburon) *Carcharhinus springeri* To 9 feet. **Range:** Bahamas, and Florida to Yucatan and throughout the West Indies to Venezuela. **Edibility:** poor.

184

Blue shark (tintorera) *Prionace glauca*
To 20 feet. **Range:** worldwide in warm
and temperate seas; in the West Atlantic,
from New England to Venezuela, including the Gulf of Mexico. **Edibility:** poor.

Nurse shark (gata manchada)
Ginglymostoma cirratum To
14 feet. **Range:** Rhode Island
to Brazil, including the Gulf of
Mexico. **Edibility:** poor.

Scalloped hammerhead shark
(cornuda, pez martillo) *Sphyr-
na lewini* To 12 feet. **Range:**
worldwide; in the West Atlantic;
from New Jersey to southern
Brazil, including the Gulf of
Mexico. **Edibility:** poor.

Spotted eagle ray (obispo, chucho) *Aetobatus narinari* To 7½ feet. **Range:** circumtropical; in the West Atlantic from Virginia and Bermuda to Brazil, including the Gulf of Mexico. **Edibility:** poor.

☐ Stingrays, eagle rays and cownose rays of the order Batoidei are common in the tropical West Atlantic. The spotted eagle ray is one of the most striking and attractive of the order. They are commonly seen singly, in pairs or in small schools, winging gracefully between coral heads or hovering lazily just beyond the breaker line. The southern stingray, yellow stingray and lesser electric ray are more often seen resting or half-submerged in reef bottom sand, where they excavate for invertebrates and occasionally take small fishes.

☐ All of our rays are quite harmless if left alone, but the stingrays and eagle rays possess venomous spines on their whiplike tails, capable of giving very painful wounds. The lesser electric ray has no spines, but it has

Cownose ray *Rhinoptera bonasus* To 7 feet. **Range:** southern New England to Brazil, including the Gulf of Mexico. **Edibility:** poor.

a potent weapon. It is reported to produce a shock strong enough to knock a man down, although most reports indicate much lesser effects. Manta rays or "devil" rays of the Mobulidae family are common around the outer reefs, and have often been photographed by divers. In spite of the name "devil ray," mantas are now recognized to be large, docile creatures, reaching 22 feet from wingtip to wingtip. They cruise channel areas and outer reefs feeding on small crustaceans and other planktonic food. Skates are flat-bodied elasmobranchs closely related to the rays. They, too, have widely expanded pectoral wings which extend forward to circle the head in a thin plate. The Texas skate shown is one of the more lavishly-colored skates.

Atlantic manta ray *Manta birostris* To 22 feet in width. **Range:** New England to Brazil, including the Gulf of Mexico. **Edibility:** poor.

Lesser electric ray *Narcine brasiliensis* To 1½ feet. **Range:** North Carolina to Argentina. **Edibility:** poor.

Southern stingray (raya)
Dasyatis americana To 5 feet. **Range:** New Jersey to Brazil, including the Gulf of Mexico. **Edibility:** poor.

Yellow stingray (tembladera) *Urolophus jamaicensis* To 2 feet. **Range:** North Carolina, Florida and the Bahamas to Venezuela, including the Gulf of Mexico. **Edibility:** poor.

Texas skate, roundel skate *Raja texana* To 2 feet. **Range:** Gulf of Mexico; common west of the Mississippi delta. **Edibility:** poor.

188

INVERTEBRATES

Invertebrates are distinct from other marine animals because they have no backbones. They include the corals, sea anemones, jellyfishes, clams, squids, crabs, lobsters and a host of other forms. Due to their great richness and diversity (mollusks alone number more than 40,000 species) only a few of the more familiar animals can be included here.

Atlantic oval squid (calamar) *Sepioteuthis sepioidea* To 8 inches. Often seen in small squadrons, darting like pursuit planes after schools of smaller fishes. **Range:** New England to Venezuela. **Edibility:** good.

Common Atlantic octopus (pulpo) *Octopus vulgaris* To 10 feet. A highly intelligent animal, often seen on the reef as it disappears into its burrow, or camouflaging itself expertly against rocks or coral. **Range:** Connecticut to the Caribbean. **Edibility:** good.

Scarlet lady, red-backed cleaner shrimp *Hippolysmata grabhami.* To 3 inches. A very colorful cleaner shrimp which often finds its way into marine aquariums up and down the Atlantic Coast. **Range:** southeastern United States to Brazil. **Edibility:** poor.

Banded coral shrimp, barber shrimp *Stenopus hispidus* To 3 inches. An industrious cleaner, this little "barber" is often seen picking and eating parasites from moray eels. **Range:** all tropical seas. **Edibility:** poor.

Spiny lobster (langosta) *Panulirus argus* To 21 inches. As it grows, the lobster molts its shell periodically in order to expand within the new shell. It is heavily fished and speared for the sweet meat in the powerful tail. **Range:** North Carolina to Brazil. **Edibility:** excellent.

Long-spined sea urchin (erizo) *Diadema antillarum* Spines to 15 inches. A bane to divers, who often pick painful spines out of hands and feet after brushing against them. **Range:** all tropical seas. **Edibility:** good. A delicacy in some areas.

BIBLIOGRAPHY

American Fisheries Society. 1970. *A List of Common and Scientific Names of Fishes from the U.S. and Canada.* 3rd Edition, American Fisheries Society, Wash., D.C.

Bauer, E. A. 1962. *The Salt-Water Fisherman's Bible.* Doubleday & Co., Inc., Garden City, N.Y.

Becker, A. C., Jr. 1970. *Gulf Coast Fishing.* A. S. Barnes and Co., Inc., Cranbury, N. J.

Beebe, W. and J. Tee-van. 1933. *Field Book of the Shore Fishes of Bermuda and the West Indies.* Dover Publications, Inc., New York.

Bohlke, J. E. and C.C.G. Chaplin. 1968. *Fishes of the Bahamas and Adjacent Tropical Waters.* Livingston Publishing Co., Wynnewood, Pa.

Breder, C. M., Jr. 1948. *Field Book of Marine Fishes of the Atlantic Coast from Labrador to Texas.* G. P. Putnam's Sons, New York.

Cervigon, F. M. 1966. *Los Peces Marinos de Venezuela.* (2 Tomos) Fundacion La Salle de Ciencias Naturales, Caracas, Venezuela.

Chaplin, C. G. and Scott, P. 1972. *Fishwatchers Guide to West Atlantic Coral Reefs.* Livingston Publishing Co., Wynnewood, Pa.

Collette, B. B. and Earle, S. A. 1972. *Results of the Tektite Program: Ecology of Coral Reef Fishes.* Bull. No. 14 of the Museum of Nat. History, Los Angeles, Calif.

Dahlberg, M. D. 1975. *Guide to Coastal Fishes of Georgia and Nearby States,* University of Georgia Press, Athens, Georgia.

Emery, A. R. and Burgess, W. E. 1974. *A New Species of Damselfish (Eupomacentrus) from the Western Atlantic, with a Key to Known Species of that Area.* Copeia, No. 4, Dec. 31.

Goodson, G. 1973. *The Many Splendored Fishes of Hawaii.* Marquest Colorguide Books, Palos Verdes Estates, Calif.

Gordon, Bernard L. 1960. *The Marine Fishes of Rhode Island.* The Book & Tackle Shop, Watch Hill, Rhode Island.

Herald, Earl S. 1972. *Living Fishes of the World.* Doubleday & Co., Inc., Garden City, New York.

Herald, Earl S. Undated. *Fishes of North America.* Doubleday & Co., Inc., New York.

Jordan, D. S. and B. W. Evermann. 1896. *The Fishes of North and Middle America.* Bulletin of the U.S. National Museum, No. 47.

191

Jordan, D. S. and B. W. Evermann. 1902. *American Food and Game Fishes.* Dover Publications, Inc., New York.

La Monte, F. 1952. *Marine Game Fishes of the World.* Doubleday and Co., Garden City, New York.

Longley, W. H. and S. F. Hildebrand. 1940. *New Genera and Species of Fishes from Tortugas, Florida.* Carnegie Inst., Washington Publication No. 517.

McClane, A. J. 1971. *Field & Stream International Fishing Guide.* Holt, Rinehart and Winston, Inc., New York, N.Y.

McClane, A. J. 1974. *McClane's New Standard Fishing Encyclopedia.* Holt, Rinehart and Winston, New York.

Metzelaar, J. 1919. *Report on the Fishes Collected by Dr. J. Boeke in the Dutch West Indies 1904-1905*, with comparative notes on marine fishes of tropical West Africa. (Reprint 1967). A. Asher & Co., Amsterdam.

National Geographic Society. 1965. *Wondrous World of Fishes.* Nat. Geographic Soc., Wash. D.C.

Poey y Aloy, Felipe. 1955. *Ictiologia Cubana.* Repub. de Cuba Ministerio de Educacion, Havana, Cuba.

Randall, J. E. 1968. *Caribbean Reef Fishes.* T.F.H. Publications Inc., Neptune City, N.J.

Sanchez, Roig, M. and G. de La Maza, F. 1952. *La Pesca en Cuba.* Repub. de Cuba Ministerio de Agricultura. Havana, Cuba.

Smith, C. L. 1971. *A Revision of the American Groupers: Epinephelus and Allied Genera.* Bull. of Amer. Mus. of Nat. History. Vol. 146: Article 2, New York.

Starck, W. A. and Chesher, R. H., 1968. *Undersea Biology*, Vol. 1, No. 1, Marine Research Foundation, Miami, Florida.

Walls, J. G. 1975. *Fishes of the Northern Gulf of Mexico.* T.F.H. Publications Inc., Neptune City, N. J.

METRIC MEASURE CONVERSION TABLE

To aid readers in converting inches, feet and pounds to metric equivalents, the following tables are provided.

Inches to Millimeters			Feet to Millimeters	
In.	**mm.**		**Ft.**	**mm.**
1	25.4		1	304.8
2	50.8		2	609.6
3	76.2		3	914.4
4	101.6		4	1,219.2
5	127.0		5	1,524.0
6	152.4		6	1,828.8
7	177.8		7	2,133.6
8	203.2		8	2,438.4
9	228.6		9	2,743.2
10	254.0		10	3,048.0
11	279.4		50	15,240.0
12	304.8		100	30,480.0

Pounds to Kilograms	
Lb.	**Kg.**
1	0.45
2	0.91
3	1.36
4	1.81
5	2.27
6	2.72
7	3.18
8	3.63
9	4.08
10	4.54
20	9.07
50	22.68

INDEX TO FISHES

DIVING TIPS
AND MAPS OF THE WEST ATLANTIC

The West Atlantic is a fish-watcher's paradise for the interested swimmer-tourist. Whether you are at Boston Harbor, Chesapeake Bay, the Florida Keys, the Bahamas, Puerto Rico, the Virgin Islands, Cozumel, Cancún, or British Honduras, the underwater world of the reefs is only minutes away. All that is needed is the ability to swim, and the effort required to adjust to swimming with a face mask and snorkel tube. These can be purchased at most sporting goods stores for under $12.00. Swim fins are advised for long skin-diving excursions. The fins give you the added push necessary for effortless cruising around the reefs. The warmth of the water in tropical seas (70° to 85°F) allows for comfortable swimming in your bathing suit. No wet suit is needed for short tours in the water.

To aid the fishwatcher in locating the range of specific fishes, and to select a vacation spot best suited for fishing or diving, I have provided maps on the following four pages that show the wide range of choices available in the West Atlantic. Without doubt, the best area for the diver is the warm, gin-clear waters of Florida, Bermuda and the West Indies, extending from the Bahamas through the Greater and Lesser Antilles to Venezuela. To cruise slowly over a coral reef in 80° water with 100 to 200 foot visibility is an unforgettable experience. Thousands of reef animals swarm through forests of elkhorn, staghorn and brain coral, and half an hour of slow and watchful cruising will reveal many of the fishes shown in this book.

Highly recommended for beginning and experienced aquanauts are the John Pennekamp Coral Reef State Park, covering 75 square miles of superb tropical reefs off Key Largo in Florida, and the Buck Island Underwater Trail and Park, just off St. Croix in the U.S. Virgin Islands. Both offer breathtaking underwater vistas. Further, many fish species usually associated with Caribbean coral reefs are swept up the U.S. coast by the warm Gulf Stream. Thus divers from Cape Cod to the Carolinas may encounter butterflyfishes, angelfishes, damselfishes, grunts, snappers, basses and many other tropical species, especially in the late summer and fall (August through October).

A few words of caution are called for, however, before you plunge into the surf. Skindiving is easy and pleasurable when practiced in calm, clear-water bays and beaches. Exercise normal caution when swimming near rock and coral reefs. If you aren't careful, wave action can pitch you unexpectedly into reef heads that may inflict painful scratches and wounds that are difficult to heal. Watch where you are in relation to the shore and nearby reefs at all times, and make allowances for wave action. Avoid over-tiring yourself, and always swim accompanied by a capable companion. Keep hands and feet out of reef holes and crevices, and avoid areas of high surf, turbulence and choppy water. SCUBA (self-contained underwater breathing apparatus) diving will provide even greater and deeper access to the underwater world, but the beginner requires detailed instruction and certification by a skilled diver before crossing this frontier. Qualified SCUBA instructors abound up and down the Atlantic Coast. Consult the phone book or your hotel registrar for information.